The Chamber
And
The Cross

Lisa K. Shapiro (signature)

Lisa K. Shapiro
and
Deborah K. Reed

Deborah Reed (signature)

THE CHAMBER AND THE CROSS
Copyright © 2014 by Deborah K. Reed
and Lisa K. Shapiro

Cover Design by Peter O'Connor
BespokeBookCovers.com

Published by Kay Publishing

ISBN 978-0-9907452-0-4
www.TheChamberAndTheCross.com

To Our Mothers
Roberta Lambert and Nicki Shapiro

Their love made us.
They nurtured, sustained and inspired us to live
with love in our hearts, and to seek love in others
and in all things.
They taught us about language and literature, and
we humbly and lovingly dedicate this book to them.

Acknowledgments

Thank you to Deborah's loving husband, Gene, who patiently endured our process and the loss of the kitchen table, and to Lisa's wise elder sister, Beth Camera, who has read more of her work than anyone.

We wish to thank the Thursday Night Writer's Group, who listened to and critiqued scene after scene, draft after draft. They sent us "back to the attic" when we needed more ideas, and coaxed us out of our comfortable sitting room when it was time to move the plot forward. For their expertise and tough love, we are grateful to Leo Dufresne, Graeme Ing, Adrianna Lewis, Dan Jeffries, and Linda Mitchell.

And to the writers and readers who have weighed in on many drafts, we owe our gratitude to Tara Perla, Mary Hill, Bonnie Woods and Paula Stein. Thanks also to Donna Bailey, Christine DeLaCruz, Catherine Kimbril, Allison Blake and all our early readers.

Prologue

It was almost dark on the December afternoon in the year of Our Lord 1452, when I first set eyes upon Bannock Manor. I had never seen a nobleman's home without protective castle walls. It was newly built, and I wrongly assumed the walls would come later.

Our journey had taken weeks and had been fraught with danger. So many had died, and most of what I held dear had been left behind in France. We were three weary fugitives who stood in the freezing rain and looked across the valley at the house. I was terrified to enter those doors.

Chapter One

Her friends always thought summers at Bannock Manor were romantic and glamorous until they came for a visit. The first view from the hill, looking across the valley, promised a stately, old home. Now that it was spring, the daffodils would be spreading through the glen, and by the time she arrived in June, the roses would be in bloom. Laura Bram hung up the phone and thought about her mother's call, and the familiar feelings of love and longing wrapped themselves like a shawl around her shoulders.

Outside Laura's window, an April rainstorm obscured her view of the gray Boston skyline. Headlights and the warm yellow lights from other apartments spilled into the watery evening. She pulled the drapes, blocking out the chill, and then turned up the heat. Tonight Carl had something special planned and she wanted to look sophisticated, yet sexy. After applying make-up, she dusted her face and bare shoulders with a shimmering powder and pulled a new, black cocktail dress from its garment bag and slipped it on. Instead of her usual ponytail, she wore her blond hair draped loosely down her back, and she swept it aside as she struggled with the gold clasp of her grandmother's sapphire pendant.

It was the right time for them, she could feel it. Laura Bram Linnehan. It had a ring to it, and yes, an engagement ring would be the world's best birthday present. She stepped into strappy heels, as dangerously high as her hopes, just as the doorbell rang.

She opened the door to Carl, and as he leaned in to kiss her, she inhaled the citrus scent of his cologne.

His brown eyes danced as he looked her up, down, and then up again. "Wow. You look great."

The new dress, not exactly a sale item, had been worth the hit to her credit card. She knew it when she saw the appreciation in his eyes. "I was hoping you'd like it," she said.

"Very sexy." His hand was warm against her back, and he dropped another kiss onto her neck before helping her into her coat. He guided her outside and she saw the double-parked limousine, the stoic chauffeur waiting while traffic snaked around the imposing car.

"You didn't have to," she said, but secretly she was thrilled.

"This is just the first of your birthday surprises." In the limo, he poured champagne and gave her a glass.

Smiling, she settled back into the circle of his arm, warm and happy, wanting to remember every detail as the city streets slipped by.

§§§

Eleanor Colfax Bram pushed open Bannock Manor's front door and put her wet umbrella in the stand. It had been ages since she'd been out this late, but the lecture series at Bristol University had been fun, and in June, she'd take Laura along for the talk on the renovation of historic homes.

In the kitchen, she switched on the light and reached for the kettle. Something was banging against the side of the house. Setting the half-filled kettle on the counter, she stopped to listen. It sounded like a shutter or a door battered by the wind, perhaps the lid of a rubbish bin. Sleeping through the creaks and rattles was one thing, but that kind of noise would keep her up all night. She peered out the window but couldn't see through the rain-streaked glass.

Pulling up the collar of her jacket, she stepped into the courtyard, keeping to the side of the house where the eaves offered a little protection. A storm was moving in fast, pitching tree branches in all directions and whipping her hair against her face. A trellis covered in dormant vines had broken loose from the wall. She laid it flat; in the morning, she would see what could be done.

From the corner of her eye she saw the bushes moving. A shadow unfolded – a man rose from a crouched position and came toward her. He wore a black coat, several sizes too big, and a dark cap pulled low on his head. He took several steps closer.

"Who are you?" She stood her ground and raised her voice above the wind. He was probably a tinker, scrounging for something to sell. "You should leave," she said.

The words were barely out when he was on her, pushing her, smashing her against the wall, his aggression so sudden she was caught off guard. Her cheek scraped, and the impact forced air from her lungs. She shoved her elbow into his gut, but he grabbed her, spun her around and sent her headlong onto the cobblestones.

Lightening flashed and he jerked back, yelling something, but he wasn't making any sense.

She rolled out of his reach, got to her knees, and then to her feet. Her palms stung, her right wrist hung limply, and a stabbing fire spread up her arm. She clutched her elbow and tried to think through the pain.

"I've triggered the alarm," she lied. "The constables will be here in a minute."

"The alarm's disconnected." The menace in his voice chilled her.

Dizzy and nauseous, she took a step backward, and another, pressing her injured arm to her chest. They were within a dozen feet of the kitchen door, and she inched toward it, never taking her eyes off him.

He rocked side to side, ready to spring.

She backed up three more steps.

He lowered his chin and lunged, blocking her route to safety.

She turned and fled across the courtyard, cradling her broken wrist. He was close behind, grunting with each step. The path up the hillside was rocky and steep, but she knew it well, and terror spurred her faster. Her side pinched, but she kept going, past the chapel and toward the castle ruins.

§§§

"Your second surprise," Carl said as the limousine glided to a stop.

When he helped her out, she felt like she was floating, and it wasn't just the champagne. He'd chosen Parker's, one of Boston's oldest establishments, and he flashed a satisfied smile as he linked her arm though his and led her into the old-world lobby. They passed beneath enormous, glittering chandeliers and into the dining room lustrous with candlelight and flowers.

Piano music drifted in from the bar as the host greeted them. "Mr. Linnehan, we have the Kennedy table reserved for you."

Laura's breath caught as the maître d' held her chair. She would have been happy anywhere tonight, but Carl knew she had a soft spot for tradition. "This is perfect," she said.

Carl tapped the tablecloth. "Table forty. I reserved it months ago. John Kennedy proposed to Jackie right here."

He had flair, it was practically his middle name, but even for Carl this was over the top. He could go for weeks absorbed in his business, and then all of a sudden, out of the blue, he acted as though she were the most important person in the world. It was like he'd called up a Hollywood director and said, The best restaurant. The most romantic table. She couldn't stop grinning.

"I've been looking forward to tonight all week," she said.

"This is your night and I wanted it to be special." He ordered lobster bisque and gave her the boyish smile that made him look like a movie star.

Suddenly she wished she could slow everything down, savor each second. He was leading up to the moment, and it was flawless, right down to the gleam in his eye.

He topped up her wineglass. "I signed a new client today. Adams thought he had him, but I got the signature first."

"I thought you two were friends. Don't you go to the gym together?"

"This is business."

She watched him through the glow of the candles, the way he radiated an aura of confidence, glad she didn't work in the pressure cooker of financial consulting.

He paused while the waiter served their entrées, and then said, "Tell me about your day."

"I had brunch with Dad and Edward. And my mother called –"

"Like clockwork."

"I'm all she has."

She pushed the worries from her mind, knowing she'd be there in a few weeks. Carl thought she was childish, going home to her mother every summer, but it was her favorite part of the year. She loved the manor house, loved that she shared a little of its five-hundred-year past. Teaching history didn't pay much, but she wanted to share that connection, that link to another time and place with her students. And it made summers with Mum possible.

She said, "I read a good paper today –"

Carl signaled the sommelier. He was as passionate about wine as he was about finance, and she waited patiently while he considered the pros and cons of each vintage. He made his selection and then turned back to her. "Sorry, honey."

She began telling him about her liveliest class and their excited discussion about Henry VIII. One of her students had written an essay taking the side of the king, looking past the obvious atrocities of the monarch's reign to the pressing need to produce an heir. Carl's brow smoothed into the patient look he adopted when she talked too much about school.

"Why don't you come to England with me this summer," she suggested. "My mother can't wait to meet you."

He pushed his plate away. "Invite her to Boston."

"I want to show you Bannock Manor."

"Tea in the rose garden." He affected a stuffy accent.

"I want you to meet my mother. You'll like her."

With a mischievous smile, he reached into the inner pocket of his suit jacket. "Happy birthday, Laura." He slid a gift-wrapped box across the table.

Her fingers trembled. It wasn't a ring box, that much was obvious. Opening the gift, she pulled a brochure out from under the tissue paper. Tucked inside were two airline tickets to Seattle and the itinerary for a ten day cruise. Surprised, she looked up at him.

"Alaska. Imagine icebergs, glaciers, whales. A cruise. Dining and dancing." He took the brochure out of her hands and unfolded it. "So – how's the first week in July?"

She pressed his hand. "Mum's counting on me." Laura worried about her mother rattling around inside that crumbling old house in the Cotswolds, resolutely trying to hold onto her inheritance.

"You don't really need your mom's permission to take a trip with me." Carl smiled. "You are thirty-one. I only get two weeks. I want to spend them with you."

"Then come to England with me."

"Why can't you do something different for once?"

"Mum and I have a tradition. It's important to me."

"Laura, listen to me." Suddenly his tone changed. He picked up his wineglass and she saw him swallowing his irritation along with a gulp of Pinot Noir. "How can we plan a future together if we can't agree how to spend our vacation time?"

Mum was expecting her from mid-June through the end of August, even counting the weeks until she arrived. Seven. "Make it at the end of August, and I'll shorten my stay and meet you in Seattle."

"My vacation is in July."

They were interrupted by the arrival of dessert, her serving of Boston cream pie garnished with a birthday candle. She blew it out, wondering how she could reorganize her summer.

The tickets lay on the table between them. A fancy restaurant, a romantic cruise, no engagement. After two years of dating, she needed to know that their relationship was heading somewhere permanent.

Maybe he planned to propose on the cruise; it was only a few months away. "This is great," she said. "I've never been to Alaska."

On the way home, he held her close, telling her about the new beemer he planned to buy. If Carl wanted something – he got it. He made a decision and made it happen.

But she knew what she wanted too, to spend summers at Bannock Manor, and someday, when she and Carl had children, to share its mysteries and stories with them. Married with kids and a house in the suburbs by the time she was thirty – too late for that. Maybe by thirty-five.

By the time the limo braked to a stop in front of her building, she was certain they could work it all out. The chauffeur opened the car door, and she stepped out, smiling, and pulled her keys from her purse.

Carl bounded up the steps two at a time. "I know the cruise wasn't what you had in mind."

She searched his face, knowing how eager she must look, how hopeful.

"Laura, I'm not ready. When the time is right..." He met her eyes, and his smile got caught between the smugness that she hated and the boyish charm she loved. "I promise, one of these days I'll go to Bannock Court."

"It's Bannock Manor," she said, disappointed that he didn't care enough to remember the name of her family home. Gently, she nudged his shoulder. "Go pay the driver, and hurry. It's cold out here."

In her bedroom, he kissed the back of her neck and unzipped her dress. "You're irresistible," he murmured, dropping kisses across her shoulders as her new dress slid to the floor.

He caressed her knowingly, confidently. When his hand moved lower, she stepped back. "I just need a moment." She grabbed her robe and headed for the bathroom. What she really needed was time to collect her emotions, unscramble love and disappointment, settle into his tenderness.

When she came out again he was already in bed, and he lifted the covers so she could see that he was ready for her. She slipped between the sheets, and his hands moved slowly down her hips; he knew exactly how to touch her, and she always responded to him.

They made love silently, his body so attuned to hers that he knew when she was on the brink. He waited until she climaxed before he finished.

"Good sex, it's like icing on the cake," he whispered. "Happy Birthday."

She snuggled against him. He'd gone to a lot of effort planning their dinner and the cruise. He did love her, and things would unfold in time – she just had to be patient.

She dozed with her head against his chest, awakening later when he stirred. "Hey, I can't stay," he whispered. "I have an early match and I didn't bring my gear."

"Want me to come?" She'd been to the club, seen his tennis matches. He was good.

"Sleep in," he said, planting a kiss on her lips.

She sat up. "About this summer –"

"Alaska's booked," he said. "I put down a deposit, and I don't want to lose it." He pulled on his undershorts. "Look, if it means that much to you, we can go to London next year. Sometimes I think you care more about that manor house than me."

"I love you," she said.

"I'll come back this afternoon and we can check out shore excursions." He finished dressing, dropped a kiss on her cheek and left.

She drifted back to sleep and dreamt she was in the castle on her mother's land. The round tower rose against the sky and the man on one knee before her placed fervent kisses on her hand. He wore leather boots, leggings and a medieval tunic. A strong wind ruffled his hair, and she reached to still the locks as they tugged and teased like bits of ribbon. For a moment she rested her hand on his bowed head, and she saw that she wore jeweled rings on her fingers.

He raised his head and the wind stilled. His soft words carried like the clear tones of a church bell. "I live for you."

He rose, but before he could kiss her, she turned her face away and gazed across the familiar landscape. They were on the castle's wall walk, and she could see the gatehouse guarding the entrance to the upper court and tower. She swayed imperceptibly toward him.

His face was lean, and his eyes were tender and full of longing.

She wanted to beg him, command him, order him to stay with her always. Desire nearly choked her, but she bit back her plea. He drew her into the shelter of the tower and out of the wind. The stairs wound upward and they climbed together, spiraling up until he paused at a window seat. Through the slit of the arrow loop she saw the rolling hills of Gloucestershire. When he left, he would ride across those hills and fields, and book his passage across the sea channel.

His lips pressed over hers and her body warmed; her mouth answered his as she grasped his shoulders, and her hand found its way to the back of his neck. Shamelessly, she pulled him closer and kissed him harder. She might have drowned in her swelling love, but he buoyed her and his kisses anchored her and bound them together.

She murmured, "I cannot live without you."

Still whispering the words "...without you," Laura began to awaken. She always surfaced from the dream as though holding onto two worlds, but when she tried to remember his name, it was gone.

Blearily, she looked at her clock. It was eight and she wanted to linger in bed. For a moment she luxuriated, stretching her arms, trying to recapture the sensation of his kisses. She could see him so clearly, the way he looked at her and smiled, the hopefulness in his eyes that turned to sadness.

She wondered why she so often had that dream.

The phone rang, and she expected Carl, but the caller ID said Bram. Her father was an early bird but it wasn't like him to disturb her on a Sunday morning.

"Hi, Dad?"

"Laura... I have some bad news."

She was alert now, and even under the blankets, she felt chilled. "Is Edward all right?"

The last time she'd heard his voice break, she'd been six years old, clutching her doll and trying to catch her father's hand. The last time she could remember her father crying, she'd been at Bannock Manor, and he'd awakened her so that he could say goodbye, taking Edward, her older half-brother, but leaving Laura and her mother behind.

"It's about your mother, sweetheart. There's been an accident." She listened to the way his deep voice changed pitch as emotion overcame him. "Megan Wiles called me a little while ago."

Her hand twisted in the blanket and she pulled it higher, covering her freezing arms.

He pressed on. "She fell. Megan found her in the castle ruins."

Under the blanket, she began shaking. "Dad?"

"She's gone, sweetheart." His voice softened. "Laura, your mother's dead."

"No. That's not possible." Blinking at the morning sunlight pouring through the bedroom window, her eyes filled with tears. The news hammered at her and she tried to fend it off, as though she could beat it back with a simple denial. "We just talked yesterday. Mum's waiting for me." A sob rose, painfully working its way to the surface, choking her. "She's waiting –"

"You need to get to Bannock Manor," he coaxed. "I'm online now. There's a flight at six-thirty that still has some seats. Do you want me to come with you?"

She did, but hated to admit it. "No...thanks." Her stomach was in knots, her body still fighting the news that her mind was slowly absorbing. How could he be so certain? "Dad, I think there's been a mistake."

"Megan wouldn't have called unless she was sure. She wanted you to hear it from me."

Coming from anyone else, she wouldn't have believed it, but Megan was a trusted friend, and her father never got his facts wrong. She clutched the phone tighter, closed her eyes and pleaded silently for him to take it back.

"Laura – we'll get through this." He took a breath. "Edward and I will fly over in a day or two. We'll be there with you."

She hung up, but her limbs felt leaden and she couldn't get out of bed.

Dad must have made a mistake. Her fingers shook as she dialed England, and it took forever for the housekeeper to answer the phone.

"Laura..." Sobbing, nearly incomprehensible, Winnie pleaded, "Come home. We don't know what to do." It wasn't possible to get anything else out of Winnie's grief-stricken ramblings.

"I'll be there as soon as I can," Laura said, as the news began to sink in. She got out of bed and started packing, throwing sweaters, jeans, panties, and her make-up bag into a pile. Her dress from the night before was still on the floor. She picked it up, but the silk slipped through her fingers and puddled at her feet. She stared at it, bewildered. She couldn't pick it up, couldn't decide what else she needed to pack. She made it back to the bed, pushed aside the jumble of clothes, and burst into tears.

When the phone rang again, she had no idea how much time had passed; long enough to create a mountain of used Kleenex. She turned her head as the answering machine picked up, but the caller didn't leave a message. After a while it rang again, but she didn't answer until she heard her brother's voice.

She said softly, "I'm here."

"Dad told me what happened to your mother. I'm so sorry."

"I can't believe it." She wiped her nose, rubbed her swollen eyes and looked at the mess she'd made of her packing. "I have to get home."

"If you need anything, anything at all, let me know." The thing about Edward was that he meant it. He would do anything for her.

"Come over with Dad in a few days," she said. "There'll be plenty to do."

She hung up, dragged herself off the bed and stared into the closet. It was April, still cold in England, and she would need extra sweaters – and something to wear at the funeral.

After she showered and dressed, she called Carl, and he came within a half hour. Pulling her into his arms, he held her while she cried. A while later he coaxed her to drink a cup of tea while he ran down a check list, helping her pack: umbrella, warm gloves, cash, credit cards. She found the number for the school secretary, and left a message that she would be away on a family emergency. Her thoughts were muddled and chaotic, and she'd almost forgotten her passport, until Carl mentioned it, and she dug it out of her dresser drawer.

When she was finally ready, her suitcases in the hall, Carl gathered her into his arms and she clung to him, shuddering, afraid to let go.

Gently, he disengaged her and reached for the bags. "It's time. I'll get the car."

She followed him out, shutting her apartment door and pushing her key into the lock. The bolt slid home, but she paused. What was she leaving behind?

Carl was waiting, the car's engine running.

With one last look, she jiggled the knob and forced herself to walk away.

Chapter Two

The coffee cup on the fold-down airplane tray was white plastic, but in Laura's mind she saw a white teacup with a rim of gold. "Bone china can last for a thousand years," her mother had once said. At Bannock Manor the cabinets were full of Wedgwood, Spode and willow patterns collected by generations of Bannocks and Colfaxes.

Laura twisted in her airplane seat, her five-foot nine-inch frame too long for standard leg room. The airliner was flying into night, and somewhere between one continent and the next she was supposed to close her eyes and go to sleep. She pressed the heel of her hand against her mouth, stifling a sob, and the woman in the next seat glanced over before quickly turning away.

A flight attendant collected the dinner trays and the cabin lights dimmed. Books were closed and blankets spread across the laps of her fellow travelers as they slept. She made a few more seat bound gyrations and gave up any hope of rest.

Carl had kissed her goodbye with a promise to see her in a few days, but the anticipation of showing him Bannock Manor was gone. The last thing he cared about was a centuries-old manor house, larger than many American mansions, and stuffed to the rafters with the treasures and debris of her ancestors. And now, when they got married, her mother wouldn't be there to share the day, wouldn't see her wearing the pearls that had been in the family for generations.

In her dressing room, her mother held up a necklace. "Do you like this?"

Laura took the double strand of pearls and held them against her throat. "They're beautiful."

"Put them on," her mother said, and nodded approvingly as Laura fastened the clasp. "They suit you very well. Keep them and wear them on your wedding day."

"Someday I will," she promised.

The pearls were packed in her carry-on suitcase and she would wear them to the funeral.

Laura had no aunts or uncles, no cousins; she was her mother's only child, and the last of the Colfax family line. She stared into the darkness beyond the plane's wingtip. They were above the Atlantic, dark night over dark water, and she felt her heart sinking at the bleakness, the emptiness of a future without her mother.

When the plane touched down, the London sky was foggy and threatening rain. Shaking off grogginess from the all night flight, Laura squeezed into the aisle with the other passengers and grabbed her luggage, then made her way through the maze of Heathrow Airport until she reached the customs checkpoint.

The agent looked at her passport and asked, "What's the reason for your visit?"

"I'm here – for a – to see my mother," she said, clamping her trembling lips and swiping at a tear.

"How long will you be staying?"

"Two weeks," she said softly.

He returned her passport, and Laura went straight to the car rental desk. Soon she was stowing her luggage in the trunk of a cramped Peugeot. "Drive on the left," she reminded herself as she circled a roundabout, fighting jetlag and the London traffic. She merged onto the M4 motorway, following the signs toward Bristol and then north on the A46 toward Tenney Village.

Once she got off the motorway, the two lane road rose and fell as it meandered through the Cotswolds villages. Through breaks in the hedgerows, she saw the familiar thatched roofs and half-timbered cottages. She knew the route well, but her usual sense of excitement was replaced by dread as she got closer to home.

Tenney Village looked as timeless as ever with the stone church dwarfed by its Norman tower, the shops along High Street, and the brightly painted sign of the White Hart Pub.

Continuing up the hill, she turned onto a lane barely wide enough for a single car, stopped and turned off the engine. She got out and walked a few paces, staring across the valley at Bannock Manor, and the ache in her chest tightened.

This would always be her real home, with its wide symmetrical wings of honey-colored limestone, multi-paned windows and steep gables on the Georgian front of the house. The back section was gray granite dating to the mid-fifteenth century, and older still was the crumbling stone castle on the far hill. It was complex and convoluted and full of memories.

Even from this distance, the manor's emptiness seemed to reach out and engulf her. She couldn't believe her mother wasn't in there waiting for her. Mustering all of her willpower, she got back in the car and drove across the valley.

As though he'd been watching for her, Nigel appeared in the entryway. The tall, silver-haired butler dabbed at his tearing eyes. "Laura, we're so sorry."

She gave him a hug, holding him a little more tightly than she'd intended. "Nigel, it's good to see you." Another look into his sad face, and she felt herself crumpling.

Winifred, Nigel's sister, rushed from the kitchen, her story burbling up like a spring. "Eleanor never came down for breakfast, we couldn't find her anywhere, and I called Megan to see if she was there." She dipped into the pocket of her dress for a handkerchief. "Megan came right over. I had no idea that anything bad had happened – until Megan came running back, hysterical she was, barely able to tell us what she'd found." Winnie's apple cheeks were awash in tears. "It was horrible."

Nigel patted his sister's shoulder, looking helpless. "The police were here all day yesterday," he said, "asking us questions; the same ones, over and over, until we wondered if they suspected us."

"What do they think happened?" Her voice sounded as raspy as Nigel's.

"They wanted details. Lots of details." His hands quivered as he described the ambulance that had taken her mother's body away.

When she pressed for more facts, he faltered and got choked up.

"We don't really understand what happened," he admitted.

She felt that if she stood there talking to Nigel long enough, her mother would come around a corner, smile, take hold of her shoulders and tell her that everything was all right.

What an awful mistake, Mum would say, and over tea she would explain the mix-up, delighted that Laura had arrived early.

Finally Nigel asked, "What are we going to do?"

"I have to talk to Megan, and the police. Will you let them know I'm here?"

Nigel reached for her suitcases, but he couldn't do the heavy lifting anymore, and she stopped him, hefting them herself. She trudged upstairs, past the portraits of stern parents and glowing children, past a painting of three young boys with cherry red cheeks and auburn hair. One of those smiling boys was her grandfather, Cecil Colfax, and the other two were his older brothers, both killed in World War II. It was one of the reasons her family was so small now. In her grandfather's time, so many young men had been killed, leaving so few of the aristocracy to carry on the old traditions and keep up the great manor homes.

And now another generation was gone.

One of the oldest portraits was of Lady Lorraine Bannock, a petite woman in a green satin gown with a ruffled, white lace collar. The wife to the first lord of Bannock Manor posed proudly, her hand resting on the mantel in the Great Hall. No matter where Laura stood on the stairs, Lady Bannock's dark, intense eyes stared back at her. She'd seen that passionate gaze thousands of times, but now the emotion captured in the depth of Lady Bannock's expression seemed different, and Laura read it as a mirror of her own feelings. Sadness.

In her old bedroom, she dug out her makeup bag and freshened up. Twenty minutes later, when she went down to the drawing room, a tea tray was waiting and so was Megan Wiles. Laura paused on the threshold, sunlight shining through the window panes, illuminating a vase of roses centered on an octagonal table. Just a few days ago, her mother would have been the one to place them there.

"Oh, Laura." Megan moved gracefully for a stout woman, wrapping Laura in her solid arms. They clung to each other, and then Megan finally released her and said what Laura was thinking. "What are we ever going to do without her?" She sat down heavily and wiped a hand over her square, plain face, as though she could erase the haggard lines.

"Please, tell me what happened." Laura paced restlessly, too agitated to sit.

Megan shared the details in a halting voice. When Eleanor hadn't appeared for breakfast, and when she couldn't be found in the house, Winnie had called. Several hours later, when Eleanor still hadn't returned, Megan came over and searched the grounds.

"The ruins were the last place I looked." She gazed at her hands. "I knew when I found her... her leg twisted... she was covered in mud."

"People don't die of broken legs," Laura whispered.

"Exposure – it was cold and rainy." Megan sighed. "The shock of the injury was too much."

Megan said more, but afterward, Laura couldn't remember much of their conversation. Her mind kept circling back to the ruins, her thoughts like a bird unable to find a perch, unable to light on any detail that made sense. People didn't die of broken legs.

The afternoon had the quality of a nightmare. Her mother's absence made the house feel strangely abandoned. Laura wandered from room to room as if searching for something, looking with a different perspective, how it must have been for her mother to live here alone, how empty it seemed. Perhaps if there had been a lingering illness, she could have prepared herself, but this suddenness was incomprehensible.

Winnie and Nigel hovered in the kitchen, shaken and grief-stricken, and as soon as supper was served, they went to their rooms.

The house was cold but she didn't try to adjust the old heating system. When she couldn't stand the chill any longer, she crept up the stairs. She was alone in this wing of the house and left extra lights on, trying to ignore the creak of floorboards. She heard movement on the stairs and again in the corridor, like an extra set of footsteps. Perhaps with more servants, more family and guests, the house wouldn't echo so. Unconsciously, she started her childhood refrain, *I won't look. I won't look.* It was the same old temptation, and she resisted the urge until the hair on her arms rose, and then she had to turn around.

When she looked over her shoulder, no one was there.

She crawled into bed, exhausted but restless, dozed fitfully, startled awake and finally slept.

On Tuesday morning before she even got up, Laura felt the stress beginning to build again. The day ahead promised to be full of social obligations and funeral arrangements.

Winnie tapped at her bedroom door. "The vicar's here."

Justin Graham and his wife Judi were waiting with an enormous pastry box in the breakfast room. "Your mother is in our thoughts and prayers," Reverend Graham said, as he put his hand on Laura's arm. He seemed to be searching for comforting words. "Would you like help with the arrangements?"

"I'd appreciate that. I've never planned a funeral before." Her voice wobbled and she tried not to cry.

Judi smiled reassuringly, and they guided her through the prickly details, everything from catering to caskets. A hearse would bring her mother home on Friday morning, and she would be buried in the cemetery where her own parents lay – between the house that she loved and the ruins where she had died.

Every decision came with an emotional as well as a financial price, and every detail seemed to spark a memory. Small scenes played out in Laura's mind: her child-sized feet carefully balanced atop her mother's as she learned to dance, mimicking her mother's voice and cadence as they read *The Secret Garden* out loud. Happy thoughts now draped in the dark crepe of mourning.

Laura put the expenses on her credit card, grateful that she had a high limit, hoping she wouldn't need all of it.

Judi set her pen down. "Your mother was such a gentle soul – shy and quiet – down to earth. I really liked her."

"Some people thought she was aloof, living here alone with just a small staff."

"She liked to keep life simple. She loved to talk about you." Judi added another task to her list. "There are dozens of people we should call. They'll want to know about the service."

"I can't. I can't make those calls." Laura buried her face in her hands. "I'd rather keep it private."

"That's not a good idea," Reverend Graham said, promising to handle many of the phone calls.

After he left, Judi stayed behind to shepherd the flow of sympathetic visitors. By afternoon there was nothing on the cake plate but crumbs, and Laura had talked to, and comforted, more teary-eyed people than she could count.

Several hours later, Nigel came to the doorway, cleared his throat, and announced the arrival of Constable Stiles.

Laura rose to greet him, her head throbbing. "Thank you for coming."

The constable's pressed uniform stretched tautly across his chest. He took off his hat, and his cropped yellow hair bristled. "I'm going to have to talk to Winifred and Nigel Wilcox again. Are they the only full time staff at the manor?"

"Yes," Laura said, "but Mrs. Dowd comes five evenings each week to fix supper." The gardener had retired last year and never been replaced, but there was no point mentioning that. She turned to Nigel and asked him to fetch Winnie.

As the constable nailed down the minutia of her mother's last movements, Laura learned that her bed had never been slept in, and she had been found wearing the same clothes from the evening before when she'd been to Bristol with Megan. Neither Winnie, nor Nigel had seen her come in that night or go out again in the morning. Her purse was as she left it, on the table in the foyer.

Laura asked, needing to know the details, but afraid of them too, "What time did she return from Bristol?"

"Eleven o'clock," the constable answered.

"Sometimes I wait up for her." Winifred blew her nose. "But she told me not to bother."

"I don't know why she went back out again." Nigel moved to stand beside his sister.

They already felt guilty, and Laura kept her thoughts to herself, but she wanted to yell at them, *Why didn't you call the police immediately?* It might have made all the difference, and her mother might have survived, but the Wilcoxes hadn't missed Eleanor until mid-morning, and by then it was too late. Mum had lain exposed to the elements from sometime after eleven at night until she died from the shock and trauma.

"Why would my mother be out walking late at night?"

"I can't say," Stiles replied. "For reasons unknown, she climbed to the castle, slipped, fell. She must have lain there until the injuries claimed her life. I'm sorry. Truly, I'm very sorry."

"Is there anything else..." There had to be some other detail, some other explanation.

"Your mother's death has been ruled an accident. The preliminary results showed a broken leg, wrist, and several ribs." He cleared his throat. "Internal bleeding as well. The kind of injuries one sustains from a fall."

Laura pressed her fingers to her temples, trying to ease her pounding head. No one knew what Mum's last hours had been like, only that she had been in pain, and alone.

When the constable finally left, she needed to talk, to pour out her grief, and she called Edward. He had always been her protector. On her first day of school in America, he'd defended her against a bully, a boy taunting her because of her English accent, making her cry.

She was crying now before Edward even answered the phone. "I don't know why," she managed to say. "I can't make sense of what happened." Gradually, she was able to vent her frustration. "No one seems to know why Mum went into the ruins. It doesn't make sense."

"When was the last time you spoke to your Mom?" he asked.

"Saturday. After brunch with you and Dad."

"We'll figure this out," he said, calming her a little. "Have you thought about what you're going to do with the house?"

"I can't think about that right now." She bit her lip, wanting to tell him not to rush her. "The funeral's Friday at noon."

He took the cue and switched gears. "I'll call Dad. We'll leave tomorrow night and arrive on Thursday."

Her big brother would show up armed with a smartphone full of contact information – who to call and how to manage her inheritance. It was just his habit to look after her.

§§§

On Thursday evening, Laura's father and brother, along with Carl, arrived at Bannock Manor in a rented Mercedes. They all appeared tired, but her father's face especially bore the look of grief and exhaustion. He hugged her, holding her more tightly and for longer than he ever had before. She wrapped her arms around him, seeking his comfort and strength, but she felt his weight as he leaned on her. For the briefest moment his forehead pressed into the crook of her neck, his face hidden in her hair, and she was afraid that he was going to cry.

He straightened. "I haven't been here in twenty years, but even coming down the lane everything looks the same." He gave her a searching look. "But of course, nothing is the same, is it?"

Edward asked, "You haven't changed my room, have you?"

"Same one." She forced a weak smile. "Just toss a few clothes on the floor and it'll look familiar."

She showed Carl to a room next to Edward's, and her father took a guest room down the hall.

Downstairs again, Carl wandered from the sitting room to the dining room and then into the drawing room. Laura wished he could have seen her family home at a better time, without a pall of grief clouding everything.

He paused before a side table, stroked his finger along the design of inlay. "Some of these antiques might be valuable."

"They are, but I never think about it like that." The manor was full of art, sculpture and furniture, but it was the people who'd lived there that captured her imagination. Their lives interested her more than their collections.

Carl inclined his head to study the plasterwork detail on the ceiling. "This is a great place to visit, but these large estates just aren't practical anymore. Look at that." He gestured toward the wall. "Cracked plaster and buckling windows. You don't want to sink money into this. Your mother –"

He broke off as Edward came in and leveled a warning look at him. "Did you offer to fix drinks? There's a bar in the servery."

"Are you going to draw me a map?"

"Head for the dining room. You'll find it."

Her brother was the only person she'd ever seen get away with bossing Carl.

Edward plopped onto one of the sofas. "I'm glad Dad didn't argue about letting me drive from London."

"It must be hard for him coming back here."

"He swore he was through with this place." Edward lowered his voice. "Lately, he's been worrying about whether Carl is good enough for his princess."

Before she could answer, Carl came in carrying a tray. "In a house like this, you need a butler."

"His name is Nigel," Laura said. "But he's elderly, and terribly upset about what happened. You'll meet him tomorrow."

Carl raised his eyebrows, signaling Edward.

"Later," Edward muttered.

"Whatever it is, you'd better tell me." She didn't want them coddling her; if there was more bad news, she needed to hear it.

Edward got up and walked to the window where the silhouette of a far bank of trees was visible in the twilight. "I've talked to a solicitor." He rolled his shoulders, like he was trying to get rid of the kinks after the long flight, but he was stalling. Without turning, he said, "You're probably not going to be able to keep the manor."

She'd anticipated news like that. The house was too much, too big, but she wasn't going to cave easily. "Go on."

"The first two hundred and fifty thousand pounds of the estate's value is tax free," Edward explained, his voice as neutral as if Laura were a client. "Everything above that is taxed at forty percent."

"Forty percent...in taxes?"

"On everything. You have to add up the land, house, art, furniture." Facing her, his business façade cracked, and he said gently, "Laura, you have three months to give a full account to Inland Revenue."

She'd been preparing herself for hurdles, but no one could assess the house in such a short time. Only three months? She stood up. "That's impossible."

Carl crossed the faded carpet and paused beside a gaming table where Laura and Edward had often played draughts, the

English game of checkers. He pulled open a drawer and fingered the playing pieces. "Did your mother make any provisions to transfer assets to you before she died?"

"I don't think so." Laura shook her head, wondering why they thought it was so important to have this conversation now. Didn't they see it was tearing her apart? She sighed, fighting back tears. "Mum was only fifty-eight."

"If you accept the position of her personal representative," Edward said, "you'll become liable for the debt of the estate."

"Don't walk into that one," Carl warned. "It would be stupid. What mortgages are on it?"

She put up a hand, trying to stop the financial interrogation. "Mum inherited. I'm sure she owns it outright."

"This isn't going to be easy," Edward said sadly.

"Pack up the pertinent documents and let Edward and me take care of things," Carl suggested. "It'll be easier for you that way, and you can get back home."

"It isn't just the paperwork," she said.

"Of course not," Edward soothed. He'd run the numbers, reached a conclusion and was giving her time to come around.

Drained, she asked, "What if I can't afford the taxes?"

The answer was on their faces, reflected in their pitying eyes. Sell. That's what they expected her to do.

Chapter Three

Early on Friday morning, before anyone else was awake, Laura slipped out of the house. Sunlight was just shining over the hillside as she followed the footpath, setting out for a walk while the dew was still heavy and the air crisp.

As she passed the rear courtyard, she remembered her father dressed like a country gentleman, a brace of plump birds slung over his shoulder and steam wafting up from their warm breasts. More memories swirled around her as she climbed the hillside behind the manor. Today they would gather to hear her mother's memorial service, but Laura turned her back on the chapel and stared across the field toward the castle ruins.

A gatehouse still guarded the castle's upper yard, the inner sanctuary where the medieval lord and his family had lived until the mid-fifteenth century. The wooden fortifications were gone, including the drawbridge, but sections of the curtain wall remained, and it was still possible to climb up to the wall walk near the last round tower. The flanking towers had fallen and most of the stones were gone, probably used to build a farmer's barn or field walls. Only the great round tower remained, its entrance twenty feet above the ground.

Laura climbed the stone stairs leading up to the wall walk that guarded the tower's entrance. Her mother's body had been found near here. Leaning against the battlements, she watched as the sun began to shred the bank of clouds above the chapel. The graveyard stretched across the hillside, and toward the middle stood a seven-foot tall stone cross, but it wasn't a Celtic cross like those found in so many English cemeteries. At the center of the flared arms, instead of a Celtic ring, a long-ago craftsman had carved a heart.

Higher on the hillside beside a beech tree, two men labored with shovels. The sod had already come up in chunks, and although she willed herself to look away, she couldn't. The mound of earth was high, the hole nearly deep enough to accept a coffin.

She fought the urge to scream, and instead, slapped her palms down hard on the wall, over and over, as tears ran down her cheeks. For centuries these stones had withstood storms and attacks, but she was defenseless. Pain ground her heart like a mason's chisel, and she crumpled to her knees, sobbing.

Cool fingers stroked her face and cupped her chin. She'd known that familiar touch since childhood, but it always caught her off guard. Holding her breath, staying perfectly still, she concentrated on the pressure of a hand against her face. Slowly she opened her eyes, but there was no sign of anyone, no sound of a tread on the stairs, no shadow of a man making his retreat. But he'd been there. She'd felt him as solidly as the stone beneath her hands.

§§§

Tension sloughed from Todd Woodbridge's shoulders like he'd shed an overcoat. One more house and his research would be complete. Lowering the window of his car, he breathed the damp air and smiled as the Bannock estate came into view. The road dipped and the elegant house disappeared, and then he rounded another bend and saw it again, and there was the medieval wing, just as Mrs. Colfax Bram had promised.

The long lane up to the house had cars parked up and down, some double parked on the grass. Something big was going on. He checked his watch; right date, right time. Funny though, she hadn't mentioned a party. A few people hurried up the drive, but instead of walking to the front door, they took a path around the side of the house.

Todd parked at the end of the long row of cars and started toward the front door, but gazing up the hillside he saw a straggling queue, dark clothes, everyone in their Sunday best. A long line of what could only be mourners snaked toward a small chapel.

He'd shown up in the middle of a funeral.

He would find Eleanor and make his apologies. Taking a few steps, he stopped, uncertain. Maybe he should just leave now.

An elderly man at the rear of the procession looked back, included Todd with a sweeping gesture, beckoning him to hurry.

Todd gazed over the crowd, searching for Eleanor, reluctant to impose on someone's funeral. The elderly man waved for him again, looking impatient. He couldn't just turn his back and walk away. The front of the line had already disappeared into the chapel. Feeling awkward, he started up the hill, keeping his head down, his eyes on the flagstones. Bright green moss, slick from the mist, grew in the spaces between the mottled brown stones.

He slipped inside, hoping to look like he belonged. The crowd jostled, shifting to make more room in the creaky oak pews. The chapel had small windows, allowing just a few shafts of pale sun inside, and the roughly mortared walls trapped the cold. It was all there, lilies in tall vases, clusters of blue forget-me-nots, and on a stand beside the flowers, the portrait of a woman in the prime of her life.

He stared at the picture, dimly aware when an usher pushed a program into his hand. *Eleanor Colfax Bram.* Reading her name on the paper, he caught his breath, absolutely stunned. When he'd met her a few days ago, she'd been healthy and enthusiastic, making plans for the future. Around him, some of the older ladies were weeping loudly, cotton handkerchiefs wadded into balls as they sobbed, blew, sobbed some more. A young woman in the front pew was barely holding it together, and his heart went out to her.

A latecomer in a baggy black coat scrunched in beside him, mumbling excuses. Todd pushed over, making room with a polite nod. The man sat down and then stared hard at the picture of Eleanor Colfax Bram.

Steeling his shoulders, Todd focused on the altar, shocked to be at Eleanor's funeral instead of chatting with her about her house. He turned to the fellow next to him, wanting to ask how she had died, but his strange smile was more unnerving than not knowing what had happened.

§§§

Above the altar, a round, stained glass window had been set into the stone, and through the chinked mortar, a rogue tendril of ivy had forced itself in, splaying its leaves over the colored glass. The roots of the tenacious plant clung to the wall, and Laura stared at the ivy while the vicar talked about the mystery of life and death.

"God has a plan, and we never know when we'll be called home," he said.

Her mother's death couldn't be part of God's plan. Why would he make her mum suffer like that? It was a pointless, devastating, horrible death. There was no answer to explain why her mother died. She had known every foothold, every dip and bend in the path, every groove in the stone stairs.

Laura sought the comfort of her father's hand as she stared at the wrought iron rack that held rows of votive candles, all lit, flames quivering. When she couldn't hold it in any longer, she gave in to the agony and wept openly.

"God gives us the strength to endure," Reverend Graham intoned. "He provides answers even when grief seems insurmountable."

She squeezed her eyes shut. There was nothing the vicar could say to soften the blow or ease her pain. She didn't think she could get through much more, but then he finished speaking, and Megan Wiles walked up to the altar. Her tender eulogy was full of humor, raising chuckles and some tears, too.

Laura took several deep breaths. It was her turn. She walked to the lectern, praying that she'd be able to speak, hoping the weight pressing on her heart would ease enough to get the words out. Throughout the chapel she saw tear-streaked faces looking pinched and red.

"I was truly blessed to have Eleanor Colfax Bram for my mother." Laura began reading, but tears made it impossible to see her notes. She knew what she wanted to say, and set them aside. "Mum was as patient, and kind, and as generous as a mother could be. She loved to read out loud, and sometimes, when I'm reading, the voice in my head is hers – I hope I'll always have that."

She scanned the faces in the pews, Winnie wracked with sobs, Nigel pressing his handkerchief against his mouth, and Gertie Barnes with her head in her hands. They all had a lifelong connection with her mother. This was a loss for them too.

Laura opened a small leather-bound book. The volume of poems was one of her mother's treasured possessions. "My mother loved poetry, and this book is as old as the manor house. The poems in it are written in French by an unknown author, and she was translating them into English." Blinking to clear her vision, she glanced down at the cramped penmanship in the book and then at the neatly typed and translated page she'd placed on the lectern. Someone else would have to finish translating them now. "This is the poem my mother read most often, and she framed a copy for me when I left England."

A blessing binds your life to mine,
Between our souls a golden thread,
The silken knot so strong and fine
That it may never fray or shred.

And distance is the dullest knife;
It cannot cut this bond of love.
Though seas divide us now in life,
In spirit we are joined above.

She thanked everyone for coming, thanked them for the kindness they'd shown to her mother, and to herself, and then took her seat. Carl put his arm around her as the vicar led them in another hymn.

Moments later, they were outside at the grave, and she was grateful that her father, Edward, and Carl stood like sentinels around her as she faced the oak casket heaped with flowers. A damp wind whipped their coats, and Reverend Graham kept his remarks brief. When he finished, he started down the hill, leading the slow procession.

A reception was waiting at the house, but she wasn't ready to leave her mother's body. Constable Stiles had recommended that she not look, not see her mother one last time, and now she regretted listening to him.

"I need a moment alone," she said to Carl and her father. "Please go on ahead."

Carl's eyes were full of concern. "I want to stay with you."

"I need a minute before..." Involuntarily, she looked into the open grave.

"It's going to rain," Carl said, and for once he looked uncertain. "Don't take too long."

"I'll be right down." She needed more time – another thirty years – but this was all she had left, just a minute or two.

She waited for the last stragglers to descend and then stood before her mother's coffin as a swift, unrelenting wind buffeted her. "I miss you so much, Mummy." She tucked the poem between the stems of the roses, anchoring it to a thorn, and then laid her hand on the smooth, cool casket. "The world is never going to feel the same without you."

Lingering beside the chapel were three men with cables and shovels, looking miserable and impatient as a dark cloud lowered and rain began pelting down.

She turned away and her glance fell on the tallest cross, weather-beaten, time-worn, with a heart at its center. How long had it been standing watch over these graves? How could she have known there was so little time left with Mum?

Winnie was waiting at the manor's back door, beckoning her to come inside. After shedding her sodden coat, she went straight into the dining room where the guests were milling around the buffet. She began mingling, receiving sympathies, listening to stories, and asking after the jobs, health and families of her guests. It was a role that had always belonged to her mother. Gradually the flow of conversation seemed more natural and she realized that her guests were doing their best to make it easy for her.

Gertie Barnes set out a platter of tea cakes. She and her husband, Ben, owned the village hardware store, and Gertie's gaze raked over the buffet with an eye toward supply and demand. Laura was used to seeing Gertie at the family store with a clipboard in hand, reading glasses dangling from a chain around her neck, her hair in a sensible plait.

She spied Gertie's daughter, a preteen on gangly legs. "How's Amy doing?"

Gertie gazed fondly at her only child. "She's bright, but at twelve she can't sit still any better than when she was five." Her expression changed, and she shook her head. "Your Mum was so young."

Over the last few days Laura had noted the way people's eyes shifted to take in the house and its furnishings, and then came back to her again. They all wanted to know what she planned to do.

Gertie smiled sympathetically at Laura, then tapped the man next to her on his shoulder. "Have you met Paul?" He looked close to Laura's age and smiled as Gertie introduced him. "Ben's younger brother Paul is staying with us while he gets his construction business started."

Laura stared into Paul's tanned face, his eyes crinkling at the edges as though he were used to squinting into the sun. He needed a haircut; wispy strands of blond hair splayed in all directions. She tried not to stare at his long nose, squashed on the end, dented in the middle, obviously broken and badly healed.

"I'm sorry about your mum." He held out a calloused palm. "How long will you be staying?"

She had planned to spend two weeks in England and then return to her classes in Boston. But now it was her turn to take a sidelong glance at the mahogany chairs, the walnut secretary, and the display cabinets with English marquetry panels. Her mother's life, her grandparents' lives, and a wealth of family history stood in every room. How was she supposed to pull apart what had taken generations to build?

"I have to think about it," she said.

He nodded as though taking the time to think things through was exactly what he would do.

§§§

Todd joined the group of well-wishers waiting to pay their respects, unsure what he would say to Mrs. Colfax Bram's daughter. One moment she looked composed, and in the next she seemed distressed, like she needed an escape. How could she stand there and talk to so many people?

"You're here." A hand pressed down on his shoulder. "So very nice of you to come."

Relief surged through him as he recognized a familiar face, even if he couldn't remember her name.

"Megan Wiles," she added helpfully, while eyeing his every day clothes with a sympathetic shake of her head. "Of course, you wouldn't have heard. Let me introduce you to Laura, Eleanor's daughter." She shouldered to the front of a small group talking to Laura, and interrupted. "Mr. Woodbridge met your Mum in Bristol last Saturday evening."

At the mention of Bristol, Laura gave him her full attention. "You saw Mum? Last Saturday?"

"I'm sorry about your mother. She was so nice, and I was looking forward to talking with her again."

"He's writing a book," Megan explained. "About medieval houses."

"Actually, I'm tracing the sources of materials in medieval English construction." He glanced at Megan, hoping she'd add the part about him doing research on Bannock Manor.

Laura stared at him, an unreadable expression on her face. "Were you talking to my mother about the castle ruins?"

"Yes."

Megan turned to him, her face pale. "That's where Eleanor's body was found."

"She mentioned the ruins, but we mostly talked about the manor," Todd said, wanting to ease the look of concern on her face.

"So, you only met my mother a few days ago?" Her tone became guarded, questioning.

"She invited me –" What could he say that might sound comforting? "I told your mother about my research, and she invited me to visit Bannock Manor." He'd been so excited about her house, the perfect house, built in the right era, and with almost no renovations to the medieval section. "She told me to come by today –"

Tears filled Laura's eyes, and the conversation dropped like a rock in an icy stream. Before he could reassure her of his good intentions, she was surrounded by a gaggle of old ladies, the same ones he'd seen in the chapel, hankies still fluttering like banners.

"I'm sorry," he repeated. "Maybe we can talk some other time." He saw his opportunity slipping away as Laura turned from him and didn't look back.

§§§

Carl had set up a drinks station on one of the sideboards. The servery behind the dining room was too remote; it was the perfect location for a servant who didn't want to be seen, but he wanted to keep an eye on Laura. Grief seemed to have robbed her of her critical faculties. She had huge decisions to make, decisions with financial implications of a magnitude that boggled even his mind, and he was used to working with giant sums of money. To make matters worse, Edward was babying her and her father seemed to have lost his footing in the family tragedy.

Carl fixed a gin and tonic, added a twist, and smiled heartily at someone with a pasty complexion. All of the guests had pasty complexions because they all spent a lifetime in a rain sodden country. The man with whom Laura was talking was the exception.

"There's no more in that one," a crackly voice said.

"What?" Carl looked down to see that he had upended an empty gin bottle. He offered the elderly gentleman a brandy instead.

The man took his snifter and wandered away, and Carl went back to staring at Laura. She was reeling and the old manor house, in spite of its crumbling plaster, seemed to anchor her. He wanted to get her the hell out of here, take her on vacation, take her anywhere, but the timing was wrong. She needed to recover some of her equilibrium and sort herself out; she needed time to reach the inevitable conclusion on her own.

"Do you need anything?"

"Huh?" It took a moment for Edward's voice to register. Carl said impatiently, "Get more booze."

"You look like you could use a drink yourself," Edward said. "Don't ever hire servants," he added mildly. "You'd be lousy with them."

Finally, the guy Laura was talking to walked away, and Carl made a beeline to her side. Her face was a mask of fatigue. "You need a break," he said. "Is there somewhere we can go?"

"I shouldn't leave," she said. "Right now, I'd like nothing more than to hide in my bedroom, but I have to do this."

"Just give me a minute. Please." He hated, hated, hated having to beg.

She seemed distracted as she led him toward the rear of the house.

He heard a clatter of pots as they passed the kitchen, and they continued along a corridor past an arched door. "Where does that go?"

"It leads to the medieval section of the house. We always keep it locked." Laura pushed on a smaller door. "This will take us into the cook's garden." They went into the private courtyard bordered on every side by plants. She didn't look at him when she said with too much certainty, too much finality, "I've decided not to go right back right away – not until school's ready to start."

He leaned against the side of the house. Some kind of vine was creeping up the wall, and he resisted the urge to yank it down. The thought of Laura spending the summer alone in this mausoleum made his temper, which he'd been keeping banked like a modest fire, flare. "That's ridiculous." His bunched muscles needed release, and he pushed against the rough wall. If it had been within his power to topple the house, he would have done it. The manor was doomed, and it was pointless for her to stay, but he squelched his impatience and said as gently as he could, "I'm sorry. But you are going to have to sell this place."

"Not right away."

"You don't understand the finances."

Her gaze sharpened; he finally had her attention.

"Do you think I'm going to give up my family home just because you and Edward crunched some numbers? This house is all I have left here, and I'm going to stay for the summer, just like I always do."

"You can't stay here alone."

"I'm not alone."

He closed his eyes and counted to ten. When he opened them, he saw that his first impression had been correct. The garden was a mess, and the manor was truly dilapidated. Worse even than the manor, however, was that Laura was being both childish and stubborn. There was no reasoning with her. He couldn't force her back to Heathrow Airport. Her face was pale, and her eyes looked raw and red-rimmed.

"You're only delaying the inevitable," he said.

§§§

It was after six by the time the last of the visitors left, and Laura hadn't seen her father for a couple of hours. She found him in the library, sitting in an armchair, his long legs crossed at the ankles, the scotch bottle and a crystal tumbler on the side table at his elbow. "Come in, sweetheart," he said when he saw her.

She remembered tiptoeing into the library as a little girl and seeing her father seated in that same chair with a book in his lap. No matter how quietly she had tried to steal in, he always seemed to know she was there. Sometimes he continued with his own reading, and sometimes he picked up a book of fairy tales and read to her while she cuddled on his lap. He must have anticipated her visits because her book was always as readily within his reach as the whisky glass was now.

Tears were slipping down his face as she went to stand beside him. He'd taken a painting down from the library wall and held it balanced on his knee. The artist had carefully depicted a stray rose against the backdrop of the garden wall.

She read the artist's name in the lower corner. Chesterfield. "I've always loved that painting."

"Did your mother ever tell you about Chesterfield? He was her first love."

"Mum was in love with a painter?" She had never thought about her mother's romantic interests.

"She couldn't get up the nerve to leave this place and marry him, so he married someone else. A few years later she settled for me."

"Dad, you're the greatest catch in the world."

He lifted the picture, and for a moment she was afraid he might fling it across the room. "She let life pass her by." He refilled his glass and tossed back a gulp.

She took the painting, returned it to its place on the wall, and then sat down on the nearby ottoman.

He sipped his whisky and seemed to be thinking about how to go on. "It was impossible to run my business from England. For six years I commuted back and forth. You were probably too young to remember."

"Is that why you and Mum divorced?"

"I also had to think of Edward. He needed a full time father, and I wanted him in American schools. Eleanor would never leave this house, no matter the price." He swallowed hard. "It was a relief when she agreed to let you live with me."

They sat in silence for several minutes, and Laura thought about the custody decisions her parents had made. As a child, she'd thought only of how hard it was on her; now she could see how painful it must have been for them, and she wondered if her mother had ever been truly happy.

"Trying to maintain an obsolete way of life is both a burden and a blessing," her father said. "Your grandfather believed in keeping the manor at all costs, and he had to sell a lot of land in order to pay the inheritance taxes."

Laura knew the history. Her grandfather's two older brothers had both died in the war, and each time a different son inherited more land was sold to pay yet another inheritance tax. By the time her mother had inherited thousands of acres had been sold to pay the debts.

Now it was her turn to pay the death duties.

"This is a beautiful home." He seemed to taste his words like the whisky, rolling them on his tongue. "But what good are dozens of bedrooms, and all those other formal rooms, if you can't make them comfortable? They're drafty, damn near uninhabitable. It's too much house for only a handful of people." He stroked the back of her hand. "Owning a manor home is like being caught in a trap – you end up gnawing away at your possessions in order to stay alive."

§§§

On Monday afternoon, Edward packed their suitcases into the rented Mercedes. "Okay, that's all of it." He slammed the trunk and gave Laura a brotherly hug. "Don't be afraid to ask for help."

Carl pulled her into his arms. "It doesn't feel right, leaving you behind."

"This isn't what I imagined your first visit would be like," she said, already feeling alone. He stroked her cheek, and she pressed her forehead against his chest. "I love you," she whispered.

"You too, and I'll call you when I get home."

She hugged him again, holding onto him tightly, battling the urge to tell him to wait; she'd run inside, pack a bag and go back with them.

Her father was the last one to come out, and the strain he felt was obvious by the dark circles under his eyes. Gazing up at the house, he said, "She's an elegant old thing. But it's just a house, and you own it now." He repeated, "You own it – not the other way around."

She clasped his upper arm. "I couldn't have made it through the last few days without you, Dad." She wanted to hold onto him, clutch at him the way she used to when she was a scared little girl. She was still scared, but she pressed her father's arm once more and let go.

He kissed the top of her head, and then turned away, but not before she saw the worry etched into the deep frown lines around his mouth.

Laura watched the men in her life climb into the car. She waved as they navigated the long lane, holding back tears until they disappeared over the hill. She'd never needed them more, and they knew it, they just didn't know what to do.

When the dust settled, and she knew they were gone for good, Laura walked back into the quiet house. It was just her and the Wilcoxes now.

Inside seemed gloomy, and she couldn't shake the chill, not even in the library, her favorite room. As the dusky light faded, she settled into one of the large, over-stuffed chairs and switched on a reading lamp. The soft light illuminated the oak floor with its geometric border design, and the large, mismatched Persian carpets. An enormous arrangement of lilies stood on an end table, saturating the air with the left over smell of the funeral. A nine-foot grandfather clock ticked away the minutes.

Turning on a second lamp, she looked around carefully, and noticed that the black lacquered cabinet was gone.

For years her mother had been poking through the rooms, selling off one antique after another just to keep the house going. Laura wished she could talk to her, ask her a million questions; why the cabinet instead of a dresser, when had it been sold and how much time had it bought? And the other questions lurking in her mind, the dangerous ones; why was she out in the storm and what had happened that night?

The sound of a throat clearing startled her, and she looked up.

Nigel stood in the doorway. "I didn't mean to frighten you," he stammered. "Mrs. Dowd asked me to give you this letter."

The cook had worked like a champ the past few days, and Laura needed to let her know how much her efforts had been appreciated. She opened the envelope as Nigel stood watching.

Laura scanned the brief note. "She's giving notice. This is her last week. I don't understand."

"She's been accusing Winnie and me of interfering in her kitchen, but we haven't. She leaves things tidied up at the end of the day, and we're ever so careful not to leave a mess."

"I can't believe she'd quit after all these years." Laura didn't need a cook, she was used to preparing her own meals, but the cook's resignation seemed so sudden and insensitive.

"She claims to have found open tins of food rotting in the pantry." Nigel looked uncomfortable. "There were a few jars of sauce on the shelves where the tops had been loosened and the contents spoiled."

"Who would have done that?" Laura asked. "Maybe some expired cans were pushed to the back and forgotten, and they leaked."

"It wasn't me or Winnie. We weren't trying to get Mrs. Dowd fired, as she claims."

"I know you and Winnie would never upset her on purpose." She set the notice on a side table. The house was going to seem emptier than ever, but maybe it was just as well that she was gone. "I like to cook," Laura said. "I'll take over for now."

Nigel continued to stand as though awaiting instructions, so quiet he was almost invisible. Finally, he asked, "Can I get you anything?"

"No, thanks." She didn't have the slightest idea what to do in the next two hours, let alone the next two months. "Nigel, I don't want you to feel that you have to check on me."

He waited a second longer and then retreated silently.

Chapter Four

He hadn't slept in days. His eyes itched and burned; reds and blues and shades of gray swirled behind his lids when he closed them. Thirsty and hungry, he couldn't stop working. He was connected with people all over the world, and the different time zones kept him busy day and night.

Life and death were in his hands.

Sitting at command central, surrounded by four large computer monitors, his eyes darted from screen to screen, his mind absorbing new movements, his fingers tapping out messages.

In the Edwardian library, a girl worked her way along the wall, rubbing her hands up and down, side to side, trying to find a hidden door, an escape hatch, any way to get out of the room. Two dozen portraits of dead ancestors littered the walls, the largest an earl on horseback, brandishing a sword, smiling, as if nothing would give him more pleasure than to impale the silly girl.

He wished the earl could come to life and kill her, but that would rob him of the pleasure of seeing her die in a trap of his own making. On her fourth trip around the room, she stopped in front of a portrait of a Victorian family all dressed in black. She touched the frame.

Nothing happened.

She was new to his server, and he wanted to handle her carefully. His fingers danced over the keyboard. 'Do you Skype?'

Her response was quick. 'No.'

Her character pulled the painting away from the wall, and it crashed to the floor.

He wanted to talk to her, give her some clues, keep her coming back. He typed, 'You're on the right track.'

After finding nothing useful beneath the low hanging pictures, she pulled up a chair to reach the next highest tier.

Slow and cautious, she snooped and shifted, knocked and poked.

While she was occupied, he directed his attention to the next monitor. The medieval castle was his favorite place. He'd built the walls and towers with painstaking detail. The dungeon held all the best devices of torture: the stretching rack, bed of nails, and a well-used iron maiden. Guys loved this stuff and always came back, always wanted to conquer the game. They didn't care how many times he killed them.

The usual players were there, fascinated by his recent changes and the surprising new ambushes. These idiots couldn't design worlds like he did; they spent their lives trying to survive the creations of others. The best part was that once he had their characters trapped, they were stuck until he finished them off. They couldn't commit suicide and start over as in other games. He was in complete control and took his time torturing them.

He tightened the crank on the rack, and a man's arms popped out of his shoulder joints. It would be fun to watch him try to escape now, with his arms dangling uselessly. Deliberately leaving the dungeon door open, he had his guard release the man from the rack. Sometimes he let the ones who escaped the dungeon get as far as the outer walls, and then he released the wolves. That was always bloody.

Switching to the third computer, he entered his password and opened *The Family Tree.*

The father, a drunken sod, crawled along the sewers, begging for ale.

The mother ate. The useless cow never had an original thought in her head. She started on another platter of food, eating until she exploded, spewing food and guts. She always died easily.

The brother and sister pleaded for mercy, but it was never granted. Why should he be kind after what they'd done to him? It would be better if they were really on the server, like the girl in the first game. His graphics were so good he could almost forget that he'd designed and programmed them.

He had first become interested in his family's genealogy as a way to discover the source of his own genius. He had traced his four grandparents, the aunts and uncles he'd never known, and the cousins who didn't give a shit. He tracked down where they had lived and what their occupations had been. Some had lived long lives – most hadn't, but what he mostly found were criminals and louts. They were all represented here, like action figures, his program so complex that he could duplicate their lives on his computer. The better he got, the more details he added.

Overall, they were an unsatisfactory lot – until he went all the way back to his great-great-grandfather. That was when he discovered the big payoff; he was distantly related to the family who owned Bannock Manor.

Chapter Five

Laura understood why her mother hadn't kept a full staff. There simply wasn't a budget to retain enough people to keep the manor running as it should. As time passed, and staff retired or moved on, their positions weren't refilled. Instead, the standards were relaxed and adjustments made. Winnie and Nigel were doing their best to keep up, but many of the rooms on the upper levels were closed up, and the neglect showed inside the house, and on the grounds outside.

Now that Laura was here, she wanted to help. Winnie and Nigel protested, but with so much to do, they soon relented.

"We always clean the books in May," Winnie said, handing Laura a pair of white cotton gloves. "These will protect the pages from the oil on your hands."

The floor-to-ceiling shelves in the library held thousands of volumes. Laura stood toward the top of the rolling ladder in the classics section, and one by one, passed books down to Winnie, who carried them to Nigel, the only one lucky enough to be seated. He flicked a soft brush against the outside edge of the pages, cracked the spine and fluttered the leaves of each book, searching for mildew or beetle larva.

She wasn't usually around in May, and this was the first time she'd ever helped with this particular job. Even wearing gloves, she loved the feel of the old leather volumes, the pages edged in gilt. She kept stopping, reading passages, the faded ribbons marking the place where a long-ago reader had left off. She'd spent her entire life around books, and yet the variety in the library, the depth of the subject matter, the range of topics and languages amazed her.

She opened a small leather-bound book to its second page and gasped. "Is this what I think it is? It looks like a first edition of Pride and Prejudice."

"It is." Winnie reached up. "I've not read much of her." Her cloth worked up one side of the cover and down the other.

Laura got the impression that, had Austen herself appeared in the library, the Wilcoxes would have carried on.

Nigel, too hard of hearing to follow Laura and Winnie's conversation, scrutinized the pages. He suddenly went rigid with indignation, and called out, "I found one of the little beasties!"

Laura craned her neck and almost fell off the ladder. "Let me see what it looks like."

The beetle larva had eaten a tunnel on its way from the binding toward the outer edge of the valuable book, littering the damaged pages with silk-like threads.

Nigel picked out the insect and held it up to the light, then carefully deposited it in a cut glass ashtray. He used the eraser end of a pencil to crush it so as not to sully his gloves. Then he dusted the soiled pages, meticulously sweeping the debris into the bin between his knees. "Too many of these and we have an infestation," he said.

Laura's feet hurt, and her legs were quivering. "Who usually climbs up and down the ladder?" she asked.

"I do," Nigel said, "but it's nice having someone younger around."

Winnie peeled off her gloves. "It's time for a rest."

"I'll make tea," Laura quickly offered.

In the kitchen, she started to fill the kettle but the water from the tap looked brownish. After running for a few minutes, it came out clear, then sputtered noisily and dropped to a trickle. After another few minutes, clear water gushed out. This was ridiculous. Until she could get the pipes fixed, they needed to start using bottled water for drinking and cooking.

How many other details needed seeing to? Laura had a funny feeling in the pit of her stomach, like she'd missed an appointment or a final exam. She'd taken so many things for granted, and suddenly it dawned on her that she didn't know how much Nigel and Winnie were paid, and they were far too polite to mention money.

When the tea was ready, she carried the tray into the library, and going against all of the manners her mother had taught her, risking an affront to English propriety, she launched into the topic of finances. "I want you to know that your salaries will continue as always, but you'll have to tell me how much." She forced herself to continue in spite of the surprised looks on their faces. "Did Mummy pay you by check? Was it weekly?"

"Your mother wrote us each a check," Winnie said quietly, brushing a few imaginary crumbs from her lap. "Every other week."

"And the amount?"

They didn't answer, and Laura stifled a sigh. She'd find it in Mum's bank statements.

"We've lived here most of our lives," Nigel said, straightening his spoon, lining it up beside his saucer. "We'd like to stay on – that is, if you're keeping the house."

She looked up to find Winnie's gaze on her.

"We know you're making changes," Winnie said quietly. "We just thought you should know – we've always expected to end our days here. It was – our agreement."

"Of course." Laura tried to sound reassuring. She couldn't imagine Bannock Manor without them. Neither of the Wilcoxes had ever married, and they had nowhere else to live. Mum had known that, and it was part of the plan, like a pension. Winnie and Nigel had been promised a place at the manor for as long as they needed it. But how could she reconcile that obligation if she didn't keep the house?

Nigel cocked his head as he studied Laura. "You look just like your Mum when she was young," he said, "with your blond hair and blue eyes."

Winnie, always easily drawn back into memories, said, "Your mum was a beauty, and the moment your father laid eyes on her, he fell in love." She paused, placing a finger on her cheek and tapping lightly, thoughtfully. "That would have been when she was twenty-nine, only a few years younger than you are now."

Laura sat transfixed, watching the subtle changes that came over the Wilcoxes as they cast their minds into the past. The years seemed to fall away from Winnie, her face smoothing as she smiled, and Nigel's hands, now that he wasn't working, weren't trembling so badly.

It was comforting talking to the Wilcoxes, their voices drifting, eyes turned inward, the teacups steaming on the library table. She wanted to know more about her mother, the things they would have seen and heard after decades of service. "Do you think Mum was lonely?" she asked. "Maybe if she'd remarried..."

"Eleanor spent years waiting –" Nigel broke off, but it was too late for him to snatch back the thought.

Laura glanced at the painting, remembering her father's anger. "For Chesterfield?"

"Yes. Chesterfield," Nigel said, with a hint of disdain. "He was far below your mother's social standing."

Winnie's voice was soft, and Laura almost didn't hear the whispered words. "She was packed, ready to go, but her father wasn't a man to be crossed. He stopped her at the door."

Laura imagined the scene: her mother on the verge of running away, and being stopped with a curt reminder about family responsibility. Later her mother must have unpacked her bags and wondered if she'd lost her chance for happiness.

"We were all relieved when Bernard proposed," Nigel said.

As they finished their tea and quietly returned to work, the Wilcox's subtle request weighed on her. She had to face the financial issues. Carl made it clear in his daily calls just how much value he placed on sound financial decisions.

And every phone call with him made Laura wonder about her own chances for happiness.

Later that afternoon, she sat down at her mother's desk and looked at the open calendar, smoothing down the page. On April twenty-second, the day of her mother's death, an entry was penciled in: Lecture on historic renovation with Megan, Bristol University. There were other entries, other plans, other events that would never be attended.

Would it always hurt this much?

In one drawer, pushed all the way to the back and tied with a ribbon, was a packet of letters, perhaps two dozen, postmarked over a two-year period when her mother had been in her twenties.

Curious, she untied the bundle and read the love letters from Chesterfield, one letter after another, soft pages worn from having been read over and over. The letters repeated pleas that her mother seemed never to have answered, more evidence of an unfulfilled love. Chesterfield, the artist, had asked Eleanor to run away with him, to leave her disapproving family and live with him in Paris.

Slowly, Laura lowered the last letter to the desk, the one in which he said, finally, that he was losing hope. Not his love, he was swift to assure her; he would always love her, but he couldn't abandon his dreams while she remained at the manor. Folded into the letter was a train ticket, the passage paid for but never used.

She put the letters back in the drawer. Her mother could have followed her heart, but she had stayed at Bannock Manor and made a suitable but unhappy marriage.

Laura closed her eyes and thought about the consequences of her mother's choices, wondering how to distinguish the sacrifices from the mistakes. Mum had kept the manor but lost what might have been her greatest love.

Laura stretched her shoulders and twisted side to side, trying to loosen the tight muscles in her back. Resuming her search, she found the checkbook tucked into the bottom drawer. It revealed a modest balance, and looking at the entries felt like an invasion of privacy. She focused on her mother's careful, elegant script, the familiar looping "g's" and precise, upright "t's."

She'd been here over a month now and should be thinking about paying the bills, but didn't know if she was authorized to use the checking account. In the back of her mind she heard Carl's accusatory tone, *You should have seen to that already.* First thing tomorrow, she'd get it done. No way was she going to give Carl the satisfaction of saying *I told you so.*

§§§

Her mother's bank was in Dursley, one of many small towns linked by ribbons of country roads. Winding lanes crisscrossed without posted signs, and a wrong turn could send unsuspecting tourists through a patchwork of fields. When she reached the town center, she found an empty space in the car park and dropped a couple of one pound coins into the meter box. As she fumbled to stick the ticket onto her windshield it began to drizzle. Quickly, she locked the car and launched her umbrella, hunching deeper into her thin jacket, scurrying toward the bank. She was chilled through by the time she reached the lobby.

The bank teller seemed to find Laura's awkward, stumbling request for information about her mother's account suspicious, and asked her to step aside while the bank manager was summoned.

The tall, silver-haired man looked familiar, and he greeted her by name. "Miss Bram. I met you years ago at a summer fête. I'm Louis Stent." He shook her hand warmly. "I'm so sorry for your loss."

Relieved that she seemed to have found an ally, Laura followed him into his office. She dug a bank statement out of her purse and handed it to him.

"Of course, I'll need to see identification." He smiled apologetically. "Our policy requires it."

After she handed over her driver's license, he brought up the account on his computer and studied the screen, frowning. "Hmm."

Her stomach clenched.

"It seems you are listed on one account," he said.

He turned the monitor to face her, touching the screen with the tip of his gold pen. "This is a joint account. You have access to these funds. Unfortunately, the savings account and any other assets will be frozen. Your mother's solicitor can help in that regard."

Nodding, Laura wondered if she looked as naïve as she felt. She jotted down the balance, automatically converting pounds into dollars. It was more than enough to manage an apartment in Boston for a while, but how far would it go at Bannock Manor?

"I've been living off my own savings," she said, "but the staff has to be paid, and I'd like to make some repairs."

"Your biggest priority should be keeping the mortgage current." Mr. Stent paused, as though searching for the right words. "The May payment hasn't been made yet."

Laura sat back. "If...if Mum inherited, why is there a mortgage?"

"It appears that your mother had no income." Underneath Mr. Stent's kind tone, Laura detected a warning. "Every few years she would use some of her equity and take out another loan."

It was so obvious, and yet somehow it had never occurred to her. She thought her mother got by selling a few antiques, but little by little, she'd been going deeper into debt. No wonder Mum avoided repairs and lived with such a small staff. Most of the time she didn't even heat the rooms.

"If you decide to sell," Mr. Stent said, "you have to back out the balance of the mortgage, and the costs of selling. There will be taxes too, as you can imagine."

It was Edward and Carl's advice all over again. The house was too expensive, the taxes too much.

"When will I have access to all the funds?"

"Mr. Pickney can help you begin the legal process. If you're careful, you should have enough for living expenses for a year or so." He paused. "Be careful about repairs though, I've seen projects that run into the tens of thousands. There's no telling what you might encounter; those old structures are terribly unpredictable."

"What if I want to keep it?" It took willpower not to wipe her clammy palms on her slacks. "Do you have any suggestions?"

"It's been popular to set up a hotel or restaurant in large, old homes. Do you have business experience?"

"I'm a history teacher."

"Oh, well, I see. I wouldn't recommend depleting your finances trying to hold onto the manor."

She signed the papers he set before her, thanked him and shook his hand. How was she going to keep the mortgage current? How many more antiques could she sell to try to save the house?

It was still raining when she left the bank, the gloomy weather matching her mood. She dashed to a nearby tea shop, desperate for a comforting cup of tea.

"Cream tea," she told the woman behind the counter. She deserved a treat of scones, clotted cream and jam. Calories be damned!

Settling into a corner table, she retrieved her notepad and started a list of ways to generate income. She wrote: sell art, sell antiques, rent rooms, rent out the manor for weddings and private parties, sell the manor. She scratched the last entry off. That would be selling herself short and unloading everything her mother had sacrificed for.

Then she remembered the groundskeeper's cottage. The cute little house was sitting empty. She could rent that out in a snap, and it might bring in enough to pay for the utilities, maybe the insurance too.

She wanted to check on the cottage as soon as she could, but it was dark when she got home, and during the next few days it rained heavily.

The Wilcoxes went about their jobs, mostly talking in the kitchen when they thought Laura couldn't hear. She'd caught snatches of whispered words about her mother's tragic death and speculations about whether or not Laura would sell the manor.

Finally the rain let up and she slipped on her jacket. Outside, pewter grey clouds hugged the ground, turning the day prematurely dark. She followed the lane as it wound through a copse of trees. It had only been a year since the gardener had retired and moved away, but the farther she walked, the more she saw how everything was overgrown. Maybe Mum should have hired someone else so the estate wouldn't look so deserted.

By the time she reached the groundskeeper's cottage, discouragement was settling in. What had once been a verdant front lawn was now a tangle of tall grass and weeds, and the hedges, usually manicured green walls, blew wildly in the wind.

Laura tugged open the door, but paused at the threshold and peered in nervously. Almost tip-toeing, she entered slowly. In the front room, the remnants of an old computer had been left behind. The case was open, the various components scattered about, and most of the letters were missing from the keyboard, like a half-eaten corn on the cob.

In the kitchen, a chipped cup sat on the counter, a layer of mold floating inside. More dirty crockery, sprinkled with rat droppings, lay in the sink. Cabinet doors hung loose on their hinges, and the stove was crusted with dried bits of food. Empty ale bottles stuffed with cigarette butts and half-eaten bags of crisps were scattered across the table.

She shuddered. Someone had been in here recently.

Poking her head into the bathroom, she gagged and backed out.

Before venturing into the bedroom, she glanced in, and was relieved to find it empty. Rain blew in where one of the windows had been left open and now a greenish-black mildew grew along the wall beneath it. Pushed into the corner was an old iron bed, its rusting springs topped with a pile of mildewing blankets.

The whole place was disgusting. Some local kids had probably discovered the isolated cottage and made it their hang out.

She squeezed between the bed and the wall to close the window, and found that dampness had swollen the wood until it wouldn't budge. Taking advantage of her full height, she reached the top of the window's frame and pulled, inching it down. She backed up to get more leverage and something sharp stabbed her in the calf.

She bit her lip, stifling a scream.

A rusted bed spring had gouged a hole in her jeans and broken through the skin. Pain from the jagged hole began pulsing, the wound trickling blood. How long since she'd last had a tetanus shot? Ten years, at least. She'd ruined her jeans, and now she'd have to go to the doctor.

Swearing under her breath, she limped outside. How could someone be using the cottage, right under the noses of the people in the main house? And no one noticed? If she found out who had left the cottage in such a state, she'd press charges.

A new priority went to the top of her list - get a new lock on the cottage door and clean it out.

Off to her left was the stable block, built in the early Victorian years. While she was out here, she should check on that too. What if she had more squatters? She picked her way around puddles until she reached the closest block of stables.

The large, square structure had an entrance wide enough for a carriage and team of horses to pass through in the north and south walls, and in the center was a large courtyard. The buildings were two stories high, with stables and tack rooms on the ground floor, and apartments for grooms and male servants above. Two of the apartments were larger, and a century ago might have been considered rather grand. They were meant to house visiting bachelors.

Dust motes and cobwebs floated in the weak light, and she sneezed. The stalls were empty; they hadn't kept horses for years. Old saddles, bridles and other tack hung on wooden pegs, antiquated combs and brushes for animals long gone, lay on a workbench. The brass placard above one stall door read Thunder, her grandfather's favorite stallion. Horses and hunts, parties and celebrations – this place had certainly seen better times.

She imagined how it might look with fresh paint, polished tack, and clean straw, how it might sound with horses clomping and snorting, and the voices of grooms calling out.

Part of her wanted to bring back the past, but that was the nostalgic, romantic historian in her indulging in a fantasy. Her father had kept a few horses, but she lacked his money and his know-how. And besides, what made her think she could succeed where he had failed?

Something scuttled on the floor above her, and she froze. It was probably just a mouse or some other harmless creature, but when she sneezed again, the shuffling sounded different, heavier. Every little thing was spooking her these days. Ignoring the pain in her leg, she rushed outside and back to the safety of the house.

Chapter Six

It was just barely turning light outside, but Laura had been lying awake for over an hour. All night long she'd tossed and turned, worrying about the house, about Winnie and Nigel, whether or not her mother should have married Chesterfield instead of her father. And Carl – she agonized over how exasperated he was with her.

Untangling herself from her blankets, she got up and went to the window. Heavy fog had settled in, matching her gloomy mood. The stables and the trees at the edge of the woods were barely visible. Spring was like that, damp and foggy in the morning, then turning sparkling bright in the afternoon. That was exactly what she needed – a change in the weather, and in her attitude. She had a million things to do today, starting with meeting her mother's solicitor.

Laura went into her bathroom and turned on the shower. It always took a long time for hot water to make its way from the water heater in the cellar to her bathroom two floors up. While selecting her clothes, she listened to the alternating sputters and dribbles, hoping the spray would turn into a nice steady stream, but the minute she stepped in, the pressure got finicky and the flow of water slowed to a trickle. She jerked the tap off, turned it on again, and after two more tries, the pipes groaned and the spray increased. Shivering, she turned up the hot lever; if someone in another part of the house flushed a toilet, her shower would suddenly turn scalding. The discolored water smelled like rust, and she hoped the floral fragrance of her shampoo would overpower it.

She got in and out as quickly as possible.

Her mother had been talking about fixing the plumbing for years, but kept putting it off. The rust wasn't new, but the graininess of the water was. Laura dressed hurriedly, and grabbed the list of questions she'd jotted down in the middle of the night. She kept thinking of more things she needed to know about her legal situation, and she couldn't worry about the water pressure right now.

At ten a.m. sharp, she walked into Mr. Pickney's office on High Street, and a small bell jingled above the door. The reception area was deserted, with nothing but an old-fashioned telephone on an empty desk. In the corner, a dusty, artificial plant managed to look sickly.

The door to the inner office opened and a diminutive man, more like a leprechaun or an elf, came out to greet her.

He extended a child-sized hand. "Laura Bram, I'm glad we're finally able to discuss this business."

It was more than just *business* to her, and her stomach was already in knots, but she managed to smile and return his handshake.

Mr. Pickney took a seat behind a massive desk, and Laura resisted the urge to peek beneath it. Did his feet even reach the floor? In contrast to his high-backed, cushioned leather seat, her chair was low, black vinyl.

He clasped his hands on top of the one folder in front of him. Laura read the curled edge: Colfax-Bram.

"My dear," he said, "your mother left a will naming you her only heir and beneficiary." He paused, as if waiting for her to be happily surprised.

She nodded, unfolded her list of questions and smoothed the paper.

Before she could ask even one, Mr. Pickney cleared his throat. "With your permission, I'll take the next step and apply to the High Court Probate Division for a grant of probate. This will give you authority to act on behalf of the estate to pay creditors, sell personal items and, of course, to sell the house."

"I haven't decided about the house yet. And, there's Winnie and Nigel to consider."

"Yes, they've been there a long time. A generous severance, say, oh, equivalent to six month's salary would be the way to go there."

She'd forgotten to look for the salary amount in her mother's checkbook and still needed to follow up on that.

"You can sell the manor in its current condition," Mr. Pickney said. "Then you won't have to be concerned with costly renovations." His eyes pierced hers. His glasses were too big for his face, and she decided he looked more like a disapproving owl than an elf. "I may have a lead on a developer who's looking for a nice property like yours."

"It doesn't seem right," she said, holding her hands tightly clenched in her lap, "that I should have to give the British government so much money when I don't have it."

"Had your mother made plans..."

She could feel her lips quivering and pressed them together. "Mum couldn't have known she was going to die so soon."

From a deep drawer, Mr. Pickney produced a king-sized box of tissues and pushed it across the expanse of his desk. "It was a very unfortunate accident," he said, his voice surprisingly kind. "She would have needed to transfer the assets to you seven or more years ago to avoid the death duties. Since that didn't happen, well, you have to pay the inheritance tax."

Her glance fell to her list. All the little questions about repairs and how to legally rent the cottage, and all the big questions, like how to take over the mortgage, stared at her. She took a breath, but Mr. Pickney was ahead of her again.

"You should give serious consideration to selling the house – the sooner the better." He leaned forward. "You don't want to spend what's left of your money now, only to have to sell in the end."

A small voice pricked her conscience – Carl's voice, not hers. *It's your inheritance – you have to get a handle on it.* "If I do decide to sell, I would want it to go to a family who will fix it up and live there. Maybe keep it for generations."

"That would be unlikely. Keep an open mind; large sums for financing aren't easy to come by. Business enterprises, such as hotels or timeshares, make good buyers because they've got their own construction crews and they won't demand unreasonable repairs." He picked up the file, opened it, and shuffled the papers. "Let's get these documents signed. Here," he said, indicating a signature line. "And here. And the next one. Sign here." One after another, the forms appeared and then disappeared with her signature, back into his manila file.

She was formally accepting the responsibilities of the estate, exactly what Carl and Edward had warned her not to do. But she couldn't walk away.

"One more thing," Mr. Pickney said, smoothing the edges of the papers. "You're required to notify your mother's homeowner's insurance about her death. It's common to have a 'lapse on death' clause, which can make the policy void. With so many valuables, it's essential that you update your coverage."

"What if someone moved into the groundskeeper's cottage without anyone knowing?"

"Don't let that happen," he warned. "Once you've got squatters, only the courts can get them out."

"I want to be clear on one point," she said. "I'm not selling the house, just starting the probate."

"Of course." He hopped out of his chair and ushered her out through the dusty entrance. "Laura, one last thing before you go."

She turned at the door, eager to be out of his office.

"Remember that you only have three months to complete the inventory for Inland Revenue. Why don't you start in the attic? Old items usually have less of an emotional pull."

She thanked him and left. Outside, the fog had burned off, and the sun was shining, just as she'd predicted, but the good weather didn't fool her. By dusk, the fog would be rolling back.

She took her time, walking slowly toward Major's Necessities, shedding some of her aggravation as she window-shopped. She loved Tenney Village, and every time she walked along High Street, she fell in love with it all over again. The main avenue started at the Norman church and ended at the White Hart Pub; only two short blocks between the Holy Spirit and whisky spirits. Along the way, the homes and office buildings were tightly packed, many sharing walls and rooflines with their neighbors. Where one section of roof had been repaired, another sagged; some storefronts sported fresh plaster while others had been stripped to stone and mortar.

Laura passed the bakery, the butcher's, and the Goodwill. When she reached Hanover's Grocers she noticed litter and weeds accumulating in the car park. The market had gone out of business several months ago, and now the nearest food shopping was in Dursley.

She was careful crossing the street. The pedestrian walkways were narrow and passing cars whizzed by only inches from the sidewalk. Major's Necessities, the hardware store, occupied a double storefront, and as she pushed through the entrance, Laura tried to remember everything she needed: nails and screws, batteries and bottled water, a new door lock for the cottage, and window latches for the big house.

Twelve-year-old Amy Barnes was standing by the book rack, dusting romance titles and peering closely at the fleshy cover pictures. Her long, coltish legs didn't come from her pear-shaped mother or scrawny father, but probably from her grandfather, whose military bearing stared down from a picture over the front register.

Without looking up, Amy asked, "May I help you?"

"Hi, Amy. Nice to see you again."

"Oh! Hi." Amy dashed down the aisle, calling to her mother, "Laura's here!"

Gertie came trotting out of the stockroom. "Lovely to see you're out and about. What can we do for you?"

"I need light bulbs – a lot of them." It was amazing how many times she entered a room and the lamps wouldn't turn on. Sometimes it was only a loose bulb, but often there wasn't one at all. She didn't want the Wilcoxes to break their necks in the dark. "And, do you carry these?" Laura pulled a broken window latch out of her pocket. "I could probably use a dozen."

Gertie plucked it out of Laura's hand and turned it over. "This is a specialty item; nice, heavy old brass piece. There's a shop in Stroud that carries vintage hardware, and you can expect to pay dearly." She handed the locking mechanism back to Laura. "How are Winnie and Nigel? It was such a shock for them."

"They're managing all right." Her mother's death was on people's minds, and it came up every time she talked to someone. Even though she expected it, the emotions still ambushed her.

Gertie stooped to adjust a row of cleaning products that had been knocked astray, and when she straightened, she brushed tears from her eyes.

Laura placed a hand on Gertie's arm, touched by her obvious affection for Winnie and Nigel. "I'll let them know you asked after them."

"I don't know how they're going to adjust. And you. How are you doing?"

"Keeping busy." Hoping to avoid the emotional quagmire they were heading into, Laura added, "We've got spotty water pressure, and it's driving Winnie mad. Do you know a good plumber?"

"Ben's brother, Paul, can do it."

Laura thought back to the funeral. The blond guy – he'd seemed nice. "How soon can he come by?"

"I'll talk to him," Gertie promised. "I'll make sure he goes up to the manor straight away."

"Laura?" Amy scooted in between them, hands on her slim hips. "You forgot to check your Mum's postbox. It's overflowing."

Getting her mother's mail had slipped her mind entirely, and her own mail at home. Now that she was staying all summer, it would have to be forwarded. Grateful for the interruption, she headed to the back of the store, which was also the local post office.

Gertie's husband, Ben, was sorting mail. Behind him were rows of individual mail boxes, and seeing Laura, he opened the Colfax box and handed her a pile of envelopes.

"Thank you," Laura said, flipping through them slowly: the electric bill, the telephone bill, advertisements, a formal envelope addressed with calligraphy that looked like a wedding invitation. Should she bother with an RSVP?

"I hope you're planning to stay on at the manor," Ben said.

Looking up, Laura braced for another awkward conversation, but then relaxed. He meant well, and Ben always got right to the point. At the funeral reception, he'd shaken her hand and said, *"It's a pity about your mum. There's none like her."* His single line of eulogy had touched her with its truth. Laura might live at the manor, but she couldn't hope to match her mother's effortless grace.

"I'm not sure what I'm going to do," she admitted.

Ben cleared his throat. "I went up to the tower after the funeral."

At the mention of the funeral service, the flood of raw emotions came to the surface again.

"I'll never forget the time we almost lost you," Ben said. "You were just a tot. Nigel came into the village pounding on doors but you weren't to be found. It was raining hard and already dark. We looked for hours."

"I remember," Laura whispered.

She remembered herself as a disobedient five-year-old, scampering up to the ruins to play. She'd lost her footing and fallen into the drawbridge pit, and her ankle got wedged between the jagged stones. The more she struggled, the more it twisted. She lay in the deepening puddles, crying while cold water seeped through her clothes, filling her shoes and making her legs go numb.

"Hallings found you." Ben's voice was soft, reverent, like whispering in church. "He was yelling for us to hurry, but by the time we got there, you weren't moving. We only found you because your baby blanket was near the top, blowing in the storm." Ben gazed at her across the mail counter. "Men saw strange things that night. Nigel bought our whisky afterward, but even with the drink we couldn't find the words to explain it."

She remembered scurrying into the ruins, even though she wasn't allowed, but she'd left her blanket at home.

"I did not," she'd cried, frustrated that no one believed her. "I did not take my blanket!"

Nigel said, "I saw him, sir, bigger than life and using the child's blanket as a signal flag."

"Hallings, you mean," her father thundered.

"No, sir. Hallings saw him too."

"For the love of God, can't anyone keep my child safe without resorting to ghost stories?"

"With Eleanor gone," Ben said, "I couldn't help thinking about it."

Absorbed in the memories, she didn't hear Gertie approach, and she jumped at the sound of her voice.

"Paul said he can come up to the manor this afternoon, and he'll give you a discount. We don't want you paying the professional rates."

"That would be great," Laura said, shaking herself and coming back to the present.

As she was heading to the front register, a man she didn't recognize came into the store. He stopped and stared at her, looking surprised. Had she met him before? A lot of people she barely knew had been at the funeral. She couldn't remember them all. He brushed past her without saying a word and headed down the electrical aisle.

Laura glanced at Gertie, who shrugged and moved to keep an eye on him.

He picked up a heavy duty extension cord, turned, saw them staring, and mumbled something under his breath. Glaring at Laura, he threw it back on the shelf.

Gertie guided Laura to the register. "Just a minute, and I'll ring you up." She quickly doubled back to the mail counter, and a moment later Laura glimpsed Ben moving toward the agitated man.

Distracted, she paid for the lights bulbs, and it wasn't until she got to her car that she realized she'd forgotten to get a new door lock for the cottage. The original one had been pried off.

§§§

Laura had only been home for a half hour when she heard a truck drive up. Looking out the window, she saw Paul Barnes slide out of the front seat. He hefted a mammoth toolbox from the back, and she hurried to meet him.

"Gertie said you need help."

She smiled, glad that he'd come so soon. "I'm not sure where the plumbing problem is. Sometimes I get a trickle, sometimes nothing at all." She was worried that he'd be put out by the size of the house, but he listened patiently, nodding as she pointed out the taps that gave her the most trouble. "I haven't checked them all," she added.

They started at the ground floor bathroom and he yanked the knob on and off several times until water came out.

Wincing at his forcefulness, she warned, "It usually takes a while." She'd been babying the plumbing along, afraid a pipe would break and send water shooting everywhere.

"The hot water's not as bad," he said. "But the cold line has dirt in it."

"Not always – it depends on what else we're using, and how much at once."

After an hour of indoor inspection they headed into the courtyard, and he analyzed the network of pipes clinging to the back wall of the house.

"Those pipes are old, and some of them leak, but I'm not worried about the drain lines – only the fresh water lines," she said. "Fresh being a relative term around here."

He grinned. "It's going to take me a while to track down the trouble." He fiddled some more with the pipes and valves.

"All the sinks, showers and tubs have sporadic pressure," Laura said. "Do you think the problem might be where the water first comes into the house?"

"I see what you mean." Paul located the main line where it connected with the back of the house, just off the kitchen. "If the pipe under this courtyard is broken, then silt and rust would get in your water. I need to dig it up right here." He drew a line with the toe of his boot.

"Can you give me an estimate of the cost?"

"Well, I have to make a list of parts, and I don't know how much pipe needs to be replaced. Unexpected problems can drive up the cost."

She hesitated. Should she get a second opinion? An estimate from a real plumber?

"I'll do a good job," Paul said. "And cheaper than anyone else."

He was Ben's brother, and Ben was honest. She decided to trust him. "When can you start?"

"Right now."

"That'll make our housekeeper, Winnie, really happy."

He pulled his truck around to the back and unloaded a wheelbarrow. "I'll rent heavy equipment if I need it." He smiled reassuringly. "Don't worry. I'll give you invoices for everything."

Spending money on repairs was going to infuriate Carl.

Pickney had told her that if she sold right away, a developer would handle the renovations. But he'd also said it was her responsibility as the homeowner to maintain the property, and they really needed clean water. Now that Paul was working on the plumbing, she could focus on making an inventory for Inland Revenue.

She made her way to the fourth floor, turning on lights, illuminating most of the dark corridors. She opened one door after another. These rooms hadn't been used since her grandparents' time, maybe longer. Sheets disguised the furnishings, and she lifted them to reveal oak and mahogany beds and dressers, tables and chairs.

She passed the narrow stairway once used by the female servants and then came to the housemaid's closet, which still held an assortment of metal buckets, brushes, dusters, and white porcelain pails designed to hold the slops from washbasins. The meager remnants in the linen lobby had been yellowing on the shelves for years. Now the bed sheets, good linens and lace runners for the dressing tables were kept in closets downstairs, closer to the rooms still in use.

Quietly, she pressed on through the maze of musty passages and rooms with small windows that admitted only the sparest light. They had been built for function, not views, designed to house dozens of housemaids and chambermaids in the era when every chore was done by hand and aristocratic families could afford an enormous staff.

In the luggage room, she found a blue, plastic computer mouse perched on top of an old steamer trunk, and the peculiar blend of the old and new made her smile. Her mother must have left it there. But it was puzzling, because Mum wasn't all that great with computers. Feeling sentimental, she left it untouched.

Prying open cracked leather satchels and faded bags, she rifled through clothes, papers and photos, knowing she would have to come back and sort through the contents carefully. She could spend days looking at this stuff, piecing together the lives of relatives, figuring out their connection to the house and her mother.

When she reached the storage room that held old nursery furniture and toys, she heard the steady tempo of rain pattering against the eaves, and looked up at the window sashes, relieved that she didn't see any visible signs of water damage.

It was hard to move in the crowded room and she squeezed between a wicker basket full of painted wooden blocks and a stand that held racquets, mallets and croquet balls, the rounded shapes smooth under her fingers. Train sets and toy tractors, a hobby horse and puppets, all loved by children and then set aside. Along one shelf, rows of metal soldiers marched toward a long ago battle.

Laura made her way to a glass-fronted cabinet that held a doll collection. Many had belonged to her mother and grandmother: fragile porcelain dolls with human hair and painted cheeks, and vinyl ones that resembled real babies. There were even cloth dolls whose sweet expressions had been fashioned by skillful embroidery. She fingered the delicate clothes and stroked the soft hair.

She saved her favorite for last, a Madame Alexander doll with a satin gown, lace petticoats, and a golden coronet atop her auburn hair. She couldn't help cradling it, pressing her cheek to its face. On her fourth birthday, her father had given her the princess doll, and from that moment it won the honored place in the center of her bed. She carefully returned it to the cabinet.

A different shelf held a gift from her mother, a childhood tea set decorated with a rose pattern, and she remembered sitting in the kitchen with Winnie, at the child-sized table and chairs, and pouring real tea with lots of cream and sugar.

In the corner of the room stood a cradle, and Laura recalled a photo taken of her lying in it when she was a few weeks old. In the picture, Edward stood looking down at her, his elbows resting on the ornate wooden headpiece. The footboard was carved with the earliest Bannock crest, the letter B between two leaping stags. Now her favorite baby blanket, looking dingy and tattered, lay in the cradle, left over from the days when she used it to rock her dolls to sleep.

Even if she devoted the whole summer to sorting the heirlooms from the ordinary, she would probably still miss something important. She dusted her hands on her jeans, sat down on one of the little chairs, and looked at the furniture and toys. If she rushed, if she wasn't conscientious enough, she might inadvertently rob her future children of their inheritance. Not only the things that made a house a home, not just the value of antiques, but the history and connection to this side of her family.

It was time to get some real work done and she started to leave the room, but something creaked behind her, and she froze. Stiffly, she slowly turned around and saw the empty cradle rocking of its own accord. She knew she hadn't bumped it, and that it had been stationary as she'd walked away. She waited for the rocking to stop, but instead the pace quickened, back and forth, back and forth.

Backing into the hall, a gust of cold air engulfed her. It had to be the manor ghost. He was trying to tell her something.

Even after she shut the door, she could still hear the cradle rocking as she hurried away.

Chapter Seven

A week after meeting with Mr. Pickney, Laura spent an entire day with an art appraiser. Dressed in slacks and a blouse, the most professional clothes she had with her, she followed the woman from the attic to the cellar, and from room to room as she snapped pictures and took measurements. She offered Laura a magnifying glass, and Laura strained her eyes, trying to see all the tiny details the woman pointed out. Some of the paintings that Laura had barely noticed before elicited great enthusiasm. The appraiser practically gushed over a small portrait of a young girl, suspecting it might be by Sir Thomas Lawrence. That was only the cursory first visit. Now the woman was back in London doing research on Laura's inheritance.

Next, she chose an expert to appraise the value of the books in the library, but she was selective. She wanted someone who really loved books, not just a buyer from an auction house or consignment company looking to turn a quick profit.

Both of the appraisers would have to come back. Collecting information on the inheritance tax was daunting, and she was getting the job done in pieces, accomplishing tasks without making any real decisions about her future, or the future of Bannock Manor. That she was not ready to do.

Today, she needed a change. She put on ripped jeans and an old sweatshirt, ready to tackle the groundkeeper's cottage.

Using gloves, Laura filled plastic bags with trash, rotting food and old computer parts. Paul was working on the trench, but had agreed to take several loads to the dump, including the moldy mattress and blankets.

The sweeping and scrubbing took all afternoon, but the cottage was starting to look cozy. With some fresh paint and a few repairs it would be a nice place to live. She imagined flowers in the window boxes, and then, because she was feeling domestic, she expanded the fantasy to include a shepherd's pie baking in the oven. Or maybe that was because she'd skipped lunch.

The little house wouldn't bring much income, not enough to do more than pay some utilities or insurance, but every bit would help.

Selling antiques and art made more money.

A lot of estate owners held their homes open for public tours or rented them out for private functions, but before she could do that she'd have to get the main house looking better. She'd also have to upgrade the electricity and the bathrooms, but it was a possibility too.

Fortunately, she had options, and the more she worked, the less she felt mired in sadness. Grief was like a swamp, and the house was an island. Either it would be her safe haven, or leave her isolated. All she knew was that she loved it and didn't want to lose it. But three months was barely any time at all to figure out so many complicated decisions, and the potential for mistakes was huge.

She heard Paul's truck approaching and opened the front door. It was already getting dark, and his headlights bounced along the rutted lane. When she got a tenant in here, she'd probably have to put down gravel to keep the road from getting boggy during the winter.

Paul climbed out of his truck, and she stood back as he poked his head inside the cottage. "Looks good." He sounded impressed. "It needed a woman's touch."

She was suddenly aware that he was no longer looking at the clean room, but at her.

"I was just thinking that you might enjoy a tot at the White Hart tonight," he said, his eyes never leaving her face.

"I'm hardly dressed to go out." She looked down at her filthy jeans.

"You can meet me in town later."

The idea was tempting. An evening with Paul at the pub might start gossip flowing, and it would bother Carl if he found out, but it was just a drink with a friend and she was ready to have a little fun.

"A drink might be nice," she said. "I'll meet you after I get cleaned up."

At seven o'clock, she arrived at the White Hart Pub and found Paul waiting out front. He kept his hand on the small of her back as they walked down the steps and into the pub. Hopefully he understood that this was just two friends having a drink.

In the dim interior, it took a moment for her eyes to adjust, and then she saw Kit, the pub's owner, behind the bar, and waved. She'd spent a fair amount of time in here over the years. Heavy pint and half-pint glasses lined up under the taps, chest-high wooden screens separated the varnished tables, and decorative china crockery adorned the walls. A set of stairs led up to a small dining room, and in an alcove beneath the stairs, Kit had a private table favored by tourists in search of romance.

Megan Wiles was planted in her usual booth near the front where she could keep an eye on everyone coming and going. As soon as she spotted Laura, she waved. "Sit here." She scooted over and patted the seat next to her. "How are you?"

"Doing okay," Laura said, sitting down.

Paul shoved a hand through his hair, leaving it sticking up in unruly tufts. He slid into the seat opposite Laura, chin jutting, clearly resentful at sharing a table.

Kit took his time, waiting until they were settled before limping over and placing another whisky in front of Megan. In a voice husky from years of smoke, he asked, "Laura, what'll it be?"

"I fancy a pint of Fuller's," she said.

"Make it two, then," Paul said, resigning himself to their group date.

"You put on a nice reception for your mum," Kit said. "Eleanor never spent much time in here – too classy for this joint." He swiped a damp spot on the table with a dingy towel. "I remember the summer I bought this place. You weren't old enough yet for the bars in the states. You spent every evening in here, sipping Guinness and acting all grown up."

If she'd figured out sooner that Kit was gay, she wouldn't have spent so much time learning to like beer. At the time, he had seemed so romantically bohemian, but now his shoulder-length brown hair showed strands of silver, and although he was still narrow through the hips, his long legs were no longer supple, his limp more pronounced every year. She couldn't remember who had told her – Winnie, maybe – that he'd been a great dancer before hurting himself on stage in London.

"I had a mad crush on you," Laura said.

"I know you did, poppit." He nodded toward Paul. "And didn't I keep the local oafs away from you, too?"

"And Mum had the spy here keep an eye on me."

"You can't believe the only reason I'd spend my evenings in the White Hart was to watch you." Megan chuckled, her cheeks and nose rosy. "What's my excuse the rest of the year?"

Kit served their drinks, and Laura looked at Paul, hoping to pull him into the conversation. "What do you usually do for entertainment?"

"I meet my mates here most nights. There's not much else to do in Tenney Village." He took a deep drink of his ale. "I'm only living with Ben and Gertie temporarily. Until I get my construction business up and running." A gleam of excitement sparked in his eyes. "I want to build affordable housing. There's a shortage, so the younger people move to the cities where they can get higher wages, but it drains the economy away from the countryside."

It was the longest string of sentences she'd ever heard out of his mouth.

"That's a great idea," Laura said, her mind flashing to the cottage and its potential.

"Quitters," Megan said. "People give up too soon and move away."

"Everyone has to make a living," Kit countered. He leaned on the bar, listening in.

"It's been hard going, getting started," Paul said, "but I'm glad I came back."

The pub door opened and Megan bristled. Laura turned and saw Mr. Pickney heading for the bar.

Kit greeted him and poured a whisky and water.

"What's the word from London?" Megan called.

Mr. Pickney cleared his throat. "There's a bit of interest in developing Tenney Village."

"We don't want Starbucks or Marks and Spencer's here," Megan said. "Let the bigger towns, places that have no charm whatsoever, hobnob with the developers."

Pickney perched on a bar stool, his short legs dangling, and Laura suppressed a giggle. He looked like a leprechaun on a toadstool.

His sharp gaze landed on Paul. "You'd get more work."

Paul shifted uneasily, reluctant to be drawn into the fray. "I don't mind the slower pace."

"We're doing fine," Megan huffed.

"We're disappearing," Mr. Pickney said. "The farms are smaller, and whether you like it or not, much of the land is owned by people in London. Tenney Village isn't a cultural center. We're the destination of holiday makers and tourists, but most of them drive through in a day or two during the summer."

Megan leaned closer to Laura and muttered, "He could talk the hind legs off a donkey."

Pickney was warming to his oratory, voice growing louder, head bobbing as he looked around to see who else he might include in his audience. Did he notice that the pub was mostly empty?

"More than that, we haven't many children," he said. "Do you think Amy Barnes will grow up and keep Major's Necessities when Gertie and Ben retire? Hanover's market has already gone out of business."

For the first time, Laura felt herself swayed by the debate. She'd heard it before – keep Tenney Village historic and preserve the community, or encourage urban growth. It was never-ending. But village politics had nothing to do with her – unless she sold the manor to a commercial enterprise.

Pickney had said that he knew someone interested in turning Bannock Manor into a hotel or timeshare. Suddenly she had a little more insight as to why he'd been so pessimistic about her ability to keep it, and so encouraging about selling.

She set her half-full glass on the table. She couldn't bear the thought of some construction crew descending on the manor like a swarm of ants, reconfiguring the rooms to build dozens of tiny apartments.

Megan nudged her shoulder. "Don't mind us, love. We're just barking and chasing our tails."

Paul got up and went to throw darts with his friends, and as soon as he was out of earshot, Megan whispered, "I think our Paul takes a fancy to you."

"No, that's not it." She'd better stop that gossip in its tracks. "He's just been around a lot lately, digging a trench in the courtyard." He'd been extra helpful, delivering a steady supply of bottled water and working late every night. He was always there, and now Winnie was feeding him regularly. It was only fair. They were grateful to have a guy around, and he liked the work.

Without meaning to, she couldn't help making a comparison. Carl was a condo dweller; he'd never dirty his hands with a shovel, or a paint brush, or hedge trimmers. And he resented it any time she mentioned Paul. Paying thousands of dollars to get the main line repaired infuriated Carl; it was exactly the kind of thing he had told her not to do.

"I got a call from Todd Woodbridge," Megan said.

"Who?"

"The writer. The bloke who wants to include Bannock Manor in his research. He tracked me down through my B&B. Says you won't take his calls."

"Oh, him," Laura couldn't believe he had the audacity to call Megan. "Why would I want that guy snooping around?"

"Because your mum liked him." Megan took another drink. "Let him come and gather his information. I'll put him up." When Laura didn't answer right away, she said, "Your mum promised him."

"I get it." Laura smiled. "No pressure. All right, give me his number and I'll add it to my list of everything that has to get done immediately."

"Oh, in the next day or two is fine, I'm sure," Megan said. "It's a good turn you're doing."

When she got home from the pub at ten, she saw she'd missed a call from Carl. She was feeling relaxed, maybe a little buzzed, and thought about waiting until morning to return his call. If she could reach him when he first arrived at his office, before he got caught up with his clients, their losses and gains, and his commissions, he was calmer and listened better. But she wouldn't sleep well with that hanging over her head.

He answered on the first ring, not bothering to hide his impatience. "It's been a hell of a day, Laura. I haven't even had lunch. How soon can you wrap things up and come home? I miss you."

"I don't know." She was working as hard as she could and was no closer to making a decision about selling. "This house is full of history; generations of children grew up here." She picked at a ragged fingernail. "There are so many things I don't want to lose, things I'd like to bring back with me."

"Whoa, hang on," Carl said. "Don't pay shipping on a bunch of stuff. You have to make decisions now."

She thought of all the things she wasn't telling him, the things she wanted to share, but couldn't.

"Tell me what you need – cleaners, packers, a moving service?" He was all business. "Just mark what you want to keep, and they can take care of the rest."

"It's more than packing, it's the loss." If only he could understand that what she was doing was complicated too. "I need to think of Winnie and Nigel. They've lived here for over forty years."

"They're not your responsibility, Laura." She heard his exasperated sigh. "You're just lonely, and you're making everything more difficult than it needs to be."

She was lonely, but the connection she had always had to the house with its crazy assortment of rooms, its shifting shadows and streaks of sunlight, its smells of fireplaces and furniture polish, all of it pulled at her. That was what he couldn't understand.

"I like it here," was all she managed to say.

"I don't think it's a good idea for you to wander around there poring over old memories. It's not healthy. You've got to put a time limit on this, Laura." After a long silence, he said, "You are going to Alaska with me, right?"

"I'm sorry, Carl. I can't leave my responsibilities here."

"It's paid for, and you and I need some time together." She heard the disappointment in his voice. "It was your birthday present."

It might have been her birthday present, but it was what he wanted, a way to keep her from spending the whole summer with her mother. Ever since she'd come to that realization, she'd been stewing. He was manipulative, and this time she was not giving in to his demands.

"Does that house have running water yet?" he asked.

"Paul hooked up a giant hose to another section of the mains, so we have water in some of the house now." Even to her, it sounded lame.

"So, how long is the famous sewage canal now?"

"Carl, let it go. You know I'm replacing the fresh water line." He was in one of his neglected moods, and she wasn't about to admit that the ditch now stretched from the back of the house to more than twenty feet across the court yard. Most of the iron pipe that Paul had uncovered was cracked, rusted, or corroded. It was turning into a huge project – just like everyone had warned her.

"Why are you doing this?"

"This house is my last link to my mother."

"That's a damn expensive link you're talking about."

"Carl, I can't keep explaining this to you."

"So, you're saying that you won't go on the cruise?"

She was saying that, and so much more. This relationship was never going to work. She knew that now. "Carl." She put as much calmness, as much firmness into her voice as she could. "We need to go our separate ways."

"Don't try to pull that crap on me."

She bristled at his arrogance, but couldn't let anger get in the way. "We don't think like a team – probably never did."

"Ever since you inherited that house you've been obsessed. It's all you ever think about."

She knew he would take it and turn it against her, convince her that she was the one being unreasonable. She was tired of his ultimatums and timelines, his threats about their future. He hated not being in control of her life.

"We don't have enough in common to get through this crisis," she said, pushing her point.

"Wait a minute," he snapped. "You're the one who's changed."

"Maybe that's true," she said sadly. "But I can't let you pull me apart."

Outside, she heard yelling, the kitchen door slammed, and then Winnie's alarmed cries. "I've got to go," she said. "There's a problem."

"There's always a problem," he snarled. "The sooner you figure that out, the better off we'll both be."

She found Nigel sitting on the edge of the trench, his trouser leg pulled up. Light from the kitchen cast a sickly glow on his skinny leg. It was covered in blood. His face looked ashen. A bag of garbage was torn open, its contents scattered about. Paul must have forgotten to replace the plywood cover over the trench when he finished working.

Winnie dabbed at the wound with a kitchen towel, scowling, carrying on about infection, broken hips and heart attacks, and not enough water. Laura had never seen her in such a state.

Nigel was wincing in pain and trying to get up.

Laura slipped an arm around his waist. "Lean on me," she said.

He struggled for a moment, and then put his arm around her shoulders. "Such a bother."

She was surprised at how weak he was as she helped him limp back to his room. He wouldn't have had the strength to climb out on his own. Thank goodness she'd been home to hear Winnie's scream.

"Do you want to go to the doctor?" The gash on his leg looked bad.

"I'll fetch an astringent and clean it for him," Winnie said. "And then I've a mind to call Gertie."

Paul was going to get an earful about this.

"I'm fine," Nigel insisted, irritated by the fuss. But his weight sagged against Laura, and then he sank gratefully onto his bed. "I'll lie down for a bit, just so you'll leave me alone."

It was too dark to see much, so the following morning Laura went into the courtyard to look at the trench where Nigel had fallen. She'd seen Paul conscientiously cover it every afternoon when he knocked off, and couldn't imagine him leaving it open just outside the kitchen door.

He was going to feel horrible when he heard about the cut on Nigel's leg.

Laura spotted a piece of ivy covered wooden latticework that had torn free from the house. It left the wall bare in that place, like a sheep shorn in one small patch. She'd seen it when she first arrived, but hadn't bothered to deal with it. It was time to start cleaning up around the outside of the manor too. After she propped the trellis against the wall, she saw Amy walking on the path toward the cemetery, pushing her bicycle.

Laura hurried to catch up. "Amy? Are you looking for me?"

"Not you." Amy lowered her voice. "The ghost." She searched Laura's face for any sign of doubt, peered dramatically from side to side, even though it was obvious they were alone. The young girl then took a step closer and announced in a stage whisper, "My dad was asking Paul about him. Now that Paul's here every day, Dad wanted to know if he'd seen anything – ghostly."

"And what did Paul say?"

"He hasn't seen anything." Amy was thoughtful. "But I think the ghost knows me."

Laura didn't blink, didn't want to threaten Amy's tentative trust. Finally, she asked, "Have you met him?"

"I'm not sure." Amy ran a hand along her cheek, fingers tracing her jaw. "Maybe."

Laura paused, remembering the time when she was seven or eight years old.

She was laughing and twirling in her mother's sitting room. In her hands she held a rose, the peach colored petals tipped with yellow, the short stem stiff in her fingers. "He brought me a flower," she sang happily.

"Who did?" Her mother used her finger to mark her place in her book.

"My knight."

Her mother frowned. "Don't talk nonsense."

"Here it is. My pretty rose."

Her mother looked hard at her. "What else does he do?"

She stopped dancing. "I feel him when he's close."

"What do you feel?" her mother asked quietly.

She put her hand to her face, stroking her fingers along her cheek. "Like that," she whispered. Seeing the flash of fear in her mother's eyes, she dropped the rose and ran to her bedroom.

Whenever Laura came home to Bannock Manor, she felt him. The ghost was always there in the background, a breeze when there shouldn't have been any wind, a change in temperature on a perfectly mild day, the slight touch of fingers on her cheek. Just as Amy had felt it.

Laura drew a breath. So she wasn't the only one the ghost made contact with. Should she be relieved by that, or jealous? Maybe when Amy was older they could talk about it. Then again, perhaps it was the kind of thing best left unspoken.

"I've been meaning to visit my mother's grave," Laura said. "Want to go with me?"

They walked along the path, past the chapel and into the graveyard, wandering between the haphazard rows, stepping over broken stones and dips where the ground sank, and past the oldest graves where the engravings were scoured away by too many storms, and too many years. If there had been any symmetry to the plots, it had vanished years ago.

"Some of the stones have rhymes," Amy said, skipping between the plots, landing here and there in her own game of hopscotch. She paused before one and read in a schoolgirl's sing-song voice, *"My body slumbers in the dust, till the last trumpet's joyful sound, then burst the tomb with sweet surprise, and in my saviour's image rise."*

"That's lovely, isn't it?" Laura felt herself drawn into the game, and after a moment's search she read, *"Weep not! The land to which I go is beautiful and bright. There shall no tears of sorrow flow, and there shall be no night."* She hoped there was a heaven and her mother was there.

Amy waved Laura onward. "This one's nearly worn away."

Laura bent closer to make out the faded script. *"They are gone and the grave hath received them, 'twas Jesus who called them away. They are gone to the Lord who redeemed them, from night to the splendour of day."*

A short distance away, they knelt beside the mound of earth that covered her mother's casket. The grave was so recently dug that the soil was still crumbly. "I haven't mentioned this to anyone," Laura said, "but my mother died on my birthday."

At first, Amy said nothing, and Laura thought she hadn't heard, but then the girl shook herself a little.

"But it's still your birthday, and that comes from your Mum." Amy leaned closer. "Do you miss her much?"

"Yes." Laura took hold of Amy's hand and gave it a squeeze, fighting back the tears. She didn't want to cry in front of the young girl, didn't want her to know how devastating the loss of a mother was, how the hole in your heart was so large that nothing, ever, could heal it.

She saved all that until she was alone in her room, and then, in the darkness, she caved in to it. "There's an old poem she taught me. Would you like to hear it?"

Amy gave a small nod of encouragement, and Laura began to recite the lines from memory, unable to keep her voice from trembling.

> This heart that once was mine belongs to you
> A paltry sum to offer as my due
> God gave it to me whole but it is worn
> Scarce strong enough to bear the duty sworn
> And though I may not travel by your side
> My memory lives within you as your guide.

It had been a French lesson, a poetry lesson and, although Laura hadn't thought about it until now, a lesson in love. She remembered sitting beside her mother, the pages of the poems spread before them.

"Even when people have died," Laura said, "I think they're really still with us."

"Like the ghost?" Amy asked.

"Maybe," Laura agreed. She gazed up once more at the tree sheltering her mother's grave. If she sold the house and the land, she'd lose this too. Her mother's resting place.

She turned to walk back through the terraced gardens, but Amy said, "Let's go up to the ruins."

Laura hadn't been up there since before the funeral. She thought of it as the place where her mother had suffered and died, and just glancing in that direction flooded her with sadness. But all through her childhood it had been a magical playground, one of the places she loved the most, where her imagination wandered back through the centuries. The castle seemed enchanted, and she understood Amy's attraction.

The ruins sprawled across a hilltop, remnants of stone and rubble walls outlining where the buildings had once huddled tightly together within the fortifications. The shell of the keep, the strongest structure in medieval times, stood at the very center. The last remaining tower rose above the fallen stones, the tallest edifice for miles around, and once her favorite spot.

Maybe, if she could get past her fear and climb those steps again, she would feel closer to her mother, or at least find a sense of closure. She'd always taken comfort in the magic of the past.

"All right," Laura agreed tentatively.

Amy was a nice kid, comfortable in her realm, and if she knew about the tragedy, she didn't say anything. She still had a girlish innocence, and Laura didn't want to take that away from her. Life would be hard enough later.

Together they walked across the field and over the gravel-filled pit, then climbed the stairs to the top of the wall walk, where a doorway led into the round tower.

Laura stopped, looked down at the spot where her mother's body had been found, and took a ragged breath.

"Are you all right?" Amy nudged her gently. "Do you want to go back?"

The wind was stronger up here, and seemed to suck up her words and wring out the sound until the world fell silent again.

"I can do it," Laura whispered.

She forced herself to enter the shadowed interior of the tower. The slabs of the stairs wound upward in a tight circle. Bracing one hand against the central supporting pillar and leaning forward, she climbed the first three steps, eyes searching for any sign that something horrific had happened here, any trace of a violent end. But instead of visualizing gruesome details, the picture that flashed across her mind's eye was of a young man in a tunic, skipping down these stairs. He turned to look back at her, an enormous smile lighting up his face.

She sighed in relief; the magic hadn't been destroyed. Curious, she asked, "What do you see when you look up these stairs, Amy?"

"Triangles. Lots of triangles."

"What?"

"The steps are triangular-shaped," Amy said. "And the center post is a cylinder. My teacher says most things can be described by geometry."

"That means you're very well grounded in reality."

"But they're not regular," Amy said. "See how uneven they are?"

The depth of the stairs varied, making it easy to trip. "Be careful," Laura warned.

The steep spiral made it impossible to see more than a few feet in front of her. She climbed slowly and near the top sat down in the base of an arched window.

Amy, climbing behind her, joined her in the nook. Peering through the arrow loop to the distant slate roofs of Tenney Village, she said, "From up here, it looks like a storybook land."

"I used to come up here all the time," Laura said, listening to the wind whistling around them. "I had all kinds of make-believe games."

Amy looked at her expectantly, waiting for more.

"I used to imagine what this castle was like when it was full of people." Laura continued, "And what it would have been like to live here."

"Sometimes I play in the ruins." Amy kicked her heels against the wall.

"You shouldn't come up here alone," Laura said. "It's not safe."

Amy bit her lip and fell silent.

She hadn't meant to sound sharp, and hoping to smooth things over, Laura began pointing out the empty spaces that had once been the castle's primary rooms. "The floors are gone because they were made of timber that's rotted away, but you can see the places in the walls where the support beams used to be." She showed Amy where fireplaces and stairs had hung at various levels.

Amy scooted out of the window and began climbing the stairs. "Let's go to the very top."

A blast of freezing wind gusted down through the tower, and Laura shivered. "No!"

Amy turned and looked at her nervously. "What's the matter?"

"Let's go back to the house." For the first time ever, terror filled her at the thought of climbing higher. She'd learned to trust these warnings. "Now," she insisted. Whether the intuition was from her subconscious, or from the ghost, she didn't know, but when the temperature dropped suddenly, her senses went on high alert.

These were the kinds of things that chipped away at her peace of mind, destroyed all her efforts at cool reasoning and logic. It would be nice if there was a rational explanation, but as another pocket of cold air engulfed her, she turned slowly and tried to see the ghost. Although he wasn't visible, she knew he was there, and he wanted her to leave the tower.

Willing herself to sound calmer, she said, "Come on, Amy. Let's get something to eat." She couldn't get behind locked doors fast enough.

Chapter Eight

The tower was a special place. From the very top, as he peered between the crenellations, he could see the roofless rooms of the old castle spreading below him to the west, and the manor to the east. He could even see the cottage where he'd stayed off and on, until Laura-the-bitch started nosing around. She was everywhere and into everything. She stole his stuff.

He hated her.

If she knew how often he watched her, how he slipped out of rooms just before she entered, or crept past her bedroom door while she slept, she'd be very, very scared.

He was itching to let her in on his game, to see real fear on her face instead of the stiff, animated expressions in his graphics.

Little tests, like pulling the plywood off of the trench to see who'd fall in, stealing light bulbs, and opening jars in the pantry, were entertaining, but too often some dildo, usually Winnie, came along and set things right. She was irritating. He'd have to do more obvious pranks, more malicious, to rattle the old bird.

Of course, Paul would get blamed.

Spying on Paul-the-ditch-digger was boring. That bloke's brain was about as pliant as the boulders he pulled from the ground. He hadn't figured out that some of the biggest stones he dug out just happened to be back in the trench the following morning. Or that when he first uncovered the pipe, it wasn't smashed, but then later it was.

Dumb as a rock.

That's what his own mother used to call him. Well, she'd never met Paul. Now she mouldered in a similar trench in her own back garden.

He watched Laura and Amy wander around the graveyard. That was a nice way to spend the day with a little girl, wasn't it?

La-de-da, they talk, they kneel, they pray, they move on. Nothing accomplished – again.

He ducked down when Amy looked his way. Peeking between the crenellations he saw her pointing. Had she seen him? She started up the hill with Laura in tow.

They didn't belong up here!

He scurried around, stuffing his things into his rucksack. If they found him, he might try to talk his way out, but he was pretty sure with two girls there would be screaming.

If he hurt them, it would be their fault. They had no right coming up here, strutting around like they owned the place. Cocky and foolish.

They climbed up to the wall walk, and then into the tower.

He crouched behind the open door to the turret, gripped his knife and perched, ready. He wouldn't be able to see them until they emerged from the winding stairs, but he would have an advantage. They would be looking out toward the horizon. With a little luck, he'd slit their throats before they had a chance to scream. He could do it. No problem.

Laura-the-bitch should know better than to come up here, especially after what happened to her mother. If she made him do this, he couldn't come back for a while. People got too upset when little girls died. But eventually it would be all right again.

He didn't want to kill Amy. She was still young, and virginal. He liked her. Once, thinking he was homeless, she offered him a bag of crisps.

He saved them.

Chapter Nine

When Laura reached the garden, the roses were growing everywhere, climbing the walls and overflowing the beds, choking the paths in a chaos of color, from scarlet to peaches and cream. Her goal was an hour or two of weeding and pruning every day. By August the garden would be in good shape, and so would she. Her jeans were already a little looser, and she was getting a tan.

That wouldn't have happened if she'd gone to Alaska with Carl.

In the ten days since she'd broken up with him, they hadn't talked. He expected her to cave in and apologize – but not this time. Some days she missed him, some days she didn't. She still heard his voice in her mind, telling her all the mistakes she was making – about him, her future, everything – but after a few hours of physical work, it faded until it was no more bothersome than a gnat.

She started on the borders, clipping the dead blooms and thinning the canes. She put her back into it, slowly and steadily accumulating a pile of debris until the path became more visible.

Everything in her life, and at the manor, was tangled and thorny. Nigel's leg was infected and he was having trouble moving around. Paul couldn't understand how the cover had come off the trench, and Winnie was so icy that he was working shorter hours to avoid her.

The more she pruned and trimmed, the longer she labored to put things in order, the more unrecognizable the landscape, as though she were venturing farther onto unfamiliar ground.

In spite of a mild breeze, she was sweating. She took off her gloves, pulled off her sweater, and brushed the hair from her forehead. The cloudless sky was the color of a robin's egg, and it felt great to be outside. Picking up the shears again, she moved to another section of the garden, working from the edges toward the middle.

Like so many traditional English gardens, the center featured a fountain, not working of course, but with paths radiating out from it until they reached the borders. Working alone, it would take weeks to get it in shape, but as she clipped and cleared the brambles, she could see more of the original design and its balanced patterns.

Pruning vigorously, her thoughts drifted back to Carl. She'd been willing to compromise – maybe too much – but he hadn't been willing to back her up, to support her. What if they'd already been married? He would have had more sway in all her decisions, and he would have acted like he owned the manor. She shuddered. That would have been disastrous. She wasn't going to spend the rest of her life trying to pacify him, and didn't plan to succumb to his unreasonable demands.

But she didn't want to grow old alone either.

A tall, shaggy weed was strangling a rose bush, and she pulled her gloves back on, ready to do battle. She tugged to loosen the root, and the rose's thorns snagged her arm.

It's him or me.

Gripping the base, she pulled and twisted. This was a tough one. "Let the damn rose bush alone," she growled.

Using a trowel, she dug at the roots until a matted knot came loose, tangled up with a rock. She jabbed at it, trying to break it away. It looked like a stone, or maybe a bone, but as she brushed the dirt away, she began handling it more carefully. It was a tool of some kind, ivory maybe, about eight inches long, rounded on one end and notched on the other. It looked like the hilt of an old knife.

As she wiped away more of the dirt, she could see an etched design in the handle, a griffin.

She smoothed her finger over the magical beast, a creature with the head, wings and sharp talons of an eagle, and a lion's body and tail. The design was accurate, right down to the tip of the long tail. The powerful body flowed gracefully along the length of the handle, wings high over its arched back. She'd seen it before; it was an exact replica of the griffin on the tapestry in the medieval wing.

How long had this been buried here? It looked old, might even be valuable. Who had lost it? Just another mystery she'd probably never solve, and for some reason that made her sad. If she sold the house, she'd lose all its secrets, just when she was feeling more connected than ever to the manor and its past.

Stiff from kneeling so long, she got slowly to her feet, stretched, and went to show Paul what she'd found.

The digger he'd rented was belching smelly, brown clouds of exhaust, and he motioned for her to stand back until he turned the engine off. "I found an old well," he said, pointing to a circular stone wall several feet below the level of the courtyard.

Laura peered into the hole. For some reason, the pit got bigger, but the pipes never got fixed. "Can you work around it?"

"Not if I want to lay pipe in a straight line."

"It probably has historical significance." She wanted to tell him to stop until she had time to think it through, but she was hot and tired and didn't feel like a debate right now.

"Not every piece of stone belongs in a museum," Paul said. "It's a used up well, not a castle." He kicked the stones with the toe of his boot. "I'll make sure it's sealed up for safety." He sounded defensive, reinforcing his claim that he hadn't left the cover off the trench. Folding his arms, he leaned against the digger. "You can't get on without water."

He thought she worried too much, and maybe he was right. "All right," she said. The hilt was cool and smooth in her palm and she looked down at it.

"What have you got there?"

"I think it's an old knife handle."

He took it from her and inspected it. "It's no good now." He started to toss it onto a pile of broken stones.

"Wait." She snatched it back before he could throw it away.

"It's rubbish."

She didn't need to make excuses, but when he gave her that look that implied she was being silly, she added, "I like griffins, and my students might want to see it."

Something suddenly caught her eye and she turned back toward the garden. Todd Woodbridge was walking toward them.

He waved. "Winnie told me where to find you. You didn't forget our date?"

Crap. She'd agreed to let him come see the house, had even written it down – somewhere. She never forgot appointments. Never. "Of course not," she lied. Embarrassed, she looked down at her mud caked knees. "I– I was working in the garden and lost track of time." She probably had weeds in her hair.

The last thing she wanted to do was show some stranger around the house, but he'd kept calling, and somehow he'd gotten Megan to vouch for him.

"He's an architectural historian," Megan had explained. *"He'll tell you everything there is to know about all the wood, stone, glass, lead, copper – whatever your house is made of – he knows where stuff came from and how it was crafted."*

It had sounded interesting. She loved that kind of information, and he'd promised her a signed copy of his book when it was published. He had been polite in an annoying, insistent, not giving up kind of way, and in the end she didn't have the heart to keep saying no.

Todd pointed to the object in her hand. "What's that?"

"One more thing for the junk pile," Paul said, throwing up his arms. "Old wells, walls, windows...everything around here has historical value. Even broken tools."

She tried to stuff it into the pocket of her jeans.

"Let's see," Todd said, holding out his hand.

A series of protests raced through her mind, but before she could land on one, she voluntarily placed it into his waiting palm.

"It looks familiar." He turned it, examining the detail on the griffin. "I can't remember where I've seen something like it before, but I know it's the hilt to a knife. He gave it back to her. "It's a beautiful piece of art. Bone or ivory." Avoiding Paul's glare, he added, "Definitely worth keeping. Might even be of museum quality."

She stared at him, trying to ascertain if he was serious or pulling her leg. Unable to read him, she decided he was sucking up so she'd let him wander around Bannock Manor.

As he followed her into the house, she was already wishing she'd never agreed to this. She didn't know much about him except for what Megan had told her. At the door leading into the medieval wing, she stopped and got the key from a dresser. Before she could insert it into the keyhole, the heavy door creaked open.

"That's strange," she said. "We always keep this door locked. Always."

Todd pulled a flashlight from the outer pocket of his backpack and clicked it on. He moved in front of her, leading the way down the passage, under the arch of another door and into the oldest part of the house. As they stepped into the five hundred-year-old great hall, the beam from his flashlight dissipated forty feet up into the arch-braced ceiling, illuminating a gallery over one end of the room.

"Wonderful." His voice was low, like he was in a church. "You've never had electricity on this side?"

"Never, but I know this part of the house by heart. I can usually get around without a light." How many games of hide-and-seek had she won against Edward? She knew the medieval wing better than anyone.

Todd swung his flashlight from left to right, and shadows sprang out of the gloom as the beam bounced off the few pieces of furniture in the cavernous room. For several moments he simply stood and gazed upward, taking one deep breath after another, as though he could absorb more about the house by breathing its air. Slowly, he walked to the raised dais at the opposite end of the hall, pausing in front of a large wooden chair. Bending down, he studied the elaborately carved family crest on the chair's back.

"Do you mind if I handle it?" he asked. "I'll be careful."

At her nod, he gently ran a finger along the raised letter B, centered between two leaping stags. "This is a symbol of strength," he said, tracing one of the stags. "The lord of the manor would have sat in this chair at the head table."

An image flashed in Laura's mind – the great hall full of people seated at long tables laden with a feast. She'd read about the history of the house, but the picture in her mind had so much detail – dancers, musicians, and smoke from the hearth fires at each end of the hall.

"The man who built this manor stood his ground and didn't back down from a fight," Todd said.

"You can tell all of that by looking at a chair?" Laura was more than a little intrigued.

He pointed to the wall panels over the dais. "Do you see where the wood is faded? Broadswords or axes would have hung there, in easy reach. This may not be a castle, but it could still be defended. Do you know anything about the original owner?"

"Not much," she admitted. "I've always wanted to learn more."

"Maybe we'll find a few clues. Is it all right if I take pictures?"

"Sure." It was hard to refuse. Just when he started sounding like a know-it-all, he smiled and gave a slight shrug as if to say, *Hey, I could be wrong.* But she was willing to bet that his guesses were close to the truth.

Todd began taking pictures with a digital camera, and Laura stepped back to give him room. A pocket of cold air engulfed her and she knew the ghost was near. Could Todd feel him? She didn't dare ask.

"When was the last time anyone lived over here?" Todd sounded normal, not like someone standing in a haunted great hall.

"A couple of centuries," she said. "My grandparents used to call the part where I live now the new wing, and it was built in the 1700s."

They moved slowly through the first level. Every detail interested Todd, from the old wooden panels to the tiny panes of leaded glass. He took endless pictures.

"One of the things I love to do," he said, pausing to make notes, "is to find the marks of individual craftsmen. I'd like to compare work by the same craftsman in different homes, but so far I haven't been able to find enough samples."

"I'm pretty sure this was one of the oldest manor homes in this area," Laura said. "Maybe you'll find a match here to one of the other properties."

"Look." Todd pointed to a beam. "Oak gets stronger as it ages, and those are oak pegs – used instead of nails. They shrink and swell with the rest of the building. Several of the beams at this end look like they might have been salvaged from a ship's hull. Ship wrecks were a great source of building materials." He turned and met Laura's eyes. "This house was built to last forever."

"So, you'll be able to use some of this information in your book?"

He could barely contain his excitement. "I'll need more time. There's so much here."

They made their way upstairs, moving slowly room by room with Todd pointing out details, large and small, things she'd never noticed before. At the far end of the second story, in one of the larger bed chambers, Laura asked for the flashlight. She pointed into a small, adjoining alcove, highlighting the tapestry hanging on the back wall, the ancient cloth sagging and frayed, a ten-inch tear separating a griffin's head from its body.

"That should be in a museum," Todd said, stepping closer, being careful not to brush against the fabric. "It looks Flemish."

Laura didn't know where the tapestry had come from, but she knew what was behind it. She hadn't been in the secret room for years.

Her knight had shown it to her when she was eight years old. In the middle of the night, he appeared in her bedroom, and when she got up to follow him, he vanished. She saw him again in the corridor and ran happily after him. He led her to the entrance of the medieval wing and nodded when she reached for the drawer that held the key. He evaporated, but she found him again at the top of the old stairs. And then she didn't need to see him. The cold air seemed to pull her along, all the way into this room and this alcove.

Week after week he'd led her here until she finally understood what he wanted. She reached out with her small hands, pulled aside the tapestry, and saw the gap where the paneling didn't meet the wall. Slowly, she slipped her hand into the space. The wall moved. No, not a wall, but a fake section of paneling. She pushed it aside but wouldn't walk into the hidden chamber. She was terrified of it.

Once, when she was positive that she was alone, she started to peek inside. Almost instantly there was a shove against her back. Spinning around, panicked, she lost her balance and careened into a wall. The mad dash back to her bedroom was a blur.

She was jolted from her memory when she heard the knight's voice say, *Don't tell.*

"Come on, there's more to see," she said, leading Todd to the end of the corridor. She pointed out a latrine closet with a wooden seat covering a stone chute. Standing back, she waited, amused, while he snapped photo after photo.

"I love garderobes," he said.

"Funny, I don't detect a hint of irony."

He looked up and laughed. "I mean it. This is brilliant engineering. They had a cistern, and pipes to carry water to the kitchens, but no bathroom plumbing, just a chute to take the waste away from the house. In the castle, it went through walls three feet thick, and emptied into the moat. If that's not worthy of an architectural prize, I'd like to know what is."

"This two-seater model probably won an award in Better Medieval Homes," Laura joked. "Make sure you get a good angle."

Finally, he backed out of the tight space. "Thanks for indulging me."

"I don't mind." Showing him around was fun. "My brother and I used to play hide-and-seek in this part of the house, and he was always threatening to throw me down the garderobe."

"And did he?"

"He could never find me. I told you, I know this side of the house better than anyone."

"Maybe you've just met your match."

They were in the corridor, standing too close. He looked down at her.

She took a step back and waited for the fluttering in her chest to settle. "Let me show you the cellars."

"Good idea," he said.

They descended into the depths beneath the great hall, and she sensed him right behind her as they picked their way across the uneven flagstone floor.

He looked at everything, craning his neck, running his hand over the beams. He stooped, inspecting the base, and then stretched, trying to see the top of each post. "It looks good," he said. "Not much rot. Amazing for a house this old." He took something that looked like a small drill from his pack and showed it to her. "This is an increment borer. I'd like to drill a core sample from a couple of beams and have them tested at a dendrochronology lab."

She stared at him, uncomprehending, her suspicion returning.

"Surely you've heard of dendrochronology?" He gave another one of his disarming smiles. "It's a must for people who own medieval homes."

She had no idea what he was talking about, and she kept her expression completely deadpan. "That's dental insurance for my house, right? I'll need to upgrade my coverage."

His laughter filled the cellar. "It's a way of dating the wood using tree rings. We can even tell what the weather was as the tree grew."

She eyed the drill. "It won't hurt the beam?"

"Not at all."

In spite of his assurance, she winced as he screwed it into the wood.

"And this," he held up what looked like a thin, long-handled spoon, "is an extractor." He pushed it through the hole and removed a small sliver of wood. "There. Painless." He showed it to her. "It's a tiny sample of the tree's rings."

She knew about tree rings, but she'd never heard about them being used to date a house, or to at least determine when the wood had been harvested. Todd drilled another sample, then took each core and placed them into containers, meticulously labeling each one.

"It's hard to explain," he said, looking serious. "Houses feel like people to me. I think they're as alive as you or me, with their own personalities, their own span of life. Some have it pretty easy, and some have it rough, just like people." He shrugged. "I'm really glad I got to see your house."

He hid so much under his joking demeanor, but she was pretty sure he was being honest now.

"Bannock Manor has always been more than just a house to me," she said. "It's my family home, my heritage –" She broke off. "It's more even than that. It's a part of me."

He regarded her with a look of interest.

Suddenly embarrassed, she said, "I only feel that way when I'm here."

He nodded. "Not in the States. It doesn't happen over there very often. I think it's because most houses aren't old enough." He gathered up his tools, carefully organizing them in his pack. "If houses had life spans, I'd say it takes a few hundred years for them to grow up." His eyes sparkled. "Then they get really interesting." His expression sobered as he held her gaze. "I'd like to come back. There's so much more I want to know." He pulled out his phone, checked his calendar. "How about the day after tomorrow?"

§§§

Two days later, Laura was working on an inventory spreadsheet. The breakfast room always reminded her of Mum, but then, what didn't? The round, linen covered table, the china cabinet with the collection of flow-blue plates, the bay window with a view of the knot garden, it was like getting a concentrated dose of memories. They slipped up on her, alighting like birds in the garden, reminding her of the way a lapwing looked when the sun hit its wings at the right angle, tints of iridescent green and purple shining through. Sometimes a picture of Mum struck her just so, a flash of vivid color that vanished when she tried to get a better look.

Mum always kept freshly clipped flowers in here, but Winnie had removed the last, wilted buds weeks ago, and she hadn't had the energy or the heart to replace them.

The empty vase had been tormenting her all afternoon. She wasn't going to get anything else done if she kept reminiscing, and her computer had long since flipped into a mindless screensaver pattern. She hit save, and then rummaged through the sideboard until she found the small pair of garden clippers.

French doors opened onto a small terrace, the weeds pushing up between the cracks and making the bricks tilt.

Stepping outside, the smell of lavender and rosemary drifted toward her. Remnants of last year's blooms were separated from the herbs by boxwood borders, and the interlocking hedges made a geometric pattern. The same pattern could be found in the borders of the library floor, so that anyone standing at the library windows could look out and see beautiful symmetry, indoors and outside. That was the intention, but now that everything was so overgrown the overall effect was lost.

"This is spectacular."

Laura whirled. "What? How –"

Todd nodded toward the clippers she was holding. "Need some help?" He slipped them from her hand.

"I can get it, but thanks just the same."

He didn't seem to hear her, and just kept walking slowly along the path, bending every now and then to inspect a blossom. She waited for the indictment, for his verdict on the overgrown garden, but he just smiled and shook the hair out of his eyes.

"Does it matter which I choose?"

Her shoulders began to relax. The sun was out, the day mildly warm. "We'll get it on the way back." She felt like walking. "Come on, I'll show you some of the grounds."

Past the stables and the gardener's cottage, she led him all the way to edge of the pasture. A stone wall divided it now, the distant sheep, cows and horses belonging to someone else, but once it had all been part of the Bannock estate.

They sat on the wall and looked back toward the manor and the castle rising beyond it.

"Impressive," Todd said. "I've seen hundreds of manors, and this one stands out."

"It needs a lot of work."

"They all need something. You would too if you were that old."

She gave him a quick, sidelong look. He just kept studying the manor, frowning slightly. He probably wanted stones from the ruins, and wood from outbuildings.

"What are you thinking about?" Laura asked.

He had a faraway look in his eyes. "It took a lot of confidence to build a home without walls around it in the fifteenth century, even when you had a castle at your back."

"I always wonder about the women and children who lived here, what their lives were like."

"This must have been a wonderful place to grow up," Todd said.

"It was, mostly. I used to climb into the tower when I was younger."

"By yourself? No other kids?"

"After Edward and Dad moved back to the States, it was just me and Mum every summer. I lived with Dad during the school year, so I didn't have a lot of friends here."

He shifted so that he was no longer staring at the manor, but at her. The sun hit his eyes and showed flecks of green. Iridescent, like a lapwing. His attention threw her off, and she stopped talking.

"Go on."

"I don't like talking about myself."

"How can you have such an interesting life, such an amazing house, and not want to talk about it?"

"Interesting to you, maybe." She said it lightly, but she was thinking about Carl's bored look, the one he got when she tried to tell him about Bannock Manor. Carl called them her *What I Did on My Summer Vacation* verbal essays.

Todd was still staring at her, eyes slightly narrowed in concentration.

"Are you counting my tree rings?" she asked. "I'm thirty-one."

Laugher seemed to come naturally to him. "I like to study people, and things. Houses too. But don't accuse me of looking at your tree rings. We barely know each other. " He looked at the castle again. "Do you still go up there?"

She didn't want to spoil the mood by telling him about her mother's death. Better to keep it simple. "Best view of the countryside," she said.

She thought he'd want to jump up and go exploring, but he seemed content to sit and talk, and she was relieved.

"When you were alone, what kind of games did you play?" he asked.

"My favorite was called 'knights and ladies.'"

"Well?"

What more did he want to know? "That's what I called it. I made it up."

"Come on," he insisted. "Let's have the rules."

"I played it alone. I was my mum's only kid, remember?"

"Don't expect me to feel sorry for you. Not when you had a castle for a playground."

"Yeah, that was pretty cool. I sat at the very top of the tower and pretended that knights from all around came to pay homage to me." She stopped talking again, afraid she'd sound vain.

He stood up, and for a moment she thought he might drop to one knee. His eyes were full of eagerness, like a kid waiting for the teacher to tell him he got the lead in the class play. "And what, pray tell, should this gallant knight do to earn the honor of your respect?"

"The knight who wins my respect –" A cold wind gusted suddenly around her shoulders, and she broke off.

"Tell me," he urged, caught up in the silly game she'd started.

"Knights don't do chivalrous deeds anymore," she said. "We damsels are pretty much left to fend for ourselves."

His hand was hovering inches from hers, and he let it fall to his side. "Yeah, you're probably right. In all my house-hunting, I've found plenty of empty armor, but not one living knight. They just don't make them like they used to."

Chilled, Laura jumped down from the wall. "Ready to go back?"

When they reached the gardens, he pulled the clippers from his pocket, selected a full, red rose, snipped it expertly and offered it to her. "For you."

As she took the stem from him, their fingers touched and she felt a spark. Startled, she met his eyes. He looked surprised too. She turned, hurried up the steps and into the breakfast room, and busied herself by filling a slender vase with water. When she looked up, Todd was watching her again.

"I have work to do," she said, trying to keep her voice neutral. "You can look around the medieval wing, just let me know when you're done."

"Sure." He stayed where he was, and his glance fell to some of the papers she'd printed out – articles on historic home restoration, grant applications, a template for a business plan. "What's all this?"

"Didn't anyone ever tell you that curiosity killed the cat?"

"Didn't you notice my Cheshire smile?" He favored her with one of his wide, devil-may-care grins.

"I'm writing a business plan to restore the cottage and turn the stables into guest rooms, so that I can raise money to pay the inheritance taxes." She rebooted the computer and turned the screen toward him.

Silently, he slipped into a chair and studied the screen, clicking back and forth between the different panes she'd set up for comparison.

After a few minutes, he said, "This is ambitious. Have you talked to the bank about a loan?"

"I haven't got that far," she said. "Most people think I'm in over my head. My father and brother want me to sell and walk away."

"Why on earth would you sell this place? The house is fantastic, and you've got roots here. You said it yourself – it's part of your heritage."

"Passion doesn't pay the mortgage." Just the fact that he cared so much, that he was on her side, gave her hope and made her believe in her dreams all over again. "According to my father and brother, this is not what you'd call a good investment." There was no point in bringing up Carl.

"Yes," Todd emphasized each word, "it is. And anyone who can't see that doesn't know what they're looking at."

She felt herself beginning to blush. "Stop staring at me like that."

"No."

"Great. The one person who supports me is monosyllabic."

"I'm just making my point." He moved a little closer.

"Okay, point taken." She reached over and powered down the computer.

"Too late," he said. "I saw the plans, and I think you've got great ideas."

"You're a dreamer."

"Just like you." He tapped her shoulder. "I don't need to know what all the businessmen think. I want to hear Laura Bram's ideas. I want to know your dreams."

Somehow, he'd gotten very close to her, and the stillness between them was suddenly interrupted by his rumbling stomach.

"Don't you hate it when that happens?" he asked.

"Poor, hungry knight." Laura giggled.

This time his grin was sheepish. "At least let me take you to the pub. I'll buy you dinner, and we can brainstorm about your plans.

He looked so embarrassed, she couldn't refuse.

Chapter Ten

Focus. Todd repeated his mantra as he followed Laura into the White Hart pub. He hadn't written a book proposal and lined up a publisher by being unfocused. He hadn't landed a grant to do research by being unfocused.

As Laura led the way toward the bar, he hung back for a moment, drinking in her long legs and girl-next-door good looks, her honey-blond hair, and eyes the color of a summer sky. She chatted with the bartender, and the guy caught her hand and looked into her eyes, but it was innocent, like watching two girlfriends. With a quick toss of her head, Laura glanced back at him and smiled.

A spark ignited, turned into liquid fire and blazed through his veins.

When he finally broke away from her gaze, he saw the bartender's raised eyebrows, and then a deliberate wink as he sashayed over, limping slightly, looking like he'd poured himself into his tight, hipster jeans.

"This way, lambs." He obviously doted on Laura, and led them to a private table in a cozy window alcove. Pulling out Laura's chair, he asked, "Sauvignon Blanc?"

"Thanks, Kit."

Todd made a mental note to remember what kind of wine she liked.

Laura ordered a Cornish pasty and salad, and he chose the roast with all the fixings.

As Kit made his way to the kitchen, Laura said, "He likes you. This table is for his favorites."

"Then it's for you."

"He's been keeping an eye on me since I first came in here. I was sixteen and trying to look a lot older."

"Didn't he toss you out for being underage?"

"He sat me in a corner booth with a virgin Bloody Mary and spent the night flirting with me."

"But he's –"

"Gay, I know."

"You're lucky to have so many friends around."

With her chin on her hand, she held his gaze. He waited while she took her time weighing and measuring him. "It's funny that you can see it, but my Dad and brother can't."

On the surface her words were wistful, but her problems were like an undertow, tugging at him, and it took all of his effort to resist jumping to the rescue. He wanted to help, but... Bannock Manor was a lifetime project. Todd waited for the right combination of brilliant and practical advice to pop into his mind. Nothing came.

Kit returned and served their dinners, topped up their glasses with a flourish, and hovered long enough for them to taste his food.

"Delicious," Laura said. "Better than any place in London."

Todd savored a bite of his roast and nodded enthusiastically. "Definitely gastro-pub."

"High praise, indeed," Kit said, looking pleased. "I'm happy to impress you, and now," he made a gentlemanly bow, "I'll leave you two cherubs alone."

Todd waited until Kit was out of earshot. "I probably shouldn't have looked so surprised."

"Oh, he loves having that effect on people," Laura said. "The White Hart is his stage."

"You know," Todd said slowly, "Tenney Village has a Cinderella complex."

She considered him over the rim of her wineglass. "Did you discover that from examining our local trees?"

"Why do I get the feeling you're making fun of my research?"

"If the tree ring fits..."

"Okay, okay." He loved the way she teased. "I only meant, you have this great little village and it's a well-kept secret."

"Dr. Woodbridge, you've just put your finger on our pulse. We like being quaint."

"You can't afford to be," he said gently. "Not anymore."

For a few minutes, she gave her attention to her food. When she looked up, she asked, "What would you do if you were in my shoes?"

"I'd be scrabbling and clawing to uncover every grant I could get my hands on. I'd take cooking lessons from Kit, and Bed and Breakfast classes from Megan. I'd figure out how to open a five-star restaurant. And I'd be researching every piece of art on your walls and in your closets. Then I'd sell the ugliest and most expensive stuff." He sipped his wine, trying to gauge her reaction. She seemed to be taking it well.

"No matter how many rooms I fix up and rent, even if I have a tea shop and give tours, it still won't be enough. Will it?"

Conversation and laughter drifted from a table across the room, and they both looked over.

"It's never enough." Todd had interviewed dozens of homeowners, been in hundreds of manor houses, and yet he suddenly cared more about Bannock Manor than any of the others. "Some people inherit a house, plus enough cash to keep it going," he said. "Others have art collections, which is a different kind of bank account. Without that, you need a business."

"And businesses need customers." She rolled the stem of her wineglass between her fingers. "I'm actually a very private person."

"How about working behind the scenes? Let the house be the stage and let professionals run the show, like at special events and weddings."

"You're really working the Save The Manor angle hard," she said, staring back at him. "My ex-boyfriend got fed up because I didn't dump it fast enough. If my house was a pet, he'd have put it down."

He remembered that arrogant guy she'd been with at the funeral reception. "How could he not appreciate all the craftsmanship? It's everywhere. In the carved doors, and glazed windows, even the floors have awesome details."

"What got you interested in old houses?"

"Tonight's about you."

"No dodging the question. If I have to, I'll get Kit to help me pry it out of you."

"That is truly scary." He grinned.

"What do you do when you're not researching and writing books?"

"I'm a lecturer at Berkeley, but it's not a permanent position, and this is my first book."

"No tenure?"

"Maybe when I'm published, then I'll have a shot at it."

"I don't picture you as the Ivory Tower type."

"You're right – it's never been a good fit for me. I grew up hiking in the foothills of the Sierras. While my friends had calendar pinups, my room was full of sketches of the Golden Gate. I thought I'd be an architect, but later realized I was more interested in historic buildings."

"What's your family like?"

"I'm an only child, so I pretty much entertained myself. I did build one house – when I was ten." He watched her eyes widen. "A dog house for my black Lab. There were times when I snuck out after my parents went to bed and slept in it with Atlas. He was the greatest dog ever."

Laura's voice was entirely innocent. "I don't suppose you put in plumbing?"

"Why is this sounding suspiciously like a job interview?"

She shrugged. "We're getting desperate at my place."

He took her hand and stroked his thumb across her palm. "I really wish I knew a way to make it work for you, Laura. I'm not going to lie. I've seen people get in over their heads with old houses. It happens all the time. With all my heart, I really want you to succeed."

Her eyes looked a little softer. "I'm glad you're on my side."

"Always." Guilt pricked his conscience. "Even if it's from a distance. I have a flight back to the States tomorrow."

She squeezed his hand and let go. "Will you come back when your book is finished?"

"Yes," he promised. "I want to see you again."

§§§

Todd smacked his travel alarm and groaned. Ten minutes later he punched the snooze again. It was already four a.m., and he was supposed to be at Heathrow at six. Barely enough time for a shower, and then he was going to have to jam to make his flight.

Sitting up, he turned on the bedside lamp, reached for his phone and checked the departures. Just his luck – everything was on time.

Instead of getting out of bed, he looked up the Apple Cottage website, just to see if there were any extra rooms available. Not that he could stay longer, but he was curious. The summer tourist season was in high gear, but Megan's little B and B still had rooms. Not good. She should be full up, but Tenney Village trotted along like a horse and buggy, unable to keep pace with the vacation superhighway. To compare, he looked up a generic Cotswolds site, and a dozen places popped up – shopping, hotels, historic buildings, public gardens and museums.

He was running out of time.

"You're crazy," he mumbled to himself as he logged onto the airline website and dug out his credit card.

A couple of hundred bucks to change his ticket, plus the price of a room for another few days was probably a stupid idea. He was way over budget, but he wanted to see her again. He wanted to get to know her better. Much better. He changed his airline reservation, then checked the time again. Only five a.m., way too early to call Laura.

§§§

Later that evening, Todd stood in the manor's drawing room, waiting for Laura. He noticed even more problems: faded wall coverings and draperies, plaster in need of repair, warped window casements and crumbling stone mullions. Yet in a house of this age, all of that was to be expected. This place was amazing.

Laura walked downstairs wearing a slinky, low cut, royal blue shirt and black slacks.

His knees nearly buckled.

"You're staring," she said, looking radiant.

"I can't help it." Taking her hand, he lightly kissed her cheek. "You look more beautiful every time I see you."

Her eyes were full of mischief. "Really?"

"Really," he said, overwhelmed by a sudden urge to drag her upstairs. Not exactly the slow courtship he had in mind, but she wasn't playing fair. Long legs, tight slacks, and a glimpse of cleavage. His imagination picked up where the clothes left off. Who could be a gentleman when a lady looked that good?

"Where are we going?" Her gold hoop earrings shimmered against her skin.

"A little village called Castle Combe. The tourist websites say it's romantic and charming."

"That's one of my favorite places." Her eyes lit up. "How did you know?"

"Lucky guess." He tried to hide his smile as he helped her into his car.

All day long he'd been trying to figure out what she would like. She was romantic, the kind of girl who lit candles with dinner. He pictured her swaying, eyes closed when she listened to music. She probably stayed up too late to finish a good book, even if she had to work the next day. He guessed she'd rather go for a walk than watch T.V. And he already knew that she was comfortable with silence and didn't feel the need to fill it with chitchat.

He'd looked up her online profile, surprised that it only mentioned the basic things about her work and family, but she was private. He didn't know if half of what he imagined was true, but he based it on the way he felt around her. When they were together, he wanted to light candles, put on music, hold her while she closed her eyes. He saw himself rubbing her feet while she read aloud, and he knew what that meant. He had it bad for Laura Bram.

They arrived in Castle Combe just as the sun was setting, and he took her hand. She slid her palm against his and smiled as they strolled through the village, past thatched cottages and honey-colored stone shops.

He started to say something, then bit his tongue, didn't want to get all geeky on their first real date.

"What?" She tugged his hand.

"I was going to bore you by telling you all about the limestone from this region."

"You mean that special color that only comes from the Cotswolds?" She widened her eyes and batted her lashes.

Laughing, he said, "Okay, so you know as much about it as I do."

"I doubt that," she said. "Tell me something fascinating."

"It's Jurassic stone, and the honey color comes after it has weathered. A lot went into making it beautiful – the workers who quarried the stone, the masons who carved it." He paused, searching for the right words to match the way he felt. "Then nature made it even more stunning."

She stopped walking and faced him, her eyes focused intently on his. She probably thought he was nuts.

Slowly, she smiled. "I love it when you talk construction to me."

"I love being with you." He hadn't meant to say it aloud.

When her smile deepened, he moved closer and met her lips, the softest, feather-light brush of his mouth against hers. Everything was silk – her lips, her blouse, her face against his, the way her hair slipped through his hand. He drew back a little and looked into her eyes. Sky blue in the center, gray at the edges, the blue of her shirt turning the irises a shade darker.

"You have pretty eyes," he whispered as he smoothed the blond hair back from her brow.

Her lashes lowered, but not before he caught the glimmer of desire. He caressed her cheek, and her head tipped so that her face was against his palm. His arms tightened around her.

She relaxed against him, resting her head on his shoulder. Inside of him, tension gathered but he didn't want to move, or breathe, or break the moment. Only his hand slipped up her spine, stroked across her back. Raising her face, she looked at him, her fingers playing with the hair at the back of his neck, gliding along his jaw. Hands on his shoulders, she pulled him toward her.

The tip of his tongue found the edge of her lips. Her breathing quickened, her tongue touched his, ignited him, and he kissed her fully, her lips dissolving under his, her body melting against him.

When he finally drew his mouth away, he kept his eyes closed, his forehead against hers as he inhaled her perfume. Gradually, her arms loosened, but before she let go, he dropped another light kiss on her cheek, trailed a string of small kisses back to her lips.

"You're irresistible," he murmured. In another minute, he wouldn't be able to tear himself away.

Her eyes had a sleepy, unfocused look. "You're... You're a good kisser."

"And you're sexy." She brought out a romantic side in him.

She touched a finger to his lips and then stepped out of his arms. "Let's walk."

They followed the footpath as it wound along the river, pausing to watch a pair of gliding swans, necks arched as they circled and preened. He slipped an arm around her waist. He'd only booked a few more days, and already it wasn't enough. He wanted another month. Forever. The word popped into his mind, and he shook his head. He lived in the States, she lived in England, and they'd only just met. He couldn't help chuckling.

"What's so funny?" she asked.

"I guess I've never really understood fairy tales. But this..." He swept an arm, taking in the footpath, the village, the setting sun reflecting like fire in the river. "If you lived in a dream, it would look like this."

"I've always believed in fairy tales."

She was staring at him in the way that made him think she could see inside of him, all the stuff he never told anyone. Except now he wanted to tell her everything.

"Do you ever feel like you've been somewhere before, or known someone, even though it's all new?" he asked.

"Déjà vu. I get it a lot, and dreams too." Suddenly she looked uncomfortable.

"What kind of dreams?" They continued walking, but now he wasn't looking at the view, just at her.

"It's silly." Her tone said she was serious.

"You know," he said carefully, "when I changed my ticket, I thought it was because I couldn't bear to walk away from Bannock Manor. But that's only part of it."

Ahead, the path turned away from the village, leading through a field, and then to the next town, and the one after that. If he wanted to, he could walk across England.

"What's the other reason you changed your ticket?" She wasn't looking at him, but gazing across the field.

The sun had set behind the thatched cottages, and the shadows lengthened.

"When I first came to England and saw one of these footpaths," he said, "I had this crazy urge to get a backpack and just take off, get away from it all and go find myself or something."

"Did you ever do it?"

"Not exactly the way I thought. This morning –" He held his breath. "I just figured out that for my whole life I've been on a path and it's been leading me toward what I'm meant to do, where I'm meant to be. It's led me here." When he glanced at her, he couldn't read the expression in her eyes. Would she tell him he was imagining things?

"I don't know what to make of it," she whispered. "But I feel it too."

He couldn't stop himself and kissed her deeply, his hands moving down her back, drawing her against him. Their hips aligned, and he responded. His hands moved beneath her shirt, and he began gently teasing her nipples through the fabric of her bra. Her head tipped back and he kissed her neck, trailed kisses toward the V of her blouse.

A dog barked, and a wet nose thrust against his leg.

"What?" He looked down, blearily focusing on the Golden Retriever. It barked again and shoved its nose against his palm.

Laughing, Laura stepped back and adjusted her blouse.

In another moment, he would have had his hands all over her.

"Gladiator, come here, boy!" An elderly gentleman came around the bend, and hurried toward them. "Here, boy," he called. "So sorry."

Crouching, Todd scratched the dog's ears and got a slobbery lick on the face.

"There's a good boy." Gladiator's owner reached them. "He's quite harmless," he said, clipping a lead onto the dog's collar.

Todd stayed in a crouch, patting the dog a moment longer, until he thought he could stand without embarrassment. "Beautiful dog," he said.

"He is, but he's too old now for duck hunting. So am I. From the States?"

"Northern California. But Miss Bram lives in Tenney Village."

Laura and the old man chatted for a few minutes, and then Gladiator trotted off beside his owner.

If the dog hadn't interrupted, Todd would have crossed a line. When he was with Laura, his self-control short-circuited. "I didn't mean..."

"Don't apologize." She linked her arm through his and they walked back to town. As they approached the main avenue, she said, "I'd like to finish this conversation another time."

"Me too." And then he scolded himself. Down boy.

The restaurant he'd picked was in a cozy inn, and the architecture was a few centuries old. As they settled in with wine and a cheddar soufflé appetizer, he looked around in appreciation. "This is the way to do it," he said. "They've renovated, but kept the feel of the era. All the elegance but with modern convenience."

"You really love your job." The candlelight glittered in Laura's eyes as she looked around at the charming décor. "I wonder if I could work the same magic on Bannock Manor."

"You can start slow," he said, but his mind was racing. He could think of a million things he wanted to do – but it wasn't his house. And he was only staying for a few more days.

She reached for his hand, gently stroking his palm.

He lowered his voice. "It's a little hard to concentrate when you do that." She started to pull her hand away, but his fingers closed around hers. "I don't want you to stop. Just saying it's hard to talk."

"Tell me more about your family," she said, as her fingers resumed caressing his. "You know so much about my life. I want to know more about yours." She leaned forward, her breasts swelling above the top edge of her shirt.

He dragged his eyes away from her cleavage. "My parents have been married for forty-six years. That's a tough standard to live up to."

"I think it's wonderful. Do you ever want to get married, start a family?"

She was the first woman who'd ever made him think about it, imagine that it might really happen. "Yes," he said. "What about you?"

"I always assumed I'd divide my time between England and America."

"Has that changed?"

The waiter arrived with their dinners, and Laura tasted her ratatouille. He watched her glossy lips and wanted to kiss her again.

"I'd like to stay in England if I can."

"I hope you do," he said.

"Would you ever consider living anywhere else?"

He risked a look up, even though his hopefulness was probably written all over his face. "It's going to be hard for me to stay away from England now."

"How long until your book is finished?"

"The research is pretty much done. I should finish a draft in the next six months." He had classes to think about too, but all of that seemed far away.

They finished dinner and lingered over another glass of wine. He paid the check, but neither one of them stood up to go. He could talk to her for hours, but talking wasn't enough. He wanted to hold her.

"I can get a room," he said, studying her eyes, trying to gauge her reaction.

"I'm tempted." She gave him one of her beautiful smiles. "But, we need to wait. We need to make sure this isn't one of those impulsive, one time flings. I – I'm not like that."

She suddenly looked vulnerable and he didn't want to push her. "Can I come and visit again?"

"Absolutely."

She was right, but he couldn't help feeling disappointed. They left the restaurant and walked slowly to the car. He hated that their evening was coming to an end. Low clouds skidded past, obscuring the moon. She turned and wrapped her arms around him, and he caught the flash of an expression.

She didn't trust him to return.

Chapter Eleven

Laura diced onions and garlic, then slid them into the skillet. They sizzled in the hot olive oil, while her thoughts swirled like a delicious aroma to Todd Woodbridge. He was so interested and supportive. He understood her desire to keep the house, and her fear.

She stirred in ground beef and Italian sausage just as Winnie and Nigel came into the kitchen. "Spaghetti tonight," she said, glancing their way. Nigel leaned heavily on a cane, and was limping. "I think it's time you had someone take a look at that leg," she said.

"I don't want anyone fussing over me," he snapped. "It's nothing a little time won't heal."

"He won't let me see it," Winnie added. "But this has been going on for two weeks, and it's getting worse."

"Do you need me to drive you to the doctor's?" Laura asked.

He waved his hand irritably, like brushing away a mosquito, and she let it drop. No point pushing it while he was in this mood. Nigel could be stubborn and proud.

Opening a bottle of red wine, she poured three glasses. "Maybe this will help."

She'd discovered that if they relaxed at the end of the day, over dinner and a glass of wine, they got chatty. Especially Winnie. It was then that the stories came out, stories about her mum, and her grandparents, gossip about neighbors and former staff, people who'd come and gone from their lives. Sometimes Winnie lowered her voice, blushing as she shared a scandalous tale from the old days, stories that didn't seem shocking to Laura at all. It was cute, and it showed how secular Winnie's life had been.

Nigel liked to reminisce about World War II, the air raid sirens, the doodlebugs, black-outs and rationing. Her historian's mind filed away the tiniest details. But he rarely talked about his time on the continent and the evacuation at Dunkirk.

Laura added more herbs to the sauce, while Winnie prattled on.

"When you were out last night, that Carl called." Winnie's jutting chin was a better indicator of her opinion than the phrase, *that Carl*. "The first thing he asked about was if the house had running water yet. I fibbed – a little. I told him that of course we did."

Carl still called occasionally, his tone and nuance never failing to convey *I tried to warn you* as he pretended interest in her undertakings. He wanted to get a dig in, to let her know how wrong she was for not staying with him and taking his advice.

"I'm not surprised he's calling the house," Laura said. I quit taking his calls on my cell."

A conspiratorial smile crept across Winnie's face. "I might have let it slip that you were out on a date."

It was good to see Winnie starting to smile again; she was adjusting to the changes, and hopefully feeling less guilty about the accident. The playfulness that Laura had always loved was coming back. Perhaps the wine helped too. "Winnie, are you trying to stir up trouble?"

She grinned, and then mentioned, a little too innocently, "Mr. Woodbridge called this afternoon while you were in Dursley. He said that you weren't answering your mobile."

So Todd was in Winnie's good graces, and he was Mr. Woodbridge, a formal title for such a casual guy.

"I can't find my cell phone anywhere." Laura had wasted the entire morning looking for it. She didn't usually lose things, but lately it seemed like they just vanished. Random items, like her hairbrush and her watch. There were other things too, she just couldn't remember them all.

"Nigel and I get along fine without one," Winnie said. "Did you know that your grandfather had a second cousin who went to prison for rape?" Winnie's conversations often took sharp turns in new directions, making them tricky to follow.

"What?" Laura turned from the stove to look at Winnie. "I don't know anything about other relatives. And a rapist? How come I never heard about this before?"

"It was a scandal for the Colfax family. They couldn't wait for the newspapers to get tired of the story. We were ordered not to talk about it, especially in the village where everyone wanted to know if we knew him."

"Did you know him?"

"Mr. Colfax didn't much care for his cousin Billy." Winnie sipped her wine. "They had a great-grandfather in common, and every time Billy came around, he criticized the family. Mind you, the bugger didn't own a stuffed pig, and could never keep a job, but he liked to remind everyone that he was almost an heir."

"Heir to what?" Laura held a spoon of marinara sauce to her lips and blew to cool it. After tasting, she added ground pepper and more oregano.

"Bannock Manor." Winnie shook her head. "If your mum had never been born, then old Billy the Bugger would have inherited the manor."

This put a whole new spin on things. Her mind instantly went to the large painting on the stairwell with the three red-headed boys; her grandfather and his two older brothers. Apparently, this Billy was their second cousin.

How could she have missed this gap in the family history? "Were there no first cousins?"

"No," Nigel piped up. "And after Billy went to prison, we never heard from him again."

While the sauce simmered, Laura started pouring bottled water into a large pot for the pasta. Since the cook had quit, she'd taken over cooking dinner, and she insisted on eating at the kitchen table with the Wilcoxes. Winnie liked her sweets, and liked to bake, but she would rather scrub floors than put together meals, claiming once the food was eaten, there was nothing left to show for the effort.

"Paul says he'll be able to lay the new pipe in another few days," Nigel muttered, as Laura struggled to lift another heavy water jug.

It galled him that the repair was taking so long, and more than a few times he'd mentioned that a real plumber would have been more efficient – if not cheaper. The lack of running water had evolved from a temporary inconvenience to an hourly frustration that had them all swearing at Paul behind his back.

She set a plate of warm garlic bread in front of them. "Only a few more days and we'll be back in the twenty-first century." Her hip bumped against the back of a chair and she felt a little lump in her pocket. "Oh, I've been meaning to ask you about this." She pulled out the plastic button from a computer keyboard with the letter 'L' on it.

"Do either of you know where this came from? I found it on the nightstand beside my bed last night."

Without speaking, Winnie got up and went to the china cabinet, took out a teacup and showed Laura the contents. Eight more keyboard buttons. "I've been finding these all over the house," she said. "I don't know what they are."

"They're from a computer," Laura said, baffled why anyone would pull the buttons off a keyboard and leave them lying around. "Could Paul have left them?"

"It wasn't him. I already asked." Winnie carried the cup over to the table and dumped out the keypads, and Nigel began sorting through them.

"Live, love, liver." He spelled out words.

"Olive." Winnie rearranged them.

"Amy's been around. Maybe she left them." Laura added the pasta to the boiling water. But Amy hadn't been over yesterday, and Amy would never have gone into her bedroom. The little plastic buttons looked harmless, but their unexplained presence made Laura uneasy. "When did you find the first one?"

"I don't know. A few weeks ago."

"Where was it, when you found it? The first one."

"In the sitting room, on the mantle."

"Was it before or after Mum's funeral?" There had been a lot of people in the house that day, and she had no idea who some of them were.

"I'm not sure," Winnie said.

Nigel rearranged the letters again, and said, "Cool."

"Look, you can spell color. C-o-l-o-r, the American way." Winnie moved around the pieces.

"Wait a minute," Laura said. "There can't be two "O's."

"But there are," Nigel said, "and two "L's."

Laura tensed up. Someone was playing a game with them, and she didn't like it.

"Why are you upset?" Winnie asked, as she put the pieces back into the cup.

"Because there are doubles, and that means these come from two different keyboards." Their faces were blank, and she knew they didn't understand. "Who would take apart a couple of keyboards and set the pieces around our house?" The thought that someone had gone into her bedroom, without anyone noticing, creeped her out.

"I have no idea," Nigel grumbled, rubbing his shin. "Winnie should have put them in the garbage bin."

Laura's mind raced as she tried to remember all the people who'd been in the house lately. Paul wasn't a computer guy, and Todd certainly wouldn't do anything so invasive. There were others, but she ruled out every one who came to mind.

"I'll take care of them," Laura said, her hand shaking as she moved the cup of key pads off the table. "And if you find any more, don't touch them, just show me."

She set the pasta and salad on the table as Winnie reminisced about an Italian restaurant she had once been to in Stratford.

Staring down at the plastic letters, Laura recalled the broken keyboard and other computer parts she'd found when she was cleaning out the cottage. At the time, she'd assumed it was teenagers and hadn't given it much thought.

This was different. Someone was sneaking about and deliberately leaving clues. The hairs on her arms bristled. How long had this been going on?

Winnie chatted on, oblivious when Laura quit eating and pushed her plate away. How many other clues had they missed?

§§§

At three a.m., Laura lay awake listening to the way the house creaked. Usually she slept through the familiar scrape of branches against the glass, and the way the wind gusted under the eaves. But now she was wide awake, thinking about the computer mouse she'd seen in the attic luggage room.

By 9 a.m. she was at the police station. The officer on duty listened to her story, looked at the little bag of computer keys, and smiled condescendingly. "You can hardly consider these dangerous."

"Someone vandalized the groundskeeper's cottage, and he's been all over the manor house." She held up the bag and shook it, frightened and indignant. "This is evidence."

"Is anything missing?"

"All kinds of things." But she didn't want to mention the silly items, like her hairbrush.

"Perhaps one of the staff is bothered about... about the recent changes. A malcontent might engage in petty theft, or try to frighten you."

"Do you know Nigel and Winifred Wilcox?"

"I do," he said, smiling. "And they would not be up to this kind of shenanigans."

"It may seem far-fetched, but..." She didn't want him to think she was completely mad. "There's no explanation for why these things turned up randomly, and there was no explanation for why my mother went into the ruins that night."

She had his attention finally, but he still sounded like he was humoring her. "I'll send someone out to the manor to have a look around."

Laura filed a report and left, feeling physically and emotionally drained.

§§§

When Laura got back home, Paul was busy placing large rocks onto a sheet of metal that covered the opening on the ancient well. The soil was muddy and tinged with rust.

"Are you already done for the day?" she asked, hearing the snappish tone in her voice.

"No. No," Paul stammered. "Some rocks fell into the well and I could hear how deep it is." He wiped his brow. "I don't want to get blamed if anyone falls in." He pried another boulder out of the trench and laid it on the metal cover.

She spotted something white embedded in the dirt to one side. "What's that?"

"This?" Paul nudged it with the toe of his boot. "Just a tree root." He picked up his shovel.

Laura grabbed his arm and leaned over the edge. "Wait." Smooth and white, it looked more like a rock than a root, with a dirt-filled indentation.

She dropped into the trench, edging Paul aside, not clear what she was protecting, but certain that she didn't want Paul hacking at it with his shovel. Kneeling, she brushed away some mud. It flaked off the porous surface, revealing something round and brittle. Laura was afraid to expose more, but unable to stop herself. "Hand me a trowel," she said.

"What are you doing?" His shovel minced a dirt clod, sending a message: she was in his way.

"Hand me the trowel. Please."

He dropped it inches from her hand. "I'm going inside."

The tension between them had been escalating as the project dragged on. He hated her interference. She got that. But this was different. She couldn't stand back and watch him smash something to pieces without looking at it, without giving it any consideration.

Scraping with the trowel, she loosened soil, slowly, carefully. Then she set down the tool and used her bare hands, brushing away more dirt.

The curvature of a skull came into view.

She could see there was more. Vertebrae from the neck nestled into the side of the trench, and she kept pecking out stones and sweeping away dirt. When the shoulder and collar bones were exposed, she stopped, horrified to think that she was actually sitting in someone's grave.

Sweat trickled down her scalp and the bitter tang of bile filled her mouth. Closing her eyes, she fought the urge to vomit, as the reality of another death sank in. Sorrow sharpened, piercing her painfully.

Who was it? How long ago?

Impulsively, she placed her palm against the skull, now warm from the sun, and offered a spontaneous prayer. She prayed with all of her heart that, whoever it was, they were at peace.

Inside, she found Paul, Winnie and Nigel having a cup of tea in the kitchen. Her composure was close to crumbling. How could they just sit there like that, like nothing in the world was wrong? Sadness pressed on her heart, and she could barely talk. Winnie began to chat, but Laura shook her head.

"I have to make a few phone calls," she said, her voice controlled. "I found something..."

And then it was all too much. Collapsing onto a chair, she buried her face in her arms. There was no relief, no escaping death. It was here again.

Chapter Twelve

Kit had never seen such a busy Sunday at the White Hart. It had only been a few days since the discovery of the skeleton at Bannock Manor, and the gossip in his pub was flowing as freely as the cask ale. The police had called in the coroner and an environmental health officer, and the authorities had established that the remains were neither recent, nor a threat to public health. Laura was waiting for a license to be issued that would allow the experts to exhume the human remains.

The health officer was tall and angular, with a long neck and long fingers, and he reminded Kit of a stork, his skin so pale that he looked moments away from expiring himself.

Kit held the bag with his take-away order just out of reach. "How old did you say the skeleton is?"

"Can't say," the man answered. "A forensic anthropologist is on her way from Bristol. You can ask her."

The lack of details didn't keep Kit from speculating. "What if it's an ancient relative?"

The health officer grabbed his take-away bag. "It's an old skeleton, probably hundreds of years old. We're lucky it's not all in a heap."

A murmur of anticipation ran through the crowd. The media had gotten wind of the story, and even though artifacts cropped up all the time in Great Britain, a circus atmosphere was developing. A whole skeleton was noteworthy. One reporter had dubbed the remains *The Medieval Man of Bannock Manor*, and the name had caught on.

When the environmental health officer left, gossiping villagers quickly clogged the gap at the bar, and Kit turned his attention back to pouring drinks. At this pace, he'd be able to do several years' worth of business in a matter of weeks. He turned out another batch of fish and chips and dreamed about spas and whirlpool jets.

The only person in Tenney Village who wasn't enjoying the extra attention and party atmosphere was Pickney. He'd put it together straightaway that a dead body on the Bannock Manor estate might make it harder to sell. Pickney had informed all who cared to listen that under British planning law, the owner was required to pay for the necessary excavation and archeological work. To make matters worse, the plumbing couldn't be repaired until the bones were exhumed, and decency also required a proper reburial.

At a table in the back of the pub, Megan was conducting court among her cronies, and Kit paused for a moment to admire her business skills. Apple Cottage was full of reporters and camera crews. The science team, when they arrived, would be staying in the manor at Laura's invitation. Kit didn't care where they stayed, so long as at the end of every workday, they made a pilgrimage to the White Hart. He polished bar glasses and pictured one scientist after another, each one drier and more desiccated than the next, panting for a pint of ale. Maybe, when it was all over, he'd vacation in the south of France. Kit's legs were positively aching.

At the end of the night, Megan bustled into the kitchen as though she belonged there, plunging her hands into the hot water and washing like a regular scullery girl.

"Take a seat, Kit," she ordered. "You look knackered."

"When you're finished," he said, "I'll serve you the best whisky in the house." She joined him at last, and he set up two glasses, pouring generously. "To the bones," he toasted. "Do you think Eleanor had any idea she had a skeleton under her courtyard?"

"How could she know?" Megan demanded.

"It explains the ghost, doesn't it? At least that's what everyone thinks."

§§§

Laura spent the entire morning on the phone. Everyone wanted to know the latest. Her father, who still knew nothing about the wandering intruder, didn't like her letting strangers stay at the manor. She tried to convince him that the researchers were necessary, that she couldn't exhume the bones without their help. And besides, it was a good idea to have more people around. He grumbled, unconvinced.

Edward had already talked to the producer of a reality television program that specialized in paranormal hauntings, and they were ready to pop their people onto the next flight. Laura refused to cooperate with his plan, and they argued. She almost never fought with Edward, but no one was being sane about the bones. The skeleton brought up everyone's nightmares, or get-rich-quick schemes, and the ideas just got crazier.

Todd was the person who was keeping her grounded, and she told him everything. He was the voice of sanity. When she'd been hysterical, right after finding the skeleton, he calmed her down. When she worried about the added expenses for the exhumation, or the delays in repairs, or Nigel's festering leg, he listened. He didn't tell her not to worry. He didn't tell her to sell the manor. Todd understood what she was saying, and what she was thinking. He grasped the pressures she faced. He offered suggestions, quick to assure her that they were only ideas.

Although they lived thousands of miles apart, he had slipped into her life, and into her heart, and she now understood the term soul mate.

"I'll come back," he promised. "The last week in August, just before school starts again."

Finally, she had something to look forward to. "I'll let you have your way with my house," Laura teased. She tried to tamp down her excitement, but it was no use acting nonchalant. Todd was coming back, and she was thrilled.

Winnie tapped at the sitting room door, looking a little frazzled. "The forensic people just arrived."

Laura ran her fingers through her hair. "I've got to go. I'll call you as soon as I know more." She hung up and hurried downstairs to greet the anthropologist.

An athletic looking woman walked briskly up the drive. "Hello. Are you Laura Bram?" She extended a hand. "I'm Jocelyn North, from Bristol University."

Jocelyn was shorter than Laura by several inches. Her brown hair, cut just below her ears, fell neatly back into place no matter which way she turned her head. Practical, especially for a woman who dug up skeletons.

"Found some bones, did you?" Jocelyn smiled as though she and Laura had been let in on a good secret. "I'm eager to have a look. It's rather like having a history book in your back garden."

In spite of the strain of the last few weeks, Laura found herself returning the smile. "I teach European history in Boston. We usually have to see our bones in museums."

"I'll take a lot of pictures that you can show your students." Jocelyn's lively eyes took in the house and grounds. "Is this your second home?"

"It was my mother's home." Laura watched a young man and woman unloading supplies from a van. "I only inherited this estate a few months ago when my mother passed away."

"I'm terribly sorry." Jocelyn regarded her with a look of genuine sympathy. "We won't drag this out, and I promise not to let my team get underfoot."

"Thanks, but I don't mind. I'll show you the house, and you can make yourself comfortable. There's plenty of room but no staff. We're pretty casual around here, and we're in the middle of plumbing repairs. The water supply is limited. We use the bottled water for drinking and cooking."

"Like camping, is it? That sounds fine. I've brought two postgraduate assistants to help with the mapping and recovery. Beth and Eric." She introduced the couple Laura had been watching, a young woman with dark hair and Mediterranean features, and a lanky man with curly black hair. "If you'd like, we'll explain what we're doing as we go along," Jocelyn offered.

Laura immediately felt comfortable. These were the kind of people she liked as friends. She had planned to introduce them to Paul, but he was nowhere around.

"This way," Laura said. "We can take the footpath around to the courtyard."

As they set up their equipment, Jocelyn explained how they would build a frame crisscrossed with wires to make a mapping grid, and lay it across the trench. "One of the problems with old skeletons is that the joints don't always hold together. With one body it's easy enough to piece things back together, if there hasn't been too much trauma, but imagine if you had several dislocated skeletons." Jocelyn made it sound as though nothing could be more fun than trying to reassemble several sets of centuries-old bones.

Even though it sounded grisly, Laura was curious about the work. "Is it common to find more than one skeleton in the same grave?"

They were standing beside the trench, and Eric was already marking the area where the pit would have to be expanded. Beth began making rough sketches showing the location of the well.

Jocelyn opened a laptop. "In 1996, when I was finishing my graduate studies, I was fortunate to have the opportunity to work on a mass grave uncovered at Towton Hall in North Yorkshire. Thirty-eight individuals were buried there. They died in the spring of 1461, when King Edward IV defeated the deposed Henry VI. Some sources claim that there were twenty-eight thousand casualties from that one day."

"I'm familiar with the Wars of the Roses," Laura said, "but not every battle."

"This one took place on Palm Sunday, and it was one of the bloodiest clashes in the history of England." Jocelyn knelt and peered down at the exposed skull. "After a fight like that, the survivors are quick to bury the dead. We made a grid, just as my team will do here. We keep track of the bones that come up in each section, you see." She held up her hands and wiggled her fingers. "The small bones – fingers and toes – have a way of turning into messy little heaps, but eventually we get most of it sorted out." She stood and placed a reassuring hand on Laura's arm. "I'll take good care of this fellow, don't you worry."

§§§

The following evening, Laura emerged from the wine cellar with a couple of old bottles. She studied the labels – chateau this and that. On a teacher's salary, she'd never bothered to learn much about fine wine. In her former life, she left those details up to Carl. The thicker the dust, the better the vintage. She couldn't remember where she'd heard it, but she hoped it was true.

She set the bottles on the sideboard, rummaged for an opener, and carefully lifted glasses down from the cabinet.

Paul came in and said, "I found more reporters sneaking around, poking their noses against the windows. The police should put up a checkpoint here."

"In another few days, the skeleton will be on its way to the lab and all the excitement will be over."

"They're taking pictures of shadows," he scoffed.

The rumors of a ghost haunting the manor had spurred the sensationalist tabloids to cover the exhumation. What would she say to an interviewer who asked her about the ghost? *Saw him just the other day and we had a nice chat.*

"I'm going to the kitchen to get cheese and crackers," she said. "I invited the research team for wine." She waved a hand at the row of glasses ready by the bottles. "You're invited too."

He did his best to hide his faltering smile. "Right," he said, disappearing from the room.

Paul could be so easy-going one moment, and the next minute a bout of shyness stole over him.

The silence after his departure didn't last long. She heard bantering and arguing, the cheery voices of the researchers tossing technical terms back and forth as they came down the corridor. For a moment she was reminded of school hallways crowded between classes, the commotion of students grabbing books, slamming lockers, running when they thought the teachers weren't looking. An unexpected feeling of homesickness made her catch her breath. She missed her students, and her friends.

Jocelyn came in, cheeks rosy from outdoor labor, lively eyes sparkling as she spied the wine bottles on the sideboard. "Nectar of the gods." She read a label and blinked. "Rare and expensive nectar. I didn't know we ranked so high."

Beth and Eric crowded up before Laura could answer.

"Quick," Eric said, snatching up a bottle. "Let's pour before she realizes we're mere peasants."

"I think you've earned it," Laura said with a laugh, "and there's plenty more if you don't mind poking through cobwebs." She passed the corkscrew to Eric. "Will you do the honors? I'll be right back with appetizers."

When she returned, bearing a platter full of local cheeses, sliced apples, crackers and a loaf of rosemary bread, a glass of wine was waiting for her. "How's the work going?" she asked.

The answers poured out as readily as the vintage wine.

"We found something interesting today," Jocelyn said. "A knife blade was beneath the skeleton, and I'm pretty sure it's the weapon that killed him. Two of the ribs show sharp force trauma, and his skull had blunt force trauma."

"It would have been a violent death," Beth said. "The cracks in his skull radiate out from the point of impact, so that might have done him in, or he could have died when the knife severed an artery. Soft tissue leaves no evidence."

Laura leaned forward. "You can figure out what killed him?"

"Possibly. It's a matter of deduction," Beth said. "Your Medieval Man also injured his right shoulder and forearm, but those bones had time to heal."

"That type of an injury usually means the individual was defending himself," Jocelyn added. "And a healed wound isn't a killing wound."

Eric, who had been eating with the intensity of a starving student, momentarily paused. "I'm hoping to make a positive match between the knife blade and the rib injuries," he said. "I can probably tell if the killer was right or left handed. As for the time period," he refilled his glass and poured for the others, "radiocarbon analysis will help us zero in on when he lived."

"Once he's out of the ground," Jocelyn said, "we'll take him to the university and reconstruct as much as we can about his life. After that, I'll walk you through the laws and you can give him a proper burial."

"I haven't found the knife handle yet," Eric mumbled through a mouthful of crackers. "It might be buried deeper."

Laura paused, her glass halfway to her lips. "I've got something I want to show you," she said, jumping up. She ran to her bedroom, retrieved the carved knife hilt from a drawer, and returned to the drawing room. "I found this in the garden a while back." She handed it over and watched Eric's jaw drop.

Without a word, he left the room, and when he came back, he was holding a plastic bag with a long, rusted object inside.

He put on gloves and removed the blade, holding it up next to the bone handle.

The others leaned forward, and for a moment no one spoke.

"I can't believe it," Eric whispered. "Of course it has to be tested, but if this is a match..." For another minute, they all stared at the pieces of the knife, and then he carefully resealed the blade and put the handle into a separate bag. "Exactly where did you find this?"

"In the rose garden. About six inches down and tangled in roots." Suddenly it didn't seem feasible that they could have once been joined. "It was nowhere near the skeleton."

"You'll have to show us the spot." He looked up at her. "Building houses, digging wells, planting and harvesting – things get moved after a few centuries."

"We'll send them to a lab for analysis." Jocelyn nodded toward the items. "It will be fantastic if the metal composition in both pieces match."

Laura took the bags from Eric and held them up. There was a little wedge of metal embedded within the ivory handle.

She couldn't wait to tell Todd about it. Her mystery du jour.

§§§

The forensic team stayed four days, and during that time Laura bought extra food, did more cleaning, and more cooking than she'd anticipated. They in turn brought excitement and enthusiasm back into the house.

When they left, the manor felt empty again.

Winnie was busy caring for Nigel. Because he couldn't stand the pain any longer, he'd finally shown her the ulcerated sore on his shin. The infection was now an open wound that went into the bone.

The local doctor immediately referred him to a specialist in Stroud.

On the day of the appointment, Laura insisted on driving him, and when he came limping out of the doctor's office, she tried to take his arm, but he stiffened and pulled away. Judging by his grayish complexion and the deep creases around his mouth, he was miserable, and doing his best to hide it behind classic British restraint.

"We need to stop at the pharmacy and get the prescriptions," she said, looking at the paper he handed her.

"I've been too much bother already," he mumbled, but didn't offer any further complaint. They had only driven a few blocks when he pointed to a building. "That's the Chemist," he said. "Right back there."

Laura circled the block until she snagged a nearby parking spot. Nigel started to get out, but she put a hand on his shoulder. "Why don't you wait here?"

"Very good." He leaned back against the seat and closed his eyes. The poor man was just plain worn out.

"I'll hurry," she promised.

Inside the chemist's, she headed to the counter at the back of the store, where six people were already standing in line. The elderly woman being served nodded repeatedly as the pharmacist explained the side effects of her medicine, and then he went over it again to be sure she understood.

Laura looked around and wondered if anyone else was in a hurry.

The line moved again, and a young mother with a wheezy looking infant dropped a basket full of medications on the counter. "Which do you recommend?" she asked.

There were still four more people in front of her, and there was a limit to how long Nigel could wait in the car.

She really wanted to go to the specialty hardware store Gertie had told her about while they were here in Stroud, but hated to make Nigel sit through another stop.

Her stomach growled as the line moved forward again. They hadn't had lunch. She was used to skipping meals, but Nigel lived by a very predictable schedule. She grabbed candy bars and bottled water from a nearby shelf. Hardly nutritious, but it was the best she could do.

Finally it was her turn at the counter, and she listened to the do's and don'ts of the prescriptions, then handed over her credit card.

When she got back to the car, Nigel was sound asleep, head tipped back, his mouth slack and hanging open. She paused, gazing at him through the window. He looked so old.

She tapped gently, but he didn't hear it. Opening the door, she said softly, "I've got something for you."

He jerked awake, arms flying up and bumping the dashboard. His skin was so thin he'd probably get a bruise.

"Sorry. I didn't mean to startle you."

"You should have said something," he groused. "Let someone have a bit of notice before you give them a heart attack."

"I'm sorry," she repeated, handing him a package of his favorite cookies and a bottle of water. "Eat a few biscuits before taking these pills." She glanced at her watch – the hardware store closed in thirty minutes. "Will you be okay if I make another stop?"

"It's all right," he said, fumbling with the cookie wrapper. "Did you buy a sweet for Winnie?"

"Cadbury's Dairy Milk, her favorite."

"Thank you," he said. "You've very kind."

He and Winnie asked for so little, and she wished she could do more.

It was late afternoon and the narrow streets were clogged with traffic, pedestrians, and cyclists gliding in and out between the cars like salmon fighting their way upstream to spawn. The fuel light flickered orange on the dashboard, and she had no idea where the nearest petrol station was. She cursed under her breath.

"Leave it for another day," Nigel said. "It's late, and Winnie will be worried. You know how she is."

"I don't know when I'll get back over this way again, and this is the closest store that carries the locks I need."

"What's the hurry?" He rubbed his forehead. "They've been like that for years."

She couldn't share her fears about the keyboard keys, and someone getting into the house. It wouldn't be fair to worry him.

"If you want to fix something," he said, "hire a real plumber and get that pipe replaced." He hadn't forgiven Paul for leaving the trench by the back door uncovered.

Paul had sworn on saints Laura had never heard of that he hadn't been so careless, but Nigel's mind was made up. He wanted Paul off the job.

She spotted the unimposing storefront just as she was giving serious consideration to her fuel light. "There it is." The store closed in five minutes, and she zipped into a parking slot. "I'll just be a minute."

The clerk looked at the lock she'd brought from the manor, and took his time going through the assorted replacements. "Unusual," he said, clearly unperturbed by the clock that indicated it was now past closing. "Very old. Amazing they've lasted this long."

He rang up the hardware, and when she saw the total, she very nearly put everything back.

Outside, the warm scent of a nearby fish-and-chip shop made her stomach rumble. She was about to suggest it to Nigel, but he was asleep again. One more stop for gas, and then it was time to get him home.

It was another hour before she pulled into the courtyard and saw the kitchen light on. Winnie was probably waiting with a cup of tea, eager to hear what the doctor said.

Nigel was slow getting out, his body stiff from sitting so long. Grudgingly, he leaned on the cane. "This is only temporary, you know."

"I know," she agreed, helping him up the steps. "Winnie, we're back," she called, pushing open the door.

By the time they reached the kitchen, Nigel was out of breath, and he sat down heavily at the big oak table while Laura put the kettle on. Winnie was nowhere around.

"Be right back." Laura headed outside to unload the car. Tomorrow, she'd use Paul's hand drill and switch out some of the window locks. She was getting pretty handy with tools.

In the courtyard, she stumbled over the large hose they were using to bring water into the house. At one end of it, a plastic fitting enabled them to connect three separate hoses and direct water to the kitchen, the basement, and a ground floor bathroom. Rather primitive, but supposedly temporary, at least that's what she believed when Paul set it up three weeks ago.

She gathered the bags from the back of the car and noticed a light shining through the cellar window. It was late, but Winnie must be doing laundry. Lugging her purchases inside, she set them on the counter.

"Winnie's in the cellar," she said, scooping tea leaves into the pot. She grabbed a roast from the fridge and started it browning. Halfway through peeling potatoes it occurred to her that Winnie was taking a long time. Maybe she didn't realize they were home.

The narrow corridor off the kitchen had several doors, one of which led to the cellar. Not wanting to startle the older woman, she opened the door slowly.

"Winnie, are you down there?"

No answer.

She started down. "We're home now."

At the bottom of the stairs, she called again and heard a faint sound, hard to figure out, but no reply. Squeezing past the battered table used for folding laundry, she ducked under a sheet draped across an indoor clothesline. The housekeeper had a peculiar philosophy about the benefits of air-drying, and rarely used the electric dryer. The cellar was dark and dank, and musty smelling most of the year, so the idea seemed senseless.

Six battered dining room chairs, usually stacked against a back wall, had been placed haphazardly in the middle of the room. Obviously, someone had been down here moving things around again. Probably Paul.

She stepped over an old wooden crate filled with empty, decades-old milk bottles, slowly moving closer to the mystery sound. The length of hose they'd pushed through the window from the courtyard and stretched across the cement floor had sprung a leak. A stream of water arced into the air and bounced against a stack of cardboard boxes filled with items for the church jumble sale. Water had wicked up the cardboard and saturated the contents. Wool skirts and jackets, silk blouses and scarves that had once belonged to her mother were ruined now.

Puddles had formed in the low points of the cellar floor, somehow skirting the drain built to carry away excess water. As she moved the soggy boxes across the room to drier ground, the bottom fell out of one and shoes poured out, her mother's high heels, and trainers, white sandals and black pumps.

Frustrated, she pushed aside a hamper and spotted something wedged between the washing machine and some laundry baskets. It looked like the hand of an old mannequin. The color was off, the fingers slightly curled. It didn't look real.

A scared-sick feeling crawled around her stomach as she forced herself closer. *Please, dear God, let me be wrong.*

She peered over the baskets and found Winnie lying in a puddle by the washing machine. Her face looked waxen and her eyes vacant. Laura crouched down and touched her cheek. It was as cold as the water-soaked cement. Trembling, she chafed one of Winnie's hands, praying for some sign of life, a twinge of lips, the rise and fall of her chest, the flicker of an eyelid. She willed Winnie to breathe.

"You can't be dead!" The sound of her voice seemed to come from a long way off.

Using her sleeve, she brushed away tears and looked around, confused. Had Winnie slipped? A heart attack?

She looked at Winnie harder, certain she'd made a mistake, but the color was all wrong, the face muscles slack. Crying and shaking, she dropped to her knees. She didn't know what to do.

Nigel was waiting in the kitchen directly above her, and by now he'd be wondering what was taking so long. What would she tell him?

He was going to be devastated.

She staggered to her feet. Clutching the handrail to the stairs, she dragged herself up, forced herself to keep moving, but at the kitchen door she stalled.

Light from the overhead lamp cast shadows on Nigel, accentuating his wrinkles and highlighting the few silver strands of hair combed over the top of his head. He looked so frail.

"Nigel..."

Turning his head, he looked at her, and quite suddenly his smiled faded. He opened his mouth to speak, but nothing came out.

She went to him, wrapped her arms around his shoulders, and laid her cheek against his head. "I found Winnie in the basement," she cried. Any hope of telling him gently and kindly shattered. "She's...She's dead."

§§§

It was after midnight when the police finally left. Laura paced, questioned, demanded answers, and when she couldn't get any, finally collapsed into tears. The whole time, Nigel sat silently in an overstuffed chair, his face buried in his hands. When Laura did glimpse his face, he wore an expression of agony like nothing she'd ever seen.

A few days later, the detectives determined that the washing machine must have shorted out, and when Winnie touched it while standing on wet cement, she'd been electrocuted. The explanation seemed so simple. They knew right away by the red streaks up her legs, burn marks and tissue damage. The electrical set up in the basement was antiquated and out of code, but they weren't going to file charges. It was an accident.

§§§

Four days later, Laura sat beside Nigel in the front pew of the chapel. He shivered convulsively and continually dabbed his eyes. Wrapping her arm through his, she felt his bones jutting through his overcoat. During the past few days he'd barely left his bed. Neither of them had been able to eat. She wanted to comfort him, wanted to give him nourishment and tell him that someday he would feel better, but she didn't have the strength.

Everyone settled into the oak pews, and Reverend Graham again led them in prayers and hymns. Less than three months ago they had gathered like this for her mother's funeral. It felt like last week. It hurt like yesterday.

Nigel looked at her, his eyes welling again. "I can't believe they're both gone."

Laura squeezed his arm, unable to reply, as she fought to remain composed.

The old house, with its crumbling towers and steep stairs, its outdated electrical, and the nightmarish labyrinth of faulty plumbing had taken its toll on all of them. Nothing here was manageable, and she didn't want it anymore. She wanted to go home to her apartment in Boston. She wanted her teaching job back. She wanted life to be easy.

When the service ended, she helped Nigel to the graveyard. She took tiny steps, steadying him, supporting him as they slowly walked to the spot where the diggers had again been at their task.

Suddenly Paul was there beside them. "Easy does it, old boy, I've got you."

Laura looked at Paul gratefully, wishing her father, or brother, or even Todd had been able to come. But it was too sudden, and they were too far away.

It was just her and Nigel now, holding on, and falling apart.

Finding Winnie dead had taken her into a new level of hell. She was afraid to fall asleep, and when she did, terrifying nightmares jerked her awake. She'd been trying to do the impossible while ignoring everyone's advice and it had ended in disaster. Staring at the brown upturned sod, she knew that her dream of living in England, her hope of keeping the manor and her mother's legacy was naïve. She'd been trying to stop a flood with a few sandbags.

"Ashes to ashes..." The vicar's words drifted over the cemetery like falling leaves.

How long would it take before her mother's grave, and Winnie's, were like the others, unkempt and forgotten? A time would come when there would be no one left who knew of them or cared.

Winnie was the one who held everything together. She had taught Laura how to bake and embroider, had stroked her hair in a way her own mother had never done. She was the little girl Winnie always wanted, and Laura wished she'd done more and taken better care of her.

"Nigel's not holding up so well," Paul whispered.

When the vicar looked her way, Laura made a small gesture, indicating Nigel, and he nodded discretely and offered a closing prayer.

After the graveside service, she and Paul supported Nigel as they walked slowly back to the house, and with every step, Nigel clung to her more tightly.

In the kitchen, ladies from the village were bustling about, laying out a tea service and heating casseroles for the reception. She tried to help, and they shooed her out. They'd known Winnie for years, they were upset, but they put a stoic face on their grief; that's what the Brits did. Keep calm and carry on.

"You look like you could use this." Paul pushed a glass of wine into her hands.

"Thanks." She hadn't seen him walk up. She'd wandered into the drawing room, absently chatting with the guests, but couldn't remember a thing she'd said. All she wanted to do was go to bed and never get up.

Gertie and Reverend Graham approached, and by their serious looks, she knew they were about to spring some new catastrophe on her.

"We all agree," Reverend Graham began, "that Nigel needs to be in hospital."

She glanced across the room. Nigel's grimace might be grief, but when she looked again, she realized it was probably pain. "I'll take him tomorrow."

"I'll take him today," Gertie said. "His coloring's not good, and he's having trouble breathing."

"I just took him to the doctor a few days ago..." She remembered her extra stop at the fancy hardware store. If she'd come right back, maybe, just maybe, she could have saved Winnie.

"It shouldn't wait," Reverend Graham said.

Gertie's look seemed to take in everything from Laura's wrinkled skirt to her red rimmed eyes. "How are you holding up?"

She felt as lost as Nigel. "Just okay."

"You can't stay here alone."

Laura continued to watch Nigel. He sat by the fire, its flickering light making his pallor more obvious, his thin hands lost in the folds of the blanket across his lap. If she sold the house, she'd be letting him down and breaking her promise about his retirement. She walked over and sat beside him.

"Nigel, do you remember when you taught me to play football?" At first she hadn't understood that he meant soccer, but soon she was enthusiastically learning the game, taking practice kicks at a goal marked by low shrubs, and sitting with him as he watched his favorite team on his old telly.

He looked at her through blood shot eyes. "That first summer when you came back..." He had to stop and catch his breath. "You were a tad snippy – you wanted to stay in Boston with your friends." He clasped her hand. "Later, when you were older and could bring a friend along..." A bout of coughing cut him off.

Laura held her own breath until he calmed again. "You're a dear, dear man, and I love you." She leaned over and kissed his cheek. "Gertie's going to take you to the hospital in a little while."

"Being in hospital isn't going to help me feel better." His hands were shaking as he rasped, "I can't leave you here alone."

"Just for a few days." Tears were running down her cheeks. "We'll get you back home in no time. I promise."

His thin lips pinched in a straight line and she couldn't tell if he was fighting grief or pain.

Gertie joined them and gently explained that it was time to go. Laura stood behind him, holding his shoulders, not wanting him to see her anguish. She could feel him caving into his illness. He didn't even have the strength to protest as Reverend Graham helped him out the front door.

Gertie remained with Laura a moment longer. "Why don't you come and stay at our place for a few days?"

"That's very kind," Laura said, watching poor old Nigel tottering away. "But I need to be here. I want Nigel to know I'm waiting for him to come home."

"It's time for him to retire," Gertie said. "He's only hanging on because he thinks you need him."

"Did he say that?"

"Everything's changed."

Laura stood at the front door watching as they drove off. If only she'd listened, she could have sold the house and sent them somewhere safe, and then none of this would have happened.

Paul came up beside her and handed her another glass of wine. "I'll come back tonight and see if there's anything you need."

She wanted to hurl the glass against the steps, but instead drained the contents. She'd made terrible mistakes. As soon as

Nigel was recovered, she would help him get resettled elsewhere, and then put the house on the market.

"What I need is gone forever," she replied.

Chapter Thirteen

In the hours after Winnie's funeral, Laura wandered through the house. She called Todd, but even the reassuring sound of his voice couldn't lift her mood. Flowers and phone calls were no match for this kind of void. She hadn't appreciated the sacrifices her mother and the Wilcoxes had made over the years. She'd taken it for granted that the manor and the people she loved would always be waiting for her return.

Stripping out of her funeral garb, she shrugged into the over-sized nightshirt. All she wanted to do was crawl into bed and pull the blankets over her head. Just as she reached to shut off her bedroom light a fleeting movement caught her eye.

"Paul?"

She stepped into the corridor, but it was empty. Barely breathing, she waited. Whatever she'd seen was solid, real, not a ghost or a figment of her imagination. She listened carefully and heard the rustle of cloth, the scratch of a step.

"Paul? Is that you?"

A man, a stranger with a pale face and greasy dark hair came out of the adjoining room. He stopped, and with an insolent smile, asked, "Surprised?"

Her first thought was that he was a lingering funeral guest, or a long lost relative of the Wilcoxes.

"Who are you?" Her heart was pounding and she swallowed hard.

"I've got plans for us," he said, his voice as coarse as sandpaper.

Terror rocketed through her, making her spine tingle but rooting her feet to the floor. "I – I'm not doing anything with you." She took a few steps backwards, into her bedroom. If she could get the door shut before...

"There's no chance of escape that way – you'd be boxed in." He watched her, his eyes never leaving hers as he stepped closer. "Don't get me wrong, I like boxes. Use them all the time. I even built a special one for you." He lunged at her. "Run, you stupid girl! Run!"

She jumped, shocked by his screeching, and started toward the stairs, but he was so close that his fingers clawed her arm, trailing the length of it, digging into her skin. Pulling away, she leapt down several steps, but he caught her and tripped her halfway, and she fell heavily against the banister.

He pushed past her, blocking her on the stairs. "I do love a good chase. Don't you?" He held up a finger. "But, there are rules."

She thought of her mother running up to the ruins. "You, you," she stammered.

Slowly, he nodded, as though encouraging her. "Go on."

Her voice was barely audible. "Were you there when my mother –"

"Ah," he said. "Her first question." His eyes glinted, beady and bright. "You only get three. Three questions that is, not three chances. The answer to that is...hmmm. You know the old saying, 'If I tell you, then I'll have to kill you?' That's the situation we're in. So you decide. Do you really want to know?" Looking smug, he pointed to her arm. "You're draining."

His nails had gouged her, and blood trickled from three long gashes. She wiped them on her nightshirt.

"Speaking of draining – water, blood – it doesn't matter; that little Winnie got the shock of her life, didn't she?"

The implication of his words was just beginning to sink in, when he said, "By the way, that was the answer to your second question, if you'd been smart enough to think of it."

He'd killed them, and now he was here for her. She swallowed hard, could barely speak. "Why?"

He beckoned, his fingernails dirty and yellowed. "Come on," he coaxed. "Come closer."

She shook her head, edging back. "N-no."

He spoke slowly, enunciating each word like a deranged game show host. "And now, a clue for your third and last question." He reached into his pocket, pulled out a computer keypad, and tossed it to her. The letter X landed on the step at her feet. "My God, you people are slow around here. I've almost gone through the alphabet twice."

She stared at the letter. So it was him. He'd been coming around here for months, leaving his crazy clues. He probably knew his way around the house as well as she did.

"I see those little wheels turning in your head. You're thinking..." He pitched his voice higher, mimicking a little girl. "Where can I hide?" He jabbed a finger to the right, then left, then up the stairs, taunting her. "Speaking of little girls, I do like that Amy Barnes. She's the only one who's nice to me in this stinking village. When I own this place, everyone else is going to know my wrath, but I'll play nice with her." He trotted down the rest of the stairs, across the foyer, and swung open the front door. "Go ahead. The way is clear."

She looked at his flabby body. Instinctively, she knew she was stronger. All the weeks of physical labor had made her lean and fit, and if she could make it outside, then she could outrun him. Again, she thought of her mom, and knew he'd played this game before.

But there was no way he was going to let her run out the front door. It was a trick.

She could probably beat him to the kitchen and get out the back. At the bottom of the stairs, she lunged right, then quickly changed course and darted left. She caught him by surprise and gained a few precious feet, and as she passed a large vase on a stand she flung it into his path. It thumped and shattered, sending ceramic shards scattering. She heard the crunch under his feet as he came after her.

He was faster than she'd thought, and at the kitchen, he snagged the back of her nightshirt, almost pulling it over her head as she twisted to get free.

"I see your boobies." He reached out a grasping hand, trying to grab one.

She clutched her shirt and tugged it down, squirming away and dodging around the heavy oak table in the center of the room. A skillet flew past her head. She turned as he picked up another one, his arms windmilling as he sent it flying.

She ducked underneath the table as a pot came next and then the teakettle, its spout spewing water that splashed across her shirt.

"This is what I like," he said, panting erratically like a rabid dog. "The chase, the futile hope for escape." He tracked her with his eyes, not moving any closer.

He liked killing people. She knew it as clearly as she could feel the water from the kettle, still lukewarm, seeping through her shirt. She wouldn't let him get her. Scrambling to her feet, her shoulder bumped the table, and she let out a yelp.

He laughed, a chuckle that sounded like mirth mixed with phlegm.

"Leave me alone!" she screamed.

"I can't now, can I?" He spat on the floor. "Not until I finish – the project."

"What do you want?" Her mind was racing. "I'll give you money."

"Oh, I want it all. You see, I am your nearest relative."

"No, you aren't!" She looked around, searching for the best way out.

"I inherit everything when you die."

"My brother, Edward, inherits from me." She didn't know where he got that idea, but she had to convince him he had nothing to gain by killing her. "Ask Pickney, the solicitor. It's all set up."

He looked dumbfounded. "You don't have a brother. You're an only child – your mother's only heir."

How did he know so much about her?

"He's my half-brother," she said carefully. "My father's son."

He looked shaken, and then he shrugged. "Your mother tried to confuse me too. She said the police were on the way, but they weren't. You're both liars." He jumped toward her. "I hate liars."

Jerking away, she slipped in the water, went down hard on her knees but didn't stop crawling as she launched herself toward the door.

He got there first, blocking the exit. "You can't trick me."

"Let me go."

"I've picked a special spot to bury you."

"You can have the house. I don't want it anymore."

"Next to my decomposing mother and sister," he continued. "You know, they've never been missed. No one ever came looking for them."

She got to her feet. She was taller than him by several inches, and she widened her stance, lowering her center of gravity, preparing to fight.

His hands were behind him, and now he brought them into view, a ten-inch kitchen knife clutched in his fingers. He pointed it at her feet. "Too bad you're bare-footed."

She didn't wait for his next move, but turned and ran down the service passage, heading for the cook's garden. At the last second, she realized he could trap her in the enclosed space. Veering down a side passage, she ran toward the medieval wing, praying that the door would be unlocked.

Behind her, she heard him crashing down the hall. Something whizzed by her ear and clattered to the floor. A knife had missed her by inches.

He yelled, "There's more where that came from."

She threw herself against the door to the connecting passage and turned the knob, grateful when it opened, and then ran headlong across the great hall. When she made it to the far end of the darkened room, she heard him coming after her. At the stairs, she hesitated. Should she go down into the cellars, or up?

"Don't disappoint me," he called out as he entered the hall. "I've been waiting a long time."

The priest's hole, upstairs. She could hide there.

As quietly as possible, she crept up the stone stairs. At the top, she looked back and saw him hanging in the shadows, like he was deliberately giving her extra time, his movements exaggerated like a garish cartoon. "If you find a good hiding place," he called across the dark expanse, "we can make this last."

On the upper floor, she ran down the hallway and into the bedchamber furthest back, the one with the alcove. Slipping her hands behind the medieval tapestry, she shoved on the oak paneling that concealed the hidden room and it slid farther into the pocket wall. Quickly, she stepped through. She yanked until it was almost shut, but then heard him coming and stopped. If he heard the noise he would know where to find her.

She eased back into the shadows, trying to disappear. The chamber, tucked behind the alcove, was as she remembered, a hidden closet about four feet by six. The walls were covered in oak carved to look like folds of linen.

He was in the corridor now, calling her, taunting her, describing all the things he'd watched her do.

"I've been waiting patiently," he said. "Now it's just you and me – and misery makes three."

She heard him come into the bedchamber and stop just outside the alcove. Her legs trembled and her heart pounded. She tried to soften her ragged breathing.

"I've made blueprints," he called out. "The manor will have unique rooms where people can satisfy their most peculiar needs." His voice sounded closer, as if he were now in the alcove. "The cellar will have a real dungeon, the attic a permanent noose. There will be a doctor's examining room, with all the tools for surgery. I have so many good ideas – I just need more people." His voice trailed off as he moved farther away. "Sounds lovely, doesn't it?"

She had to get the sliding panel completely closed before he came near again. She pulled, and it shifted. Tugging harder, it began to move, making a soft grating sound. The opening narrowed. Ten inches left, then six.

A shoe shoved into the gap. Fingers wrapped around the upper edge. Then his shoulder pushed in, and he forced it open wider. "Is this the best you could do?"

She braced her weight against it, trying to keep him from sliding it open. He was pushing hard, but she leaned in with her shoulder, holding it steady.

He forced his hand in, and then his palm smashed into her face. Pain radiated from her nose, across her cheeks and forehead. Her eyes watered. She lost her grip and stumbled out of his reach.

"Not bad!" he said, squeezing inside. "This is probably the only hiding place I didn't know about. Thanks for showing it to me."

She backed against the opposite wall as he pulled the sliding door completely closed. They were swallowed in darkness.

Suddenly he grabbed her wrists, pinching them tightly. "But it wasn't such a clever place after all, was it?"

She broke free and flailed at him blindly, pulling his hair, kicking and clawing.

He backed off, laughing. "You've made some very stupid moves."

She realized that he didn't have a weapon. Racing to the sliding panel, she started to tug it open.

"You're so predictable," he said, inches from her ear. His arm wrapped around her neck and yanked her back, then closed the wall up again.

He was strangling her, his forearm smashing against her throat.

She rammed her elbows into his stomach as hard as she could. It took several times before his grip loosened. He was still behind her, and she pushed back, digging in with her heels, forcing him against the rear wall of the chamber.

He grabbed her hair and twisted her neck so that she was forced to look at him. "Game over."

She tried to gouge out his eyes, but only managed to rake her fingernails down his cheek.

He squealed and let go of her for a second. She ducked low, ramming her head into his gut, thrusting with her feet to increase the pressure, forcing his back into the ornately carved wood paneling.

Behind him, a section of wall shoved in and they both lost their footing.

A hard blow to the back of her head knocked her to the floor. Nausea and pain kept her down, and she felt warm, sticky blood.

"Is this a door?" he asked, in a cool, conversational tone.

She was on all fours, too dizzy to move.

He kicked her in the ribs, knocking her over. "Where does it go?"

"I – I don't know."

"You're lying! You knew this room was here!" He grabbed her arm, pinning it behind her back, wrenching her shoulder until it felt like it was going to pop. Without loosening his grip, he kicked the wall several times. Rusty hinges squealed.

"Incredible. There's a door here. It's a secret room, behind a secret room. I couldn't have planned it any better myself."

He let go of her arm to look inside, and she grabbed the opportunity to scramble out of his reach. He planted a kick on her backside, and she went sprawling, face down. Before she could right herself, he grabbed her ankles and started pulling her into the inner room.

Kicking with everything she had, she thought she might still get out.

Laughing, he danced in circles around her, slipping in and out of range, dodging her kicks. He got hold of her right ankle, wrenching it to the right with excruciating pain.

Still on her back, she thrashed, kicking and screaming, her bare feet glancing off his thick thighs. She was running out of time. She aimed for his groin and missed, but her heel struck his gut and she felt the air whoosh out of him.

He doubled over, hissing profanities. A second later, his boot stomped the top of her thigh.

A cramping pain shot through her leg, stopping her assault.

Grabbing the neckline of her nightshirt, he yanked her further inside. She struggled to get up, but he pulled the cloth so tight it was choking her. She heard the door shut with a heavy clang, and then metal scraping. There was a clunk as if something heavy had fallen into place.

"How convenient." His voice echoed in the darkness. "A key was sitting in the keyhole, just waiting for us."

She wrenched away, feeling the cloth burn her neck as it tore. She stood, trying to shove him aside. "Don't lock us in here!"

"Done!" he said, elbowing her away from him. "Cozy, isn't it?"

"Let me out." Her voice lowered as she tried to keep it from shaking.

"You need to be punished."

"Let me go." She tried to sound firm, even threatening.

"Hmmmm... Nope."

She stood panting, trying to listen to his movements, to keep track of him in darkness. When it sounded like he was getting close, she slithered in another direction.

He circled the small room again and again.

"I'll open the door," he said after a while, sounding uncertain. "I'm going back on the other side, but you, my dear, will remain in here."

She drew a deep breath and tried to still her shaking limbs. As soon as he opened the door, she would do whatever it took to escape. She wasn't going to stand still while he locked her in.

She heard him fumbling at the door, grunting and heaving. "I can't get this fucking key to budge." He pounded against the door, swearing, until she heard a snap, and then something metallic dropped to the floor. "Fuck!"

He began beating on the door with his hands, and she shrank back, trying to stay out of his way.

"We're screwed," he screamed. His rant continued as he struggled with the door. "The key broke off. I can't get the bloody lock open."

Laura pressed herself into the opposite corner. After a while, it sounded like he sank to the floor, muttering to himself. With her toes, she felt the area around her, searching for the key.

"You don't deserve this house." The suddenness of his comment startled her.

She wanted to keep him talking so that she'd know where he was. "How did you kill my mother?" Her tone was surprisingly calm.

"Why should I tell you?"

"Because she was my mother," Laura whispered. "I deserve to know the truth."

"She was running through the castle ruins, up and down, hopping here, climbing there." His voice became sing-song, as if he were repeating a fairy tale. "At the top of the wall walk she slipped."

"Were you chasing her?"

"It was only a game," he chuckled. "She shouldn't have jumped."

"You said she slipped." Images of her mother trying to outrun him played in her mind like a movie.

"I'm not sure," he chirped. "She flew through the air with the greatest of ease, like the daring young man on the flying trapeze."

She flexed her fingers, wanting to hurt him, to feel the life drain out of him. "What about Winnie?"

"An extension cord. I cut off one end and wrapped the wires around a screw on the washing machine. Easy. Simple. Just add water, plug it in, and wait." His voice held a tinge of pride. "Afterwards, I took the cord away."

That bastard had gotten away with two murders, and no one even suspected him.

"I was waiting for you that day," he continued. "Not the old windbag."

She shifted, still searching for the key with her feet. If she could, she'd lock him in here until he rotted. But she had to get out.

"Shocking, huh?" He snickered. "Now that you know, I can't ever let you out of here." His laugh got louder and pitched higher. Suddenly he was laughing so hard he seemed unable to stop. "Not that I was planning to. This place is perfect."

The cut on the back of her head was throbbing, and a trickle of blood ran down her neck. She had to stay calm, think clearly, be ready, but she was feeling dizzy again. It felt like her blood pressure suddenly dropped and she was going to pass out. There was no choice but to sit down – just for a minute.

She heard him moving closer, then felt his hand on her leg. She inched away, pulling her nightshirt down tight around her thighs. Her hand brushed something cold, and she grasped it. The rough metal object was about the size of a cigar with an oval loop at one end, the other jagged metal. It had to be the broken key.

He leaned close to her. "I – I –" His hands wrapped around her hips and he lowered his face onto her lap. "I want –"

She hesitated, her grip tight on the metal piece.

"– to smell you." His face nuzzled her.

She gritted her teeth against the feel of his head digging into her lap. Bile rose in her throat.

His fingers gouged between her thighs.

Recoiling, she pushed him away and stumbled to her feet. "Don't touch me!"

He stood too, trying to find her in the darkness. "There's nothing you can do to stop me." His outstretched hands fumbled across her chest.

Bracing herself, knowing she couldn't waiver or he'd retaliate, she lashed out, stabbing with the sharp end of the key where she thought his face would be. It connected, and he screamed. She hit him a second time, plowing the rough metal down the side of his jaw.

He grabbed at her but he was off balance.

She slammed her knee between his legs and felt him double over, then smashed the metal piece hard on the back of his head.

He snorted and sucked in a breath. "I'm going to kill you."

She rammed the sharp metal into him again and again, hacking relentlessly.

His teeth sank into her knee and he held on like a vicious dog.

Ignoring the pain, she didn't stop, but jabbed the crude weapon into his ears, his face, the side of his neck, over and over, until he collapsed onto the floor.

With all of her weight behind it, she stomped the heel of her foot into his jaw. Then she did it again. Switching to his ribs, she lost count of how many blows she dealt him. She only paused when she realized he was no longer grunting or making any noise.

Her whole body was braced to fight, her muscles tight as she forced herself to back off. She was ready, her senses alert, and if he so much as whispered, she'd be on him again.

He was down, motionless.

She still wanted to hit him, but made herself hold back.

"Can't move." His voice quivered.

She wanted to open the door but if she got close he might grab her again. Waiting against the far wall, she marveled at the power her rage had generated. She'd been like a grenade moments after the pin was pulled.

After a while her adrenalin began to ebb, and she slowly sank back down to the floor again. Her hands and feet stung, her wrists and ankles ached, she was nauseous.

"Why did you do it?" she asked, wiping her sticky fingers along the floor. It was his blood on her hands.

He whimpered.

"Who are you?" she demanded, hoping he really was hurt, that he couldn't rise again and come after her. He deserved every blow she'd given him and a thousand more.

"I can't feel my legs," he said.

He was probably trying to trick her.

In the darkness, she couldn't see exactly where he was, but knew he'd fallen close to the door. Terrified he'd creep up on her in the dark, she stayed flat against the wall, listening for every sound he made. As soon as it was safe to get past him, she'd try to open the door. Shivering, she wrapped her arms tightly around herself and waited, still gripping the piece of metal. She wouldn't hesitate to use it again if she had to.

After he'd been motionless for a long while, she stood up. Nudging him with her toe, she tested his responses. His leg seemed limp and lifeless. She poked the other leg and it was the same, no response. There was no resistance, no talking or moaning. He was still alive though; she could hear him breathing. Grabbing him by his boots, pulling first one, then the other, she dragged him to the side of the room so he would no longer be blocking the door. He was heavy and unconscious.

Next, she felt along the walls until she located the door. Its nail studded wood was easy to distinguish from the graininess of the stone walls. She stepped in something slippery under her bare feet, and forced herself to ignore it. The important thing was to get out. Trailing her fingers along the door's surface, she felt three large metal hinges on the left side. About mid-height, a large rectangular area was covered in iron and in its center she felt the jagged end of the broken key poking out of the keyhole. There was nothing to grip, and each attempt scraped more flesh off her fingertips.

Behind her she heard a moan. Reaching down, she picked up the key shaft and prepared to use it again.

His breathing became shallow and rapid, like panting. "Need a doctor."

If he thought she was going to let her guard down, or feel sorry for him, he was dead wrong. "Who are you?"

"I'm stuck." He began to cry.

"Tell it to the police when we get out of here."

§§§

For the next several hours she screamed for help, and during that time he never moved. He was seriously injured and needed medical help. Fear that he wouldn't get it soon enough worried her, but not as much as the thought of him recovering.

Time and again, she reassured herself that Paul would eventually show up at the house to do his work. He'd see the mess and call for help.

But searchers might never find this chamber. She never had, and she'd known where to look. The outer room, the only one she'd known about, had always given her the creeps. She'd never gone inside, or mentioned it to anyone. Now she wished she'd shown it to Todd. He would have been so intrigued, and could have told Paul, or the police, where to look.

Moving systematically, she felt along the walls. The square-cut stones were the size of large cinder blocks, interlocked, and held in place by a grainy mortar, solid, rough and cold. On one wall, about five feet up from the floor, she found a shelf. Tracing her fingers along its surface, she felt a box and a very large book. Something soft brushed against her hand and she jerked it back. She reached out again and felt vines with leaves on them, and little fuzzy shoots. Tendrils of ivy had managed to worm their way inside. The exterior of the eastern, medieval section of the manor was covered in ivy. When she lifted her face, she felt the reassuring hint of cool air coming from somewhere high above. That was a relief – fresh air and another way out.

The man on the floor let out a soft wail, like a sickly baby, and she cringed.

§§§

After a couple of hours at the White Hart, Paul got up the nerve to drop by the manor. It was going to be difficult, but he wanted to convince Laura to let him move in. He knew what she felt for Todd, and didn't have a hope of interfering with that, but for the time being she shouldn't be living alone in that big house.

He found the front door wide open, and in the light from the entryway he saw a toppled table and broken vase.

"Laura?"

He stepped in, calling her name, moving quickly through the ground floor rooms. Nothing else seemed out of place until he reached the kitchen. Cupboard doors were hanging open, drawers pulled out, and knives on the floor. He yelled again and a sick, dizzying feeling made the room turn like a kaleidoscope. He was sobering quickly, and fear was a stone in his gut.

He ran up the stairs to Laura's bedroom. No sign of a struggle in there, everything neat, a book on the nightstand, and a stack of folded laundry on her dresser. He called her name as he moved from room to room, but there was no sign of her.

His hands were shaking so badly he dropped his phone, snatched it up again and called the police.

§§§

Laura sat huddled in the darkness as the hours dragged by. She'd tried everything imaginable to dislodge the broken key head. She'd even tried to work lose the metal plate that contained the locking mechanism, but nothing she did had any effect. The rough old iron was tightly secured and built to withstand any manner of assault. Her hands were raw and blistered.

What if Paul decided to take the day off, or a couple of days? He'd done that before. It might be a while before she was even missed.

Todd would get worried when he couldn't get ahold of her, but what would he do? Contact Megan?

She thought of Megan, and Nigel, her brother and father, Gertie and Ben, Amy. There was no reason any of them would be alarmed if she didn't appear for a few days. After all, it was the day after Winnie's funeral, they would think she needed down time. Fear of being forgotten gnawed at her. Rationally, she knew it wouldn't happen, but nothing about her life was even remotely rational lately. Anything could go wrong, and did.

After a while she dozed, then jerked awake, trembling and sweating from a nightmare. Only it wasn't a nightmare, she really was locked in a pitch black room. She rubbed her arms and curled her legs up close to her body.

He was still alive, laboring for each breath. If they didn't get out of here soon, he wasn't going to make it. The thought of being locked in the small space with a decomposing body drove her to get up and try again.

She had to find something that would help her escape. Her legs were stiff, but she got to her feet, stumbling a little as she felt along the wall until she found the shelf again. She touched the book, but in the darkness couldn't see what it was; an old bible perhaps. The box was made of wood, fastened with a metal clasp. It stuck, but she managed to pry it open, and her fingers brushed over a velvet lining. A rolled parchment lay inside. She picked it out and set it carefully on the shelf. In the bottom of the box was a small fabric bag. Opening it, she poured what felt like a cross on a chain into her palm.

How long ago had these items been put in here? Judging by the build-up of dust and grit, it had been decades, if not centuries.

Soft, almost too low to hear, she heard a groan. It came again, and she tensed, but after a few moments he lapsed into stillness.

§§§

By the time the police arrived, a cold fog had settled around the house and a heavy drizzle descended. Paul watched men with flashlights fan out across the property calling Laura's name. They circled from the house to the outbuildings, walking through the garden, stepping over and into the rose bushes, tramping up and down the hillsides and throughout the castle ruins.

Inside of the manor they'd found blood on the stairs and near the front door. Now they were focused on the grounds. Eleanor's death, and Winnie's, were on everyone's mind. If something bad happened to Laura, he'd never forgive himself.

On the path that led toward the rose garden he thought he saw someone. Thorns snagged his jeans but he barely noticed as he held the flashlight tighter, readying it as a weapon.

"Who's there?"

The silhouette of a man with long hair and wide shoulders stood beside the wall of the medieval wing, but in the darkness Paul couldn't discern his features. He swung his light toward the stranger's face, but the glare seemed to bounce right back at him. For a moment he was blinded, and when he could see again, the figure was gone. He charged to the spot where the man had been, swinging the light wildly, the beam dancing in crazy patterns over the bushes, and bouncing off the ground.

"What are you doing?" Officer Stiles called out.

"I saw someone."

Stiles turned slowly. "I just came up the path; I was right behind you."

"You didn't see him?" Maybe his mind was playing tricks. He'd had a lot to drink earlier.

"No." The constable's breath puffed in clouds around his face.

Shaken, Paul followed Stiles back inside to look over the house again. They worked their way into the medieval great hall, casting flashlight beams into the shadows high overhead.

Officer Stiles called out as they moved slowly up the stairs to the second floor. They kept searching, circling through the rooms twice without finding anything suspicious. They looked into an alcove with an old tapestry hanging on the wall, but other than that it was empty.

"I'm going to have Kit open up the White Hart so we can organize search teams," Stiles said, as they were finishing.

Paul paused in the corridor. His eyes were tired and it was difficult to focus through the darkness. "She's got to be around here somewhere. I'll stay here."

"I want you at the White Hart," Stiles said. "We'll leave a team behind to keep searching."

"But –"

"You can't stay. I'm not sure how safe it is."

When they got to the pub, Paul's brother was there, along with most of the other villagers.

"The police are going door to door in the village," Ben said, shaking his head sadly.

By dawn everyone was crowded around tables and squeezed into booths, hands clutching mugs, their eyes full of worry. Kit poured coffee and tea while a constable divided the volunteers into search groups.

§§§

Gradually a shaft of light far above her head brightened the chamber, so faint and thin that at first she barely registered the change, but slowly the blackness of night gave way to morning. Laura stood up slowly and shook her arms and legs, trying to coax more circulation through her body. She was hungry and thirsty, and had to use a corner in the room to relieve herself.

Now that it was light, she could see that her night shirt was spattered and filthy, her hands and feet disgusting.

The side of the man's head and neck were covered in gashes and bruises, and blood oozed from his wounds. His face was swollen, his arms flung out awkwardly. His eyes remained closed, but pink, frothy bubbles appeared around his lips. A wrenching gasp seized him, and she turned away, not wanting to watch him suffer.

Had he stood by and watched her mother die? Had he enjoyed it?

Maybe later she'd feel remorse, but right now she was relieved that he was unconscious. It gave her time to figure out a way to escape.

From the inside, the narrow door was covered with dozens of large nails and looked like it was built to withstand a battering ram. Without tools, it would be almost impossible to extract the broken end of the key, but she tried anyway. There was nothing to grip. The whole locking mechanism was huge and probably hadn't been lubricated in centuries.

The ceiling was about twelve feet up. Craning her neck, she could just make out the circular opening high in the wall that let in a shaft of light. It was about the size of a man's fist and partially filled with strands of ivy. Leaves fluttered as fresh air wafted into the room. This chamber must be about three stories above the manor's rear courtyard, and she'd have to get close enough to the ventilation hole in order for her calls to be heard. She tried to hoist herself up on the shelf, slipped and landed hard, yelping when she jarred her knee.

The only thing to use as a step was the book. She hated to risk damage to something so old, but she didn't have a choice. Even with a step up, the shelf was too high. She tried again and fell, sprawling closer to the unconscious man. She rolled away quickly, repulsed at the thought of almost touching him.

She was tempted to quit, to give in to the rising feeling of hopelessness and fear, but she forced aside the panic.

He mumbled incoherently.

She looked at his shirt and thought about how much warmer she would be if she took it. She didn't want his jeans. He'd soiled them; she could smell it. He was gross, and she'd rather be cold than touch anything of his.

Ignoring the pain, she got up again and placed both hands on the shelf. She dug her toes into the mortar between the stones, searched for the next toe hold, found it, and then another, hauling herself higher an inch at a time. Clinging tightly to the groove between the wall and the shelf, she hooked her right knee up. She paused to catch her breath, and then eased her other leg up. The rough stones bit into her skin, but for the first time she was able to get both knees onto the shelf. To reach the hole and carry out her plan, she had to stand and make it to the air shaft.

With her upper body pressed against the wall, she managed to get one foot on the shelf, and then gradually raised her other leg until she was standing. Precariously, she inched along the shelf. When she was even with the airshaft, she peered into it, but from her vantage point she couldn't see down, only across the tops of the trees.

She reached inside and cleared away some of the ivy. The wall was about a foot thick.

"Help!" She screamed at the top of her lungs. "I'm trapped behind a wall in the alcove." Was her voice loud enough to reach the outside? Tears burned her eyes and she blinked them away. "Help me!" she yelled again. She imagined her words bouncing and rebounding off the stone, fading to a whisper before anyone could hear her.

She called until her legs began shaking, and then, afraid of falling, she carefully climbed down to wait. People would be searching. She was exhausted, hungry and thirsty, but she would be found.

Picking up the velvet bag, she opened it and examined the cross. It had a heart of yellow gold in the center and arms of white gold, and looked like a miniature replica of the standing cross in the cemetery. What was the story behind this room and these objects so carefully hidden? Who had they belonged to?

She draped the chain over her head and the cross settled over her heart.

Unrolling the parchment, she studied the picture of a young man in medieval clothes, a dagger tucked into his belt.

Her historian's mind gathered in more details. This portion of the house was constructed in the mid-fifteenth century, the secret chamber fashioned so well that a casual observer would see nothing but a tapestry hanging in an alcove. If they thought to look behind that they just might discover the oak paneled wall could slide like a pocket door and reveal a hidden room. But they would never guess that beyond that was another room, a second secret chamber. It was so soundproof that someone might be close by and never hear her cries for help. After years of teaching history, it was easy for her to imagine why a family in medieval times might need an impenetrable hiding place. It was just big enough to protect a wealthy family if an enemy ever paid a violent house call.

She pulled the book, a large, leather-bound manuscript, onto her lap. Maybe she could find some information about this room, and a clue about how to escape. Positioning herself to get the best sunlight, she turned one page and then another, staring at the flowing script in what was apparently an old diary. It had belonged to Lorraine Bonville Bannock.

She felt a soft sensation, like a hand brushing her shoulder. The ghost was here. She looked up, but couldn't see anyone. When she turned back to the book, she felt it again, a light brush of fingers across her shoulders and on the back of her neck. She could have pointed to a presence, except that she was staring at empty air.

When she was a child, the ghost had persisted in waking her up and leading her to the alcove. He didn't stop until she'd looked behind the tapestry, discovered the sliding panel and the antechamber beyond. Was this inner room what he'd been waiting for her to find?

Well, he couldn't help her now.

The man on the floor was dying, and she didn't want to sit quietly and watch. She couldn't waste the daylight hours. Setting the book aside, she looked at the blood-smeared door. Using the broken key shaft, she began scraping it on the wooden floor in front of the door, hoping to gouge a hole large enough to crawl through. It hardly made a scratch, but she continued to work at it. She didn't know what else to do.

As she worked, she thought about prisoners who spent years tunneling their way to freedom. Without food and water she wasn't sure how long she'd last.

Chapter Fourteen

At first Laura wouldn't allow herself to think about dying, but a full day and a second night passed with no sign that anyone was trying to rescue her. All the hours she'd spent balancing on the shelf and screaming out the air vent had only resulted in bruises and cuts. At least half a dozen times she'd lost her balance, and once her knee suddenly gave out. Each time she'd fallen back to the floor.

She spent hours scraping and clawing to carve a gap under the door, and she began to think about what might happen if she didn't succeed. Their bodies might never be found until the house was demolished. He was even quieter, his chest barely moving as he breathed. The moaning and gasping had ceased hours ago, and she was sure he'd slipped into a coma.

Now that it was dark again, she anticipated another night of uncontrollable shivering. Thoughts of her mother's body, and Winnie's, seeped into her consciousness and she tried to push them away. Her stomach cramped up and a headache pounded just above her eyes.

She wasn't a quitter! She was healthy and strong, and she was going to live, get married and have four or even five children. She paused, and spoke out loud. "Four or five kids? Now where did that come from?"

Raising her arms high and wide, she stretched and twisted side to side. Her bruised muscles protested but she ignored them and kept exercising. "Come on," she coached herself. "Stay warm." She jogged in place, but her right knee and ankle ached from her falls. She just wanted to stay warm through the night, and tomorrow she'd find a way out.

When she was too tired to take another step, she lay down on the hard floor as far from her assailant as possible. She didn't sleep well, and every time she dozed, strange dreams plagued her. They were colorful and frightening, set in medieval times. She was in a carriage racing through thick fog and someone was after her. He wanted to annihilate her bloodline, her entire family.

She awoke in the cold, dark room, her heart pounding, and thought of Todd, and how good it would feel to curl up against his warm body. Had he missed her yet? Was he worried?

§§§

By the time Todd arrived at Apple Cottage, Laura had been missing for three days and four nights. Something horrible had happened to her, but no one had a clue as to what.

Strain was deeply etched on Megan's haggard face as she handed him the key to her last available room. "Laura's father and brother arrived yesterday," she said. "They're at the manor."

"I'll head over right away."

"They haven't found anything." She paused, her voice thick as her eyes filled with tears. "I can't believe she just...vanished."

Todd nodded, and his throat tightened as he swallowed hard, trying to keep his own emotions in check. He climbed the steep narrow stairs to a small, stuffy room on the third floor, put his suitcase on the bed and pushed open the window overlooking High Street.

The village appeared deserted. Were they scouring the countryside looking for the Laura? Or was everyone behind locked doors?

He grabbed his jacket and went directly to Bannock Manor.

Laura's brother, looking as somber as Megan, let him in. "Thanks for coming," Edward said. "It means a lot that you made the effort."

"I couldn't stay away." Not wanting to waste another minute, Todd asked, "Do you mind if I look around? I want to check out the obscure places that the police might have missed."

"They've been everywhere, dusting for fingerprints, pulling stuff out of closets, digging up part of the cellar."

Todd thought about all the media attention that had been stirred up by the discovery of the medieval skeleton. It could have attracted any number of crazies. "We need to find her."

The worry in Edward's eyes reflected Todd's own fear. "Go ahead, look around all you want, except the library. My dad's in there." His eyes darted toward the brightly colored tape on the wall leading upstairs. Someone had made notes on each piece, labeling spattered blood stains and hand prints. "I don't think he can take it if they don't find her alive."

Todd spent the next three hours wriggling through a foot-high crawl space between the second and third floors. He climbed over heating ducts and mouse-nibbled electric wires, stirring up a century's worth of dirt. He saw old coins, combs, and buttons that had slipped between the floorboards. Repeatedly he called for Laura and then paused to listen. Twice he tracked down muffled voices, hoping it was her, only to discover the sounds of the family were echoing from another room. Inch by inch, he maneuvered his way through the Georgian wing of the house, sneezing as dust caught in his throat and clogged his nostrils. Hot and thirsty, he spotted light coming through a wooden latticed grate several feet ahead and crawled to it.

When he emerged, he found himself in a large bedroom with floral drapes and bedspread, and an old fashioned vanity covered in lace. On the nightstand was a framed photograph of Laura when she was about five or six, her blond hair in braids and a gleam in her eyes, as though she was keeping a wonderful secret.

He picked it up and stared at the little girl. She'd grown into an extraordinary woman, one who turned heads with her smile. He missed her, missed her bright energy, her unshakable optimism. "Hang in there, baby. I'm going to find you."

He'd never been in this room before, and after a cursory look, realized it had to be her mother's bedroom. He had liked Eleanor the minute he met her; he had fallen in love with her daughter instantly.

Back in the corridor, he hunted down more grates, but instead of crawling through them, he stuck his head inside and used a flashlight, calling for Laura. Again and again he called, hearing desperation in his own voice. He checked every crawl space he could find and came up empty handed.

At nine-thirty, when it was too dark to see much and he was getting shaky, he went to the White Hart. He climbed onto a bar stool and ordered a pint.

"What'll you have for dinner," Kit asked.

"Anything. I don't care." There had to be somewhere else to look, somewhere the others had missed.

"Some fish and chips?" Kit persisted.

"All right," he agreed, hoping Kit would leave him alone. He listened to the other shell-shocked patrons mumbling about what they thought they knew or what might soon be found. One man was pushing the ghost theory, saying Bannock Manor had always been haunted, and the uncertain future of the house had riled the spirit.

Todd didn't believe in soul mates, or love at first sight, but it was almost like that with Laura, the way they'd connected so quickly. She filled an empty place inside of him with her warmth and humor, and the silence of the last few days was breaking his heart.

§§§

It was hard to remember how long she'd been trapped. Was it three days, or four? Her hair was matted, her scalp itched, and the gash on the back of her head was getting infected. She was cold all the time. One corner of the chamber was fouled from waste, but now she was too dehydrated even for that. The muscles in her arms and legs twitched and cramped, her tongue felt swollen and tender, and she had a pounding headache.

Pulling the neckline of her nightshirt up to cover her mouth and nose, Laura stared at the man who had locked them in here. There was no mistaking that he was now dead. His cheeks were sunken and his jaw hung slack. The stench of his rot was increasing.

No one was going to hear her cries for help, she knew that now. She was going to die alone. Today, tomorrow, sometime next week, who knew? Probably in another day or two she'd be so sick from the infection, she'd be too weak to care.

She crawled over to the body and unbuckled his belt. She tugged it out of his belt loops, pulling hard to work it out from beneath his body, hoping the saturated portion in the middle would dry quickly. Searching his pockets, she extracted a wallet and a comb, some keys, but no cellular phone. He'd been immobile for days, and she should have thought of it earlier.

All this time he had been fully dressed, while she'd had nothing to wear but an oversized tee-shirt and panties. She unlaced his boots and pulled them off, disgusted by what she was forced to do. His socks were stiff, and she tried to ignore the smell as she slipped them onto her feet. She momentarily considered his shirt, then decided against it.

She opened his wallet and pulled out some money, not much. There were no credit cards, but she found a driver's license. Oliver Colfax. He thought he was her relative, thought if he murdered her and her mother, he would be the heir. Well, Oliver wasn't going to be anyone's heir now.

He was forty-five and lived in Birmingham. Did he have a family? If it was true that he'd killed his mother and sister, then maybe the police were already looking for him. Would they even know to come here? Maybe somebody knew something that would help her.

With the last of the sunlight, she wanted to try and hang the cross outside the air shaft. If it got someone's attention, it might signal her location. She lifted the chain from around her neck and threaded it through the belt buckle. Stepping onto the book, she braced her elbows on the shelf and boosted herself up. She was weak and her muscles burned, but she hooked her right knee up, and then pulled the rest of her body onto the shelf. It took four or five attempts to get her quivering legs to stand. When she reached the air shaft, she slipped the cross inside and wiggled the belt forward, slowly pushing the cross closer to the outside.

Half way in, it tangled in the ivy and wouldn't budge. She pushed and pulled, but the cross was stuck. The more she tried, the more it knotted in the vines.

Her vision blurred; she was too weak and too dehydrated to continue standing, and she barely made it down off the shelf before the room went fuzzy

§§§

Todd stood against the wall of the once elegant, now shabby drawing room as Laura's family waited for the press conference to begin. The massive search had been underway for five exhausting days. In both Great Britain and the U.S., the public was following the story as television crews sensationalized each tidbit of village gossip and local lore. Every hour was crucial, but it seemed as if the urgency of finding Laura was getting lost in the drama. What if she was hurt and needed medical attention? What if she were being harmed? Todd refused to allow himself to think that she might be dead.

Edward paced nervously in front of a window, his jaws clenched as he watched the growing crowd of reporters assembling on the front lawn. Their father leaned against a writing table, fidgeting with a letter opener. If he wasn't careful he was going to hurt himself.

Gently, Todd took the heavy, dagger-like letter opener out of his hands.

Bernard looked like he was going to protest, but then he said softly, "Laura talked a lot about you. And the fact that you dropped everything to come and look for her..." He paused, swallowed hard and glanced out the window. "I'm grateful – that's all."

"I'll never stop looking," Todd said.

After a moment, Bernard turned and held his gaze, and they both struggled to hang onto their shredded composure.

Todd had already combed through all the rooms in the attic, ripping dust sheets off antique furniture and pushing boxes aside. The police had been there before him, but he searched again. He looked at the architecture and the slant of walls, the odd spaces, the deep cupboards. More times than he cared to admit, he thought about how easy it would be to hide a body in this house.

Outside, Scotland Yard made a public announcement to at least twenty different television crews, most of the village, and perhaps fifty or sixty search and rescue teams. There were no new leads and no clear suspects. There was one person of interest, but they hadn't been able to locate him yet.

§§§

As light once again made its way into the chamber, Laura slowly opened her eyes. The night had seemed endless. There was nothing more she could do. The lock wouldn't budge, no one heard her calls, and after days of working, she'd only carved a slim gap under the door. They were never going to find her, and she was dying.

The weakness, lethargy and cramps were getting worse, and each time she dozed, it took her longer to come fully awake. Her swollen joints ached, her mouth and throat were agonizingly dry, and her skin was as stiff as the parchment pages of the old manuscript. But it was the gash on the back of her head that caused the most discomfort. Every movement of her head, any time she touched her scalp, pain radiated around her skull, an itchy, pulsing, raw sensation.

Dying was harder than she could ever have imagined. Sometimes, usually when sunlight was in the room, she felt tiny twinges of hope. But mostly ugly fingers of despair clawed at her throat. Pain gnawed. She hadn't made a difference in the world, there hadn't been enough time.

She opened Lorraine's memoirs to distract herself.

I am tormented by my sins.

I am haunted by the lies and secrets I hold tight against my heart. How could a young girl know that each deception would spawn another? I can think of no other way to gain forgiveness than to confess, and yet, in confessing, I will cause more pain. I shall write my story, laying down all my secrets, and perhaps someday those I hold in affection may understand. Even now, I cannot say if my decisions were right or wrong, only that I wish to be understood...and forgiven.

Closing her eyes, she leaned back against the wall and thought about how she'd passed Lorraine's portrait on the stairs a thousand times. The woman in the painting had always fascinated her, but until now she'd known nothing personal about the first mistress of Bannock Manor.

Lorraine had written an account of her life during the fifteenth century, just as the war between England and France was drawing to a close. From her reading, Laura learned that Lorraine had been an only child from a noble family in Normandy, France. Her father had been allied with the English, who had slowly but surely lost control of their French territories.

Under different circumstances, this would have been an amazing find, a firsthand account of the end of the Hundred Years' War, exciting beyond measure, a sensation among historians. But now there was nothing to get excited about. The book, like her, would probably stay undetected in the chamber.

Laura roused herself and continued reading.

On May Day in the year of our Lord, 1450, when I was a girl of fifteen, I first became aware of the dangers outside the walls of my home at Chateau Brèche. By nightfall my world was forever changed.

I awoke to the smells of baking bread and roasting meat. From my window in the keep, I saw servants carrying firewood and fresh water, eager to finish their chores before our May Day picnic. On this day the customs between men and women are lenient, and couples may stroll freely through the woods, holding hands and collecting wild flowers, and a man and a woman may exchange a kiss without shame. I was in high spirits as I dressed, and I teased my maid, Matilde, about her chances for romance.

I was on the first cart as it left the castle gates. The sky was a vibrant blue, and the hills of the French countryside looked fresh and green. In the cool woods, sunlight dappled the trees, the shouts of men, and the laughter of women, filled the air.

I saw Jacques, and when my cart came to a stop nearby, I hopped down. He was working with the other men, cutting green boughs to adorn the great hall. He watched me as I played and sang with the other girls, and though he held no title, I was flattered. Papa and his English visitor had stayed behind at the Chateau, and Matilde was enjoying the company of a groom.

I was not used to such freedom and soon slipped away. I chose a narrow path and had not gone far when I came upon a speckled fawn. It gazed at me from baby-soft, brown eyes. I looked around but saw no sign of the doe that should have been nearby. Perhaps, like me, it had no mother. With a flick of its ears it pranced down the path, and I followed as quickly and as quietly as I could. I was close enough to see the flecked brown and white markings and the little tail that bobbed like a signal flag. I felt daring, exploring by myself, and I imagined that I could capture the fawn and make it my pet. It trotted away on its tiny hooves and I tracked it, leaving the path as it moved through the trees. All at once it froze, raised its head and dashed away.

Suddenly an unfamiliar man stepped from behind a tree and grabbed me. Before I could scream, his thick, hairy hand covered my mouth and clamped down so hard that I struggled for breath. I fought wildly. To still me, he put the tip of his knife to the side of my throat and pressed it into my flesh until warm blood ran down my neck. I stopped struggling, the knife eased, the hand covering my mouth moved away, and I gulped for air.

When he tried to kiss me, I smelled his sour breath and broke away screaming. He caught me after a few stumbling steps, grabbed my arm and yanked me to the ground. He was on me, slapping my head, pulling up my skirt, straddling my hips. He raised the fat blade of his knife and threatened to cut off my ear if I did not lie still. My shaking made him laugh. His stench of musk and horses made me choke.

A second man came toward us, leading a pair of horses. He was dressed in black, even his leather armor. He had a long dagger in his belt, and ordered the man kneeling between my legs to put away his knife.

A stone was digging into my back, and I lashed from side to side, trying to keep his horrible touch from impaling my most private flesh.

The newcomer drew his dagger and commanded him to stop, and when the ruffian atop me saw the drawn blade, he loosened his grip.

The man in black yanked me to my feet and ordered me to quit crying. Before he could get a cloth binding on my mouth, I screamed with all my might until the back of his hand struck my face. I tasted blood.

He tied the binding, and then with cool deliberation grabbed my right hand and described how he would cut off the tip of each of my fingers.
A third man joined us, dressed in a good cloak, a jeweled sword in his belt. His horse seemed to sense my fear, shaking its head and pawing the ground. This well-dressed man signaled the other two.
The man holding me tied my hands behind my back, then tossed me over his shoulder as if I were a sack of grain. As he set off through the woods, he informed me that the truce between the Bonville and Dannes families was at an end.
I was to be a hostage.

Laura looked across the small room at the rotting corpse. Like Lorraine, she had been victimized by someone she didn't even know, someone who thought they would gain power by her death. A fly had made its way through the vent hole and was buzzing around the stinking body. Images of maggots slithering over rotting flesh crawled into her mind.

She spoke out loud, and her voice sounded odd. "Someone, please find me." A painful lump caught in her throat. "Dad, I need you."

When would they find her body? How many years? Her mind flashed to the skeleton buried under the courtyard. They would never know what had happened to her either.

Laura examined the book again. The vellum pages were thick, and when she flipped through the heavy book, she saw that there were pages missing. She studied the spine more closely. The last third of the book was gone, and from the looks of it, it had been done in haste, with a knife, leaving jagged edges.

Compared to that, what she was going to do was minor. She tore a page out of the middle of the book. The single sheet was about the size of a large magazine page. She folded it lengthwise and slowly wedged it under the gap she'd carved into the floor beneath the door. She hoped that if someone found it, they might realize there was another room behind the wall.

The effort exhausted her. She lay down and propped the book open to block the sight of the dead man, the loathsome Oliver Colfax, and began to read again.

They carried me deeper into the woods, and when they stopped to set up camp, I was left alone with the man who had first tried to hurt me. I watched in terror as he unlaced his pants, describing what he planned to do to me. With my hands still bound behind my back, and a gag in my mouth, there was nothing I could do to defend myself. I was Papa's only heir, and when I was ruined, it would be the end of our family.

From beyond the trees I heard a scream, and then a horse charged us, eyes rolling and foam spraying from its mouth. It pounded straight toward me, and I braced for the crushing impact.

A body in black clothes was caught behind the horse, and the weight of it slowed the plunging animal. His head was lolling, the neck half severed, his spurting blood vessels leaving a damp trail in the earth. The man who wanted to rape me caught the reins and cut loose the body. A knife was wedged in the neck, but when he bent to pull it out, he staggered and sank to his knees. He collapsed at my feet, the back of his head split by a hand axe.

The last remaining soldier rushed toward me, drawing his jeweled sword. He pulled me in front of him, held me tightly, and steadied his blade against my throat. Two bodies lay at our feet.

The stampeding horse, the dead men, it happened so fast I did not understand, but then I saw Jacques Dannes step from behind a tree.

Jacques wove in and out of the bushes, slowly moving closer, forcing the soldier to turn one way and then another, always keeping me between them. My captor stumbled over his fallen comrade and briefly lost his balance.

I broke free.

Jacques was on him in an instant, and the clang of swords rang loudly through the forest.

I dared not do anything that would distract Jacques' attention, and tried to keep out of the way as they struggled back and forth across the clearing.

I heard a grunt, and then the sword fell from Jacques' hand and bewilderment played on his face. He had been trained to protect me, had spent his whole life trying to impress me, but he stumbled back, wounded and unarmed.

I ran to Jacques, but our enemy grabbed me and threw me to the ground. When I tried to wriggle away, he kicked me and I felt my ribs crack.

Jacques lunged, knocking the other soldier away from me, but with a sudden thrust, his sword caught Jacques in the arm and ripped him open from shoulder to elbow. His blood rained over me.

The pain in my side held me motionless.

Jacques' face contorted, and with a guttural cry, he sprang at the soldier, smashing blow after blow. His good hand closed around the soldier's throat. They fell to the ground, but he did not loosen his grip. They stayed locked in a death struggle until Jacques, in a move so swift I could hardly follow it, grabbed the dagger from one of the dead men and forced it down into the soldier's neck. He put all of his weight behind it until the body jerked. Jacques fell right beside him.

His breathing was shallow, his face white, and when I moved next to him, his eyes fluttered open. Slowly he reached up and pulled the gag away from my mouth, and then using the bloody knife, he cut the rope from my wrists.

I wasted no time. I cut his tunic into bandages, but even bound in several layers, blood seeped from his wounds. With the battle over, one of the horses wandered back. Clutching my side and gritting my teeth against the pain, I got to my feet, caught the reins, then led the horse to a fallen tree so I could mount. I tucked my skirts around my legs and told Jacques that I would ride for help.

I feared that by the time I returned, he would be dead.

His voice was weak, little more than a whisper. "Know this before I die. I love you."

Laura gently stroked the page. It was Todd's face she saw as she read about Jacques Dannes. Her crying was tearless and silent as she grieved for the future they'd never have. Thinking of Todd, she whispered the phrase aloud, hoping it would find its way into his heart. "Know this before I die. I love you."

She buried her face in her hands and wept for her mother too, for that terrible and unexpected loss. And for the pain her disappearance would cause her father and brother. She rubbed her eyes as she mourned for Winnie, who had died so needlessly, and for Nigel, who was now left alone.

There were so many things she wanted to do, so many experiences she'd never have: marriage and babies, growing old with someone she loved. And she couldn't save Bannock Manor.

With the last of her strength, she dragged herself to the wall and tried to hoist herself up to the shelf. She had to try one more time to move the cross, get a signal to the outside world. Her limbs shook and she could barely stand.

Pulling herself up was agony but she ignored the way the stones gouged her flesh. Her ankle throbbed and her muscles quivered but she didn't let go.

Clinging with her fingers, she dug her toes into the mortar between the blocks. She got her knee up, spread her arms to steady herself, and then got her other knee onto the shelf. She paused to catch her breath. Now she had to stand.

Her ankle gave way, her foot slipped, and before she could catch her balance again, she crashed to the floor. Her head smacked down hard, and the breath whooshed out of her. Streaks of white swam in her vision, and when she tried to blink them away, every nerve ending in her face exploded in pain.

She curled into a ball, holding the back of her head. Her neck and shoulders were on fire, and when she drew her hand away from her scalp, her fingers were smeared with blood.

In front of her the air seemed to blur and change colors. She blinked and managed to raise her head, still staring at the odd cloud taking form. Suddenly she wasn't sure if she was awake. She touched the wall beside her and felt the rough stones. She rubbed a hand over her face. Her skin felt cold, and her lips were cracked.

The form continued to solidify until she was staring at a man. He wore leggings and a knee-length tunic slit along the sides. He was so real that she could see the decorative embroidery on his lapels and the broadsword belted at his waist. She stared at the heavy weapon, his solid chest, and then gazed at his face.

"*Don't you know me, Lorraine?*" he asked softly, gently.

"My name is Laura."

"*As a child, you called me your knight.*" He smiled tenderly and knelt before her. He smelled like the outdoors, like the forest.

"Help me," she cried.

He looked at her with such sadness. "*Lorraine, forgive me.*"

She wanted to protest again that her name was Laura, but she didn't have the strength. She closed her eyes and inhaled the scent that always reminded her of coming home to Bannock Manor. When she opened them again, he was no longer visible, but she felt the familiar touch of his hand on her cheek.

If he existed, then there had to be something beyond physical death.

Her heart fluttered erratically, and then she sensed that she was drifting on a wind current, over the tree tops, high in the sky. It should have frightened her, but she wasn't afraid anymore. She could still feel his fingers against her skin, and then his touch faded too, until she couldn't feel anything at all.

Chapter Fifteen

The sounds of people talking and carts creaking carried up to her and she listened as she never had before. The yeasty smells of baking bread and the aroma of roasting meat floated into her room. She was afraid to get out of bed – afraid of the pain in her ribs and the pounding in her head. And she was afraid to look outside.

Standing slowly, her body hunched like an old woman, hands pressed against her ribs, she moved to the window. Several stories below, people were working. A woman, the tail of her headscarf flapping as she walked, carried a large round of cheese. Two men were delivering sides of meat from the smokehouse to the kitchen. The cellar doors opened, and workers rolled out butts of beer and casks of wine. The castle grounds were a hive of activity as soldiers lined up for inspection before the change of guard.

Everything appeared so normal.

At the sound of a door opening, she turned.

"At last – you're out of bed." A woman bustled about the room, gathering stockings, a comb, ribbons and a scarf. "Lorraine, it's time to get ready."

And then she remembered.

Matilde closed the shutters, blocking out the fading sunlight. "Someone very special has been anxious about you."

"Jacques?"

"No, ma chérie. Not a boy – but a man. An English baron."

Her bedcovers, lined with rabbit fur, were heavy and warm and she longed to be back inside their safe cocoon.

"Oh, no. You can't go back to bed. The May Day feast has already been postponed for three days."

"I can't go."

"You're only fifteen – you'll heal quickly." Matilde moved about the room lighting candles. "Donna-Marie is brewing tea to ease your pain."

"I don't want to be drugged by one of her potions. They can celebrate without me." Her eyes welled. "How can I face them?" She knew she sounded like a petulant four-year-old, but everyone would be looking at her. "When they see my split lip, and the marks on my face and neck, they'll wonder..."

Lifting a blue silk dress from the trunk, Matilde said, "You're going to look beautiful."

Lorraine was as stiff as a wooden doll as Matilde pulled the gown over her head. When the outer corset was in position, her maid tugged the lacings tight. "My ribs! I can't breathe." She no longer cared that the fabric was from Flanders or that the gown had been made especially for this occasion. "It pinches me, and see how low the bodice comes? Take it off – I don't want to go."

Matilde began to comb her hair. "A scarf will hide the blemishes until they heal. At least your color is coming back."

When Lorraine's long brown hair was free of tangles, Matilde divided it into four strands, plaited each with ribbons and wove them into a graceful design on the back of her head. Matilde secured the headdress and then draped a lace scarf gently around her neck and shoulders.

"Be thankful that your honor is intact," Matilde whispered.

"I don't feel...intact." She moved to a chair near the fire and set a screen in place to protect her gown from flying sparks.

Donna-Marie came in carrying a mug of steaming tea, followed by Michel, her father's steward.

The healer offered her the cup. "This will dull the pain."

"How is Jacques?" Lorraine refused the brew. "Will his arm mend?"

"I flushed the wounds with brandy, sewed him closed and covered the stitches with a plaster made of honey."

Lorraine asked, "Will he be at the feast tonight?"

"Yes," Michel answered. "Your father wants to thank him. It is time to go." She followed him into the corridor where torches burned in iron holders. "This evening your seat is by Lady Cecile. Her husband has done very well in the tournament today." He continued to instruct her in a low voice as they walked. "Your father's esteemed guest is an Englishman. Lord

Bannock." He bowed to her as she took her seat at the head table. "Signal me if you need anything."

The ewerers came forward with pitchers and basins, and the diners washed their hands. The butler poured spiced wine, and the soup was served. Platters laden with carved meat and pies stuffed full of roasted poultry filled the table, but she had no appetite and sat with her hands folded in her lap.

Lady Cecile, the wife of Sir Theobald, used her cutting knife to spear a juicy portion of meat and laid it on the trencher bread in front of Lorraine. "You'll feel better if you eat something." The guests were busily helping themselves. "If the meat is not to your liking then perhaps a little of the fish?"

Lorraine's stomach churned, and she clamped her lips. The table was too crowded, the voices too loud, and the air was full of smoke from the fires at each end of the hall. The floor had been swept and strewn with clean rushes, but as the meal progressed, the dogs scavenged for droppings and greasy scraps of used trenchers. Behind her, two bitches snarled over a bone. She tried to follow the conversations. Sir Theobald was talking to Lord Bannock, a large man with red hair and a beard, a great chest, protruding belly and hands as large as bear paws. Unbidden, the sight of another man's filthy hands came into her mind, and she closed her eyes in an effort to block out the memory.

"Lorraine?" Lady Cecile's voice reached her.

She opened her eyes and saw every head at the table turned toward her.

"Didn't you hear the baron's question?"

She made an effort to join the conversation. Lord Bannock was staring at her, and so she asked politely, "Sir, do you like Normandy?"

"Ce n'est pas terrible."

She smiled with the others as he made an effort to put her at ease.

"I like it better now that I'm not here to fight a battle," he said. "Did you know that your father saved my life?" He smiled, as if to charm her. "I stayed here a long time ago, but you were a very young child, scampering about and climbing into your father's lap every time your nurse scolded."

"I don't remember."

"You wanted nothing to do with me – I frightened you. I hope that is no longer the case."

Lorraine looked helplessly at her father, but he only signaled for the butler to pour more wine. Lord Bannock held up his goblet and finally stopped staring at her.

Lady Cecile gave her a strange look. "Childhood passes so soon."

A quartet of trumpeters raised their horns and added to the din. How much longer would she have to endure this? The knights began pounding their goblets to the beat of the drums, and she saw Jacques seated among them instead of in his usual place at the back of the room. Their eyes met. What did he think of this?

Her father let the commotion go on for several minutes then stood and summoned Jacques to the high table. In a voice that filled the hall, her father bellowed, "Jacques Dannes, you've done a great service to the Bonville family. Tell us how you rescued my daughter."

Jacques stammered and attempted to give a modest account of the fight, but the knights drowned him out, shouting questions and begging for details. They wanted entertainment. He glanced at her apologetically. His right arm was bandaged, but he raised his left and silenced the crowd. "I surprised the first man and slit his neck open with my knife. Then I frightened their horses, and when they bolted, I killed the second man with an axe to the back of his head." The excitement of the battle seemed to overtake him, and his voice grew louder. "I killed the third man with his friend's dagger."

"By all the saints, that's the way to fight," Bannock shouted.

The men encouraged Jacques, and he seemed to be enjoying their admiration. It mattered little to them that she had almost been raped. Unconsciously, she touched a small cut on her neck where the knife blade had pressed.

She watched as her father removed his leather belt and unsheathed the long dagger. He held it up so that everyone could admire the bone handle carved with the design of a griffin. "This dagger bears my family crest. It's your reward for saving the honor of my household." He slid the dagger back into the sheath and handed the belt to Jacques. "Bon, voilà. Put it on."

"Thank you, my lord." Jacques bowed his head. "I vow to always serve you."

For the past eleven years while she had kept company with her ladies-in-waiting, her maids and tutors, Jacques had been among the serving boys and then in the barracks with the other knight-aspirants. They inhabited different realms, but he watched her. As a child she hadn't taken any special interest, but recently she had been drawn to him. He was taller than the other men, his cheeks smooth-shaven, his dark hair curling around his ears. She watched him, too.

Michel appeared at her elbow, and she was about to ask him to escort her back to her room, but he said, "Your father wants you to join him and his guests."

Nervously, she followed Michel as he led her up the stairs to her father's private chambers.

Animal pelts covered the timbered floors, tapestries hung on the walls, and a crackling fire cast shadows on the faces of the waiting men. The guard at the door shifted his weight, and his leather scabbard creaked. Inside, Lord Bannock stood on one side of her father's carved chair, and her godfather, Sir Theobald, stood on the other.

She was seized by panic and her legs began to buckle. She pulled back, but Michel whispered, "Be strong!" His hand at her elbow steadied her. "This is important."

Had they learned something about the attack?

Roland, the captain of the guards, closed the door, and the sounds from the great hall faded.

Michel poured wine, and her father offered a toast. "Lord Bannock, to a great alliance!"

Bannock raised his cup. "To you, Sir. May your grand-children be many!"

Her father beckoned her closer. "My dear, we live in dangerous times. The Bonvilles of Normandy have held the land and castle of Brèche from the time of Henry I, son of William the Conqueror. But the powers in France have changed, and our allies are disappearing. York is in exile and it's no longer safe to support English rule in Normandy."

Bannock's hand wrapped the hilt of his sword. "Marquis Bonville, you saved my life, and now it's my turn to repay you."

"How many men can you send to fight for me?" Bonville asked.

"Two hundred. For as long as you need them."

Her father turned to her and gave her a tender look. "Lorraine, when I depart this world, Lord Bannock will be able to maintain our holdings." His tone was firm as he stared into her eyes. "In return, you will pledge your allegiance to him, as his wife."

It took all of her will power not to cry out. Why hadn't anyone warned her?

Her father placed her trembling hand into the Englishman's palm. "Brian Bannock, I promise you the hand of my daughter, Lorraine Bonville of Chateau Brèche. All of the lands and holdings that will be hers upon my death shall be yours, in keeping for her, if you vow to honor and protect her."

Her father couldn't be doing this to her. She didn't want to marry this – this disgusting foreigner.

Bannock knelt. "My lord, I vow to honor and protect your daughter and holdings."

"Excellent!" Her father looked pleased. "Lorraine, when you're married to Lord Bannock, he will take you to England. And then one day all this shall be passed to your children."

"My lord." Michel approached the table with parchment scrolls. "The documents."

Papa was giving her to a hairy, old man. She felt the blood drain from her head. "Papa –" Suddenly Lord Bannock's arms were around her, holding her upright, his meaty hands pressing against her fractured ribs. He smelled of horses and sweat, and she knew she was going to be sick.

"You're pale." Bannock scooped her up and carried her to a chair. He set her down slowly. "Forgive my boldness."

Her father hovered while Sir Theobald rushed to get brandy. Bannock took the cup and pushed it against her lips. The fumes stung her eyes, and she had no choice but to swallow or the amber liquid would have spilled down the front of her gown.

Bannock said, "You weigh no more than a sparrow."

She wished she had died in the woods, rather than have to feel his touch again.

Her father guided Bannock back to the table, picked up his quill, and dipped it into the ink well. With a flourish he affixed his signature, and Lord Bannock did the same. He held the red wax over a candle flame, let it drip onto the parchment, and then carefully pressed it with his brass seal. When he was finished he smiled and said, "Lorraine, your future is secure."

Sir Theobald clapped him on the shoulder. "You've made a good match."

"Bonville, let me take her with me now," Bannock said. "I have a fortified castle, and I'm building a new house."

"She'll stay with me for one more year. When she is sixteen, she can marry."

They didn't even look at her while they negotiated the terms and timing of her marriage. She was being sacrificed! Bartered for soldiers!

Once she got her father alone, she would plead with him, make him see his mistake. She looked down at the document that promised her life to this man. She was familiar with the Bonville griffin but had never seen Bannock's coat of arms, twin stags above the letter B.

"When we marry," Lord Bannock said, "your badge will be joined to mine."

She kept her eyes on the parchment. Her future was whatever her father determined it would be.

She couldn't bear it anymore and stumbled from the room, glaring at everyone she passed, daring them to speak to her and suffer the consequences. She yanked open her chamber door so forcefully that it crashed against the wall.

Matilde clutched her sewing to her bosom. "What is it?"

"I won't do it! I will not marry that pig." She slammed the door as hard as she could, ignoring the ache in her ribs that made her want to double over. "I would rather die than let him touch me. I hope he dies!"

"If you talk like that, you'll bring on evil."

"Evil is already here and Papa has just handed me over." She wasn't going to cry, but she would find a way to punish them both. She picked up a jug, flung it, and it crashed against the wall. "I hate Brian Bannock. I won't marry him. I'll kill myself first."

Lorraine knew she was frightening Matilde, but she didn't care. She stomped back and forth. "I don't want to live in England. They're ignorant—just look at Bannock, he's a beast. I'll run away! I'll make Jacques take me somewhere where they can't find me. I would rather live as a peasant." She threw herself onto her bed and cried, "You sit there like a tree stump. Doesn't anyone care how I feel?"

Matilde tried to calm her. "Your father had to make a strong alliance for the safety of us all."

§§§

The following day, after the formal announcement of the betrothal, Lord Bannock departed for England. All around Chateau Brèche, people celebrated his name, and Lorraine heard them calling him a savior – the English nobleman who could protect them against the treachery of Etienne Dannes.

She couldn't bear the thought of spending her life with Bannock, and went to her father's room, begging him not to send her away.

Her father reached for his cup of wine. "If I could keep you by my side, I would gladly do so." He moved to the cushioned bench by the fire, and she sat beside him. "Bannock was right when he suggested that I send you to England now. You're not a child anymore. I don't have many allies, and my enemies want to take advantage of my weakness." The weary acceptance in his voice made her want to turn away, but he took her hand. "Perhaps you don't understand what's at stake."

"At least you've made the peasants and merchants happy."

"If I lose my estate, their fortunes and possibly their lives will be lost. Etienne is clever. He knows that the king of France would like to be rid of nobles like me, those who are too friendly with the English."

No amount of pleading could change his mind. He had given his word, and all of her foot-stomping and tears couldn't soften him. "In hundreds of years, our home has never fallen," she said.

He wrapped his arm around her shoulders. "My chateau was built with Norman hands, and it will be defended with Norman courage."

She left his room and walked slowly down the stairs. The stress that showed on her father's face frightened her. All his restless hours were wearing him out. No matter what time of day or night it was, he had a candle burning while he studied his maps and wrote letters trying to gather friends to his side.

Chateau Brèche wasn't grand; it had been built as a compact stone fort on a hill, with a labyrinth of cellars below ground and a five-story keep at its center. The great hall was on the first floor, and the second story was divided between a storeroom, a guard room and an office. The third-floor rooms were for visiting gentry. Her room and her father's were at opposite ends of the fourth floor, the safest part of the chateau. Matilde slept on a pallet beside her bed, while a dozen other female household servants shared the rooms on the top floor. They considered themselves lucky to be inside the keep.

Holding the rope railing, she worked her way down the three flights of stairs, even though each step caused a sharp pain in her bruised side. Still weak, it took her a while to reach the courtyard, but sitting on a bench in the sun was worth the effort. Since the attack, she'd hardly been outside.

People passed by, filling their buckets at the well. Women lowered their eyes and curtsied when they noticed her, and the men tipped their caps. Two young women, one with an infant bound to her back, gossiped companionably as they lowered the wooden bucket and wound it up again. Their features were so similar she wondered if they were sisters.

She felt a pang of envy for these women with their simple lives, even though they had husbands to please and babies to pacify. What would her life be like when she had children of her own?

The women stopped talking and cocked their heads.

Lorraine heard the pounding of hooves racing across the barley fields. The riders were coming toward the chateau. At first she thought it was the return of a scouting party, but this wasn't the typical canter at the end of a journey. They were galloping. Her mouth went dry; people stopped what they were doing and looked toward the open gates.

The soldiers clattered across the drawbridge and into the yard, and the peace of the day erupted into chaos. The leader shouted for Roland and Marquis Bonville.

Roland ran from the barracks just as her father emerged from the keep. It seemed as if everyone was shouting. It took a moment for the babbling to subside enough for her to hear the news. At a farm near the border between Castle Dannes and Chateau Brèche, the scouts had found one of the tenant holdings burned to the ground. A father and both of his sons had been murdered, the mother and daughter raped. When the scouts arrived, the shaken wife had given them Etienne Dannes' message – he would soon be lord and master of Chateau Brèche.

Lorraine rushed to her father's side. His rage was barely under control as he addressed the gathering crowd. "No scoundrel will be allowed to murder peasants and rape women! We will fight back!"

The woman with the baby strapped to her back, the one Lorraine had been watching at the well, stepped forward. Her face had gone pale. "Marquis Bonville, if you please, sir – I live on the border. The family that was attacked, was it mine? Was it Claude and Chloe Jardin?"

The other women crowded closer, bracing for the news.

A knight jumped down from his mount and addressed the Marquis. "My lord, I can verify that it was the Jardin holding." He turned to the trembling woman. "Your mother and sister live, but –"

She screamed and fell to her knees. The baby's head bounced against her shoulders as she wailed until one of the women took it into her arms.

Lorraine watched, unable to look away. She didn't know the Jardins, but she felt a kinship with this girl. They both had been violated by Etienne's men.

His victims seemed random, but his target was clear; he planned to destroy the Bonvilles. People gathered into knots, murmuring words of comfort, blessing themselves with the sign of the cross and talking about revenge.

One of the brewers shouted, "Will we go to war?"

An older man called out, "We can't leave a woman and girl out there alone!"

Lorraine's father tried to calm them. "Soon we will have extra troops for our defense. In the meantime, those on the border may come inside the walls."

Some people nodded, but most turned resolutely away. It was early in the season, and they wouldn't abandon their fields so soon after the planting. Losing a harvest was almost as bad as losing a loved one – in the end, the loss of food might put more lives at risk.

Lorraine took a few steps across the courtyard, but Matilde caught her arm. "We should go back inside." Matilde hated it when things were unsettled.

"I'm going to the barracks," Lorraine said.

"You can't!"

The barracks, armory and drill ring were off-limits to women, but Lorraine was willing to risk the impropriety. "I have to see Jacques. If he ruled Castle Dannes instead of Etienne, none of this would be happening!"

"He's not in the barracks." Matilde looked guilty. "He's with Donna-Marie. He has a fever, and his arm is swollen. Roland carried him there last night."

"Why didn't you tell me?" Lorraine turned toward the gatehouse.

"We were just attacked – you can't go outside the walls!"

"The attack was on the border." She pretended to be calmer than she felt. "Go back to my room. I won't be long."

She took the path that paralleled the orchard to the healer's cottage. Inside, a long wooden table filled the main room, and above it, bundles of cut herbs were drying on a hanging rack. The cottage smelled like mint and rosemary. A kettle steamed on a hook over the hearth, and Donna-Marie was building up the fire. She nodded but continued with her work. Lorraine peeked into a crockery jar on the table and recoiled. Leeches.

Jacques lay in a small bedroom, opposite a window that let in both light and air. He was sleeping, and she admired the way his lashes curled. A sheen of sweat covered his forehead. She wanted to caress his cheek, but the gesture was too forward, so she tentatively stroked his arm. She leaned closer and whispered a prayer. A few moments later she heard a movement in the doorway and pulled back. Donna-Marie was watching her.

"Will he survive?" Lorraine asked.

"Unless the infection spreads. You can help me clean the wound."

She wasn't sure she wanted to, but she didn't want to be sent away, either.

The healer disappeared into the kitchen and returned with a bowl of steaming water, a stoppered bottle, and clean strips of cloth. She set everything down and without pause unwrapped the bandage. As the material pulled away from Jacques' skin, Lorraine saw that it was crusted with dried blood and a yellow-brown stain. She pressed her hand to her mouth and tried to breathe calmly. The wound stretched from his shoulder to just above his elbow. She murmured another prayer. The gash had been sewn together, but the black stitches were wide apart, and the skin between them bulged, puffy and red. Yellowish pus seeped from the edges.

"It hasn't closed," Lorraine said.

Donna-Marie pulled the stopper out of the bottle and dropped some of the astringent onto the wound. Jacques' eyes flew open.

"Keep him still," the healer said.

Lorraine went to the head of the bed and put her hand on his good shoulder. Her touch calmed him a little. "Ssh. It will feel better soon."

"Don't make promises," Donna-Marie warned. She swabbed the wound, and Jacques groaned.

"Why isn't the skin growing together?"

"It will when the infection clears, but the muscle was cut through to the bone, and I had to sew that as well. If the infection is in the bone, there's little I can do." She continued to clean the wound as she spoke then layered it with fresh bandages.

Jacques' eyes closed and he moaned again.

Lorraine changed the water in the basin, hoping she'd get a few minutes alone with him. Donna-Marie carried her supplies back to the kitchen, and Lorraine drew the stool closer to the bed. "You're going to be all right now." He stirred, and she took his hand. "Don't fall asleep yet."

He stared at her, his eyes unfocused, then gave a weak smile. "I dreamt you were here."

She let go of his hand when the healer came back into the room, hoping she hadn't been caught.

Donna-Marie began to wash Jacques' face. "He thinks he's going to take his brother's castle away." Her tone made it clear she thought Jacques was speaking nonsense. "He's delirious, going on about Castle Dannes." When she finally finished tending to him, she picked up the basin and whisked it from the room.

As soon as they were alone, Lorraine whispered, "When we were in the woods..."

He stared at her.

"About what you said to me...." He was nodding off again, and she shook him gently. "Do you remember? You said something to me." He'd thought he was dying, and had confessed his love. She whispered, "I feel the same."

He opened his eyes, but the glaze of fever was back. "I'm going to kill Etienne." His gaze slid over her, but he was no longer focused on her face.

She brushed his dark curls and momentarily let her fingertips linger against his mouth.

Donna-Marie pushed a mug of hot cider into her hand and nodded toward her patient. "Fevered men say strange things."

Lorraine asked the question that was worrying her. "Why did Roland bring him here? Why didn't you go to the barracks?"

Donna-Marie returned to the front room and began snipping herbs, dropping the clippings into a pot of simmering water. "Roland was asking questions. I tried to warn him that the boy wasn't making any sense."

Lorraine followed her and asked, "What kind of questions?"

"How well did he remember the Dannes defenses? I suppose if he thought Jacques was going to die, and since he's the only soldier at Brèche who's ever lived at Castle Dannes, Roland wanted to learn what he could." Her spoon tapped the sides of the pot. "Jacques was only a boy when he came here. Why trouble him with things he can't recall?"

Chapter Sixteen

In the valley surrounding Chateau Brèche, the fields were ripe with oats and barley, and the orchard was in bloom. The shearing was done, and the smell of new wool was in the air along with the scent of apple blossoms and lavender. Lorraine was as eager as everyone else for the market fair to begin. It was Midsummer's Day, and the peasants and farmers had gathered at the gates before dawn; now they crowded the yard. Busy stalls displayed candied fruit, sweet cakes, and bread with spiced meat baked inside.

As the day grew warmer, wine, ale and cider flowed from great casks. The merchants hawked their crafts, weapons, jewelry, and lengths of linen and woolen cloth. With so many people milling about the guards were alert for cutpurses, scanning the plain, eager faces for signs of a spy, a stranger more interested in the battlements than butts of ale.

The Bonville soldiers patrolled the forests around Chateau Brèche, and in the last month there had been no further sign of menace from Castle Dannes. Yet Lorraine knew that even on fair day, when everyone spoke gaily and laughed easily, the threat of an attack lingered like smoke.

She made her way slowly through the crowd, nodding to each merchant as he cried out the nature of his goods. One held up silk cloth for her to admire while another tried to catch her eye with the glint of a golden pendant. A small peasant girl stepped into her path and dipped a curtsy, and Lorraine pressed a coin into the child's palm. A dozen urchins scampered around her, thrusting their grimy palms into the air. She shooed them away and noticed Jacques waiting in the shade of the guard tower.

He cleared his throat. "My Lady, perhaps you need a guard today?"

She was wearing one of her best gowns and hoped he liked the way it hugged her waist. "I want to stroll through the orchard and would be most pleased to have your company."

He fell into step behind her, keeping one hand on the hilt of his dagger as he followed her through the portcullis gate. They crossed the drawbridge and walked along the road, leaving the dusty yard and the press of the fair crowds behind.

She set a brisk pace and soon turned onto the footpath to the orchard. "If you care to walk beside me, it would be easier to converse," she said.

"Roland will allow me to be your guard – but not your companion." Jacques made a point of looking around. "I must remain alert to danger."

"You saved me from those..." She halted. "They were so vile! I hate to think of what...."

In a low, soothing voice he said, "I made sure they'll never hurt you again."

She ducked under a branch. "I wish my father's men would kill Etienne!"

"Etienne's deeds shall not go unpunished." He moved close beside her, protectively. "Your father is waiting for Lord Bannock's help before he strikes back."

"Lord Bannock's not here!" She caught Jacques' hand. "You deserve vengeance more than anyone. Castle Dannes could belong to you."

"Bastards have no claim."

How could she make him see how important it was? Her future, and his, depended on the truce between their families. Their fathers had created an alliance so carefully, and now, because of Etienne's greed, she was being sent away.

"If Etienne dies without issue, you would inherit the Dannes estate. Then you would have everything Lord Bannock has, and perhaps I would never have to go to England," she said thoughtfully.

"I cannot hope to inherit, but someday I will be knighted." He stretched to his full height. "I'll prove to your father – and Roland – that I am honorable and loyal." He pointed toward the drawbridge. "One day, I'll ride through those gates on my way to battle. I'll be sitting astride my own war horse and wearing a new suit of armor."

He looked so fierce that she wanted to tease him. "Come on. I'll race you to the other side of the orchard." Before he could answer she darted away, forcing him to chase her. She was in high spirits and called over her shoulder, "I thought you'd be faster than that!" Her hair fell out of its net as she twisted through the trees and scampered just out of his grasp. She reached the orchard and whirled on him. "It's good to be outdoors again. I've missed it – and you." Her chest rose and fell rapidly, but Jacques was scarcely winded.

He leaned against an apple tree. "We're not supposed to be alone." He looked beyond her shoulder. "Someone could be watching."

She closed the distance and took his hand. Slowly, more slowly than she had ever moved, she brought his right hand to her lips. Gently, she pushed back his sleeve to expose the lengthy scar, still raised and tender, snaking up to his shoulder. She rested her cheek, ever so lightly, against his wound. "I owe my life to you."

He stroked the back of her head and his hand lingered on her shoulders. "I hope never to disappoint you."

She wanted to kiss him and knew he desired her, but did not test his restraint. Finally, when she could stand it no longer, she said, "I wish we could always be together."

He knelt on one knee. "I pledge myself to you for eternity."

Even though it was a pledge she knew he would be unable to fulfill, she wanted to believe in him. She trusted him. When he picked up her palm and kissed it slowly, the intensity of her body's response surprised her.

He rose to his feet and they meandered through the orchard, not holding hands but brushing against each other, walking so close that she could feel the warmth of his body.

When the sun dropped low on the horizon and the heat faded, they made their way back to the gates of Chateau Brèche. The market was ending, and preparations were under way for the evening's festivities. In a cleared field, a stone ring had been piled with timbers ready to be lit for the midsummer fire. It would burn all night, and the dancing and singing would continue until the revelers, weary of wine and song, fell asleep by the fire or crept away for more intimate arrangements.

Lorraine had just begun to think she and Jacques might join the dancing when Roland approached. He gave Jacques a stony glare. "Where have you been all day?"

"I – I was escorting Lady Lorraine. She wanted to walk in the orchard."

"Alone?" Roland looked from Jacques to Lorraine. "With no chaperone?"

"It was me – I insisted," Lorraine said. "I know Jacques would never do anything to.... to cause me harm." It had been a wonderful day, and Jacques had acted so honorably. She was tired and thirsty, and Roland was ruining everything. "I'm weary of being cooped up inside the keep."

"Lady Lorraine, we wouldn't want people to think that Jacques has taken liberties." In the weak light of dusk, she saw the apprehensive look on Jacques' face. Roland turned to him. "You're late for guard duty."

Jacques hurried away, and she watched him with a sinking heart.

Roland said, "I'll take you to the keep."

Without arguing, she followed. If France was as bad as this, how much worse could England be?

§§§

In the weeks after the midsummer fair, Lorraine had no chance to leave the chateau. The skirmishes on the borders resumed, and more families had been forced to leave their holdings. At night the newcomers, along with the usual servants, slept in the great hall, and their livestock filled the stables to overflowing. By September so many peasant families had moved inside the castle walls that their small, one-room huts had sprung up like mushrooms after a heavy rain. Each morning the women dragged their spinning wheels and looms, wash buckets and cook pots outside so they could work in the sunlight. Children, unaccustomed to so many playmates, chased each other through the warren of shacks. But they all stopped what they were doing and watched Lorraine whenever she walked through the courtyard. Their attention made her shy. The number of soldiers on duty had been doubled, but she still saw little of Jacques.

One Saturday she was on her way to the chapel when a group of young men began showing off. They formed a line and wove into a circle dance, taking the parts of both boys and girls. A crowd of onlookers quickly formed, hooting and clapping, urging them on. The smell of strong ale reached her. A bored musician, seeing the opportunity to pass a hat, began to play, and the dizzy boys tripped over their feet. When more practiced dancers joined in, the assemblage clogged the yard. People halted work, and Lorraine found herself surrounded. The odor of unwashed bodies permeated the air, and she felt as though she would suffocate. When a man bumped against her, she screamed. The feel of a strange body against hers brought back that terrifying day in the woods, and she put a hand over her mouth, fighting the urge to cry.

He made an awkward bow, uttered a hurried apology and staggered away.

"Lady Lorraine, are you all right?"

She blinked up at Jacques. "So many people live within the walls now. I'm not used to the crowds."

"I know a place where we can go." He led her away, being careful to keep a discreet distance between them. "The boys are like ponies left in the stables too long. They have too much energy, but they don't mean to make trouble."

"I didn't used to be so nervous."

"As long as you're within these walls, you're safe."

On the north side of the compound, the hillside was steeply terraced, and the cemetery spread over the lowest and widest level. Her mother and baby brother were buried there, and it was the resting place for generations of Bonvilles. Jacques led her behind a tall monument built to honor a fallen warrior, and she sat down on its marble base. From this vantage point the long valley looked peaceful, but somewhere on the border, scouts were patrolling the lands between Dannes and Brèche.

Jacques said, "I wish I could take you someplace far away from here."

"What will happen if Etienne attacks our chateau? Papa is worried – I can tell. What will happen if he's killed?"

"Your father has hundreds of men-at-arms, and soon he'll have even more."

Did she hear bitterness in his voice? She took his hand, turned it palm up and studied the lines, then bent and placed a kiss on it, amazed at her boldness.

The look in Jacques' eyes changed, became more piercing, and he shifted uncomfortably. "We should go before Roland starts looking for us." But when she looked up, he was leaning toward her, eyes half-closed. He kissed her softly.

It was a lingering kiss, and passion surged through her. She whispered, "I didn't know a kiss could feel like that."

"Oh, Lorraine." He sounded worried. "Forgive me." He stood up and offered his hand. "I shouldn't have done that. I'll take you back."

She wanted him to kiss her again, but he was already turning away. In another few minutes she'd be back in the crowds, separated from him by a wall of people. "Jacques. Wait. Every day I watch for you – don't leave yet."

His eyes were cloudy. "If we're seen like this, there will be trouble, and it will be that much harder for us to meet again." He wavered, but took a step toward her. His arms went around her, and he took a deep breath. "I have to go."

She knew he was right, but she was already thinking ahead to when she could see him again. "I'll find a place where we can be alone."

His smile faltered. "Where?"

"I don't know yet, but I'll find a place."

His fingers teased the ends of her hair. "Only you would be so bold." His hand slipped to the back of her neck, and they leaned together again.

For the next few days, Lorraine tried to focus on her studies, but her thoughts kept drifting to Jacques. His changing guard shifts complicated her plans. Even if she could figure out a place for them to meet, she had no idea when it would be possible.

Sitting by the window in the solar where the lighting was best, she stared at a blank canvas. The carpenter had stretched linen fabric to a wooden frame, and she had spent the previous week applying thin layers of wet gesso. It was now ready to be painted. Lorraine was well-educated for a girl and art lessons were her favorite. Twice a year an art tutor from Paris came to teach her technique. She wanted to paint a picture of Jacques but didn't dare, so she decided to paint the Norman countryside with Chateau Brèche in the background.

A nearby table held several small dishes and vials filled with colored pigments, and she carefully measured clarified egg whites, ground chalk, and the powdered, reddish-brown resin called Dragonsblood. After mixing the ingredients to make a smooth paste, she dipped her brush into the new color she would use for the soil.

Matilde sat in a corner napping, but Lorraine spoke to her anyway. "If this is a good likeness, I'll take it with me to England. When I'm homesick, I can look at it and remember happier times."

She peered through the window, trying to judge the view and the proper perspective for her painting. A long line of horse-drawn carts were on the road approaching Chateau Brèche. Standing up to get a better look, the paint brush knocked against her gown. She wiped the smudge but only succeeded in smearing the dark paint into the pink woolen fabric.

"Wake up," she called to Matilde, "Something's happening."

Matilde surveyed her sleepily. "Yes, you've ruined your gown."

"Outside – I've never seen so many carts before." Lorraine watched as a dozen carts lined up by the cellar door and Michel supervised as the crates and barrels were unloaded.

Matilde lumbered to her feet and joined Lorraine at the window. "They must be afraid of more attacks. I think your father is preparing for a siege."

"Maybe he's just taking precautions." Lorraine watched barrels disappearing into the storerooms. "Does anyone ever live through a siege?"

Matilde shook her head, uncertain. "Not if they run out of food or water..."

A fully supplied keep could withstand months of siege, but sometimes walls were breached, stables caught fire and wells ran dry. She didn't want to think about that happening here, and said, "Go back to sleep, Matilde."

Lorraine picked up another bowl, measured finely ground azurite and blended it with egg tempera. She needed blue to paint the sky. For sizing, she added the paste of boiled parchment. When the color was as soft as a robin's egg, she dabbed her brush and spread blue along the top third of her canvas, all the while keeping a watch on what was happening in the courtyard below.

After the last cart horse pulled off, she put away her art supplies and went downstairs. When no one was looking, she slipped inside the cellars. A man passed her, pushing a wheelbarrow full of turnips, but he kept his head down, minding his own business. Farther along, the stone floor ended, and she found herself walking on a sloped dirt passage that twisted and turned, opening onto dozens of subterranean storage rooms. The cold air was musty, and her candle flickered.

She came to a room protected by grillwork, and behind the locked gate she saw the wine cellar. Through the iron bars she glimpsed bottles and crocks covered in mold. Even the walls were growing mold. She covered her mouth and nose and continued downward. In another room she saw rounds of cheese the size of cart wheels. She pulled a second candle from her pocket and lit it from what was left of the first. When she looked up again, a man was standing in front of her.

"What are you doing here?" she demanded.

He tipped his grimy cap in a gesture of respect. "I work in here." His dark eyes were beady and his back hunched. He reminded her of a hedgehog.

"How far does this go?"

He scratched his whiskered chin. "A fair ways."

"Is it safe down here?"

"Occasionally the ceiling collapses – usually during an extra wet winter when ground water is seeping. I have lots of problems then. Michel doesn't allow too many people down here." He cocked his head. "Does Michel or the Marquis know where you are?"

She decided to befriend him. "What's your name?"

"André, mademoiselle. I'll guide you back, but be careful, it's slippery."

"Please – can you show me a place to hide if we're attacked?"

He considered her request for a moment. "Veuillez me suivre." He took her to a room full of wine casks. Behind the oak barrels and cut into a side wall was another small room. Its opening was camouflaged by the angles in the earthen walls, but it was close enough to the cellar entrance that she could find it on her own.

"If the keep should ever fall, you can hide in here," André said. "I'm the only one who knows about this room."

"Tell no one else about it," she said, her eyes boring into his. When he nodded acquiescence, she favored him with a smile and left him to his work.

When she returned to the yard, she paused to catch her breath, letting her eyes adjust to daylight. The hem of her gown was soiled, and the brown paint splotch marred the front, but the midday meal had already started, and it was too late to change. Self-conscious, she decided to slip through the kitchen rather than use the main door to the great hall.

She had noticed that a new servant always carried her father's cup, poured his wine and served his food. He was a bland-faced man with milky skin, thinning hair and a disappearing chin. He was in the kitchen now, standing beside Michel, inspecting a portion of meat and vegetables on a serving platter. Quickly, she stepped back out of sight. Usually the food was served communally, the meat and pies carved at the table, but lately her father's food was served separately. While Michel watched, the pale man took a serving knife, polished it on a corner of his tunic and cut a sliver of meat. He chewed carefully, swallowed and waited. Then he took a spoon and dipped up a mouthful of the boiled cabbage and onions.

He was tasting her father's food!

She retreated outside and kept going until she was behind the bake house. The ovens were fired up, and she leaned against the warm, brick walls until a measure of her composure returned.

Her father was worried about a siege – and about being poisoned. She wanted to tell Jacques. Shielding her eyes, she looked up at the wall walk but didn't see his lanky figure. He could be in one of the guard houses or on a distant part of the battlements, but he was most likely in the great hall with everyone else. She forced herself to go back inside.

When she took her place at the table, Michel frowned at her lateness, but her father seemed not to notice. His meal was already before him, but he ate sparingly and then put down his knife. No wonder he was losing weight.

Jacques sat with a cluster of guards, and as the meal ended, they got up in groups of two or three and left.

When she thought she could catch his eye without being too obvious, she stood up but saw that Michel was speaking to him privately. A group of knights moved past blocking her view, and then she saw Michel hand a coin purse to Jacques. He tied it to his belt and quickly left the great hall.

Lorraine hurried outside and walked as fast as she dared toward the stables, but before she got close, Jacques came out leading a saddled horse. He mounted and rode out through the gates, never noticing that she was trying to get his attention.

§§§

Jacques had been resting in the great hall, glad for a seat on a bench and the chance to lean his back against the wall. He was surprised when Michel Steward pulled him aside, but he had more status since he'd saved Lorraine's life.

It mattered; he wouldn't pretend otherwise. Some men were foot soldiers all their life, and the unlucky ones ended up as mercenaries, hiring their sword to anyone who would give them a wage. Others became squires but progressed no further, always serving a master, never gaining their independence. Only a lucky few became knights, and to achieve that distinction, a man had to stand out, bring honor to himself and his lord. For the first time in his life, Jacques believed he might someday own a warhorse, have armor fitted to him, wield a broadsword and then, when the battle was done, return to land that belonged to him. He was hopeful, a feeling that was almost as good as being in love.

The summer roads were dry, and it was an easy passage from Chateau Brèche to the town of Domfront, but the journey was a half-day's ride, and it would be dark by the time he made it back. On such a fine day it was easy to forget that Lord Bannock existed, easy to pretend that Lorraine's betrothal wasn't real.

He could tell he was close to the town because the fresh air dissipated, and was replaced by the stench of latrines. Small hovels crowded between the lane and the fields.

He spurred his horse onward, but soon had to pull up again; the lane was clogged with tinker carts. He cursed. The only way around was to cut through a field, and if he ruined a crop he might be fined.

It took twenty minutes to pick his way to Tanner's Lane with its oily smell of hides. The meat market was in the street beyond. Here the buildings were tall and narrow, and each successive story jutted further out, leaving the lane below in constant shade. Dangling from the overhanging eaves were great hooks that held pig and cattle carcasses waiting to be butchered. The gutters beneath them ran purplish-red with blood.

Turning up another lane, he followed the clang of a hammer striking metal until he managed to find the blacksmith's forge. Jacques dismounted and tethered his horse.

Marquis Bonville wanted swords and armor – the money purse contained a list – and if the smith couldn't make enough, then he was to buy whatever he could from the Italians. Their weapons were expensive, but their craftsmen were so good that a man wearing Italian-made armor was as safe as if he were guarded by angels.

When the blacksmith saw how young Jacques was, he tried to raise his prices, but the purse contained just the amount that Michel had determined was fair. After a brief show of haggling, the merchant accepted the price and took the purse.

Jacques was about to step outside when he heard a voice on the street call out, "I need a sword sharp enough to cut off the head of an Englishman without spilling his cup of ale."

There was no mistaking the laughter that followed. He hadn't heard that sound in eleven years but knew it in an instant. It was a coarse, cruel laugh that he would remember until the day he died. He slipped deeper inside the blacksmith's shop until the voice moved farther up the lane.

When he went outside a few minutes later, he kept his horse in front of him, with one hand on the saddle and the other on the hilt of his dagger.

He remembered what it was like living with Etienne. "I'll slice your ear off if you tell, you whining, good-for-nothing bastard. Stop your sniffling, you little girl." And then another blow would land – always on his back, never on his face. Etienne always struck him where their father wouldn't see.

As a six year old, he had curled into a ball, unable to fight back against his seventeen year old half-brother. When he was eight, his father brought him to Chateau Brèche and placed him out of Etienne's reach. Long after the bruises faded and the fear receded, he could still hear the taunts in the back of his mind. "Your mother cleaned the chamber pots that my mother filled! Even she didn't want you, bastard boy. Don't worry, I won't ruin your pretty face."

His boots seemed stuck to the ground as though it had suddenly turned into a bog. He was cowering behind his horse. His own voice rang in his head. *Fight back!*

He risked a quick look up the road and saw Etienne standing outside a tavern. He seemed smaller, less imposing. He was – short. As an older brother, Etienne had seemed all-powerful. Watching him now, Jacques noted the differences between them. Etienne was blond, like his mother, and wore fine clothes and a pointed beard in the fashion of courtiers.

Jacques was dressed like a common soldier in a brown linen tunic drawn in by his belt, woolen leggings and leather boots. Because he was traveling, he also wore a jerkin made of boiled leather that doubled as cheap but effective armor. He'd grown much taller than his half-brother and he'd inherited their father's dark, curling hair. Etienne's face was broader, but his eyes were set too close together, and his lip twisted easily into a sneer.

Etienne's companion came out of the tavern, and they turned away, but not before Jacques saw the silk badge on the man's tunic. He was one of the king's guards; Etienne had support from the king of France. And in return, what had he promised? Perhaps the death of one of the last noblemen still loyal to England.

Jacques forced himself to wait until Etienne and the royal guard had turned down a side lane and then swung himself into the saddle. On his way out of Domfront, he didn't waste time on the clogged central road but cut over to a dirt track that ran parallel to a field. When it rained, this path would be impassible. As it was, it was badly rutted, and he couldn't go as fast as he wished. He'd been sweating since the moment he'd seen Etienne, his hands trembling, and the horse began to shy. He slowed, calmed himself and the animal, and reached the open road beyond the town. Then he galloped as fast as he dared to Chateau Brèche.

§§§

The door of Lorraine's room was slightly ajar, and she stood behind it, listening for the men to leave her father's chambers. Jacques, Roland and several others had been in there for hours, and she strained to hear the dire news they were discussing. When she finally heard the latch turn, she silently closed her own door until the sounds of shuffling boots and mumbling voices moved down the stairs.

After all was quiet again she slipped out. She wanted to talk to Jacques. It was late, and at the landing there was only a single torch to light the way. With each step the glow became fainter, and on the first floor she found herself standing in total darkness. Sensing someone nearby, she froze and held her breath.

From the shadows, she heard a low voice. "Shhh. It's only me, Jacques."

She reached through the dark, and his fingers found hers. He pulled her into the nook beneath the stairs, and they stood listening, their bodies touching, but all was quiet.

She whispered, "How did you know I would leave my room?"

"Because I know you."

"I've found a place where we can talk." She stroked his cheek, and her thumb rubbed his lower lip. "Let me show you."

"You're impossible to resist." He kissed her hand, and then held it tightly as he followed her to the cellar entrance where another torch was burning.

She pulled a candle from her pocket and lit it with a trembling hand. Though she had been waiting for this opportunity, she was nervous. They made their way through the maze of cellars deep beneath the keep, until she found the room André had shown her. Once, the sound of something moving gave them pause, but it was only a rat. They saw no one. Holding the melted stump of burning candle, she reached into the dark hole and showed him the space. He brushed away the spider webs and entered first. She followed, setting the candle into a wall niche and pulling another from her pocket. She lit it and glanced around.

Jacques looked amazed. "How did you find this?"

"I wanted a place to hide if our enemies ever got inside the walls." She lowered her eyes. "I wanted somewhere private where we could meet. André, the cellar keeper, showed this to me."

Jacques took off his cape and draped it over a large oak cask, then lifted her and set her on top. "You're clever, but if we're caught in here alone..."

She had planned this, envisioned what it would be like alone with him, but now she was shy. "What's going to happen to us?"

He stared at her, and she saw hunger in his eyes. "Tonight?"

She laughed, covering her nervousness. "Tonight, tomorrow, a month from now, even next year." Leaning against him, she wrapped her arm around his neck. "I wish we had the power to choose our own future."

"Your father can't wait until I have land and a title of my own. There isn't enough time." He pulled back. "He'd never let us marry. He loves you too much."

"There are other ways to get land and title without inheriting them."

"Only the king can bestow those favors, and the king doesn't like the Bonvilles. I'm in service to someone he wants to get rid of." His expression was gloomy. "I'm just a bastard. Expendable."

"Jacques, please." She saw his confidence deserting him.

He cupped her face. "If your father knew the thoughts I have about you, he'd exile me."

She ached for him, and nothing mattered but his touch. She kissed him, tenderly at first, then harder as her excitement grew. He tightened his embrace and kissed her eyes, her cheek, her neck. When his hand grazed her breast, she moaned, and the sound startled them both. They pulled apart.

"I love you." He was breathless. "But I don't want to ruin your life."

"If we were married," she said, "we could always stay here."

"You know we can't. Things might have been different if your father had sons; he could have made other alliances."

She pleaded softly, "I don't want to go to England."

He reached inside his tunic, brought out his cross and showed it to her. She had never seen him without it. "My father gave me this on the day he brought me here. It's the only thing I have from him." The cross was large and heavy with arms of yellow gold and a filigreed heart of white gold fixed at its center. "He told me the cross represents eternal life, but the heart at the center represents love – a father's love for his son. He sent me away because he loved me and wanted to protect me from Etienne's abuse. I was only eight and afraid to leave my home, but he wanted me to be safe. That's what your father wants for you."

He tucked the cross back inside his tunic and said, "I saw Etienne in Domfront today."

They heard footsteps, and Jacques quickly blew out the candles. They sat in darkness, afraid to make a sound. The distant glow of a torch came closer as someone walked along the tunnel. They continued to sit quietly, gently stroking each other's arms, until they heard the tread again, this time coming from the opposite direction.

In the deep blackness, she couldn't see Jacques but felt his breath on her cheek and his chest muscles move under her hand. His strength was reassuring, and some of the tension left her when she felt his lips against hers.

"We need to go back now," he murmured, and helped her down. "Hold onto my hand. We'll have to feel our way back."

They bumped and stumbled through the dark and twice found themselves going in circles. It was impossible to tell how long they'd been gone, and she was afraid Matilde might worry and sound the alarm, but when they finally reached the cellar door, the night was still quiet.

She longed to pull him to her one more time, feel his lips on hers again, but she didn't dare. They might be seen. Her only comfort was knowing that they could go down into the cellars again.

But it was wrong – and dangerous. He knew it, and so did she. She bid him a hasty goodbye.

The following day she sought out the sanctuary of the chapel. The gargoyles seemed to stare accusingly at her, their sneering faces taunting, questioning her sincerity as she entered the place of worship. She did her best to ignore them.

When she was sure she was alone, she knelt before the statue of the Virgin Mary and crossed herself. "Blessed Mother, please help me. I want to remain pure, but...my body betrays me with desire."

Could she really confess to the Virgin Mother that Jacques was all she thought about? His hands, his lips.... She tried to push away the shameful feelings and began her prayer again.

"Blessed Virgin Mother, please give me strength." She rested her forehead against her clasped hands and begged, "Please."

When she was a girl, lonely and crying for her mother's touch, she had come here and pretended that this statue was her mother. The loving face smiled down at her, the arms always extended toward her, as if ready to embrace her.

"Dearest Mary," she added, "Please protect Papa and Jacques from danger."

The domed ceiling of the chapel was painted light blue with golden stars to represent heaven, and over the altar hung a tall crucifix. Onto it was nailed a carved statue of Jesus; his face wore an expression of suffering.

He died for our sins. I need to live in a manner worthy of Him.

Chapter Seventeen

In January of 1451, frost sat on the fields until late morning, and a thick layer of ice formed in the water buckets. Lorraine was at her window when a scouting party from Chateau Brèche charged through the gates, calling out for Roland. She ran outside and joined the gathering crowd. The yard was a confusion of horses, knights, barking dogs and onlookers as everyone pressed closer to hear the news. Another holding had been burned, another family murdered, but this time the attackers hadn't ridden away after the slaughter. An organized band of soldiers carrying the Dannes banner was riding toward Brèche.

Roland issued orders, and the chaos became more organized. Soldiers swiftly mounted the battlements, taking positions along the crenellated castle walls. Fresh horses were saddled while the men gathered up swords, lances, crossbows and quivers full of arrows. Lorraine saw her father with Michel – they were heading for the armory.

Papa shouldn't go!

She darted after him, but her path was blocked by the mayhem. When she reached Roland's office, she ignored the guard captain's irritated frown. She didn't care what the men thought. Her father was dressing for battle. He looked pale, and perspiration beaded his forehead.

"You can't leave – we need you here!" she cried.

Her father met her eye. "What kind of leader would send his men into battle while he stayed behind?" He shrugged into his arming doublet, a long-sleeved, padded jacket, tapered at the waist, flared at the thighs, designed to fit snugly under his armor. She wanted him to stop. Ever since May Day, she'd been dreading the prospect that he would go to battle, but the likelihood had increased with each successive attack. His expression softened. "Be strong for me, ma chérie."

She watched as Michel stooped and buckled spurs and articulated metal shoes over her father's leather-clad feet. Greaves, tube-shaped and hinged, were fitted about his legs and secured to the boots. Seated on a horse, a knight's legs were the most vulnerable to attack by foot soldiers. Custom-fitted pieces of armor were attached to cover her father's thighs and knee caps, breast and back plates were hung from his shoulders, and finally large pentagonal plates covered the seam between his upper and lower body armor. The metal looked heavy enough to crush him, but Michel continued to layer the pieces in place. Lacings, rivets and leather buckles secured metal vambraces to his arms and pauldrons to his shoulders. At last, he slipped his hands into his gauntlets.

When Michel held the chain mail coif above her father's head, her resolve crumbled.

She flung her arms around her father's neck. "Please – please come back to me."

"You must be prepared...." He searched for the right words. "If anything happens–"

"He doesn't need distractions right now." Michel drew her away. "Be strong."

She watched as the coif was positioned to protect her father's throat and the back of his neck. She bit back another protest. A padded hat was fitted onto his head and the helmet placed over it, the visor not yet lowered. She could still see his worried face, and she seared it into her memory.

She whispered, "I love you, Papa," but he didn't seem to hear her.

In the courtyard, the horses pawed at the ground, the steam puffing from their nostrils and forming clouds in the frigid air.

Her father mounted and then leaned down to her. "Stay in the keep until I return." He brushed her hair back, and his gloved hand lingered on her cheek. Holding himself rigid in the saddle, he trotted to the head of the procession. When he gave the signal, over a hundred mounted men began to move.

The men-at-arms filed past, the squires bringing up the rear. Jacques was too poor for plate armor, but he wore chain mail and boiled leather, and he carried a short sword and battle axe. She waved as he rode past. He looked in her direction and nodded, and she might have discarded all caution and run to him, but Matilde's hand on her arm restrained her.

"Stay back or you'll be trampled," Matilde warned.

"I have to tell him –"

"Hush. Let him go."

The army cleared the drawbridge, and then the people from the village came hurrying across, bringing as much food, bedding and other household goods as they could carry. When the villagers were safely within the walls, the gates swung closed, and the portcullis door, with its deadly spikes, rumbled down.

Dust swirled around Lorraine as she pushed through the crush of people. She made her way to the keep, climbed the stairs and reached the solar window in time to see her father and the Brèche army riding across the fields. They headed for the high ground above the valley, where they could strike at the enemy from the cover of the forest.

A few at a time, the gentlewomen, many of whom were married to the knights, joined her in the solar. Their fingers were busy with needlework, and they bent their heads together, conversing in hushed voices, but every noise startled them, and one or two stayed by the window, watching. Lorraine glanced at her half-finished painting, but she left the paints unmixed, the palette dry.

Lady Cecile sat beside her. "If our men should lose this battle, some of us may be forced to reconsider alliances." She picked up Lorraine's hand, turned the palm up and studied it as if hoping to see her future.

"I'm not sure what you mean," Lorraine said.

Lady Cecile let out a heavy sigh and turned to face Lorraine. "Sir Theobald and I are proud to serve the Bonvilles, but –" She plucked a stray thread from her gown. "If we should lose this battle, or if he is killed, my life as I know it is at an end."

Lorraine looked at the older woman and saw the fear on her face. That same expression was mirrored on the faces all around her. Conquering armies took what they wanted and raped the wives and daughters of their enemies.

"If only Lord Bannock had sent the troops he promised." Lady Cecile dabbed away her tears.

Lorraine felt a flash of guilt. She'd been relieved Lord Bannock hadn't returned, but he could have helped them.

§§§

The men returned at sunset. Her father was still alive, still at the head of his troops, but his shoulders were bowed in weariness. The proud figure of Sir Theobald rode beside him, followed by Roland and the other knights. Lorraine stood on her tiptoes, nudging taller women aside as she tried to see out the window. Where was Jacques? What if something had happened to him?

The soldiers straggled along, some riding more slowly and nursing hastily bandaged wounds. Occasionally a rider led another horse, its saddle draped with the limp body of a slain man. The fallen lay face down across their mounts, and some horses carried more than one body.

Behind Lorraine, a woman screamed and crumpled. Others pushed around her, trying to see, and more voices were raised in wails of grief.

The chapel bell began to toll.

She finally saw Jacques at the end of the line, leading a horse, its rider face down and lifeless. The urge to run down to the courtyard was overpowering but she resisted, knowing she wouldn't be welcome there. Not yet. The men needed time to shed their armor, tend their horses, wash and prepare the bodies of their comrades for burial. Donna-Marie was already making her way toward the barracks. The men had their wounds, the women their tears; later they would share their stories and take comfort with one another.

Stumbling toward a chair, she pressed a hand to her mouth and stifled her sobs. Lady Amalie sat down next to her and hid her face in a kerchief.

Lorraine asked, "Did you see your husband?"

"I know his horse," the woman sobbed. "The silk tunic he wore into battle – I sewed it with my own hands." She pointed to the window. "I saw his body lying across his horse. He's dead."

Lorraine wanted to offer comfort, but everything she thought to say sounded false. How could she grieve with these women who had lost so much? Around her, ladies were throwing themselves in each other's arms, sobbing. Their children were brought in, and the wailing took on a hysterical pitch.

Messengers brought the news from the barracks; twenty-one men had died.

When Lorraine finally left the solar she headed to the one place where she knew she could be alone. She lit a candle and descended the cellar stairs. The solitude would be welcome after so much weeping.

She sneaked into the cellar and was almost to the little room when she thought she heard something. She stopped to listen. After a few minutes, she called, "André?" As soon as her voice broke the stillness, she wished she could call it back. It might be anyone, and she was alone, undefended. What if a spy had found a way into the chateau and was hiding down here?

"Lorraine." It was Jacques. He took her hand, led her into the hidden room, and placed her candle in the niche.

"I didn't know you'd be here," she said.

He pulled her to him, and she soaked in his warmth. He smelled of leather and sweat, dirt and blood. She hadn't realized she was shivering until he ran his hands over her arms and stilled them.

"All I could think about was coming back to you." He talked in short bursts, describing the hiss of arrows, the clash of swords. "It happened so fast. They outnumbered us, but we held the high ground." He let go of her and paced the small room, too restless to stand still. "They attacked again, and we beat them back a second time. I saw your father take two men with a single stroke of his broadsword. He's a fearsome fighter." He turned his face away. "I killed three of them."

"But, you've killed before. Sometimes it's necessary." She touched his back, and felt his muscles rigid with tension. The fight had not yet drained away. She whispered, "Did you see Etienne?"

"Only from afar, but I don't think he saw me. I know he survived this day."

When he reached for her, he wasn't rough, but he wasn't gentle either. His lips were hard and his mouth insistent. She didn't pull away. He needed this; she could tell by the way he held her.

Jacques spread his cloak on the floor, sat down and pulled her onto his lap. He closed his eyes and kissed her. His hands roved over her back, down her hips, up to her breasts. She gripped his shoulders but was nearly helpless against him. When he cupped her bottom, his breathing turned ragged. He fumbled with the hem of her heavy gown and stroked her calf. When his hand slipped up her leg, desire coursed through her body. She wanted to stop him but couldn't.

She whispered against his mouth, "I was so worried for you."

His hands fumbled with the lacing of his pants, and then he pulled off his tunic. Gently, he pushed her back until she was lying down.

She tried to stop him, but her protest inflamed him further. He rolled on top of her and trailed kisses down her neck. The last of his control disappeared, replaced by something more urgent. His tongue thrust past her lips, and her mouth opened wider as she returned his kisses. Through the thin fabric of his under tunic, her hands found his flesh, stroked his back, and then the hard muscles of his buttocks. His hips began to thrust against hers, and she was caught up in desire. She wanted him, needed him, now.

A look of pain crossed his face as he rolled away from her. "I'm sorry." He sounded tortured as he stood up and pulled his clothes back on. "I shouldn't have used you –" He helped her to her feet, but wouldn't meet her eyes. "I didn't mean to lose control."

Grateful that he had returned to her safely, she said, "I want you, too."

He pulled her shawl around her shoulders and looked into her eyes. "You have to go back." Taking her chin in his fingers and caressing it, he whispered, "We can't be seen down here like this."

She longed to spend the night in his arms and in another moment would have given herself to him. "We can never do this again," she agreed. "No matter how much we want to. It isn't right."

Their final kiss held the force of their resolve, and the intensity of their desire. When they pulled apart Lorraine burned with her need for him. Holding his hand tightly, she reluctantly followed as he led them to the cellar entrance.

Jacques slipped out first, disappearing into the darkness. After a few minutes, when all remained quiet, Lorraine crept out and made her way back to her room.

She already missed him.

§§§

By spring more peasant families were living within the chateau walls. The guest rooms in the keep were crowded with the families of knights whose lands along the border were vulnerable. With fewer tenants planting their fields, the harvest for the coming year would be smaller. Michel had not yet ordered strict rationing, but less food was served at the meals.

Lorraine and Jacques had fewer opportunities to be alone. Children of tenants and children of squires played together on the stairs and chased one another around the yard. Any patch of ground a family wasn't camping on was given to their livestock, and waste quickly accumulated in whatever space was left.

Lorraine longed for the fresh air of the orchard, but the gates were always closed now. On warm days the stench of overcrowding was almost unbearable, and she wondered how much worse it would be by summer.

Entering the crowded great hall for the mid-day meal, she sat at the high table just as Sir Theobald and Lady Cecile came in.

They took their places beside her, and Lady Cecile asked, "Where is your father?"

"He's still in his room. Roland just received new maps, and they were anxious to examine them. He'll be down after –" The end of her sentence was drowned by a crash from the kitchen.

She thought a careless servant had dropped a platter, but then the sound of splintering wood reached her, and a scream, cut short, followed by another piercing cry. She rose to see what had happened when a rough hand pulled her back.

"Get down!" Sir Theobald shoved her under the table and pushed his wife down beside her. "Stay there!" He had his sword in his hand.

She scrambled underneath as two armed men charged the high table. Sir Theobald cut down the first, but the second man's sword impaled him. Theobald was a big man, and the blade caught him in the belly and tipped down toward his bowels. He cried in rage and swung mightily, but the assailant thrust deeper. Theobald sank down, kneeling in a puddle of blood and bile, looking at the heap of guts spilling from his open belly.

Lorraine pressed a hand to her mouth and gagged.

Lady Cecile screamed and crawled toward her husband, trying to hold him up, but she was crushed under his weight and instantly drenched in his blood.

A third attacker sprang onto the table, kicking over tankards of ale and knocking a haunch of beef to the floor. Nobles and commoners ran in every direction, shoving in panic as they fled. He surveyed the room, and she knew he was looking for her father. They had come to kill him. His gaze pinned her. He leapt from the table, grabbed her ankle and jerked her out. She kicked at him and thrashed wildly from side to side.

"I'll take you, anyway," he snarled.

Suddenly the point of another sword appeared, protruding from his chest. The tip came out and up, moving toward his eyes, which filled with confusion a moment before they glazed. He collapsed, leaving a smear of blood across the table.

Roland pulled his sword free. "Lady Lorraine!" He shouted, helping her to her feet. "Are you all right?"

Stunned, Lorraine looked around. *Where had they come from? Who were they?*

Lady Cecile sat on the floor, holding her dead husband's head in her lap. Lorraine looked up as the kitchen door swung open and she saw more dead bodies in there.

"I must get you out of here," Roland said, quickly guiding her out of the great hall.

"They came to kill Papa, didn't they?" On the verge of hysteria, she spun around, scanning the frenzied crowd. "Where's Papa?"

"We're going to find him."

They found her father still in his room, and he paled visibly when they told him the news.

"Theobald dead?" The Marquis shook his head and slowly sat down. "I've known him all my life. He was like a brother to me. I should have been there."

"Begging your pardon, my lord," Roland said, "but you'd be dead now too."

§§§

A few days later, Lorraine knelt at Sir Theobald's grave and placed a bouquet of wildflowers on the mound of freshly turned soil. More than two dozen new graves scarred the hillside, and from all around came the cries of grieving women and frightened children.

Lady Cecile had turned into an old woman overnight. Without children of her own, she was forced to follow Lady Amalie's family to the south.

"Papa will appoint a caretaker so you can keep your land here," Lorraine said, certain her father would never turn away the women who had been married to his knights.

"What good would it do to appoint a caretaker if no one can defend the holdings?" Lady Cecile replied softly.

"But...the south," she said dismally, realizing that people were beginning to think that her father was losing control of his estate. "The king of France controls the southern territories."

"All of France is united now," Lady Cecile said. She kissed Lorraine on each cheek. "Bon chance, chérie."

"Bon chance," Lorraine whispered, as her friend walked away.

§§§

As the weeks passed, Lorraine grew used to the sight of carts leaving. The titled families fled to places safer than

Chateau Brèche. Even the peasants who had come inside the walls started to slip away. Those who hoped to earn a living on distant estates collected their belongings and followed the nobles. The summer wore on, and those who remained tended their crops, but each week more news came of another abandoned home, another untended garden growing only weeds.

Lorraine was tired of watching life through a window. One afternoon she was in her room staring down at the debris left by the families who had hastily decamped. They had left behind chicken coops, slop buckets, bits of timber, and compost heaps through which pigs and dogs rooted for food. A foul stench of human and animal waste assaulted her. There were fewer servants to maintain the old way of life in the castle, and garbage continued to pile up.

By contrast, the trees on the distant hills were in full leaf.

A figure in the cemetery caught her eye – a mourner, perhaps. She sharpened her gaze on the marble dais at the base of a statue, and recognized Jacques hunched over a book. She hadn't spoken privately to him in several weeks. Blushing, she thought about the last time they had been alone together, and how close she had come to giving herself to him. It seemed wrong to think of that now, after so much tragedy.

She left the keep and went to him.

He was holding a quill and writing, and then he looked up, smiled, hastily blew on the pages and closed the book.

She hadn't meant to startle him. "I saw you through my window." She sat down.

"Roland finally gave me a day off," he said.

"What are you writing?"

"It's nothing." Looking embarrassed, he shifted the book from hand to hand. "I write verses."

He was quiet, and after a moment she offered, "Would you rather be alone?"

"No." He caught her arm, and then, realizing his mistake, dropped it. "I've missed you." He capped the inkpot and stowed it in his satchel, dried his quill and put it away.

She leaned her knee against his, wanting to touch him. "What kind of verses do you write?"

"They're mostly for you." He shrugged and thumbed the pages. "Like this one." In a soft voice he read:

> A blessing binds your life to mine
> Between our souls a golden thread
> The silken knot so strong and fine
> That it may never fray or shred
> And distance is the dullest knife
> It cannot cut this bond of love
> Though rank divides us now in life
> In spirit we are joined above.

When he was finished, he stared across the valley.

Flattered, she didn't want him to take her silence for disapproval. "Will you read it again so I can memorize it?"

He repeated it twice, and she recited it after him. When she could say it flawlessly from memory, she smiled and felt happier than she had in weeks. He wrapped his ankle around hers, and she adjusted her skirt to hide his leg.

They sat that way for over an hour, and every so often he chose a verse, as though telling her through his writing that he loved her. Whenever he stopped reading, silence filled the space between them, but it no longer felt awkward. They stayed for as long as they dared, not kissing, but taking comfort in the presence of one another.

Chapter Eighteen

In the autumn of 1452, the mists took longer to fade in the morning, and at night the moon hung glassy and white, promising frost. The harvest was bad again, and those remaining at Chateau Brèche grew poorer still. Fewer tenants worked the land, and the wheat and oat stores wouldn't last much longer. It was the blood month, the season of slaughter, and everyone took part in butchering, salting and smoking the meat. This year, more cattle were butchered than usual because there wasn't enough grain. And better to slaughter them now, before Etienne's soldiers could steal them.

The prospect of a dreary winter was made even gloomier with the news that England was on the brink of civil war. A band of traveling minstrels arrived, timing their performance just as Mass ended and the midday meal began. Perhaps they were hoping for a place to stay the winter, but Michel was not going to feed any more mouths. They passed the hat and gave the news from abroad. In England, the noble houses of York and Lancaster both had a claim to the throne.

Lorraine knew that Lord Bannock, like her father, was loyal to the house of York. If he was pledged to fight in England, then he wouldn't come to Normandy. For two years, the citizens of Brèche had waited for his help while Etienne's soldiers systematically burned out, raped and killed the tenant farmers.

Marquis Bonville was unable to collect his rents and had no money to pay his troops, and they defected until only a few dozen were left. As the living conditions within the chateau became unbearable, his health continued to deteriorate.

More than a year and a half had passed since Lorraine's betrothal, but no word had been forthcoming from Lord Bannock. He had not sent the promised troops, and no one knew when he planned to return. Once she made the mistake of suggesting to her father that he cancel the engagement, but the comment caused a fit of anger that ended in a spasm of coughing.

Lorraine watched him turn from a vigorous man into a frail one, a soldier who no longer rode out to battle, and for this she was grateful, but to him it was a humiliation. He hated to concede anything, but more and more of his time was spent sequestered in his room. Since the attack in the great hall that had claimed Sir Theobald's life, they ate their meals in his private chamber.

Each evening the routine was the same. A manservant placed a portion of each dish on a plate, and they all waited while the taster stepped forward to sample it. She was so used to the bland-faced man now that she hardly paid him any notice. He chewed, swallowed, gave a small nod and stepped back.

One evening, her father speared a piece of meat on his knife and then scooped up a bit of the dressing made of nuts and stewed summer fruit. Someone coughed, and she looked up. Her father's knife was an inch from his lips when Michel lunged at him. The knife, the meat and the dressing flew from his hand.

"Poison!" Michel pulled him away from the table.

A servant grabbed the back of Lorraine's chair and pulled her away from the table. "Don't touch the food!"

The taster's pale face had turned red and his lips a sickly blue. His mouth opened, and he made a gurgling sound. Eyes bulging, his whole body jerked and twitched as though run through with an arrow. Lorraine couldn't take her eyes away from him. He was trying to suck in air, but it seemed that no matter how hard he tried, he couldn't inhale. His legs gave out, his color drained into a waxen sheen, and he fell dead.

Michel did his best to keep the incident quiet, but Lorraine heard the servants whispering. No one was safe, and more of them ran off.

Rather than wasting his energy on breaking down the chateau walls, Etienne had found a way to break the spirit of Brèche's people.

Lorraine's seventeenth birthday went unnoticed.

§§§

Unable to sleep, Lorraine drew back the shutters from her window. In the dim moonlight, she saw the faithful sentries on the battlements, and her heart went out to them. They must be freezing on such a cold night.

Jacques was up there somewhere, standing double watch as usual. It had been weeks since they'd had time alone, and then, they met for only a few minutes in the cellar's tiny room. A quick kiss, a pledge of love, no mention of the future – that was all they had. It wasn't enough. She thought of him constantly, watched for him, lingered in places where he might see her.

Closing the shutters, she wandered into her father's room where a fire blazed but hardly dispelled the chill that permeated the stone walls. More and more of her time was spent at his side, reading to him, and watching his health fail.

She observed silently as he shuffled to the table, leaning heavily on Michel's arm. The trusted servant added Donna-Marie's medicinal herbs to the watered wine, and waited while her father drank it.

He sipped a little soup and dipped his bread to soften it. Whoever had added the poisonous cowbane to his food a few months back had never been caught, and another taster hovered at his shoulder now.

Her father no longer ate much, and weight had melted from his frame. Pushing his bowl away, he reached for her hand. "I'm going to send you to England."

"How can I leave you now?"

He gave a dry cough that turned into a gasp for breath. "I'm not going to get better. For all I know, I'm still being poisoned – though my enemies haven't had an easy time killing me."

"I'm staying with you, Papa."

"It's not safe, chérie. You're to marry Bannock."

"Lord Bannock broke his promise. Where are his troops? He's too busy in England to help his old friends."

Her father's temper sparked and his hand struck the table. "He made a vow to protect you, and if he cannot come here, then you must go to him."

Another fit of coughing consumed him, and she rose to help. He brushed her aside. She nodded to the taster, signaling that he was no longer needed, and with a slight bow, he backed out of the room.

Her father's next cough became a strangled cry. It broke off abruptly, and he sagged into Michel's arms.

"Quickly," Michel called. "Get Donna-Marie."

Terrified, Lorraine raced to the small room that the healer had been forced to occupy since moving inside the castle walls. When they returned, her father lay on his bed, his face ashen.

Donna-Marie touched her fingers to his neck and then pressed her ear to his chest. When she straightened, she said, "The heat is very weak."

Her father stared at her, and she read the fear in his eyes and saw pain etched in the corners of his mouth.

"Do something," she cried, grabbing Donna-Marie's shoulder.

"There's nothing more I can do," Donna-Marie said softly, shaking her head. "He may not live through the night."

Lorraine looked to Michel, but his expression told her he too feared the worst.

Her father struggled to breathe, and Lorraine waited through a terrible pause. For a long moment his chest neither rose nor fell, and she found that she was holding her own breath, waiting, gasping when he inhaled again. As the minutes crawled by, the time between each inhalation and exhalation lengthened, and each seemed more jagged than the last.

She prayed as she held her father's hand, but he was still slipping away. She sensed it the way she felt a change in the air when a storm was coming. Fighting back panic, she whispered in his ear, "Live, Papa. Live for me." If his will wasn't strong enough, then hers would serve them both.

Hours passed as she fingered her rosary. The knights entered one by one, clasped her father's hand and offered their prayers.

"God save Chateau Brèche."

"God be merciful."

If she defied her father and stayed, would they fight for her as they had for him? Could she command their respect?

Donna-Marie placed a pungent poultice on her father's chest, and Lorraine watched his labored breathing.

She awoke to the sound of voices outside and realized that she'd fallen asleep in the chair beside her father's bed. He lay very still. His eyes were closed, and she couldn't tell if he was breathing. Lowering her cheek to his face, she felt a moist puff as he exhaled. His mouth smelled of fever, but he was still alive.

A commotion sounded in the courtyard below, and before she got to the window, Michel and Roland came into the room.

"Qu'est-ce qui se passe?" she asked.

"We have news from our spies," Roland said.

Jacques shouldered in behind them, looking windblown as though he'd just come from a hard ride. She wanted to run into his arms but instead braced herself for more bad news.

"Word has already reached Castle Dannes that the marquis is on his deathbed." Jacques was breathless. "Etienne's army will be here by dawn, with support from the king's soldiers."

Michel's voice was barely above a whisper. "We'll all be hung for traitors."

"We have to hold them back!" Lorraine insisted.

"We will defend you, my lady," Roland assured her. "Our men-at-arms are loyal to the Bonvilles."

Jacques walked over to the bed and stared down at her father. "They had their spies here too."

Michel drew him aside and Lorraine moved closer. "You must take her away before they get here," she overheard the steward say.

"I won't leave him," she interrupted.

Ignoring her, Michel addressed the captain. "Roland, what is your plan?"

"I'll have the guards prepare the battlements with firewood and oil. We'll need as much water as the men can haul."

She tried to run after Roland, but Michel stepped in her path. "Lady Lorraine, you're going to leave before the battle begins."

"I am not leaving here." She glared at him. "And I'll never surrender Chateau Brèche."

"We can't defeat the royal army, and Etienne's terms will be harsh."

She turned to Jacques.

"Lorraine, I know him." Jacques' face was streaked with sweat and dirt, and he wiped his brow on his sleeve. "He plans to kill the Marquis, and he might kill you too."

"It's time for you to do as your father wished and go to England. You must survive," Michel said urgently. "If you stay here, you could be killed. Or forced to marry Etienne and give him heirs. Either way, Chateau Brèche will be his legally." He gripped Jacques' shoulder. "Take her to Lord Bannock."

§§§

Michel chose Lucas and Jacob, two of Bonville's most trusted guards to escort Lady Lorraine. They hefted her heavy trunks onto a cart and it creaked and settled.

Lorraine was the daughter of a marquis, the intended bride of a rich baron, and she was being sent off to be married with only a meager dowry. He'd ordered Matilde to pack Lorraine's wardrobe – as much silk, satin and finery as she could lay hands on, but it was only a fraction of Lorraine's possessions. It might bring shame on the Bonville family name, but with the little time they had left, nothing more could be done.

From the pantry he gathered the silver plate and gold salt cellars and sent a man to fetch casks of port and brandy. The rest of their wealth might soon be in the hands of Etienne Dannes.

People ran in all directions, sending up a cacophony of screaming, crying and shouting. Michel moved steadily through the chaos and saw a young boy about to be trampled by a horse. At the last moment, a hysterical woman pulled the lad to safety.

The soldiers moved with purpose and the archers were ready in the towers. Their arrows would send a good number of the enemy into the hereafter. Chateau Brèche would not fall easily, but if Etienne could not take them by force, then he would lay siege.

Michel had witnessed such a horror only once. He had been a young steward waiting outside the walls of a castle, ready to record the plunder. He expected to feast his eyes on treasure, but the people stumbling out of the battered gates were half-mad with starvation. Inside, the wreckage was worse. Horses had been slaughtered, the well had run dry – there was nothing left but decay.

Michel ran a hand over his throat. Would his head be cut off, or would he be hung?

"Sir?" Lucas pointed to the cart. "It can't hold any more."

Michel lifted the lid on a waiting trunk. The material for Lorraine's wedding gown lay neatly folded inside. "Load this." He waved away a barrel. "Leave the port wine."

Lucas looked doubtful but did as he was ordered.

By the time Lorraine arrived in England, her father would surely be dead and her estate in the hands of the enemy. Michel was counting on her bloodline and Bannock's word that the wedding would go forward. When he had done everything he could to assure her future, then he could face his death.

Jacob harnessed the horses – four to draw the heavy cart and four more for the carriage. Torches flickered and the animals tossed their heads. It was almost time.

Michel ran back inside the keep where maids were packing the household goods, and hiding the valuables deep into the folds of linens. Most of it would have to remain behind.

Scanning the terrified faces, he spotted the stout young woman he was looking for. "Matilde, if you please."

She curtsied. "Master Steward."

"It's time to leave." He was glad she would go willingly. "Grab your satchel! The carriage is in the courtyard."

"Master, where are we going?"

"To England, God willing."

He was about to go to Bonville's room but paused at the window, slid the bar from its brackets, and opened the shutters. Men were moving along the wall walks, and commoners were on the battlements. Farmers shouldering pickaxes and spiked poles were ready to support the men-at-arms. He set the bar back into place. It was folly to fight the king's army.

Lorraine looked up as he entered the bedchamber. Michel thought he would have to argue or remove her by force, but she was waiting for him calmly. She had spent the last several hours caring for her father, bathing him, spooning drops of water into his still mouth, and rubbing warm beeswax onto his parched lips.

Her eyes were swollen and red, and her lips trembled as she spoke. "Michel, does he know I am here?"

"If he could talk, he would tell you that you are the light of his life," He touched her shoulder. "And he wants you to survive this fight."

Lorraine pressed her cheek against her father's. "Please, please, get well Papa. I need you," she cried.

Marquis Bonville hadn't opened his eyes or spoken for several hours. Michel watched Lorraine frantically kiss her father's whiskered cheeks again and again as she begged him to respond.

"I cannot leave him." She swiped the tears from her eyes. "He'll have to go with me."

"It would be wrong to drag him away from here – to die along the road," Michel said. "Let him die in his own bed. He's peaceful and comfortable now.

He watched her silently battling her emotions. He could only guide her – not command her.

Lorraine gently kissed her father's lips, made the sign of the cross on his forehead, over his heart, and on each of his shoulders. "I love you, Papa." She was sobbing now, her shoulders shaking. "I'm going because you want me to." Kissing her father one last time, she stood and squared her shoulders. She looked carefully around the room as if memorizing it.

She faced Michel, and the anguish on her face broke his heart.

"I shall never forget your service to my family," she said.

§§§

Lorraine would never have agreed to leave, but it was the only way to protect Jacques. If he stayed, he would be killed by Etienne.

She had seen the certainty in Roland's eyes, briefly, before his lashes had concealed his concern, and his despair. Chateau Brèche, home to the Bonvilles for centuries, was going to fall.

She was ashamed that she was leaving. Her father was dying, and the people she had always taken for granted were going to suffer a terrible fate. When she saw that the carriage and cart were loaded and ready to leave, she wavered, but then saw Jacques mounted on his horse. Matilde peered through the carriage window. She counted two drivers and six mounted escorts – they were all waiting for her.

Michel guided her through the press of people and assisted her into the carriage. The coachman took his reins, and the horses started forward.

Michel reached for her hand. "It's your duty to marry Lord Bannock."

"I will marry him if he'll have me." The carriage moved faster. "Au revoir!"

Michel's hand slipped away. As they drove through the gates, she turned back, looking wildly from side to side, trying to catch a last glimpse of the steward, the yard, her beloved chateau. The horses drew them farther away from everything she'd ever known and from all she held dear. She watched as the chateau's towers receded into the wintry night.

§§§

The carriage raced through the darkened countryside, and Lorraine was bumped and jerked from side to side. A freezing rain started, and the wheels skidded on patches of ice. They may have escaped the attack on the chateau, but Etienne's soldiers could still hunt them down. She felt sorry for the men on horseback, weighed down in their heavy, sodden cloaks, sleet slashing at their faces.

At dawn, the carriage jolted to a stop in a clearing deep in the woods. Through the thick fog, she could make out the forms of the guards as they spread out around the carriage. Beside Lorraine, Matilde slumbered fitfully, occasionally starting as though in a bad dream.

The door creaked open, and Jacques peered in. "Are you warm enough?" he whispered.

She clutched his nearly frozen hand. "Yes, but you are so cold." He began to pull away, but she held him. "Wait. Stay awhile." She was afraid to release him, afraid that each moment might be their last.

"I'm on watch," he said, looking back over his shoulder.

"Is there any sign of Etienne's men?"

"Not yet. We'll stay hidden in the woods during daylight, travel only at night, and pray this fog stays with us."

Matilde, head drooping onto her chest, snored softly.

Jacques leaned farther into the carriage, and in the cramped space they were only inches apart. She touched his lips, chapped from the wind, stroked his jaw, and then drew his mouth to hers. The familiar warmth spread within her, intensified. He was the center of her world now. They held the kiss until Matilde stirred, and then reluctantly, she sat back, a long sigh escaping her.

His eyes were half closed as he looked into hers, leaned forward again, and kissed her deeply. When he pulled away, the warmth of his touch lingered on her skin.

A frosty wind swept inside and cold air filled the space where his warm body had been. "I wish you would come inside and rest," she said, knowing he couldn't.

He didn't answer, just slowly shook his head and smiled, before shutting the door.

She tucked a blanket over Matilde's shoulders, and then her own, savoring the heat from his kiss. They had to stay very quiet, and when she finally dozed, she dreamt that she slept in his arms.

Cold rain continued through most of the day, making it impossible for the men or horses to rest. The ice crust from the night before had melted, leaving the land a muddy quagmire. It seemed as though they were caught in a timeless place, a place filled with dread.

Twice, Lorraine and Matilde climbed out of the carriage and, holding their skirts high, walked a short distance into the trees to relieve themselves.

At dusk, the gray light faded quickly into dark, and for a brief interlude, the rain stopped. They continued on their journey, but every few yards the wheels of the carriage and the cart sank into the mud. The horses pulled them free, only to have the wheels sink into the next rut. They made such slow progress that the landscape outside the window, obscured by the dark, seemed not to move. Yet they were moving, she could tell by the protesting creaks of the wheels.

The storm continued as they progressed toward the coast, and gradually the landscape changed. They emerged from the forest and began climbing a steep mountain. When lightning broke the darkness, Lorraine looked out Matilde's window and glimpsed the edge of the road, and beyond that the land dropped away sharply. The horses struggled to keep their footing as they inched up the mountainside, and the women held on tightly as they were knocked from side to side.

The rain was pounding against the top of the carriage and it was too dark to see anything outside when the wheels caught in yet another rut. The carriage rolled backward and then began to slide sideways. Lorraine braced herself as she felt the horses straining. A sharp crack sounded, she felt a jolt, and wondered if they had rolled over a fallen tree limb. The carriage tilted sharply toward the right, Matilde was pitched against the door and Lorraine was thrown onto her. The carriage teetered unsteadily.

The horses whinnied and tugged. The men shouted at them. There was another loud snap, and the carriage jerked a few more inches to the right, rocked precariously and then toppled onto its side.

Lorraine fell on top of Matilde, pain ricocheting through her skull as their heads banged together. The carriage began sliding, crashing over bushes and picking up speed. Horses screamed and snorted as the weight of the carriage dragged them down, their hooves thumping as they struggled to break free of the harnesses.

Matilde, pinned beneath Lorraine, was screaming. "My arm. My arm!"

Lorraine grabbed the door frame but her hand slipped and she fell back, her elbow knocking into Matilde's face. Fighting to untangled herself, she scrabbled for anything to pull herself up, but the carriage slammed into something hard and spun in a different direction, knocking her sideways.

It was dark, and she couldn't see much, but they were still moving, still sliding. There was no way to know if they were heading over a cliff or into a river. The walls began to cave in, and the door beneath them started to break away. Mud and branches were forced inside.

The carriage slammed into a tree and came to an abrupt halt. Lorraine's head snapped back.

Men were calling for them to hold still.

Matilde wrenched her head up, panting, trying to keep her face free of the muck. "My arm... I think it's broken."

Moving gingerly, aware of every shift in the precarious balance, Lorraine got to her feet. She tried to lift Matilde, but her arm was wedged beneath the toppled carriage. "We have to get out of here."

Some of the horses were fighting to get back on their feet, while others sounded as if they were strangling in their harnesses. One desperate mare kicked repeatedly at the front wall until it caved in. A hoof struck Matilde's shoulder and she screamed louder, using her free hand to shield her face.

The whole tangled mess shifted and slid a few more inches.

Lorraine struggled to free Matilde without rocking the carriage too much. She heard the men coming closer as they raced down the hill.

"Put the horses down!" someone yelled.

When lightning flashed again, Lorraine saw the body of the carriage driver a short distance away. From the awkward angle of his neck, she knew he was dead.

One of the guards tied a rope around his waist and worked his way down the hillside. Several times he lost his footing and used the rope to break his fall. When he was almost level with them, he wrapped one arm around a knobby tree, drew his sword and pointed it at the nearest horse. The ensnared animal, as though sensing its doom, began struggling harder. The hoof slammed into Matilde again, and an entire wall of the carriage collapsed.

"Save us," Lorraine screamed.

Above her, a voice called out, "Hold tight. We're coming for you." And then she heard him yell to his comrade, "Do it! Slaughter the horses now."

The guard let go of the tree, wrapped both hands around the hilt of his sword and bore down on the kicking horse, plunging the point of his weapon into the animal's arched neck. The horse screamed, using up the last of its breath in one more shudder and one last vicious kick. The sword twisted in the guard's hand and he lost his grip on the hilt. His foot slipped, and he went down under the remaining tangle of horses. Smelling blood, they went wild and thrashed in a helpless frenzy.

Before Lorraine could cover her eyes, she saw the brave man battered to death.

"Pull! Pull up!" Jacques cried desperately.

From the top of the cliff, the other guards tugged on the rope, but they were too late. The body was caught in the mass of animals, and their struggling shook what was left of the carriage even more. Suddenly it slipped several more feet down the embankment, and Lorraine braced herself.

She heard yelling and saw three more guardsmen. They plunged down the slope without sparing time for safety ropes. There was a flash of blades as they set about their grim work, and within minutes the wild shrieks of the animals stopped.

At her feet, Matilde moaned in pain.

Jacques called, "I can reach them now!" He was above her, peering through the opening. "Lorraine, are you all right?"

"Matilde's hurt. Please help her."

"I have to take you one at a time." He handed her a rope. "Wrap this around your chest."

"Take Matilde first."

"I'll need someone to help me with her." His tone was firm. "You first. Right now."

She did as he asked, letting him secure the rope under her arms and draw it tight. As he lifted her, she saw that he kept his weight on the carcass of a horse, barely touching the carriage at all.

"Haul!" he yelled to the men up the hillside.

She didn't move and thought it wasn't going to work, but then felt a tug and the rope bit into her chest. Jacques guided her clear of the wreckage and then half-carried and half-dragged her back up toward the road. Several times she lost her footing and was pulled on her stomach through mud and bushes until he could get her on her feet again.

When they finally reached the top, he untied the rope. "Thank God we got to you in time," he said. "A few more feet and you would have gone over the cliff."

"Get Matilde," she said, gasping for breath. It began raining again, a hard pelting rain, and she started to shake. "Please don't let her die."

Jacques took off his heavy cloak and wrapped it around her, and then pulled her to the side of the road.

"What is it?" she asked.

He put his finger to his lips to silence her, and then she heard the rhythmic galloping of horses coming toward them. "Hide," he ordered, pushing her into a thicket of trees. "Don't show yourself unless I come for you." The fear in his voice frightened her more than the sound of approaching horses. He pushed her deeper into the woods and repeated, "Stay hidden."

§§§

Jacques grabbed his sword as six mounted soldiers crashed from the woods. He spun around, taking stock of his men. One lay dead in the road, but two others dropped the rope they'd been pulling and joined him, ready to fight. Three more were down the hill attempting to rescue Matilde.

The man in the lead shouted, "Marquis Bonville is dead and his steward lies headless beside him. You, Jacques Dannes, are under arrest and shall hang for their murder."

They surrounded Jacques, their horses tossing their heads and snorting, excited for battle.

"The charges are false. The Marquis was alive in his bed when I last laid eyes on him." Jacques raised his sword and took a step back, hoping he sounded more confident than he felt. "Etienne's greed set him against the Bonvilles."

The leader dismounted, ignoring the accusation. "You also stand charged with abducting Lorraine Bonville and sacking Chateau Brèche." He used the hilt of his sword to break the lock on a trunk and held up a silver cup with a griffin on the handle. "This is from Brèche. It's all the proof I need to condemn you." He smiled cruelly. "Your own brother will knot the noose around your neck."

Jacques and his men were on foot and out-numbered, but he had to stay alive. Lorraine needed him.

§§§

From behind a fallen tree, Lorraine heard the king's soldier announce his news. As she watched the skirmish begin, tears blurred her vision, and she stifled a sob. Her papa had been a devoted father and a virtuous man, and she prayed that he'd died peacefully, before they stormed the chateau. Three hundred years of the Bonville family line, and now it was all going to end in slaughter.

She heard the clank of swords and the cries of pain as blades sliced through men. At first Etienne's soldiers stayed mounted, but they couldn't maneuver on the narrow road. Three Bonville men slipped in and out of the trees, hacking without mercy. One of Etienne's men went down with a spurting leg wound and was quickly finished, and the other riders dismounted and gave up their advantage.

The battle was now only five to three in favor of Etienne's soldiers, but the Bonville men were exhausted from days on the road. Neither side gave ground, but then one of Jacques' men slipped and was killed before he could recover his footing. Another Bonville man found himself facing two opponents and was dealt a fatal wound.

She caught sight of Jacques as he impaled one man, but he now stood alone. Too horrified to watch, too terrified to turn away, Lorraine stayed quietly hidden. Three figures crawled from the edge of the cliff and hauled a stretcher into the woods. A moment later she recognized Jacob, Lucas and Jean as they emerged again and quickly moved up behind Etienne's battling men.

Lightning flashed directly overhead, lighting up the forest, and almost immediately a crack of thunder boomed. Panicked, she ducked back down and stayed where Jacques had put her.

The tallest man went down with a sword through his chest, and another screamed, clutched his neck, and dropped to the ground. The men were covered in mud, and it was impossible to tell them apart. She saw another fall, and another. When the last three men were left standing, they gradually lowered their swords and looked around.

Without the ring of metal, the woods, even with the pounding rain, seemed shockingly quiet. Lorraine waited. Jacques had told her to wait. If he had fallen, then she would vanish into the woods and take her chances, but she would never surrender to Etienne.

She couldn't tell if the survivors were from Chateau Breche or Castle Dannes. Three men dragged the fallen bodies to the side of the road and tumbled them down the embankment. Next, using brush, they cleared the road of all signs of a fight. When they were finished, they disappeared down the hillside.

Pulling Jacques' sodden cloak over her head, she crouched down, trying to be invisible. If it were Etienne's men moving about, once they discovered that she wasn't in the carriage, the search for her would begin.

Curled inside the cloak's dark depths, she trembled uncontrollably.

And then he was there, shaking her and softly calling her name. "Lorraine, it's time to leave."

She could barely stand up. "Jacques. Thank God it's you." She saw the horror of the battle fresh in his eyes.

"Jacob and Lucas are alive," he said. "Matilde's hurt badly. Everyone else is dead." He led her to the cart where Matilde lay covered in blankets and wedged between the trunks. "You will have to ride in the open cart with her."

Lorraine gazed at the unmoving form of her maid. Matilde had been with her for most of her life, hadn't even protested when ordered to leave Chateau Brèche, and now she might die.

Matilde's face was swollen, her eyes closed. She lay completely still.

With a lump in her throat, Lorraine stroked Matilde's cheek. "What are her injuries?"

"Her arm was pulled out of joint," Jacques said. "There's a gash on her head. I don't know how many times she was kicked by horses." He helped Lorraine into the cart, took a corner of his cloak and wiped mud from her face. "We have to get away from here. If anyone asks, we'll say that we are husband and wife." He smiled apologetically as he tucked a blanket around her. "No one is looking for a humble married woman."

"Being your wife is all I ever wanted."

He pulled her tight to his chest for just a moment, and then released her. "We're not safe here."

"Perhaps when we get to Calais..."

"Etienne will never stop looking for us. For you. His claim hangs on your life."

Before he turned away, she saw the worry in his eyes.

Two extra horses waited by a tree, waiting for a rider that was never coming back. Jacques tied them to the back of the cart and then climbed onto the wooden seat. Looking over his shoulder at Lucas and Jacob, he snapped the reins. "Let's go."

Chapter Nineteen

The day's mist had darkened to a watery dusk when Lorraine saw the port lights and the lanterns in the windows of Calais. She had never seen such a large town. The air reeked of fish, and the gutters streamed with sewage. They rode past the docks, the shipping offices locked up tight for the night. In the stormy darkness, the business was all inside. Sailors, out of work until the storm passed, spilled from the taverns, some of the men so drunk that they remained standing only with the help of their companions.

Jacques hailed a man who looked sober and called, "You there! Do you know where a good inn is located?"

"In High Town," the fellow replied.

On the hill overlooking the port, the wealthy district stood separate from the waterfront, and Jacques headed that way. Calais was nothing like the small hamlet that surrounded Chateau Breche. Although it was late, men and women were strolling about, and it was noisy. The cobblestones were slick from the constant drizzle, and they picked their way slowly up the steep lane. The buildings, three and four stories tall, were shrouded in fog, the upper floors looming out over the street.

She was exhausted by the time they arrived at the inn called L'Auberge de la Colombe. Candlelight flickered through the glass windows and illuminated the painted sign of a bird hiding its beak behind a white wing.

Jacques rapped on the door until an upstairs shutter opened.

A woman's voice said curtly, "We're closed. Find your lodging elsewhere."

"We've traveled for days. My wife and her maid are cold. How many rooms do you have?"

"Not enough for a group of wet men." The shutters began to close.

Throughout the long cart ride, Lorraine had silently watched Matilde pass in and out of consciousness. "We'll catch our death if you don't help us," she yelled up to the woman. "You'll answer to God if you turn us away!"

Taken aback, the innkeeper paused. "Who are you that I should help you?"

Jacques spoke up. "Our carriage overturned, and the women are hurt. We need shelter."

The innkeeper was silent for a moment, looking down on them, considering. At last, she said, "I only accept gold or silver coin – in advance."

"Yes, Madame." He held up the coin purse Michel had given him. "We can pay."

"I have two rooms, and your men can sleep in my stables." She appeared at the door a moment later, a tall woman with a gaunt face.

Lorraine shivered in her sopping clothes and prayed none of them would fall ill.

The innkeeper closed her long fingers around Lorraine's arm and drew her inside. She glared at Jacques. "She's nearly frozen!"

"We lost our carriage," Jacques said.

"She's just a young girl." The woman squinted at Lorraine. "I am Madame Margot. And how may I address you?"

"Our family name is Dubois," Jacques lied as he paid the innkeeper.

Madame Margot collected their coins, including expenses for their food and hay for the horses. Having decided to let them in, she proved to be a good hostess and ordered the women's trunks brought up to their rooms. A housekeeper was summoned to heat water for baths and to prepare a meal. Madame Margot personally ushered Lorraine upstairs while the men carried Matilde.

When all their possessions were unloaded, Madam Margot gave blankets to Jacob and Lucas and sent them to sleep in the stables. Remaining in the room, she watched as Lorraine opened their trunks and searched beneath damp layers of clothes for dry gowns.

"I can hang a rope across the room to dry your clothes before you travel on," she said, as she helped Lorraine unlace

Matilde's gown. "It's a shame that such fine fabric got soiled with so much mud, Madame Dubois."

It took Lorraine a moment to realize that Madame Margot was addressing her. "It's been a difficult journey," she managed to say.

"Why are you traveling in such a bad storm?"

Lorraine couldn't talk about the tragedy that had befallen them. She looked down at Matilde, awake but moaning helplessly on the small bed, and tucked the blankets around her.

"It hurts much worse than before," Matilde complained.

Madame Margot hurried out and returned with a bottle of tonic. She poured a dose into Matilde's mouth and then a little more. "This will make you sleep."

In a short time the tonic took effect and Matilde was snoring away.

"You and your husband have the next room," Madame Margot said.

Grief, fear, and relief swirled through Lorraine, the torrent of emotion in her heart as strong as the storm outside the windows. She needed Jacques. She wanted to hold him in her arms. Without a word, she followed the innkeeper into the adjoining room.

It was much larger, warmed by a bright fire, and before the fire stood a bathing tub filled with hot water. Across from the hearth was a large bed.

"As soon as you are done bathing, I will send Monsieur Dubois up with your supper," the innkeeper said.

Lorraine stared at the bed nervously, her mouth dry. "Merci."

When Madame Margot left, Lorraine took off her wet clothes and stepped into the tub. A bar of lavender scented soap had been left on the mantle, and she longed to linger in the warm water. Instead, she washed quickly and put on clean clothes.

A small trestle table and a bench were in the corner of the room, and she sat there to wait. Guilt flooded her as she stared at the bed, knowing she should not sleep in the same room with Jacques Dannes.

There was a tap at the door, and she peeked into the hall. "You can't come in here," she whispered to Jacques.

"I've got hot food – enough for the three of us."

The aroma of chicken and onions drifted into the room and her stomach rumbled. She couldn't remember the last time she'd had a hot meal, and this one smelled delicious.

He set the tray and a bottle of wine on the table. "How is Matilde?"

"Sleeping. Madame Margot gave her tonic."

"After we eat, I'll carry her in here, and I'll stay in the other room."

They devoured the meal and then lingered over the bottle of wine. They hardly spoke, but as they emptied one glass of wine after another, their fingers touched, and they leaned toward each other across the table.

Lorraine felt her eyelids drooping, and this time she looked at the bed longingly.

Jacques stood up. "I'll move Matilde in here."

§§§

In the next room, Jacques tried to wake Matilde, but she only moaned, lying heavy and unconscious. After trying for several minutes, he gave up and returned to find Lorraine already asleep, her dark hair tangled on the pillow. He knelt beside her, softly caressing her warm cheek and delicate nose.

She stirred, and he quickly moved away. He stripped and stepped into the tepid water in the bathing tub. He didn't want to smell like lavender but was grateful for a chance to bathe, and instantly began to relax.

When his head began to nod, he forced himself up, donned a clean pair of leggings from his pack, and then washed his muddy clothes in the tub. He wrung them out and draped them over the bench to dry. He was exhausted, and the room was cold. He should leave but instead, he sat on the edge of the bed. Lorraine lay asleep under the covers, and before he could stop himself, he stretched out, lying on top of the blankets.

How many nights had he dreamed about Lorraine sleeping peacefully beside him? He felt the outline of her body and when she didn't stir, he laid his head beside hers and studied her face. Inhaling the scent of her hair, he knew that from this night on, he would always see her like this in his dreams.

§§§

During the night Lorraine awakened and stretched. Her eyes adjusted to the darkness, and she saw that the fire had burned low. She tried not to stir, unwilling to let go of the wonderful sensation of Jacques' body against hers. If only she could lie with him like this for the rest of her life and forget about everything except his warmth and strength. She snuggled into the arc of his arm.

He was awake on top of the covers, and he nudged her to turn over so that he could massage her neck and shoulders. His fingers kneaded her taut muscles, moved down her spine, and everywhere he touched, she felt a glowing heat build, and another kind of tension fill her.

She stayed beneath the blankets, with her back to him, but she scooted her hips into his, and his body folded protectively around her.

He nuzzled her neck, then his hands slowly moved down to her hips. He was so close that even through her gown and the blanket, she felt his response.

In the past, they had learned to meet this point and move a little beyond it. Their bodies seemed to know instinctively how long they could tease the passion, how long they could stay at the brink of desire before retreating. She rolled to face him, and he stripped away the blanket. Impulsively, she pulled off her gown so that only her chemise covered her body; he wore pants but no tunic. She ran her hands over his bare chest, and his hands roamed under her chemise and over her hips until his palms cupped the flesh of her backside. There was nothing between them but thin cloth, and it was time to retreat. She knew it, and she could tell he knew it by the way his shoulders tightened. This was the moment when his arms would grip hers, when he would kiss her forehead and whisper something sweet before pulling away.

His mouth found her ear, and there was a new note in his voice as he spoke her name. "Lorraine. Tell me to stop."

They separated, and she could see how his face was changed by passion, how his body trembled. She reached for him, but it wasn't to clasp his hand, wasn't to stroke his cheek or tease his lips apart.

She reached for the laces of his pants, and he sighed. "You mustn't do that."

She spread her fingers over the flat of his stomach and watched his muscles quiver. She felt him changing, hardening, and it made her soften. Her thighs were wet and she took his hand and guided it, utterly shameless in her need to have him.

§§§

Jacques was poised on the brink of an impossible decision. They were alone. They were meant for each other. In the deepest part of his heart, he knew the truth and made his decision. Lorraine was meant to be his not only for a night but for all time. He slid his fingers between her legs and claimed her as his own.

She moaned, and her hips rose, inviting him closer.

He wouldn't deny her this pleasure. Restraint was in the past. Regret didn't exist. Her mouth opened as his tongue entered and tasted her. The kiss deepened as he climbed on top. Pushing inside of her, their bodies fused. He felt her resistance; he felt her acceptance. He forgot the danger, forgot the unhappiness of the past two years. He remembered only that he loved her, and he knew it more with each stroke of his body. As carefully as he could, as gently as he knew how, he made love to her.

§§§

Lorraine was afraid. She knew the primal fear of taking a man into her body, of being unable to resist his entrance into her, but she no longer wanted to stop him, couldn't resist him, and her body moved as his moved. She was terrified, even while her arms clung to him, even while her hips surged toward his. She was helpless against his rhythm, the rhythm that was becoming hers as he pushed past her body's last barrier.

She felt a sharp pain, and then he was completely inside of her, and his body stilled; he seemed to stop the rush, the whirlwind, as he peered down at her. His kisses had been fierce, but now he kissed her slowly and tenderly. He kissed her shoulders, her breasts, all the while holding the rhythm at bay and holding his body still.

"Lorraine," he whispered, "You mean everything to me."

He scarcely moved, and it drove her mad.

Her body bore his imprint, and deep inside her womb she prepared to receive him. She softened and relaxed, and he sensed it. He bore down on her with the rhythm of life, the rhythm of love, and her body caught the ripple that spread from his loins to hers. Her hips thrust up as his descended, rising again and again, until she found her release and cried out. Even then passion didn't relinquish its grip but rippled through her belly and breasts, making her fingers tingle and her muscles sigh. He stayed within her, stayed over her, and his breathing revealed his pleasure.

She held him as he shuddered.

He possessed her and she was changed.

§§§

Matilde awakened at daylight. At first she couldn't remember where she was, but then she rubbed her eyes and winced. Her eyes and cheeks were swollen and tender, and with a groan she recalled the disastrous carriage ride. The innkeeper's tonic had worn off, and her arm and shoulder throbbed. Her body protested every move, but she badly needed a chamber pot.

She found one under the bed and used it gratefully. Then she sat on the edge of her bed and examined the small room. It was tidy and clean, but she was alone.

Quietly, she opened the door to the adjoining room and looked in. Jacques and Lorraine were asleep in each other's arms. Her calmness surprised her, but then she'd seen the looks that had passed between them. She had let herself assume that Lorraine's feelings were merely those of a girl flattered by her first suitor, but she'd been mistaken.

"C'est honteux," she whispered. "They are fools, but I shall never speak of it."

She couldn't send Jacques away. It wasn't her place to give him orders, and besides, they would never reach England without his help. Yet if Brian Bannock suspected that Lorraine had been used by another man, he would refuse to marry her.

What would become of them then?

If Lorraine thought that Jacques could take care of her, she was wrong. The life of a mercenary soldier stretched before him, a lonely road with nothing during the day but battle and nothing at the end of it but a pallet by himself. He could not keep a wife, for he had nothing to give her and no way to make a living except by his sword.

"He's only a bastard," Matilde whispered to the smoldering fire. Shutting the door, she retreated back into her little room. When the time came for Lorraine to be with Bannock, when she had to fulfill her obligations as his wife, then Matilde would be ready. Lorraine wasn't the first woman to make such a dangerous mistake, and with careful planning, Brian Bannock would never know.

Chapter Twenty

Lorraine awakened slowly. Even before she opened her eyes, she felt Jacques looking at her and snuggled deeper into his arms, seeking more of the tenderness that they had shared throughout the night. She heard rain beating outside and his heart beating in his chest. Warm in their bed, with the shutters closed against the storm and embers glowing in the hearth, she felt that the chill of the world would never find them. Last night she had been afraid of the pain, but now she understood that their bodies were made for each other. Shame had vanished, replaced by love. The last few days had been terrifying, and she would never again naively believe that the world was safe, but as long as she was with Jacques, she was at peace. He loved her.

He placed soft kisses on her eyelids and cheeks, but when she gazed into his face, his expression was serious.

She tried to coax a smile. "What troubles you?"

"What future can we possibly have?"

In spite of his concerns, their bodies were perfectly aligned, and he was already growing firm against her. Her hips moved, and she began to open for him. She was ready to receive him, and all that was necessary was his willingness. "Well then, marry me."

"I have nothing."

"No one knows who we are and there's no one to stop us. We can sell everything. We don't need silver plate or lengths of satin. We'll sell the brandy, too."

"The silver and brandy are your dowry," he said. "And the satin is for your wedding gown."

"We can buy a cottage on the coast, and you'll learn how to fish."

"You weren't born to be the wife of a fisherman. You should have beautiful treasures and a home where you'll always be safe."

"With you I am safe."

"I can't fight against Etienne and the king of France with only two soldiers."

She wished Jacques hadn't brought up his name. If Etienne ever caught them, he would have Jacques killed. It was the only reason she would agree to continue on to England.

If she couldn't be Jacques' wife, she would at least have him now.

He whispered her name as he entered her. He moved slowly, and when she reached her peak, he slowed even more, easing back from the brink of release. She raised her hips and once again he brought her to the edge, the place where she abandoned all thought, except desire. Again he slowed. He wouldn't let her finish. She wanted to beg him, but when she opened her mouth he kissed her. She wrapped her legs around his hips. The flood broke over them and she clung to him, wishing she could hold onto him forever.

§§§

Lorraine was still sleeping as Jacques dressed and headed for the kitchen. He was hungry enough to eat an ox, but the innkeeper gave him porridge. She watched him gulp his food and seemed to take pity on him, refilling his bowl and adding a little sausage.

"How is your wife?" Madame Margot asked.

"She is well, thank you," Jacques choked. "My wife and her maid are still asleep."

"I'll make sure they get breakfast – and your men too if you'll send them to the kitchen."

Jacques roused Lucas and Jacob from where they slept in the stable. "I'm going to find us passage across the channel," he said as he saddled his mount. "Be on your guard while I'm gone."

"Sir." Lucas handed him the bridle. "We wish to stay behind when you sail for England. We have families at Chateau Brèche. They might be waiting for help. If they survived."

Jacques paused and took his time before answering. Without Lucas and Jacob, there would be no one to guard Lorraine and Matilde. Pirates sometimes captured ships at sea, and robbers preyed on people foolish enough to travel alone.

Jacques considered the dangers, but he knew Etienne would stay in France. He could not risk leaving his newly acquired land, and once Lorraine reached England, she would be under Lord Bannock's protection. It would be dangerous to travel without them, but he couldn't deny their need to take care of their families.

"Will you stay with Lady Lorraine until we are safely aboard a ship?"

"Yes, sir," Lucas said. "It's our honor."

Jacques agreed, hoping their families had survived the attack on Chateau Brèche. As he rode down the hill toward the seaport, he felt a moment of bitterness. He had never been a full member of a family, nor had he ever really belonged in any home. He was the bastard son of a nobleman, and now he was an outlaw.

He shook off his self-pity. My only duty is to Lorraine. But he wished that every day might begin as this one had.

§§§

Wind drove the rain across the open water and into the harbor as Jacques went from one shipping office to the next.

He was always greeted with the same reply. Come back when the storm clears. When the weather is better and business slows, then perhaps you may have passage.

He saw crates of delayed cargo piling up; it could be days or weeks before anyone had room for a party of travelers.

None of the sailors in port seemed disturbed. They were cozy in the taverns and with the bar maids. Jacques entered one tavern after another, standing inside the doorway with his cloak on, away from the firelight, listening to men talking. He heard sea yarns and tall tales but no mention of Chateau Brèche. Those troubles were a world away from the port of Calais.

He returned to the inn, hung his dripping cloak on a hook in the kitchen, and looked around for a piece of bread or cup of ale. Everything had been swept clean, the stores locked away, and Madame Margot and her staff were nowhere to be seen.

Wearily, Jacques climbed the stairs and knocked at Matilde's door. There was no answer and he peeked inside. The tonic bottle was on the table and Matilde snored, deep in a drug-induced slumber. Dark bruises mottled her face. She was a strong woman, but it was just as well that they weren't traveling today.

He pushed open the door to Lorraine's room, hoping for a fire and a few scraps of food, but what he saw rooted him in place.

The wooden floor of the old room sloped toward the hearth. Lorraine sat on a blanket in front of the fire, and the light cast golden hues in her hair. Spread before her was a feast: a platter of meat and freshly baked bread, a wedge of cheese and a bowl of dried fruit.

She poured wine into goblets. "Come in." Her smile promised so much more than food.

He closed the door and slid the bolt into place. "How did you manage this?"

"Madame Margot asked if I would like supper in my room. She thinks it's natural for us to be together."

§§§

Lorraine held a morsel of cheese to Jacques' lips. He nibbled it and then nibbled her fingers. She laughed and fed him another tidbit, and as he bent his head to take it she brushed the hair out of his eyes. His nearness made her heart quicken.

Her father and her childhood home were gone, and she had to decide for herself where she would live. England or France? If they didn't live near the sea, then they could buy a small farm with an orchard. They had been given this chance, and they'd be fools not to take it.

Jacques finished eating, and as he stared into the flames, his eyes began to droop. "I had better go to the stables and check on the men," he said.

"Every time you walk out the door, I'm afraid I'll never see you again." She handed him his book of verses. "Will you read to me?"

She studied his face while he flipped through the pages, and after a few minutes she moved closer and began kneading his shoulders. He found the verse he wanted and read:

Our lives will soon unfold in different lands
We stare across a sea from distant sands
But even though we live on separate shores
I promise to remain forever yours

She moved beside him. "It doesn't have to be like that."

Jacques drew the cross from around his neck, placed it over her head, and spoke the words that his father had once said to him. "This is a token of my love. The cross stands for eternal life and the heart is for eternal love."

He carried her to the bed, undressed her quickly, and kicked away the last of his clothing. He settled himself over her nude body, and the golden cross pressed between their hearts. He kissed her throat and shoulders, suckled her breasts, traced kisses down her belly, and slowly entered her.

§§§

The days passed and the rain continued, and Jacques grew restless. More guests arrived at the inn, and lodgers lingered in the drawing room and dining room. The dark, heavy beams and low ceilings trapped the pipe smoke, and the crowded rooms smelled of unwashed bodies. Each time the door opened, a blast of frigid wind blew smoke from the fireplace through the room instead of up the chimney. Most of the lodgers had red eyes and runny noses.

Lorraine sorted through the trunks, aired out their clothes, and packed the garments that had been washed and dried. She cared for Matilde during the day and lay in Jacques' arms throughout the night.

He wished for a lifetime of such moments. He imagined her singing in his household and thought about the children they would have. Their first son would be named Frederick, after her father.

One afternoon the sky cleared, and Jacques threw on his cloak. Lorraine glanced up from her mending. "Where are you going?"

"To the docks." Reluctantly he turned away.

The storm had weakened, and more ships were setting sail. As long as Lorraine remained in France, she was in danger of being captured by Etienne. It was only a matter of time before they were hunted down. Jacques hated his brother and knew how cruel he could be. If Lorraine had to marry someone besides himself, she would be better off with Brian Bannock.

At the docks, merchants crowded the streets. Everywhere Jacques turned, he was in the way. Sailors shoved him aside as they hurried to get their cargos aboard the outgoing vessels. The men who had lolled about drinking ale now worked with a purpose, and the shipping clerks, counting out coins, waved him away when he inquired about a berth. At every ship the answer was the same – no passage.

Dejectedly, Jacques made his way back to L'Auberge de la Colombe, his mind occupied with memories of his love-making. In the quiet hours before dawn, Lorraine had whispered, "Marry me."

He was haunted by those words. Was it possible? Or was he a fool for even thinking he could take care of her?

In England they would be traveling in a strange country without any guards, and they had only Bannock's long-ago promise that he would give Lorraine a home. Like Marquis Bonville, Lord Bannock undoubtedly had political enemies. Life in England might not be much better than in France. The only certainty was his love for her.

Jacques stopped in the middle of a narrow lane so suddenly that a cart driver cursed and careened around him, but he barely registered the near miss. He made up his mind. They would slip away to a small village, find a priest and get married.

When he got to the inn, he ran inside, eager to find Lorraine and tell her his plan. Madame Margot intercepted him, pulling him into the empty drawing room, where a fire crackled in the grate.

"I've been waiting for you," the innkeeper hissed. "Did you think you could fool me with your wicked deception? Your likeness is posted throughout Calais." Her hand shook as she thrust the parchment at him. Beneath his picture were the words, Decree of Arrest. Jacques Dannes is ordered to surrender for the murder of Marquis Frederick Bonville. "They claim that the man who killed the Marquis also kidnapped his daughter. Do you deny it?"

He thought furiously, but before he could invent a story, Lorraine walked calmly into the room. "I deny it," she said. She studied the parchment then moved the screen aside and tossed it onto the fire where it curled and blackened. "He is neither a murderer nor a kidnapper. I am Lady Lorraine Bonville."

Madame Margot nodded, and a look of understanding crossed her face. "The fine clothes. I should have known you were not a working man's wife." She trembled with rage. "You had no right to deceive me."

Lorraine held her head high, but Jacques could see the tears starting in her eyes.

"I am sworn to take her to England. She is betrothed to a baron." Jacques pleaded, "Will you help us?"

"If you are found on my property, my holdings will be forfeit." Madame Margot walked toward the door. "By this time tomorrow, your face will be known in every port along the coast."

Jacques felt desperate. The warrant was issued for him alone. "I'll leave. Let her stay."

"No." Lorraine looked panicked. "Don't leave me."

"I know a captain who may provide transport," Madame Margot said, "but it's going to cost you dearly."

§§§

For a second time they packed frantically, and when the cart was loaded, Jacques lifted Matilde onto a horse, climbed up behind her and shielded himself behind her bulk. Madame Margot guided them to the last office on the dock, one so dilapidated that Jacques had ignored it on his earlier rounds. The worn sign said Crown Hallé, and the man who greeted them looked more like a pirate than a reputable captain. Twin daggers were tucked into his leather belt. One of his eyes was as blue as a calm sea; the other was milky white and blind.

Madame Margot talked to him privately.

Jacque dismounted but kept his face hidden under his hood.

On the grimy dock, Jacob and Lucas bowed to Lorraine. Each guard took her hand by turn, kissed it and wished her a safe journey. She struggled to look brave as she thanked them and released them from their service.

Jacques paid the two men. They nodded in appreciation and mounted their horses.

The captain eyed Jacques' coin purse. "Can you pay the price of passage?"

The fare he named was double what it should have been, but Jacques paid it, and the captain wasted no time.

"On board with you now. There's money to be made." He beckoned to the ragtag crew. "Load the trunks and help the ladies. Be quick!"

The captain said something to Madame Margot and winked his good eye, and Jacques said a silent prayer that they had not been betrayed.

Madame Margot touched the captain's face. "Safe passage." She climbed onto the cart and took up the reins. "God save you," she said to Lorraine. With a snap of the reins, the cart drew away.

§§§

Lorraine stood on the wharf beside Jacques and peered down at the swirling water. Unlike the clear river that ran alongside Chateau Brèche, this water was cloudy and smelled of rotting fish and sewage. Patches of an oily, iridescent film slithered on the waves and mixed with grayish foam. Dozens of seagulls circled overhead, screeching loudly and landing brazenly close. One swooped so low it startled her and she dropped a glove; the beady-eyed bird snapped it up as though it were edible. Suddenly the creatures were everywhere, flapping their wings and screaming.

She waved her arms, trying to shoo them away, and scurried onto the gang plank, hoping to escape them. A swell hit and the narrow board rose and fell as though she were on the back of a sea serpent. Holding tight to the guide rope stretched taut between the ship and the dock, she gingerly made her way onto the deck.

Captain Hallé laughed and urged Matilde to follow. "I've already collected my fees and don't care if you come or not, but your mistress might be disturbed if you stay behind."

"I'll drown," Matilde blubbered. "I can't swim."

Lorraine couldn't swim, either, and the creaking ship sounded ready to break apart. She doubted the ship was sturdy enough to make it across the channel.

The captain ignored Matilde's whining and threw her over his shoulder. "Hold quietly, Madame, or I may drop you into the sea myself." He stepped lightly up the gangway, as gracefully as if he were dancing, and hooted in amusement as he set the sputtering Matilde on deck.

Lorraine fought to keep her balance as the floor beneath her feet shifted. Jacques was still on the wharf, staring warily at the swaying plank. A sailor slammed one of her trunks down beside her, and she jumped. The screeching gulls drowned her shriek.

At Captain Hallé's order, men began releasing the mooring ropes. In another moment they would pull up the gangplank.

"Jacques! Hurry," Lorraine screamed. "He'll sail without you."

The men on deck laughed and made a show of untying the lines and jiggling the gangplank.

Jacques ran onto the plank, and it shuddered under his feet. He froze, his arms outstretched for balance as he stared into the water below.

The crew taunted him and shouted insults until the captain ordered them to action. The sails rose up the mast, snapping as they unfurled in the frosty wind. The ship heaved, and Jacques leaped onto the deck just as they began to pull away from the wharf.

The men worked in clusters, straining to control the angle and direction of the long poles secured to the bottom of the sails. Creaking wood and flapping sails added to the chaos of shouting as the ship slid away from the pier.

Lorraine's hair whipped against her cheeks, and her cloak billowed. She watched Calais fade into the haze. God willing, she would one day return to her homeland, and to Chateau Brèche. When the coastline was no longer visible and the sky as black as the sea, she asked, "When will they show us to our rooms?"

In the scant moonlight, Jacques' face looked pale, and he stumbled for balance as the deck rocked beneath him. "I'll ask the captain."

A young sailor with black, broken teeth escorted them below deck. Lorraine felt the eyes of the crew on them as they passed, and she risked a look into their faces. Some stared in open curiosity, and one man leered, thrusting his hips toward her provocatively as she hurried to get past him. Fortunately, Jacques was ahead of her and didn't see, or he might have pulled his dagger on the pig of a man.

"Bad luck for women to be aboard," Black Tooth said. "Our men would just as soon throw you into the sea."

He opened the door to a small room tucked along a narrow corridor. It contained one chair, a table and a bed. The blankets piled on the bed smelled vile, and there were rat droppings on the table.

Lorraine's stomach lurched and rolled along with the ship, and she collapsed onto the chair. "Does the window open?"

The boy rubbed a hand through his greasy hair and nodded to a small, square window above the bed. "If the blanket gets wet, it'll take days to dry." He turned his rotted grin on Jacques. "Keep an eye on your women; our boys get ideas."

Jacques followed Black Tooth from the room, but before shutting the door, he turned to Lorraine. "I'll be just outside if you need me."

Matilde removed her woolen mantle, spread it on the bed, and sat down heavily. The bow of the ship raised high on another swell before plunging down again, and she moaned as spray splashed the dark window.

Lorraine pulled her cloak more tightly around her shoulders as the ship shuddered up another wave and slammed down the backside. If the ship broke apart, it would be hopeless to try to swim. Their heavy clothes would drag them to the bottom of the sea.

"I was afraid Etienne would find us before we left France," said Matilde.

Lorraine answered with more confidence than she felt. "We won't ever have to worry about him again."

"Promise me that you'll marry Lord Bannock."

"Don't ask me to make a pledge I cannot keep," Lorraine said.

"You gave your word to your father."

"Everything has changed."

Lorraine moved the chair closer to the tiny window. The only thing visible was gray water and an occasional glimpse of the sky. As night deepened, she could hear the water hammer against the side of the ship, but the world outside was black. She kept her back to Matilde so she wouldn't have to see her disapproving look.

After what seemed like hours, Lorraine stood and stretched, but the ship heaved and she was thrown against the wall. Her shoulder felt bruised, and she thought about the injuries Matilde had been coping with for the past week.

"How are you feeling?" she finally asked, sitting on the bed beside her maid.

Matilde harrumphed and looked away.

A loud bang on the cabin door made them both jump.

"Who's there?" Lorraine called.

She heard Jacques shouting, and then the door slammed open. She tried to stand, but the motion of the ship tossed her against Matilde. The sailor who'd been staring at her earlier, the one with the lewd grin, struggled to get in.

Lorraine screamed and grabbed a heavy crock off the table.

Jacques fought to keep him out, pressing his dagger against the man's throat.

"Let go." Black Tooth waved the tip of his drawn sword between Jacques and the sailor, threatening his shipmate, "Come below again, and I'll let him gut you." He stood aside as the sailor bolted out. "Keep your dagger handy," he ordered Jacques.

"If the women are harmed –"

"Touch the crew, I'll kill you," Black Tooth said. "Then what'll happen to your lambs?" He tipped his cap in a belligerent manner and left.

Lorraine was about to fling herself into Jacques' arms, but Matilde held her firmly.

"Guard the door," Matilde said to Jacques.

He nodded, his face pale. "Lorraine." He sounded hoarse.

"Outside," Matilde said.

Jacques backed out, and Lorraine had no energy left to argue with Matilde. They spent the rest of the night huddled on the bed, listening for sounds of fighting outside their door.

In spite of her certainty that sleep was impossible, Lorraine awoke at dawn and rubbed her eyes; grains of dried tears and ocean salt stained her cheeks. From the porthole she caught a glimpse of the sky turning pale blue, and the rhythm of the waves felt calmer.

Jacques brought mugs of ale and stale bread with a warning to stay below until they reached the coast of England. The sailors were still mumbling threats.

Finally, he knocked again and informed them they had arrived. Lorraine felt the ship bump against the pier and heard men's shouts as they secured the lines.

They emerged onto the deck into a day that was cold and clear. The English port was bustling, and dozens of ships were docked, taking on or unloading cargo. Push carts were piled with fresh fish, and eager merchants haggled over goods.

Amid the confusion, they were set on the dock beside their trunks and left to fend for themselves. It felt as if the ground were still swaying. Lorraine listened to the guttural sound of English. Dock workers jostled against them, and people stared.

"Look out!" Matilde screamed, pulling her aside as something splattered at their feet. A live fish flipped end over end, and nasty stains splotched Lorraine's gown. She looked up in time to see the sailor who had tried to accost her lift his hand in a rude gesture.

Instead of feeling relief to be on land, Lorraine was afraid. For two years, thoughts of England had haunted her, and now that she was here, she didn't know what to make of it. She glanced at the strange surroundings. "I wish we hadn't come."

"Would you rather spend your life running from Etienne and his assassins?" Matilde clutched her arm. "I don't want to be here anymore than you, but a good match is not to be tossed away on a girl's dream."

After some haggling, Jacques purchased a horse and a plain, unpainted carriage with tattered curtains that smelled of mildew. He loaded their trunks, helped the women climb inside, and they set off again.

Lorraine wondered how they would be received. Bannock had agreed to marry an heiress, not an impoverished woman.

Hours passed, and the coast fell away. Through the carriage window she saw stone and timber cottages, land divided by hedges and stone walls, and fields dotted with grazing cows. On a hill above a village, a castle guarded the countryside. They bounced along the rutted roads, heading north. When they stopped to ask directions the villagers drew back, suspicious of their accents. The war between England and France had left people bitter. She would never be accepted in Bannock's household.

Darkness fell, and they searched for an inn. They were turned away four times before they found lodging, a shared room for Matilde and Lorraine while Jacques slept in the carriage to guard their belongings.

Lorraine slept poorly, and after a breakfast of watery porridge, they continued on through an expanse of forest. They traveled over hills and crossed pastures full of grazing sheep.

"It's beautiful," Matilde said.

"The land is pretty," Lorraine observed, "but the people don't like us."

As the days passed, she watched the scenery and contemplated her duty. From the moment they had set foot on English soil, Jacques had behaved toward her only as a devoted servant. Matilde had already accepted their fate, and it seemed that Jacques, too, understood that the choice for her had been made long ago.

§§§

Night was falling on their third day in England as Jacques drew up the carriage in front of an inn. Each abode was a little less hospitable, a little shabbier than the last. He shook his coin purse and tried to judge how far they still had to go.

He secured lodging while Lorraine and Matilde waited outside. They took a room on an upper floor, and once they were settled, he drove the carriage around, unhitched the horse and tethered it. He hated transporting Lorraine in such a poor carriage, but what it lacked in finery, the horse made up for in strength.

They had established a routine. The women ate while he tended the horse, and then Lorraine brought him supper.

It was bitterly cold, but she lingered. "Stay inside tonight and sleep by the fire. It's too cold to stay out here."

"I have to keep watch," he said. "To guard what's left, or you'll have nothing to bring Lord Bannock." He could tell by her expression that she was torn.

"I'll sit with you while you eat," she said, "and afterward, I can keep watch while you rest."

She made the same offer every night, and he refused each time. He was afraid of what would happen if they were left alone. "Go inside," he urged. "At least one of us should be warm."

"I'll bring you an extra blanket."

She returned with two blankets, and he wondered if she'd taken them from an empty room. In this weather, a patron robbed of a blanket might solve the crime at the point of a dagger. He didn't ask but took one willingly, adding its warmth to his thin cloak. She pulled the other one around her and put her head on his shoulder. He felt warmth coming from her slender body, like a tiny brazier. He worked an arm free and wrapped the end of his blanket around them both. The wooden seat was hard, but with her beside him it didn't matter.

They were in a foreign country; he didn't understand their customs, didn't know their laws, and could only speak a little of their language. Every night he thought of how lost he was, and how poor, and how much Lorraine needed the protection of Lord Bannock. Every night he battled with his emotions – gratitude that she had a champion, despair that it wasn't him.

She shivered, and he held her tightly. He never tired of staring into her dark eyes, and the longing he read in them was unmistakable. When she lifted her face to his, he cupped her chin and said, "Why did you ever fall in love with me?"

Her lips brushed his. He opened his mouth, and their tongues met. She snuggled closer, and his resolve abandoned him. He promised himself that each kiss would be the last, and yet each taste kept him coming back for another. He was like a man in a river who keeps surfacing and gulping air, only to sink again. Love was drowning him, he couldn't release her, couldn't free himself.

The carriage was cramped and the seat was too short and narrow for either of them to lie down. He cradled her head and shifted his weight. She was beneath him, and he balanced one leg on the bench, braced the other on the floor, and was suddenly too desperate to care about comfort. He no longer tried to pretend that one more kiss would be enough.

They were behind the inn, invisible to the main room. Through the foggy windows he could see the flickering of candles, but the corner room where Matilde slept was dark. And yet if they were caught, he wouldn't be able to defend himself. No one would believe that a husband would take his wife like this, in a carriage. No, they would accuse him of taking what wasn't his, and if they learned that Lorraine was betrothed to Lord Bannock...

She stared into his eyes. "Don't leave me. Please – don't ever leave –even when –" She didn't say *when she belonged to another man*. "Maybe he won't want me."

"Of course he'll want you."

"Promise me you'll stay."

"I promise." How could he refuse?

His mouth covered hers while she fumbled to loosen his leggings. He kissed her neck, pulled the gown off her shoulders, and licked the hollow where her throat ended and her cleavage began. He tasted salt. He trailed kisses to her nipples, and she arched beneath him. He lifted her gown, and his hand moved slowly from her ankle to her knee then slid up between her thighs. She parted her legs and he stroked her. She moaned and moved her hips under his, raising herself, and he almost burst when he felt her wetness. He would have her one more time.

When he entered her, he crossed the threshold where he could no longer think clearly. Her delicate rippling began, spreading toward him, pulling him deeper. He climaxed quickly, muffled his cry against her shoulder, and stayed as he was, braced over her. She was still moving and he reached down, touching softly with the tips of his fingers until she cried out.

He must have fallen asleep because when he awakened, she was pulling her gown up to cover her shoulders. He slid his hand into the bodice of her dress and touched her breast. "Once more. I need you once more before I give you up forever."

Just before dawn, she left his arms and stole back to her room.

Chapter Twenty-One

On a freezing afternoon, their fifth day in England, the three weary travelers reached Bannock's land. Jacques halted the carriage at the crest of a hill, and they all climbed down to look across the valley. Atop the opposite hill, a castle of weathered gray stone stood sentry, and above its tallest tower, a flag bearing the Bannock crest snapped in the wind. Pastures swept up toward forested hills, and on a small rise at the north side of the sloping valley, just below the old castle, stood the new manor house.

Unlike the castle, enclosed within its protective walls, the manor stood on open land. Bannock must have been confident to build a home with only the castle at its back. Lorraine stared in dread at Lord Bannock's domain. The man who owned such a home would wield a great deal of power.

Matilde reached for her hand. "I hope Lord Bannock will honor his pledge."

"I hope he doesn't," Lorraine whispered back.

The wind picked up and rain began to fall, but instead of scrambling back into the carriage, they remained where they were.

Jacques looked tired, and his eyes were bloodshot. He picked up Lorraine's hand and held it to his cheek. "You were born a noblewoman," he said. "Lord Bannock can protect you – I cannot." Rain dripped from his chin, and he looked defeated.

"Without you, nothing else matters," she said.

He kissed her palm and then pulled her toward the carriage. "You're getting soaked." He helped her inside and searched through his travel bag until he found his book of poems. "My love is in this." He pressed his book into her hands.

Lorraine clutched Jacques' book and fought back her tears.

He assisted Matilde into the carriage and quickly shut the door.

They proceeded to the gatehouse, and Jacques announced to the guard, "Lady Lorraine Bonville to see Lord Bannock."

The guards acted as if they were commoners or gypsies and even after lengthy questioning remained unconvinced that the betrothed of Lord Bannock would arrive in such a worn-out carriage. Lorraine hadn't expected their identity to be in doubt and found the interrogation humiliating. She was also afraid they might be arrested, but finally they were allowed to proceed to the manor house. The carriage began to move again, only this time they were surrounded by a dozen mounted soldiers. With each rotation of the wheel, each jerk and bump of the ancient carriage, she was closer to facing Lord Bannock.

She pressed her hands tightly against her stomach, hoping to settle the churning nausea, but the bile continued its climb up her throat until suddenly she stuck her head out the window and vomited. As she wiped her mouth on the hem of her chemise, she heard one of the men mumble something that made the others chuckle.

"You're as white as a bowl of milk." Matilde looked worried. "Lord Bannock might think you're sickly."

The carriage stopped in front of the house, and a crowd quickly gathered. Most of the women appeared shy, holding their children and staying a safe distance away, but the men gawked openly.

Lorraine watched the front door open, and an older man with gray hair and a mustache came out onto the topmost step. One of the soldiers dismounted and talked to him privately. His gaze remained fixed on Jacques, and his face registered distrust. She'd held so tightly to the possibility that they would never actually arrive, and now she wondered why she had even let him bring her here.

Jacques jumped down from the driver's seat and stood between the carriage and the servant. He waved his hands, forgetting his English, and attempted to convince the man of their identity. Frustrated, he turned to Lorraine, and she quietly supplied him with the English words.

Matilde, her face still covered in bruises and cuts, kept her head down, clutched her rosary and mumbled prayers. Lorraine could feel her quivering.

The imposing man opened the carriage door and glanced between the two women, deciding which one to address. "Good afternoon, Lady Bonville." He looked directly at Lorraine. "I am Simon Masterson, Lord Bannock's steward. Please forgive any awkwardness, but we have to be cautious." He watched her closely, and his gaze took in every detail. "Lord Bannock left a month ago for Wales and never mentioned that you were coming. He'll return next week for Christmas."

Clearly he expected a response from her, but she didn't know what he meant and didn't like being confronted by such a stilted, pompous servant. Her throat constricted and her cheeks burned. Was he telling her to come back next week?

After an awkward pause, he held out his hand. "Perhaps you would be more comfortable inside." He summoned servants who began unloading the carriage, and as she and Matilde emerged, more servants arrived. Simon directed Matilde to follow a maid to the domestic quarters.

Lorraine tried to intervene. "I must have her with me."

Simon Masterson seemed unperturbed. "Bannock Manor is under my keeping while Lord Bannock is away. Your maid will be more comfortable in the domestic quarters, where she will have someone to see to her injuries. Your guard –" He cast a disparaging look at Jacques. "He will be housed in the castle."

She was about to argue, but Jacques pulled her aside. "Stay calm," he whispered. "Show them that you deserve to be treated with authority and respect." Simon moved closer, and Jacques soothed, "I'll be nearby."

She looked past Simon's shoulder and saw that the crowd was growing larger. The peasants were creeping closer and angling their necks, watching. It had stopped raining, but the December afternoon had turned cold and her gown was heavy and damp. Reluctantly, she followed Simon up the steps.

Inside the foyer, she glanced down at her clothes and saw herself as she must appear to him, a common girl in musty garments, without a proper escort.

Simon closed the heavy door, shutting her inside. He didn't invite her to sit but questioned her further about her family, her home, and other details that an imposter wouldn't know. She knew that Michel would have done the same if a poorly turned-out carriage had arrived bearing unexpected visitors.

"Sir, if you distrust me so much, send me away. I will return when Lord Bannock is here." She knew that as soon as she was gone from this cold place, she would never come back. "I really don't care what you think of me."

"Where are the rest of your belongings?" It seemed he still had a point to make.

"Lost when we sailed from Calais." She recalled Jacques' advice to stay calm and bit back her temper. "Whether or not my remaining dowry is acceptable is for Lord Bannock to decide."

"If you will kindly wait," the steward said, "I will see to the arrangements." He opened the door to a room and waved her inside. He made a slight bow and left, shutting the door behind him.

The moment she was alone, she shook her heavy skirt and released a cascade of mud onto the flagstone floor. It was odd to have a receiving room on the ground floor; the two large windows would be quite vulnerable to assault. Again she wondered why Lord Bannock had built his new house outside the protection of castle walls.

She sat beside the window and watched four soldiers march across the drawbridge and into a gatehouse. A peasant man pulled a small cart piled high with sacks of grain. Two maidens carrying a heavy, woven basket between them crossed the lower courtyard.

She waited and waited and then began to pace. Was Simon Masterson being deliberately rude? She was a guest and should have been offered refreshment and shown where to clean up. How much power did he have? Michel would have been watchful but never so ungracious. She paused in front of the window, hoping to see Jacques or Matilde. A brown-haired woman walked past and glanced in, and her placid expression turned to surprise when she spotted Lorraine. The woman quickly walked away, and Lorraine resumed her pacing.

A sharp rap sounded, and the door opened. "We have your rooms ready," Simon said. He led the way up a flight of stairs and into a small sitting room. Beyond it was the adjoining bedchamber. "I cannot give you leave to wander about without an escort."

How dare he treat her like a thief! She glared at him but decided to ignore his insinuation. "If you'll be so kind as to have my trunks brought here, I'd like to change." She added, "I'll need my maid."

"I'll send a chambermaid to help you."

"I prefer my own maid."

He turned at the door. "I will send up Tess, our head housekeeper, to get you settled."

When he was gone, she picked up an embroidered pillow and threw it at the door.

The two rooms that Simon had allotted her were small and overlooked the kitchen and bake house. They were the sort of accommodations reserved for lesser gentry. The sitting room was comfortable, with a small fireplace, two chairs and a table, and the whitewash on the walls was clean, without the buildup of candle soot. The bedroom was barely wide enough for a narrow bed and wardrobe.

It was growing dark as she peered into the rear courtyard. Their carriage had been brought around, and Jacques stood beside it, looking lost. He couldn't see her, and she was afraid to call out.

We have made a terrible mistake coming here.

Someone knocked on the door, and she jumped. It was Simon, followed by two servants. He introduced Tess first, a thin, older woman in charge of the chambermaids and scullery girls. Next he motioned to a girl with a generous figure who looked a few years older than Lorraine. "Joan will be your chambermaid."

Joan curtsied. "Milady, may I show you to the garderrobe?"

She followed Joan to a tiny room adjacent to an exterior wall. A built-in stone chute was topped by a wooden seat with a hole in the center. Lorraine gagged as the cold wind blew upward carrying a foul odor, but she wasted no time making use of the indoor latrine.

Afterward, as she ate supper alone in her room, she worried about Jacques and Matilde. Tomorrow she would find them, and they would make plans to leave. She heard a light tread in the corridor, and a step paused outside her door.

Simon called, "Good night, Madame."

She heard a key turn in the lock. Lorraine tiptoed to the door and tried to move the latch, but it wouldn't budge. He was still there, just on the other side, although he didn't say another word. After a few minutes, she heard his steps move away.

She was clearly unwelcome here, but didn't know if it was because she had arrived unexpectedly, or that she'd brought so little dowry, or just that she was French.

During the next several days, she was chaperoned whenever she left her room. Each morning her stomach turned sour, and she threw up in a chamber pot that she discreetly emptied down the garderrobe chute. What bothered her more than the English food was the fact that she wasn't allowed to see Jacques or Matilde, and she worried that they were being mistreated.

And every night Simon came and locked her door.

§§§

Brian Bannock held up his right arm and signaled his men to halt. He pulled back on his horse's reins and looked at his home on the far hillside. The late afternoon sunlight broke through the clouds, and he smiled at the view. Under the protection of Cragmoor Castle, the newly built house enhanced his status. His horse pranced restlessly, anxious for the comfort of the stable, and Bannock concurred. It was good to be home. They galloped across the valley to the manor house.

A stable boy came running as Bannock dismounted. Simon emerged from the large, intricately carved front door and set a torch into a wall sconce. "Welcome home, my lord."

Bannock entered the foyer and began peeling off his chain mail hood. "I'll be glad to be free of this extra weight." He pulled the metal collar over his head. "Have supper brought to my room," he ordered, as he headed up the stairs. "I am weary beyond endurance."

Simon followed behind. "What is the news from Wales, my lord?"

"York is at Ludlow Castle, and Lancaster controls London. Parliament is still loyal to King Henry, and the king favors Edmund and Jasper Tudor. Their kinship with the king weakens York's influence."

"I believe the Tudor brothers have too much power." Simon gathered the discarded clothing as he went. "How long will you be home this time?"

Bannock reached the landing. "I shall stay long enough to make sure my estate is in order and celebrate Christmas with my people." He took a deep breath. "There will likely be war between York and Lancaster."

"That could threaten the unity of England."

Upstairs in his private sitting room, he devoured a huge platter of food. Simon shifted nervously, and as he poured a second goblet of wine, Bannock barked, "What is it? You're more jumpy than a hound after a hare."

"My lord, there is some news," Simon said. "A young woman arrived last week, and she claims to be Lady Bonville."

Bannock set down his goblet and pushed out of his chair. "Lady Lorraine is here? But how did she get here? Get me fresh clothes and give me more details. Is Marquis Bonville here?"

Simon rushed about the room, laying out clothes. "She came with only one maid and one soldier as a guard. They arrived in a shabby carriage. I suspect they are imposters."

Bannock put on his best tunic, pulled up his leggings, and fastened a wide leather belt about his waist. "Tell me what she looks like."

"She is small and looks very young. She has long, brown hair, and her manner is quite skittish. Joan reports that she is sickly. The few clothes she has are of a fine fabric, and she travels with some valuable jewels, but those may have been stolen. All three of them are French but understand English. When she arrived, I questioned her carefully and took the liberty of searching her belongings before her trunks were carried to her room. The young man is under guard at the castle, and the maid is in the domestic quarters. I have given them no opportunity to rob you."

Bannock slumped back into his chair. "Did she say what happened to her father? Or why she did not wait until I came for her?"

"According to our guests, Chateau Brèche was attacked and Marquis Bonville killed, but this girl could be anyone from France taking advantage of the disaster. It's happened before."

Simon's cautious nature had saved Bannock's life many times. But if this was Lorraine and her father was dead, who had possession of the chateau? The chateau and its land were supposed to be his when he married her. The title passed with the land. He needed to know what had happened. "Have Tess bring her to the withdrawing room. I shall know in an instant if it is Lorraine Bonville."

Downstairs in the long, narrow withdrawing room, Bannock paced nervously. The room hadn't been used while he was away, and now it was cold and drafty. It would be hours before the freshly laid fire could dispel the chill.

He only stopped pacing when Simon appeared. "Presenting Lady Lorraine Bonville, of Chateau Brèche."

It seemed to take an eternity, but finally she was there in the room. Her changed appearance shocked him. He remembered her as a healthy and robust girl of fifteen, and he'd often thought that by the time he married her, she would have filled out into a woman. Instead, she looked like a starving waif with a pale face and dark circles under her eyes. He was careful not to let his disappointment show.

He crossed the room and welcomed her. Her eyes narrowed, and her smile drooped for a moment when he kissed the back of her hand. Her flinch reminded him of the day they were betrothed. He had known then that she didn't want to marry him, and this meeting felt the same. What could a young girl understand about a great alliance between two families? He would own large estates in England and Normandy while her father's heirs could carry on the title under English protection.

She looked up at him and attempted to smile. "Thank you, my lord." She pulled her hand free.

She wasn't aware how easily he could read her emotions, and he chose to ignore her transparent dislike for him. "You must tell me everything."

Her eyes lost some of their timid expression. "You promised to come back with troops to help us, and we waited as long as we could. When my father became ill, Etienne Dannes lost no opportunity to strike."

"Etienne Dannes attacked the chateau?"

"We barely had a chance to defend ourselves. Jacques Dannes helped me escape before the fighting began. I am alive, thanks to him."

Bannock listened as Lorraine blamed him, accused him of failing to protect her and everything dear to her. She told him her frightening tale and cried as she described how her carriage overturned on a muddy mountain road. She trembled when she recalled how most of her guards had been killed.

"I thought Jacques and Matilde were dead. I was alone in the woods."

There was no mistaking the depth of her grief, and there was also no denying the admiration and loyalty she felt for Jacques Dannes. "I wrote to your father and explained my delays, but he never sent word that your situation was so grave." Bannock walked to the fireplace and stared into the flames, taking the time to compose himself. "You cannot blame me for all that has happened."

She seemed anxious that he understand the magnitude of her loss. "We had no friends left to fight for us, and no one came to our aid. You did not come for me. My people were killed, and my home is lost." She crumpled into the nearest chair and covered her face with her hands.

Bannock looked toward the sideboard where Simon and Tess waited and motioned for them to leave. Servants spread their own version of gossip. He was more concerned about the lack of chaperones during her long journey than a lack of chaperones right now. He stared into the fire and thought about what he'd just heard. He was furious about the lost dowry, and wondered if he was still obligated to marry her. She was all that was left of the Bonville contribution to their marriage.

Exasperated, he asked, "What do you expect me to do?"

"I will understand if you want to cancel the betrothal." She sat up straight, stiffening her spine. "We can leave in the morning."

How naïve and innocent she was. It would be a serious social and legal breach for him to break off the written marriage contract, and the ramifications would be catastrophic for them both. The only way he could justify canceling the betrothal was to accuse her of being a harlot or some other grievous offense. He'd have to publicly announce that he couldn't accept her as his wife. After that, it would be a social disaster for another man to marry her. Society would abandon her, and her only remaining options would be a convent, marriage to a commoner, or prostitution.

The consequences for him were almost as serious. Any gentleman who cancelled a betrothal contract was considered a rogue, and members of society would not risk a daughter's reputation on him.

Everything he'd spent his life working for was at stake. First he'd purchased Cragmoor Castle with gold from the French campaigns, and then he'd restored the gray stone walls and battlements. He had earned his knighthood in battle, and his wealth and influence had grown steadily. The king had bestowed on him the title of Baron, and knights had pledged themselves to his service. Lords sought his favor and his troops, and peasants worked his land. His beautiful manor house was almost complete.

All that remained to secure his position was marriage into nobility, and Lady Bonville had many generations of titled nobility flowing in her veins. He had spent his life raising his social status, and now he was ready for a wife and heirs. He had already waited too long for marriage, but he must be certain that his wife's allegiance was to him. He'd decide within the week what action he wanted to take.

Turning from the fire, he looked at the young woman who didn't understand the fragile nature of her future. He chose his words carefully and responded to her with deliberate vagueness. "I cannot let you leave here only to wander the world with a maid and a single guard. Next week is Christmas, and by then we will have had time to make the necessary plans."

§§§

The day following Lord Bannock's return, Lorraine noticed the difference immediately. Everyone was busy.

Neighboring landowners, noblemen and their families would be staying for the holidays, and all the craftsmen and servants were hard at work. From her window, she watched a swarm of activity as people hurried in and out of the cellars beneath the kitchen.

During the previous week, she had barely left her rooms, but today breakfast was served in the dining room. Unlike Chateau Brèche, where their meals and most activities were in the great hall, Bannock Manor had a room just for meals and nothing else. The dark-paneled walls were carved to look like folds of cloth, and instead of a dais at one end, there was large table in the center, surrounded by comfortable chairs.

Lord Bannock sat at one end of a long mahogany table. "This morning I have estate business, but this afternoon I'd like to show you around." He tore a piece of bread from the loaf. "Do you ride?"

She didn't want to spend time with him; she wanted to see Jacques. "Why haven't I been allowed to see my guard?"

Bannock was a bulky man, his face and arms covered with brown freckles, his red beard streaked with gray. "I asked you if you rode!"

The thought of being with him repulsed her, but she had to be careful of his rising temper. "I'm still recovering from my journey." She could tell by his expression that her response angered him, so she continued in a different vein. "I would feel better if my maid were with me. I haven't seen her since we arrived."

Tess was summoned, and Bannock ordered, "Have Lady Lorraine's maid moved inside the manor. She can sleep in the attic with the female servants. After that is settled, help Lady Lorraine become familiar with the house and grounds." As he left the table, he said, "Maybe now your health will be restored."

Lorraine was in her sitting room a short while later when Matilde, her arm in a sling, barged in and launched herself at her mistress. They clung to each other happily. Matilde's dark hair was neatly combed and plaited on her neck. Her smile was the same as always, showing her big front teeth, and her eyes bulged the way they did when she was excited.

"When is the wedding?" Matilde asked.

"We talked for a long while last night, but Lord Bannock did not tell me his plans." Lorraine sat on her bed. "Tell me about Jacques. Have you seen him?"

"Please, don't be a fool," Matilde pleaded. "Marrying Lord Bannock is what your father wanted, and besides, we've nowhere else to go." She was about to say more, but there was a knock at the door.

"I've come to show you around." Tess set off at a brisk pace and Lorraine and Matilde hurried to follow her. "Now that Lord Bannock is back," Tess said, with a glance over her shoulder, "there's a rush to get everything finished."

At the opposite end of the house, Tess paused before a door. "This is the master's chamber, and your room is next to it."

Lorraine hesitated on the threshold.

"Go in," Tess encouraged.

The large bedchamber was furnished with an oak table and four matching chairs. A fire was banked with warm embers, awaiting Lord Bannock's return. Lorraine ran her fingers over the satin-smooth top of the table. A tapestry depicting a hunting scene hung on one of the walls. She averted her eyes from the massive oak bed with its carved posts and canopy, crossed the room, opened a door, and stepped into the mirror image of the master suite. The wardrobe, table and chairs were smaller than the masculine furniture on the other side.

"This alcove is for storing your gowns and chests." Tess rested her hand on the rough stone of the exterior wall. "A carpenter will finish the paneling before you move in."

Lorraine stared at the door between the two suites. The arrangement was so obvious. Lord Bannock could open this door and come for her. She closed her eyes and clutched at the door frame as the room began to spin. She couldn't do this.

"Are you all right?" Tess asked.

She steadied herself, took a breath and opened her eyes. "I'm fine," she lied.

Matilde and Tess were on either side of her, exchanging worried looks.

"Maybe we should see the rest of the house," Matilde suggested.

In many of the rooms, carpenters and stone masons were putting the final touches on mantels and moldings. In the great hall, a balcony stretched along one end of the rectangular room, and the Bannock Crest was carved in relief on the ceiling. Lorraine looked up and saw hundreds of tiny, diamond-shaped window panes anchored between lead frames.

Chateau Brèche didn't have glass in the window openings. In the winter, thin, semi-transparent vellum was installed while wooden shutters kept out the wind and rain. In the summer, the windows were uncovered to let air circulate.

"Look at the light." Lorraine pointed to the sunlight as it poured through the windows and broke into rainbows on the paneled walls.

Tess smiled proudly. "Lord Bannock hired a London man to design this house."

At the back of the great hall, they walked down a set of stairs into the cellars and emerged into a series of cavernous rooms. Great pillars supported the ceiling and bore the weight of the house above. If the richly decorated rooms in the manor house attested to Lord Bannock's wealth, so did the rows of stores in the cellars. Lorraine saw sacks of wheat, barley and oats. Dozens of crocks stored olives, spices, oil and sugar. Just the salt alone was worth several soldiers' yearly wages. One room held huge quantities of dried fruit. The next room contained big wooden bins of onions and cabbages.

Lorraine noted the abundant supplies and asked, "Does Cragmoor Castle also have a storeroom?"

"The castle has enough to support us during a siege, but most of this comes as taxes from the peasants and tenants," Tess said. "We also have a smokehouse and bake house."

"Why are there no walls around the house to keep out enemy forces?" Lorraine said, walking toward the open door.

"Unlike France, England is now united." Tess puffed up like a peacock. "Manor houses are for civilized countries."

"But, it doesn't seem safe."

"Here, we need only protect ourselves from robbers." Tess kept her superior tone, even when she resumed their tour. "Would you like to see the courtyard and gardens?"

"I know how busy everyone must be with all the preparations for Christmas. I'll walk in the sunshine with Matilde."

"I should introduce you." Tess seemed apprehensive.

Dismissing Tess with a toss of her head, Lorraine pulled Matilde into the courtyard. "I don't want to take any more of your time."

She could see the castle with its practice yard on the hill, the outbuildings and fields. In the center of the courtyard, a group of workmen were digging, and a great mound of earth lay heaped on the cobblestones.

Matilde tugged on Lorraine's sleeve and pointed to the gaping hole. "Joan showed this to me. When the new well is finished, water can be stored in a cistern at the house. They won't have to haul water from the castle well much longer."

They inched closer, trying to get a look while staying out of the way. The hole plunged deep into the earth. The workers stopped and bowed their heads in deference to her, shuffling uneasily as Lorraine crept to the edge, but one look into the depths was enough, and she retreated to a safe distance.

Shielding her eyes from the sun, she looked up the hill. "Let's climb to the castle."

"I don't think we should go up there," Matilde said.

"From the top of the tower, I'll be able to see the whole countryside. You don't have to come."

Matilde pulled her shawl tightly about her shoulders. "Don't go up there. Please."

"This is the first time I've been outside in a week. Simon and Tess watch everything I do."

Matilde looked anxious.

"You can wait in my room," Lorraine said. "I won't be long."

As soon as Matilde went back inside, Lorraine's gaze sharpened again on the castle. Within seconds she was across the courtyard, through the gate, and climbing the steep path toward the upper yard. As she passed the drill ring, men glanced at her and then resumed their training. They appeared to pay her little attention, but she was very interested in them. She wanted to know how many troops Lord Bannock commanded.

Soon she was high enough on the hillside to see the fields. Forested hills stretched away into the distance, and a swift stream wound down through the valley. Stone walls crisscrossed the meadows and provided a windbreak for sheep.

Wind whipped through her hair, and she wished she had donned her cloak before leaving the house. Climbing higher, she saw two guards standing quietly at the castle gatehouse. She held her chin high as she passed them.

Without the threat of an invasion, the bridge over the moat was down, and she crossed it. The portcullis gate was wide open, and she walked through. This castle was smaller than Chateau Brèche, and the keep, at least from the outside, looked uninviting. No wonder Lord Bannock had built a new house.

She stayed close to the wall and followed it around the perimeter until she was at the base of one of the four round towers. The breeze tugged the folds of her gown as she hurried up the stone steps to the wall walk and opened a heavy wooden door. She climbed the circular stone stairs, passing small, empty rooms as she wound her way higher and higher.

Lorraine found a small door that led into the tall, narrow turret and knew it was the highest point of all the castle buildings. Her fingers were stiff with cold and she could barely grasp the iron handle as she braced her right foot against the wall and used her whole body to pull. The door opened a crack, and she scrambled through before it slammed behind her. She climbed another set of stairs until she came to a window seat recessed into the outer wall. Wind whirled through the arrow loops as she sat down to catch her breath.

The countryside reminded her of the hills of Normandy, and she thought of her father. It would have pleased him to know that she had made it safely to England.

She looked down on the manor and felt wretched. She was sorry she would break her father's pledge, sorry to cause embarrassment to Lord Bannock, but she could not marry him.

Suddenly she knew she wasn't alone. She listened, every nerve alert. Seconds stretched into minutes before she saw Jacques climbing the stairs toward her. She jumped up, laughing. "How did you get away?"

"I'm not allowed to go beyond the outer walls." A strong wind ruffled his hair, and as he got closer, she reached to still the locks. "I didn't think you would come." His soft words carried like the clear tones of a church bell.

Joy surged through her as she slid her freezing arms inside his cape and held him tightly. "And I've had a thousand thoughts of you," she said. Her head tipped back as he kissed her throat. Her body stirred as the familiar spark began to build. When his hand stroked her breast, she moaned. He nuzzled her and traced kisses across her cheeks.

She wanted to be with him more than anything else in the world, but it was too dangerous. She whispered, "You have to leave."

His expression was tender and full of longing. "I will never leave you."

She wanted to beg him, command him, order him to stay. Desire nearly choked her, but she bit back her plea. "It's not safe."

His lips pressed over hers, and her body warmed; her mouth answered his as she grasped his shoulders, and her hand found its way to the back of his neck. Shamelessly, she pulled him closer and kissed him harder. She might have drowned in her swelling love, but he buoyed her, and his kisses anchored her and bound them together. Being with him was the only thing that mattered. "I cannot live without you," she murmured.

They both heard what sounded like the squeak of a door and froze. Jacques slipped down the steps and returned after a few minutes. "It was only the wind."

He braced his back against the wall and slid down to a sitting position. "Remember when we used to go to the wine cellar at Brèche? We couldn't stay apart."

She straddled his lap and fluffed her gown around them. "I want to feel you close to me." It only took a second, one look in his eyes to know he wanted her too. She lifted his tunic and unlaced the front of his leggings. He was swelling rapidly as she freed him. Without breaking eye contact, she moved above him and carefully lowered herself as he entered her.

He opened the front of her gown and slipped it off her shoulders. His fingers felt like icicles, but she relished the shock of his touch. He suckled her breasts, and she moaned.

She knew they should stop, but they couldn't, and their movements quickened. She was caught up in the passion, and soon she was trembling in his arms.

Jacques' eyes were tender and full of longing. "Will you marry me?"

"Yes."

Chapter Twenty-Two

Lord Bannock usually had a sense of peace when he was at Bannock Manor, but today, his first day home, he was already frustrated. Word of his return had traveled fast, and many of his land tenants had been waiting weeks for him to resolve their problems. He'd spent most of the day in his justice room, dispensing judgments and settling disputes in the shire.

Ben Wilson was a land tenant whose flock was dwindling by two or three sheep each month, even after the spring lambing season. His neighbor's flock seemed to be growing. Wilson marched about the room proclaiming loudly that wolves would feed on each flock in equal measure. He'd found no carcasses, yet the sheep mysteriously disappeared from his fields. The outraged farmer was going to take justice into his own hands if Lord Bannock didn't stop his neighbor's thieving and get his sheep back.

Bannock promised he would visit the neighbor's farm by the end of the week to look things over. If one of his tenants was stealing from another, Bannock's punishment would be harsh. He stuck his head out the door and saw half a dozen men milling in the corridor, waiting for an opportunity to share their worries. Damn them! He'd only been home one night, and he wanted time to sort out his own problems. Etienne Dannes had stolen a whole Norman chateau and all of its holdings, including the title of Marquis.

The next caller, John Davidson, slipped into the room with his head hanging low and his hat in his hands. Davidson hadn't paid his rent in two years, and he couldn't make his rent again this year. He was sorry, but he wanted to remind Lord Bannock that his wife had died three years ago and left him with six wee ones to raise, and he hadn't been able to find a new wife willing to live in his old cottage and care for the babes.

Bannock watched impassively while tears rolled down Davidson's cheeks. The two youngest ones had got loose a month back and drowned in the pond. The four that remained were still too young to be put into service, but their father offered, hopefully, that in a few years the girls could work in Bannock's house to help pay the rent.

"I cannot allow the rents to fall more than three years behind." Bannock reminded him of the well-known rule. "If I let your family stay for free, all the others will stop paying rent, too. For the past three years the weather has been favorable, and if you cannot make a living here in good years, how will you carry on during years of drought or flooding? I have taxes to pay to the King, and my soldiers depend on me for their wages. I keep a strongly fortified castle so that you and all the rest may live without fear of attack."

Bannock wished John Davidson hadn't come today. He didn't want to turn a man and his young children out of their home in winter, but he couldn't risk appearing weak before his tenants. "I'll give you until New Year's Day to come up with one year's rent."

"But Milord, 'tis just a fortnight away."

"Farm the children out to families who have lost young ones and need help with the work." Lord Bannock opened the door, dismissing the pitiful man.

Imagine a man complaining that he has too many children, too many to care for, and yet here I am at forty-one years without a single legitimate heir – no one to take care of me in my old age or to take over all of this when I die. I should have sons by now, sons to train for knighthood, sons to fight with me and watch my back in battle. A man with sons can make alliances with other families and spread stability through his land.

The day dragged as Bannock brooded in his justice room. Men took turns laying their burdens before him. Some problems were handled swiftly with a fine charged to the offending party, but other problems were more difficult, and he wanted to hear them with a clear head. For many of these, he delayed the decision for another day.

It was almost supper as he sat listening to yet another problem tenant. Ross Jones had been summoned after several of the other tenants had pleaded for Bannock to intervene. Jones beat his wife and children, as many men did, but the harsh punishments his neighbors had witnessed were inhuman.

Years ago, Bannock had learned that his pent-up anger was a valuable weapon, and today he used his growing frustration against Jones. He walked around his desk and with one swift movement lifted Jones out of his chair and shoved him against the wall. He squeezed the man's shoulders until it seemed the bones would snap.

"You'll be the one hobbling about with broken arms and legs if there's any more cracked bones in your household," Bannock snarled. A man had the right to control his wife and children, but brutality would not be tolerated. "Simon will be checking on you and reporting back to me." When Bannock released him, he tumbled to the floor and then scrambled out, mumbling apologies.

Simon came in and shut the door. "My lord, there is another problem. We must talk about Lady Lorraine."

"Yes, things are not as I expected."

"It's much worse than you think."

"Simon, you have never trusted women."

"They often give me reason to distrust them." Simon poured a tankard of ale and handed it to Bannock. "I was watching Lady Lorraine from the oriel window. She was in the courtyard and dismissed Tess, and her own maid, and then slipped off alone. She climbed the hill to the castle before I lost sight of her."

"I told her to learn her way around. Perhaps she was looking for me."

Simon's expression of doubt irritated him.

"The French boy came out of the stables and followed her. They were together a long while. Then the boy returned, and after several minutes, I saw Lady Lorraine coming back to the house. She's been hiding in her room ever since."

Bannock slammed his fist on the table with such force that Simon jumped. "Am I to have a woman who would rather run off with some bitch's mongrel pup than marry me? She may not care if she disgraces herself, but I will not allow her to foul my reputation. She's not to leave this house again without me. Have her eat alone in her room tonight, as I do not wish to throttle her."

Simon left to carry out his orders.

Bannock's next tenant to bring a complaint was Old Miller. His daughter was with child, and he blamed Will Johnson. Miller pleaded with Bannock to force young Will to marry the girl and take her to live in his household. By now her belly was large, and it was too late to avoid a scandal, but the old man hoped to preserve his family's good name.

Bannock sat at his desk and pretended to listen to Miller carry on about his daughter, but he was preoccupied with Frederick Bonville's daughter. Had Lorraine bedded with Jacques? He did not want scandals and bastards in his household, either.

"If the baby is Johnson's, then he'll have to marry her. I'll have the priest take care of it quietly."

"Thank you, sir. Thank you." Old Miller backed out of the room, bent low and groveling. "It's a relief, sir, it is. Thank you again."

Bannock waited until he could walk down the corridor without pounding his fist on Lorraine's door and confronting her directly. That would only cause more scandal.

As soon as he reached his bedchamber, he poured a cup of whisky. He remembered how he had vowed, on bended knee, to honor and protect the daughter and land of his good friend Marquis Bonville. He raised the top of his desk and pressed on a hidden latch. At his touch a drawer opened, and he took out the betrothal parchment. He and the Marquis had both signed copies and pressed their family seals into the wax. He had made it known to everyone that he was going to marry Lady Lorraine Bonville, but now she was making a fool of him. How difficult would it be to find another woman of noble birth to bear his sons?

As the night wore on, Bannock refilled his cup again and again. Whisky splashed on a corner of the parchment, and he stared at it. By the time the bottle was empty, he knew he had no choice. He'd given his word and sealed it formally. Their fates had been sealed when the parchment was signed. He would marry Lorraine, but he would let her know what he expected of her.

Even though it was late, he sent for Simon. "I need a woman, and Joan's heavy breasts will be a comfort."

"My lord, she has already gone to bed."

"I want a woman, and I'll have one now!" Simon hesitated, and Bannock demanded, "Bring her to me!"

For once he wanted someone to do his bidding without arguing. He wanted a wench. Besides, he always gave Joan pleasure. And soon the time would come when he would teach Lorraine about her duties.

§§§

On Christmas Eve, Simon began his rounds earlier than usual. He went first to the castle, where the feast preparations were underway. The manor house wasn't big enough to hold all of the guests, so the festivities would take place in the castle's great hall. He arrived just as the foresters were bringing in the Yule log. The men shoved the great tree trunk into the hearth as far as it would go. It would burn day and night until the Feast of the Epiphany. The twelve days of Christmas brought a break from work for the laborers, but for Simon and the household staff, it meant putting in more hours. Every room in the manor and castle was filled with guests, and the overflow of people spilled into the great hall. Many had spent the night on blankets before the hearth.

Several maids had already set to work sweeping out the old rushes and sprinkling the floor with a fresh covering mixed with scented herbs. Joan ran in, pinning up her hair. She reached for a broom and then looked up, and as she met Simon's gaze, she blushed. Things had gone well last night, he judged, and hoped Lord Bannock would be in better spirits today.

He summoned a group of boys to set out the trestle tables and benches while more workers placed green holly boughs and ivy vines along the mantels. Later the minstrels would arrive, and they were always hungry. Simon ordered the cooks to prepare extra loaves of bread and pots of cooked oats. Officially the celebrations began with the lighting of the Yule log, but everyone was feeling festive already.

Behind the castle kitchen, Richard, the head cook, turned a spitted pig and a deer over the roasting fires. His assistants were preparing game birds, pies and savory stews, and the tenants had contributed chickens, eggs and cheese as part of their rents.

Simon found Lord Bannock in the justice room reviewing his ledgers. "How are you feeling today, my Lord?"

Bannock pointed at the columns of profits. "It's been a good year, and I want to give generously to my knights."

"I've taken the liberty of ordering new clothes for the senior servants. Perhaps you'll want to give them their gifts tonight. It might work out well if you presented the knights with their new cloaks and belts tomorrow evening."

"Whatever you think best, Simon." Bannock looked moody and tired. "I count on you to handle these things."

Simon decided to take a chance. "What decision have you made regarding your marriage?"

"I want to be married as quickly as possible after Epiphany. Our Christmas guests can stay on for the wedding."

"With respect, my lord, I think you should delay. She's not a good match."

"She'll grow up once she's married. And once that boy is gone, she'll learn to rely on me."

"I wish you would send all three of them away," Simon said. "We have to keep her under constant watch. She skulks around the house trying to slip out, and Tess can barely keep up with her."

Bannock turned to gaze out the window. "I do not want to die in battle without a son to inherit my holdings. I am not going to make the same mistake as Marquis Bonville. His daughter has noble blood, and I will teach her loyalty."

"But –"

Bannock held up a hand to silence him. "Little girls grow up. They have duties, and they become mothers. They learn their place in life. All I need from Lady Lorraine is for her to give me sons."

§§§

On Christmas day, Lorraine sat in the carriage next to Lord Bannock as they rode to church in Tenney Village. She wore a burgundy silk gown that had been made for her, but it may as well have been sackcloth. She loathed the gown, and the fact that Bannock was wearing a matching tunic.

Everything he owned had to be created in his image, even her.

She seethed quietly, seated demurely with her hands in her lap, her eyes downcast. She'd risked only one glance at him. That was enough. His eyes burned with fury. How could a man with so much hatred dare set foot in a church? Lorraine's fingers strayed to her throat, and she touched Jacques' cross beneath the bodice of her gown.

Bannock stared at her, and she let her hands fall into her lap.

When they reached the church, he helped her from the carriage. She heard a clamor all around her and wanted to duck back inside, but Bannock held her arm and made her stand beside him. Across the road, standing three and four deep, villagers jostled and pointed. A young girl, scarcely older than Lorraine, caught her eye and waved shyly. Uncertain what to do, Lorraine waved back, and the crowd broke into cheers.

Bannock nodded and smiled, and held her hand as he led her up the steps. At the door, he turned to face the crowd. "Wave to them," he ordered.

She raised her hand, and the villagers clapped and roared approval.

A voice called, "Bannock!"

Others took up the cry. "Lord and Lady Bannock!"

She wasn't yet Lady Bannock, but they didn't care. She looked across the cheering throng and searched for Jacques. He was standing at the very back of the crowd, his dark head visible above the others.

Bannock's grip on her tightened. "You belong to me."

They entered the church, took their seats in the front pew, and then the knights entered in order of rank. Simon soon joined them and introduced a gaunt, elderly man dressed in brightly colored silks. "Lady Lorraine, may I present Sir Bertrand of Blakesdell."

The knight made a surprisingly deep bow for such an old man. He took Lorraine's hand and kissed it. "An honor to meet you, my lady."

Bannock greeted him heartily. "Bertrand, welcome home. How was your journey?"

"Utterly boring." Sir Bertrand winked at Lorraine. "I've brought back Flemish art and plenty of gold. The wool from your sheep commanded a good price, Lord Bannock."

"Excellent!" Bannock clapped a hand on his shoulder. "If you were bored because you weren't attacked and robbed, then I pray your work is always dull."

"The French may yet disrupt our trade, but we can talk of that another time."

"Sir Bertrand, now that you are home," Bannock said, "perhaps you will serve as an escort to Lady Lorraine?"

"I have an escort!" Lorraine wanted to bite her tongue, but she couldn't take back the outburst.

Simon interrupted, smiling. "Bertrand knows every inch of the estate."

Lorraine fought to control her temper. She didn't need to be spied on every moment, but Bannock and Simon had other ideas. The Mass began, and it was just as well that she couldn't speak. She was afraid of making another angry comment. Now she was going to have a doddering old knight following after her.

Too upset to take comfort in the Mass, she knelt and tried to pray, but instead, her mind explored ways she could leave Tenney Village, the manor house and Lord Bannock. She wanted to marry Jacques.

The somber service droned on, and the heavy incense made her stomach churn. Just when she thought it was almost over, the priest made the announcement. "On January tenth, Lady Lorraine Bonville of Normandy will marry Lord Brian Bannock."

She couldn't catch her breath. Her chest heaved, her heart beating too fast. She thought she was going to faint.

"This is what your father wanted," Bannock whispered. "This is where you belong."

The wave of dizziness passed. She glanced around and saw everyone looking at her, but no one seemed aware of her distress.

Bannock hadn't bothered to tell her about her own wedding day. The date had been set for just after the Feast of Epiphany, a mere twelve days away.

"That's not enough time for the reading of the banns." She kept her head down, avoiding the curious stares. "Even in England the priest must make an announcement for three consecutive Sundays prior to a wedding."

"The announcement will be posted on the church door." Bannock held up his heavy coin purse and smiled down at her. "The banns can be bypassed if I pay for a marriage license."

"We should wait until midsummer to marry." She refused to look at him, didn't want him to see how desperate she felt. Perhaps appealing to his pride might sway him. "More people can travel then, and we'll be able to have a grand ceremony."

"I may be in London by summer." His gaze moved to her breasts and then to her waist. "I want you with child by then. There's no reason to wait any longer."

His hungry look sickened her, and she turned away, but she could still feel his eyes on her, could feel his calloused fingers on the back of her wrist. It was all she could do to remain in her seat.

After the service ended, they emerged from the church into the shadow of the great Norman tower. Bannock shielded her, pushing his way to the carriage through the crush of well-wishers, and she was forced close against him.

When they reached the manor, she took her place next to Bannock at the high table. She endured the rituals as they washed their hands, the wine was poured, and the soup was served. Platters of food arrived and were replaced with more as soon as they were emptied. Bannock devoured one trencher of meat and then another, quaffing cup after cup of wine.

During a lull between courses, Bannock beckoned his knights to approach, and presented them with Christmas gifts. Each man received a surcoat, cloak or belt. They bowed graciously, praising him, swearing their allegiance.

In spite of herself, Lorraine admired his generosity. His estate obviously made a good income, and he shared his fortune with those who served him.

The feast seemed endless, and even after most of the food was gone, people continued drinking and laughing. Game boards came out, and at the far end of the hall, peasants began playing knucklebones. Everyone was vying for a position and calling out a bet. It didn't take long for Lorraine to learn the simple rules. One player tossed a bone into the air then tried to snatch up his neighbor's bone pile, catching his bone before it hit the table. The men laughed all the harder when a dog, fangs bared, snapped up a bone from a man who wasn't guarding his pile. The unlucky fellow swore, cuffed the dog, and then recoiled from the snarling teeth.

"You lost that one, fair as a maiden's tits, you did," his companion declared.

"Guard your bones, I say," another man taunted.

At the high table, Bannock set up a different game. He turned a wooden knob, revealing a hollow center in the board, and let the game pieces, dark and light marble balls, fall into his hand. Sir Bertrand sat down across from him and began placing white balls in indentations on the board. Bannock had two gray marble balls that he placed on the board opposite Bertrand's pieces.

Lorraine leaned forward to watch the play. It was a strategy game, that much was clear, but she didn't understand the seemingly random moves.

"Bannock always plays the fox," a man said.

She looked up to see one of the knights, a handsome young man, leaning over her shoulder. She tried to remember his name.

"I'm Robert," he said with a slight bow.

She murmured a greeting and turned her attention back to the game.

"It's Fox And Geese, my lady. Lord Bannock has the foxes, and poor Bertrand, well, he's an old goose, isn't he?"

She looked at Robert and saw that he was smiling fondly.

"If a fox jumps a goose, he captures him." Robert pointed to the collection of white marbles that Lord Bannock had gathered in an empty cup.

As she watched, Bannock jumped a gray ball over a white one, collected it, and dropped it into the cup. He picked up the cup and rattled it, but Bertrand ignored him.

"Is Sir Bertrand letting him win?" Lorraine whispered.

Robert laughed softly. "Laying a trap, I'd say. The only way the geese survive is by surrounding each fox until he's penned in."

Bannock played aggressively, capturing Bertrand's pieces as fast as he could, but Bertrand was cautious and methodical, sacrificing a lot of geese. The play went back and forth for a long while.

"Bannock's outnumbered," Lorraine said.

"Right," Robert agreed. "It's almost impossible for the fox to win. That's why Bannock likes it."

Bertrand closed the final gap so that the last fox was surrounded.

To Lorraine's surprise, Bannock laughed.

He poured a cup of wine for Bertrand. "You're older than my castle, Bertrand, and one of the smartest men alive."

"The mummers are starting," Robert said, as a hush fell over the hall.

The board game at the high table had engrossed her attention, but now Lorraine saw that other tables had been pushed aside, and an acting troupe began an elaborate pantomime of the Christmas story. Even without words or music, it was easy to follow as Joseph and Mary searched for a place to stay until they found lodging in the manger.

In the darkened quiet of the great hall, Lorraine saw Jacques on a bench along one of the walls. He met her gaze and smiled. Her heart twisted in her chest as she yearned to go to him, to touch him, to hold him in her arms. Being separated from him was painful, and she could see it on his face too. He missed her.

Bannock didn't say anything, uttered no sound that would have disturbed the performance, but his hand locked around her wrist and stayed there until the last mummer took a bow, and the hall, silent for so long, erupted in cheers.

Only then did Lorraine risk another glance at Jacques, but he was gone, and the bench where he'd been sitting had been moved to make room for dancing.

She pulled her arm free from Bannock's grasp. "I'll go to my room now," she said.

To her intense frustration, Bannock signaled Bertrand, who was instantly at her side. "Please see to it that Lady Bannock goes directly to her bedchamber."

Bertrand made one of his deep, ingratiating bows and offered his arm to her. She gritted her teeth and allowed him to lead her from the hall.

When they reached her room, she paused on the threshold. "You gave Lord Bannock a good game, Sir Bertrand."

He inclined his head. "It is wise to know when to retreat, my lady."

As soon as the door shut behind her, Lorraine heard the familiar scrape of a key in the lock.

§§§

Jacques slept in the castle guardhouse under the watch of the shift captains, but he wasn't allowed to train with the soldiers and was shunned by them all. At the stables, the stable master heard his French accent and shook his head no. Desperate to prove himself useful so that he would be allowed to stay, Jacques finally convinced the blacksmith to give him a try.

The forge was far behind the stables, a safe distance from the other buildings, and it was there that he learned to hammer horseshoes and repair riding tack. During the day, stripped to the waist and standing by the hot fire, he tried to keep his mind on his work. He wanted to keep busy, hoping that the harder he worked, the less heartache he would feel, but even when he fell onto his pallet at night, exhausted and disappointed, he was consumed with thoughts of Lorraine.

On his fourth day, Charles, the blacksmith, after observing that he was competent, sat on a keg and sipped from a crock.

"You are not as bad as they say," Charles said. "For a French man."

Ignoring the insult, Jacques' hammer struck rhythmically against the molten metal.

Charles wiped spittle from his lips. "Enjoy your stay while it lasts, you poor bastard. Simon plans to turn you out after the Feast of the Epiphany. He can't wait to be rid of you." While Charles spoke, he rummaged in a leather sack. His hands shook, but he managed to find a broken sword blade. "This was made by the French. It's not as good as English craftsmanship, but it killed a man just the same."

"Why not melt it down?"

At first the blacksmith didn't seem to hear the question, but after a long pause he said, "It killed my son." He spat at Jacques' feet. "He should be here instead of you."

The whisky was taking its toll, and the bag was about to slip from the blacksmith's grasp. Jacques caught it and hung it on a hook next to a ring of keys. "What are those keys for?"

Charles swayed drunkenly. "I've a set as good as Simon's, one key for every lock on the estate."

§§§

Lorraine couldn't get away from Sir Bertrand. He was with her every time she stepped foot outside the manor house. She knew that the farther he walked, the more he limped, and that he liked nothing better than for her to sit in the solar with the ladies so that he could prop his leg on a stool and rest.

When his attention faltered, she tried to slip away, but he soon roused himself and came after her. She took a perverse pleasure in going for long walks, just to see how long he could hold out, but he never complained, even when his face was twisted in pain. Each day she explored Bannock's property, desperately searching for a means of escape.

On the day of the Feast of Epiphany, wood was stacked for a huge bonfire in a field just beyond the house. She was about to go outside when Bannock stopped her.

"The bonfire is for commoners," he said.

"I want to see it. Your tenants enjoy it when I spend time with them." If there was any hope of finding Jacques, it had to be tonight when she could mingle with the crowd.

Bannock relented but made her wait for Bertrand.

As soon as the old codger came, she set off toward the field as fast as she could walk, not caring what the pace did to his sore leg. They arrived in time to see the flames catch the great pile of timber. A shower of sparks rained down, and the crowd roared with excitement. Soon the fire was so high it illuminated the hillside. She saw Jacques standing by himself at the edge of the field. A few minutes later she saw him again, climbing the hill toward the castle. He crossed the drawbridge.

The music began: drums, horns and lutes playing a dancing tune. Lorraine caught Bertrand's hand and whirled him into the line. He looked surprised as she pushed him toward the men's row, and she took her place opposite with the women. They came together, and she curtsied. They moved apart. They came together, linked arms and twirled then broke apart, and the lines moved in opposite directions. The dancers clapped in time with the music. Lorraine twirled the next partner and the next.

She caught a glimpse of Bertrand, and noted when he left the line, completely exhausted. He limped to a large stone near the fire ring and sat heavily, puffing and rubbing his leg.

Lorraine kept dancing, moving slowly down the line toward the edge of the field. She whirled with the last dancer and then kept going, running as fast as she could toward the castle, and toward Jacques.

She was out of breath by the time she reached the base of the wall walk, but she bolted up the stairs that led to the tower, and pushed through the door.

Jacques caught her in his arms and kissed her. "I didn't think you'd come."

"We don't have much time."

He held her at arm's length. "They're going to send me away tomorrow."

"I'll go with you." She clung to him. "We'll sell my jewelry and go where no one knows us or cares who we are."

"I'll steal a horse from the stables." His arms tightened around her. "Watch for me tomorrow night, and when I have everything ready, I'll light a candle by the well and hold it up for you to see. Wait until the courtyard is empty, then come to me."

"Simon locks my door at night."

"I can get a key. Send Matilde to meet me at the blacksmith's forge. Tell her to come after dark. Find the key that opens your door and send the rest back with Matilde."

"What if I can't get out in time?"

"If you're not there by dawn, I'll wait for you in a shepherd's hut in the valley. We passed it on our way here." He kissed her, pulled the dagger from his belt and pressed the hilt into her hand. "If you have to travel alone, you'll need this."

Her fingers traced the carved pattern of the Bonville griffin. "This was my father's dagger."

"It was always meant to protect you."

§§§

Sir Bertrand lay flat against the stone of an archer's seat. His bones ached and he would probably be limping worse than ever tomorrow, but it was a small price to pay to defend his lord's honor. Lady Lorraine had disappeared into the upper part of the turret. He heard the faint murmur of conversation, and waited. His back was in agony. Hearing the scrape as the door in the upper turret opened, he held his breath and slipped deeper into the shadowed crevice. The whispers grew louder and he recognized Lady Lorraine's voice; she was speaking with her French guard.

"Je t'aime," she called softly to her hidden companion as she fled down the stairs, and then there was the rush of cold air as the door at the bottom of the tower opened and closed again.

Bertrand waited. A short while later the lean figure of Lady Lorraine's escort descended. Bertrand remained motionless as the boy walked slowly past his hiding place. He could have drawn his sword and disemboweled him, but it wasn't his place to take the life of a traitor. That honor was for Lord Bannock.

§§§

The following morning, Lorraine hummed to herself while Matilde helped her dress. "I have a favor to ask you." She smiled at Matilde's fearful look. "No, no, nothing bad. Jacques is going to borrow a set of keys from the blacksmith. I want you to bring them to me."

"What are you planning?" Matilde backed away, shaking her head. "If I get caught, they'll hang me for a thief."

Lorraine pulled on her stockings. "They are not going to hang a maid for following her lady's orders." She rolled the garters to the top of the stockings and adjusted them. "Simon has no right to treat me so."

"It's only a few more days, and then you'll be married."

"I cannot gain respect if I'm locked away in a small room."

Finally, she convinced Matilde to meet Jacques and get the keys. After her maid left, Lorraine wrapped the dagger in her cloak, bundled her jewelry together, and stuffed it all into her wardrobe chest. When the time came to leave, she would take as many clothes as she could wear, her jewels, her cloak, and Jacques' book of verses. That was all she could carry.

§§§

Simon slipped out of Lorraine's room and saw Matilde coming down the corridor. She had a folded garment in her hands.

When she saw him, she stuttered, "My lady's laundry."

Simon scowled at Matilde, and then watched as the clumsy fool nervously stumbled and almost dropped her washing. She had no idea the dagger that Jacques had given Lorraine was now tucked into his boot.

"If I ever find out that you've betrayed Lord Bannock, I will turn you out of this house," Simon warned. "I'll make sure you are homeless, penniless and helpless. If you want to stay here you should rethink your allegiances."

He paused to let his words sink in and saw the terror in her eyes. Satisfied, he brushed past her and hurried to the justice room.

§§§

Matilde lifted the lid on Lorraine's wardrobe trunk and dropped the heavy ring of keys inside. She had learned the truth about their plans, and although both Jacques and Lorraine had begged her to leave with them, she wasn't about to set off on another dangerous journey. They had nowhere to go, and if they were caught, Bannock would be merciless. If he tried to turn her out, she would beg his forgiveness, even if she were demoted to a scullery maid. She wiped her shaking hands on her apron, wishing there was something she could do to dissuade Lorraine from leaving.

§§§

Bannock listened to Simon's report and felt his face turning hot. Had it been any other knight, he might have doubted the veracity of the report, but Bertrand was trustworthy. And Simon had checked his story.

Simon held the evidence, the Bonville dagger with the carved handle. "I found this in her trunk."

Bannock took the dagger and cursed. There was no mistaking the griffin on the hilt. He'd seen Frederick Bonville give this dagger to Jacques. Simon hesitated, and Bannock asked, "What else did they say?" Simon held his tongue until Bannock thundered, "Tell me what they said!"

"Forgive me, my Lord. They plan to run away."

§§§

It had been dark for hours, and snow fell steadily as Jacques scurried from shadow to shadow, heading for the courtyard. The retaining wall around the new well wasn't finished, and stones and loose dirt were piled beside it. Shivering, Jacques crouched behind the rubble and watched the back of the house. The only horse he'd been able to steal was the old beast that drew the baker's cart, and it was tethered and waiting at the shepherd's hut, along with some food. He pulled a candle from his pocket. Even in the falling snow, its glow would be visible. He was grateful for the snowfall because it would cover their footsteps.

Jacques began to move toward the torch that burned in a sconce beside the service door. He hadn't gone more than a step when the door opened and two of Bannock's soldiers came out. He quickly ducked back down. They looked around and then disappeared up the path, heading toward the castle.

Minutes later the door opened again, and Bannock stepped into the courtyard. He cocked his head as though listening. Snowflakes landed in his hair and blew around his uncloaked shoulders.

Jacques ducked down again, his heart hammering.

§§§

Lorraine watched from her window, waiting for Jacques' signal. It was so black outside she was afraid to blink for fear of missing the candle's flame. In the dark room, she stood sweating under two chemises and two gowns, but the layers of clothes would keep her warm during her escape. The key hung by a ribbon underneath her skirt. It was heavy, longer than her hand, and with a complicated design at the locking end.

She heard another key unlocking her door, but it was only Tess. "Lord Bannock asked me to check on you, and I can see why. You'll take sick if you stand by that cold window all night." Tess drew the shutters across the window, slid the bolt into place, and then turned for the tray she'd brought. "Why are you still dressed?" Tess pushed a mug of hot cider into her hands and bustled around the room, turning down the bedcovers and rearranging things.

"I want to be alone," Lorraine stammered.

"Lord Bannock asked me to keep you company." Tess came closer. "May I help you get ready for bed?"

"No!" Lorraine backed closer to the window. "I – I –" She wanted to scream at Tess to leave her alone. "I might take a walk."

"You're not leaving this room; Lord Bannock's instructions."

§§§

Jacques was staring so hard at Bannock that he didn't hear the step behind him until it was too late. A hand fell on his shoulder, and then an iron-like grip pinned his arms. He struggled but couldn't free himself.

Bannock stepped around the well. "You're no match for me, boy."

The heavy fabric of his cloak hampered his movements almost as much as the grip on his arms.

Bannock pitched his voice low. "You'll pay for your betrayal."

One of the soldiers dug his knee into Jacques' back, and the unlit candle fell into the snow.

Bannock held up the dagger. "Why did you give this to Lorraine?"

"For her protection!"

"I protect her now."

Jacques struggled out of the soldier's grasp and broke loose. The man caught his cloak, dragged him back, and wrapped his arm around Jacques' throat. He couldn't breathe and kicked ferociously.

"Hold him," Bannock cursed. He struck Jacques across the face. "Thieving bastard!"

Jacques spat blood and shook his head to clear his vision. He saw the flash of the knife, but his flailing did no good.

Bannock stabbed underhanded, driving the blade into Jacques' ribs. He shoved the knife with such force that Jacques' feet left the ground, and he would have collapsed but two men held him from behind.

He heard the snap of the breaking blade even before he felt the pain. His vision clouded. He tried to speak, but only blood bubbled out of his mouth. He gazed into Bannock's face and saw no hint of remorse.

"She would never be my wife as long you are alive."

Jacques' head sagged and the men let him fall.

"Bury him in the trench tonight, and I'll order the well finished tomorrow."

Jacques lay in the snow as the soldiers began digging his grave. He heard the clinking of the shovels as they scraped at the frozen ground. Snow fell on his body, his face. He didn't want to die – not now, not tonight. Lorraine was waiting for him. He had to see her, to explain. He shivered violently.

From beneath him, a stream of blood was carving a groove in the snow. Tiny wafts of steam rose from the warm blood and swirled into the air. When he tried to breathe, he felt the blade shift, and heard a frightening sound of air escaping from his chest. More snow covered him, and his bones ached. He willed his body to rise, but it couldn't.

The fear slipped away, replaced by a deeper ache, a bitter sadness. He wanted to call out, but couldn't make a sound. Lorraine would never know. Above him, Bannock's men labored. His body shuddered, and another sharp pain tore at his lungs. He was so cold. Suddenly the shaking stopped, and a weight crushed his chest.

Chapter Twenty-Three

Lorraine paced back and forth across her small sitting room, and the iron key bounced against her thigh. When she realized how nervous she must appear, she stopped abruptly. "I want you to leave," she said to Tess.

"Lord Bannock ordered me to stay." Tess remained planted in her chair. "All night."

"Then I'm going to bed." Shaking with tension, she walked into the bedroom. How dare he.

She slammed the door, but Tess opened it and pulled her chair between the two rooms. Her intentions were clear; she worked for Bannock.

"If I'm not going to have privacy, I'll remain dressed." Lorraine blew out the candle and flopped down on the bed, but she didn't stay there. How long could Jacques wait outside on such a cold night? As the hours crept toward dawn, she paced between the window and the door trying to stay awake. When she finally sat down, her head dropped to her chest and she dozed.

As light sifted into the room, she awoke to find Tess still watching her. Lorraine averted her eyes and sat up, and then, with an exaggerated yawn, climbed out of bed. She kept her back toward Tess so the housekeeper wouldn't see the fear on her face. "I need to put on fresh clothes," she said. "Will you please send Matilde?"

"You won't see her until after tomorrow's wedding. Lord Bannock was in a rare rage last night, and he put it clear to us that we would all pay if you were not at the church tomorrow."

I hate him. Lorraine opened the shuttered window and looked down at the empty courtyard, and her eyes filled with tears.

Someone knocked at the door, Tess opened it and admitted Joan. The two women exchanged a knowing glance.

"The seamstress will be here soon to give Lorraine a fitting," Joan said as she took the key from Tess and relocked the door behind her. Joan added wood to the fire. "Your room is nice and warm. She'll be glad to work in here."

If they found she had a key, they'd take it. "I need to use the garderrobe," Lorraine said.

"What do you think the chamber pot is for?" With one foot, Joan slid the ceramic pot from under the bed. She looked at it pointedly and gave a mocking smile. "I won't be helping you with that."

Lorraine shut the door in her face, and in the few moments that she had to herself, she quickly removed her extra layer of clothes and hid them with the key. She closed the wardrobe chest as Joan pushed into the room.

"The seamstress is here."

Lorraine stood on a stool for more than an hour while the seamstress piled on layers over her chemise: silk under gown with a stiff skirt and then a satin overskirt held in place with straight pins. The seamstress pulled and pinned the material and pricked Lorraine's flesh until she was afraid her blood might stain the gown. Finally, the heavy brocade was lifted over her head and fastened at the back by dozens of tiny bows.

Joan pulled the laces so tight that Lorraine could scarcely breathe.

Lorraine ran a hand over the satin brocade of her wedding gown, and a lump rose in her throat. Her father had purchased the fabric for her, and seeing it reminded her how much she missed him. It seemed ridiculous that the cloth had made it all this way, and so many lives had been lost.

I have to get out of here. Her stomach roiled, and she clamped her lips against the rising nausea. The weight of the heavy garments dragged at her, and she felt trapped in the suffocating cloth.

"I need some air." Lorraine stepped off the stool and ran to the window. Outside, a gang of men mortared stones around the new well. She tugged at the dress, not caring if it tore. "Take this off me." She collapsed into a chair as the room began to spin. She buried her face in her hands. Had Jacques already left?

"Let me help you," the seamstress scolded. "Crying will only make it more difficult."

Simon's voice sounded on the other side of the door. "I would like a word, if I may." His tone suggested that he wouldn't be refused.

Joan pulled an old gown over Lorraine's head and shoved stockings and slippers onto her feet. The seamstress gathered up her materials.

Joan and the seamstress scurried out as soon as Simon came in.

"We should review the guest list." He handed her a parchment, the ink so fresh it stained her fingers. "At the reception tomorrow, you'll have the privilege to meet, among others, the Lords Berkeley, Norfolk and Mowbray, and their wives." Simon explained the lineage of several prominent local families, and her attention drifted. He rapped his knuckles on the arm of her chair like an impatient tutor. "You don't have any idea what is expected of you, do you?"

"If you mean that I am expected to curtsy until my knees ache and nod agreeably with everything the lords say, then I think I know my place very well."

"Entertaining Lord Bannock's guests is just one thing you must learn to do." Simon leaned close. "Pleasing your husband is another."

He was trying to intimidate her and if she was stuck here and gave in now, she'd spend the rest of her married life cowering to him. Lorraine forced herself to meet his gaze. "I will be Lady Bannock, and you are a servant."

Simon rose slowly. He glared at her, his anger palpable. "I know what Lord Bannock needs, and it will go easier for you if you placate him."

She bit back a retort as he stalked out the door. Why bother fighting with him? With luck, she'd be gone by tonight. She pulled on a second chemise and tied the ribbon with the key at her waist. She hid her jewels and Jacques' book of poems in her cloak, then stared out the window, waiting for dark.

Her plans would be ruined if Tess stayed with her again.

Lorraine watched carriages arrive carrying nobles and landowners. Carts delivered large quantities of food and ale, and the servants hurried back and forth from the bake house to the manor and up to the castle. The male servants carried trunk after trunk for the arriving guests. She saw Bannock admonishing the stone masons, directing them to finish the retaining wall around the well. Every time she looked, he was down there, watching the progress of the workers.

He smiled at her before she could duck away. Why was he lingering in the courtyard like that? He kept looking at her window.

By the time Joan brought her supper, Lorraine was ravenous. The maid didn't speak, just left a plate of cold meat and bread, a mug of ale, and a pitcher of water to wash in.

A while later, she heard a brief knock, the latch turned, and Bannock came into her room.

"You shouldn't be in here," she said, flustered by his sudden appearance.

He seemed unconcerned by the impropriety. "By tomorrow night you'll be sharing my bed." His swagger made her wonder if he'd had too much to drink, but when he came closer she didn't smell whisky, just his distinctly male odor. "I've brought you a wedding gift." He opened a velvet bag and showed her a pearl necklace.

She said nothing as he fastened the double strand of pearls around her throat.

"I want you to wear these tomorrow," he said, pushing his face close to hers.

She recoiled, but he placed his hand behind her head and kissed her. She gasped and wiped her mouth. "Don't!"

He laughed, captured her face and kissed her again.

She shoved his chest but wasn't strong enough to break his hold. Her fighting seemed to amuse him because he laughed even more, then grasped her chin and forced her to look into his face.

"If you fight me tomorrow, I will hurt you." He strode out.

She unhooked the necklace and dropped it on her dressing table. And then, as an afterthought, she opened the satchel and added it to her other jewels. She could always sell it.

Lorraine touched the key at her waist, reassuring herself that it was still there. Jacques would be at the shepherd's hut by now, waiting for her.

She sat on her bed and waited for dark, praying that no one else would come and torment her. She wouldn't lie down, wouldn't risk falling asleep tonight. When all was quiet, she spent another half hour listening at her door. At last she decided to use the blacksmith's key. She pushed it into the lock, but it didn't turn. Panicked, she tried again, but the key wouldn't budge.

Each key on the household ring had been a different size and weight, and she had tested nearly all of them until finding the one that worked. Could she have pulled the wrong key off the ring? She tried again, holding her breath, moving the key gingerly, slowly, testing it first one way and then the other. There. She felt it catch even though it hadn't slipped all the way in. She closed her eyes, concentrating, and jiggled it, but the key still didn't turn. She eased it back, then a little farther in, and finally felt the teeth settle into the lock. It grated and turned, and she pushed open the door.

From the corridor came the sound of light steps, and she heard Tess and Joan chatting. Her heart was pounding as she closed the door again.

"Tell the cooks to start heating water earlier tomorrow," Tess said. "And get the scullery girls up, too."

"They're up before dawn as it is," Joan complained.

"Use the hearth poker if anyone lags," said Tess.

Lorraine leaned against the door, holding tight to the latch. As she expected, Tess checked to make sure it was locked, but Lorraine held it firmly and it didn't move.

"Lady Lorraine," Tess called, "do you need anything else tonight?" When there was no answer, she said to Joan, "She must already be asleep. She was awake most of last night and didn't look well today."

"She's too frail," Joan said. "A man likes a bit more flesh on a woman. Why would he choke on a sparrow if he could dine on pheasant?"

"Don't say anything," Tess advised.

"She's too scrawny, and I don't mind who I tell."

"Hush." Tess sounded amused. "I'll sleep out here on the floor. Last night I never slept a wink in that chair, and I had so much to do today."

"See you in the morning, then. I would like to get some sleep myself." Joan's voice faded away. "Unless his lordship wants my company again."

So Bannock bedded Joan, and Joan wanted her to know it. The loud boasting had been for her ears; everyone else must already know.

She tiptoed to the window. A group of knights staggered drunkenly up the hill to the castle barracks. The stable boys, followed by their dogs, wandered off to bed. It was too dark to see the distant outbuildings, but she could discern the faint glow of the blacksmith's forge far beyond the stables.

It was much later before the sounds in the corridor faded for the night. Tess had been snoring rhythmically for over an hour.

Lorraine opened the door cautiously, grateful that in the newly built house, the hinge made no sound. Stepping over the sleeping housekeeper, she pulled the door shut and headed for the stairs. All was quiet at the landing as she crept down the first flight, making her way to the great hall. The peasants slept scattered about the room. Lorraine held her breath, terrified that a cry of alarm would sound. One careful step at a time, she tiptoed across the length of the long room and down the stairs that led into the cellars.

She hid behind the grain sacks until she was certain she was alone, then made her way to the outside door.

She chose a spot where she could hide without being seen from the house. The horses and lads were quiet, but a dog barked. She hurried on. Near the bake house, she heard boots crunching on the frozen ground and stepped into the cover of bushes just as a pair of guards strode past. A branch gouged her ankle and she stifled a gasp.

"Did you hear something?"

"Perhaps someone's getting cozy in the bake house. It's too cold even for robbers. Leave them be."

Lorraine was afraid to breathe. Just when she thought she couldn't stand it, the sound of cart wheels grinding over the icy road caught the guards' attention.

"Hold there! Hold, I say."

She peeked out and saw a guard put up his hand. A tinker's cart pulled to a stop, the tin ware, cups and knives jangling like dull bells.

"You're out late," one guard said.

"The cook wanted all of his knives sharpened." The old tinker slurred his words and lurched in his seat. "I worked my arse off, and I needed a bit of rest after supper."

"And a lot of ale. You're already celebrating his lordship's wedding. You had best stay at the castle 'til daybreak. If you fall out on the road, you'll be frozen before the sun wakes you."

"My horse knows the way if I doze a little."

"Well then, good morrow."

The guards hastened toward the warmth of the guard house, and Lorraine heard the door slam as they shut themselves inside. The jingle of the tinker's cart continued down the road.

Moments later she dashed after it, staying in the shadow of the trees at the edge of the lane. The wheels of the cart stuck in a rut, and before they pulled free, she climbed into the back and curled into a tight ball, covered by her cloak. She heard the whip snap and the cart began moving again. The jangle sounded louder and her teeth chattered. The cart swayed, rocking to the pace of the old horse.

She couldn't see and had no way to judge when they were near the fork in the road. One path led toward Tenney Village, the direction the tinker would surely go, and the other fork led through the valley, past the shepherd's hut and beyond, toward Tetbury.

She waited until she thought they had gone far enough, and was just getting up her nerve to jump when the cart slowed to a stop. She tried to discern what the tinker was up to when the sound of snoring reached her. Slipping off as easily as she had climbed aboard, Lorraine ran for the cover of the trees.

The guard's warning that the tinker might freeze worried her, so she picked up a stone and threw it at the horse. It missed, but the animal whinnied.

"What? What is it, old fella?" With a snap of the reins, the cart pulled away.

The woods were dark and the snow deeper here. The tinker used a lantern hooked over a pole to light his way, but she hadn't even brought a candle. The moon was a sliver in the sky, drifting in and out of the clouds, and her eyes adjusted enough to let her make out the road.

Lorraine walked until she could no longer feel her frozen feet. She stumbled and caught herself, only to trip on a tree root a few steps later. She landed hard on one knee, and when she lifted her skirt, blood smeared on her fingers. Limping another few yards, she sank onto a fallen tree. It was a mistake; she might freeze to death. Her cloak did little good against the bitter wind, her teeth chattered and her knee throbbed. It was harder to walk through the snow than she had anticipated, but she had to keep moving. She lurched to her feet and continued walking. Somewhere ahead she would find the hut, and Jacques.

When she first heard the whicker of a horse, she was shaking so hard it didn't register and she just kept walking. Several minutes later, she thought she heard something again but couldn't be sure. The horse whinnied once more, and she crept cautiously toward the sound.

Relief flooded her when she saw the hut with a lone horse tied out front. It pulled at its tether and snorted a warning, but no one came out. She inched toward the door and pushed it open. Jacques' belongings were in a corner. She picked up his bedroll, wrapped it around her shoulders and inhaled the scent of him. Where was he?

The simple hut had a dirt floor and no windows, and the walls were wooden planks weathered to gray. It wasn't much bigger than a horse's stall, and she thought about bringing the animal inside for warmth but decided against it. The mare was too nervous, and if it started suddenly, she couldn't control it. Kindling was ready in the hearth, but the smoke might attract attention.

She searched through Jacques' bag and found four apples, a loaf of bread and a thick wedge of cheese. She dug in her satchel to get the knife but couldn't find it. She dumped everything out and looked around carefully. The knife was gone. Fear settled into the pit of her stomach.

Wind whipped around the hut, and the horse nickered. Maybe their plan was foolhardy. If Jacques didn't arrive by dawn, she would have to move on before they could track her.

She stomped around the little hut, hands tucked into her armpits as she tried to keep warm. Eventually, she sat on the bench, huddled in Jacques' blanket, praying he was somewhere safe.

It seemed like hours later when she heard barking dogs and galloping horses. Through a chink in the wall, she saw men on horseback circling the hut, and smelled the pitch of burning torches.

A soldier yelled, "We know you're in there."

She backed into the farthest corner.

"We're going to burn this hut down whether you're in it or not!" The rough voice taunted, "Come out, young miss. Or you'll be roasted."

The tethered horse out front whinnied and tried to pull free.

"You can marry Lord Bannock, or we can give your cooked flesh to the wolves, but we can't leave you behind alive."

A heavy boot broke through the door, and a pair of dogs charged in, their fangs inches from her legs. She jumped onto the bench, but it tipped and sent her sprawling. She landed on her back and threw up her arms as the dogs went into a frenzy. They were over her, snapping and snarling as she tried to roll away. At a sharp command, the dogs backed off. She lay where she had fallen on the dirt floor, afraid to move.

A man in armor reached down and yanked her to her feet. "You'll be back before daylight, before the guests know what you've done." He grabbed her around the waist more tightly than necessary, dragged her outside and threw her roughly onto his horse. He climbed up behind her, his forearms pinning her as he snapped the reins.

Lorraine jabbed at him but only bruised her elbows against his chainmail sleeves. One of his comrades cut Jacques' horse free and then threw a torch into the hut. She twisted in the saddle. All around her the men were in armor, metal visors pulled over their faces, their identities hidden.

"My jewels," she cried, "I left them. The pearl necklace Lord Bannock gave me is in there!"

A knight jumped off his horse, ducked inside and was out again in an instant, holding up her belongings. He lashed the bag to his saddle and remounted.

Cold wind stung her face as they galloped toward Bannock Manor, and icy air rushed down her throat and choked her. She clung to the saddle with both hands, unable to brush away the tears that were coursing down her cheeks. Would Jacques know what had happened?

They arrived at the manor just before dawn, and she was taken back to her room.

Tess was waiting, rigid with fury, and Lorraine saw fear mixed with anger on the housekeeper's face. "If they hadn't brought you back for the wedding, I'd have been dismissed. I've nowhere else to go." Spittle flew from Tess' lips. "I could have been beggared because of you!"

Lorraine didn't say a word as Joan and Tess prepared her for the ceremony. A bathing tub was brought in and half-filled with tepid water. They were furious, scrubbing vigorously with harsh lye soap to remove the smoke and grime from her pale skin. The soap burned the cut in her knee, and the gash opened again and bled into the water.

She examined her skin, but the knights hadn't really hurt her. Of course, they wouldn't dare. All of their tactics had been to scare her. Other than the cut, she had no marks on her skin.

Tess took the cross from around her throat and set it aside. "You'll be wearing pearls."

Her bleeding knee was tightly wrapped in strips of linen. She would not complain. If she showed any weakness they would use it against her in the days ahead – and she would never let them break her.

Joan yanked a wooden comb through her hair, jerking Lorraine's neck with every tug. After several minutes, Lorraine knocked Joan's arm away and the comb flew across the room. "Do that one more time and I'll pull yours out by the roots," Lorraine said.

Joan huffed, but was a bit gentler as she braided Lorraine's hair and coiled the strands into an intricate weave.

She never asked for food or drink, but when a meal was finally brought, she ate greedily.

When she was dressed in the ivory gown and everything was ready, Tess held up the pearl necklace that Bannock had given her just yesterday. It seemed a lifetime ago.

"What about my other jewels?"

"Lord Bannock took them," Joan snapped.

§§§

The sun was shining on the tenth of January, 1453 as Lorraine climbed into Lord Bannock's carriage, but her mood was somber. He glanced once in her direction, his eyes full of fury, then turned his face away. She was afraid, but tried to appear calm and dignified as the wedding procession made its way from Bannock Manor to the church in Tenney Village. They passed cheering crowds. Young girls looked at her with envy, men nodded respect, and children scrambled to catch the coins and treats tossed into the air. Even old soldiers who hated the French crowded forward to see Lord Bannock and Lady Lorraine.

As they got close to the church, she clutched the carriage window and stared into the horde. Jacques was there, he had to be. She was alert to every movement, scanning the crowd for a glimpse of his head, taller than the rest, but couldn't find him. In a matter of minutes it would be too late.

The carriage stopped, and Bannock helped her down, claiming her arm as they walked toward the church entrance. People pressed toward them shouting blessings, and he nodded, smiling.

Jacques was nowhere to be seen, and every step brought her closer to losing him. At the entrance of the church, she stopped and tried to yank her arm free. "I – I need a moment," she said. "I'm feeling faint."

Bannock's eyes bore into hers, as his right arm came firmly around her waist. "Keep moving, and keep smiling."

They entered the crowded sanctuary, walking down the center aisle to the altar and the waiting priest. As the ceremony began, she stared straight ahead, fighting back tears. When the priest asked her to say her vows, to promise to obey and be loyal, to forsake all others, she couldn't choke out the words.

She began to shake. Bannock squeezed her right hand in his, tighter and tighter, until her knees almost buckled.

Unable to look at him, she locked her eyes with those of the anxious priest as he began again, slowly coaching her along, a few words at a time, until she'd committed the rest of her life to a man she loathed.

Afterward, the steeple bell began its thunderous peal announcing the marriage, its rhythm battering her heart.

The wedding feast was a blur. Lorraine sat beside Bannock at the head table while lords and ladies congratulated them and offered toasts. She sat stiffly while all around her people danced and laughed. When it got dark, hundreds of candles were lit and the great hall was filled with twinkling lights. She never saw or asked after Jacques or Matilde. She never left Bannock's side. He made sure of it. The ceremony was over, and she was his wife, his property. Everything she owned belonged to him.

It was late when the wedding guests assembled into a rowdy parade to accompany her to the bedchamber. They hooted and slurred crude remarks. Some of them made gestures mimicking fornication. She fought to keep her expression passive, to give nothing of her emotions away.

When they left, she would be alone with Bannock.

He was drunk and allowed the revelry in his bedchamber to go on for too long, but finally he sent everyone except Simon away.

"Lady Lorraine must have a maid to help her remove her gown," Simon said, as he assisted Bannock to undress.

Lorraine nervously crossed through the connecting door and into her side of the suite to wait. She couldn't get undressed without help. Tess or Joan would probably come, or perhaps Bannock would simply rip the gown off of her. What did he care about satin brocade? The thought of Bannock's touch repulsed her. At least he couldn't take away her memories. Unconsciously she reached for Jacques' cross, but felt the pearl necklace instead.

When a knock sounded at the outer door, Lorraine called listlessly, "You may enter." When she saw it was Matilde, she jumped up. "I was afraid I'd never see you again!" Relief immediately turned to horror. Matilde's face was covered in purple bruises and her gown was filthy. She smelled as though she had fallen into a latrine. "What happened to you?"

"How did you expect them to treat me after you ran away?" Matilde burst into tears. "You disgraced Lord Bannock, and I was punished." She held up a hand, displaying a gnarled finger. "They pulled the joints apart." It was the finger used for wedding rings.

"You? But the fault was mine."

"If you disobey the rules, Lord Bannock will punish you." Anger flashed in Matilde's eyes. "And when he orders your punishment, Tess orders mine. I had to clean the garderrobes too – all of them."

Lorraine felt horrible but had to ask, "What do you hear of Jacques? Have you seen him?"

"He was sent away."

"He wouldn't leave me." She lowered her voice. "I found his horse and some of his things. Perhaps he is locked up somewhere."

"Look at me! I am not even allowed to have a bath or a fresh set of clothes," Matilde cried. "Why do you insist on dishonoring Lord Bannock? They'll keep punishing us."

The stench of Matilde's skin, the foul odor emanating from her filthy clothes, did more to convince Lorraine than words. "I'm sorry," she said. She went to the washstand and poured clean water into the basin. "At least you can clean your hands and face."

"We haven't much time," Matilde whispered as she washed hurriedly. "Tess is only letting me tend to you because she wants you to see my condition. This is a warning of how things will be if you, if you..."

"All right," Lorraine said quietly. "I understand."

Now that her hands were clean, Matilde began to unfasten the bows and pins holding Lorraine's dress in place. "You know what you must do."

"Not with ...him."

"You can't waste time wishing for what you've lost – what will never be again." Matilde looked around nervously, then whispered in Lorraine's ear, "You must look after your child."

"What are you talking about?" But even as she said it, her hand went to her stomach. "That's why I've been ill?" She whirled and pushed Matilde's hands away. "I have to leave –"

"Don't be foolish." Matilde grasped her shoulders. "You're lucky to be married and not cast away."

"But if I'm bearing a child… " She stood up, looking around, trying to decide what to take. "I have to find Jacques." Even as she whispered the words, she knew that leaving was impossible, and she sank back into her chair.

"He's gone, and you'll never see him again."

"No!" Her voice caught on a sob. "I don't believe you – he wouldn't leave without me! I know he wouldn't."

"Lorraine, you have nowhere to go. You must take care of this baby." Matilde said softly, "Don't risk losing all that you have left of him!"

Lorraine sat silently, thinking, while Matilde stripped away the last of her wedding clothes and helped her into a sleeping gown. Next her hair was unbound, brushed, and tied with a ribbon.

"Lord Bannock must never know that this child is not his," Matilde warned, her lips close to Lorraine's ear.

Lorraine shuddered to think what might happen if he found out.

Matilde reached into the pocket of her apron and extracted a wad of cloth. Her quick fingers plucked at a knot, and it fell open to reveal a purplish lump.

Lorraine recoiled. "What's that?"

"A bit of pig intestine filled with chicken's blood. I sewed the ends closed. Bannock will expect to see proof that you are a virgin. Here." She pulled a shawl from Lorraine's wardrobe, tied up the cloth with its disgusting contents, and settled it around Lorraine's shoulders. "Make sure this is within your reach tonight. When the time comes – you'll know when it is – Lord Bannock will be worn out from his exertions. When he falls asleep, break open the pouch with your fingernail and smear the blood between your legs."

§§§

Bannock pulled a chair close to the hearth, poured a cup of wine and waited. It had been a long day, and he had drunk a lot. His anger had seeped out of him, and he was feeling generous. Lorraine was shy, and he wouldn't rush her. He sipped his wine slowly, not wanting to be so drunk that he would be rough his first time with her. He wanted her to know the pleasures between a man and woman.

He would indulge her with the best that his home had to offer. The best bed, the warmest coverings, the richest gowns, even the most beautiful tapestries. If it was cold they would have a bigger fire, if she was thirsty she could have all the ale or wine she wanted. She could have everything just as she liked it, exactly to her heart's content. And he could have her.

He looked at the closed door, heard the faint murmurings of their voices. His impatience was beginning to mount. He thought about pushing it open and demanding that she take her place in his bed, but he wanted her to come to him, and so he waited.

They were already married in the eyes of God, and in a little while he would bind her to him physically, making her his wife in body, making her completely his own.

§§§

Matilde kissed Lorraine's cheeks, first one and then the other. "Bon chance," she whispered.

Lorraine's hand trembled on the latch of the bedroom door but she couldn't make herself open it. Suddenly the door opened from the other side, and Bannock was standing there. She felt herself dwarfed in his presence, her small hand disappeared into his large one. He guided her into his room. Two chairs were drawn up before the fire. He offered her a cup of wine.

"No thank you," she mumbled.

"Are you cold?" he asked.

She shook her head no, took a step toward the bed, and drew the shawl from her shoulders. She folded it hastily and tucked it beneath one of the pillows, remembering Matilde's instructions. "Perhaps I'll need this later," she said awkwardly.

"I won't let you get cold." He moved toward her.

She had gone to the bed to place the shawl there, but her action had merely hastened the moment when she would have to get into the bed.

Bannock came up beside her and scooped her into his arms. "You are hardly bigger than a lamb." All traces of hardness and malice were gone from his voice as he placed her on the bed.

§§§

Bannock was glad she had come to him. Now that it was time, he didn't want to fight. She was afraid, and he would be gentle so as not to spoil her and turn her into the kind of woman who, because of brutality, could never enjoy a man.

Her eyes were closed, and when he touched her shoulder, she stiffened. He drew her closer, and the feel of her slender figure in his arms instantly aroused him. He knew many, many ways to indulge a woman. He guided her to lie with her back to him, leaving a little space between them, and massaged her neck and shoulders through her gown. His hands moved methodically, rubbing across her back, down her side, back up to her shoulders. He caressed her, waiting for her to relax.

She needed time. She was a girl of high passion and would learn to respond. His fingers worked more firmly on her flesh, and his hands moved a little lower, then lower still, until they were brushing over her hips.

Gradually, he realized that he could massage her all night long and it wouldn't have the desired effect. Her muscles were rigid with tension. She wasn't ready, but he couldn't wait much longer. He grasped her hips and pulled her closer, pressing himself against the swell of her bottom. She let out a gasp of protest. He turned her so that she was beneath him, slipped his hands under her nightgown and pulled it over her head.

She didn't try to stop him but squeezed her eyes shut.

"Lorraine." His breath was ragged. "Open your eyes." His lips found her earlobe, her neck, her shoulder. He traced kisses to the top of one breast, and asked softly, "What pleases you?" He took her nipple into his mouth and suckled it. He felt her arch, but it was pain, not pleasure, that he saw on her face. He sighed, suckled a moment more, and then drew his mouth away, keeping most of his weight on his arms. He tried kissing her chastely, but she still didn't respond, just kept her eyes shut tight.

He longed to see her look at him with desire, longed to feel her hands reach for him the way he was reaching for her. He put his hands between her thighs and tried to open her legs.

"No." She struggled, thrashing against him.

He placed his knee between her legs and wedged them apart. "Don't fight me."

She whimpered, wrapping her arms across her body as though she could shield herself.

"Lorraine, I'll try not to hurt you." His attempts to appease her only caused more panic. He stroked with his finger, searching in vain for any sign of arousal. There was none. His passion overrode his judgment, and he thrust his tongue past her rigid lips.

She came alive then, fighting, biting and clawing. And then she screamed.

Her attempts to drive him away made him press more firmly. He trapped her body, drew up once and positioned himself at the center of her.

It was time to consummate this marriage.

She put her hands over her face, her chest heaving, and gave another shuddering sob. He entered her halfway. She tried to wrench away, but he pinned her shoulders. He weighed her down, and she gasped for breath. He thrust deeper. Her face was white and pinched, her eyes open, but she stared at a point past his shoulder. He grabbed her wrists, held them above her head, and drove more fully into her. He felt her body resist, and even though he knew he was hurting her, he was beyond stopping.

She wouldn't look at him, wouldn't touch him, but he felt her slowly opening.

As the pressure within him built, he buried himself in her, then drew out almost all the way, before plunging inside of her again. Over and over he pulled back and then drove himself into her. At last, he spent himself, but continued to clutch her until his spasms stopped.

She was crying. Her whole body wracked with sobs.

He closed his eyes, and rolled off of her. In the darkness, he felt her moving. She was groping for the bedcovers. He leaned up. "What are you doing?"

"I'm just getting my shawl." She sounded scared.

He reached for an extra coverlet, laid it over her, then fell back onto the pillows. "Get some rest. The night isn't over."

§§§

When Lorraine had been with Jacques, she opened to him without effort. Now, as much as she willed herself to accept Bannock, her body couldn't yield. The more Bannock battered at her, the more she tensed. The pain had been excruciating.

It was as though Brian Bannock wanted to be certain that all of his seed was delivered into her. She felt it, hot and painful, and when he finally let go she wanted to curl up and die.

But she remembered Matilde's instructions, grabbed the shawl from where she had stuffed it behind the pillows, and fumbled until she found the little pouch of blood.

Bannock began to snore.

She worked frantically, jabbing the little pouch again and again, yet it wouldn't burst. Trembling, she grasped at her throat; her fingers grazed the pearl necklace. She unfastened it and used the clasp to gouge a tear in the pig intestine. The sticky blood oozed onto her fingers. She smeared it between her legs then wiped her fingers in the shawl.

Slipping out of bed, she found the chamber pot and started to throw the skin inside, but it would be seen by Bannock in the morning. She put the lid back on and looked around, wondering where to hide it. The room was dark and unfamiliar.

"No need to be shy about it, woman. Use the pot and come back to bed."

"I need to wash up." Naked and cold, she stumbled to the wash stand, her legs sticky with more than the chicken blood. There didn't seem to be anywhere to hide the messy glob. She poured some water into the washbasin and washed her hands and face, the pearl necklace, and the thin layers of membrane.

Bannock began to snore.

Leaving the pearls on the washstand, she tossed the intestine into the fireplace. It sizzled for a second and then was gone. Every step was painful as she made her way into her new room, and crawled into her own bed.

She was awakened by a heavy hand on her shoulder.

"Why did you leave?" he asked, irritated. Without waiting for an answer, he lifted her out of the warm blankets and carried her back to his bed.

He went to the fireplace, stirred life back into the embers, and then poured himself a cup of wine. His gaze rarely left her. Slowly, he sipped his drink, his smirk challenging her, his piggish eyes daring her to run. His robe hung open, deliberately, and she saw his flaccid shape begin to swell. When she averted her eyes, he chuckled and climbed into bed beside her.

She smelled wine on his breath and slid away.

He grabbed her knees, gripping them painfully and tried pulling them apart. "Let me see." There was a warning note in his voice.

Lorraine stifled the urge to scream, to tell him that she had made love to Jacques dozens of times and it had been beautiful, not like the brutish rutting with him. She hoped he could see the hatred in her eyes.

The room was dark, the fire cast shadows, and Bannock gave a low curse. He pulled her by her ankles toward the edge of the bed and stretched her legs toward the fire. He looked again and muttered something, touching his fingers lightly to the patches of dried blood on her thighs.

He was satisfied; she saw it on his face. He tossed his robe off and climbed onto the bed, pulling the covers around them both.

She had done her duty and tried to get up.

He caught her arm. "You're not going anywhere." He fondled her breast with his big hand. Her skin rippled with gooseflesh. "You're cold." He took her more tightly into his arms.

She resisted the impulse to fight him. As he continued to grope her, she felt his mounting need pressing against her thigh. He reached for her hand and placed it on his leg. She gritted her teeth, knowing he expected to take her again.

"You have to learn how to be a good wife." Bannock's eyes locked with hers, and then slowly, deliberately, he pushed her onto her back. "Touch me," he demanded.

She was afraid to disobey. As if from a distance, she watched herself caress his shoulders and the rough, reddened skin of his arms.

"More," he insisted.

If she still had the knife, she would have used it. Instead, disgusted and revolted, she moved her hands to his penis and stroked him until he moaned. When he tried to touch her, she clamped her legs together, but he climbed on top of her and wedged himself between them. He didn't seem to notice that her hands lay still at her sides as she waited for him to finish.

She would survive this night. She had Jacques' baby to live for.

Chapter Twenty-Four

The cold winter months passed slowly, and March brought more rain and gloomy days. Lorraine stayed in her room and fantasized about Jacques' return and the joy he'd feel when he learned that she carried his child. Gently, she placed her palm over the small swelling of her belly and prayed for a healthy baby.

But, when would he come back?

This baby was going to arrive too soon after her wedding to be mistaken for Bannock's.

The door to her room opened, and she started to rise, but Bannock gestured for her to stay seated. "You look nervous," he said as he came in. "I'm not such a beast as that, am I?" He moved the screen away from the fire and tossed in another log. "It's too wet outside to get much more done today."

The flames blazed, but the peace she'd felt moments ago went up in smoke.

Bannock's face was cast in shadow. "You're like a stranger in this house." He moved closer, never missing an opportunity to corner her. "You can't spend all your time in here." He set the fire screen in place, moved to the window, and parted the heavy draperies.

Lorraine had seen him do this a hundred times. When he was outside, he looked at the house, and when he was inside, he gazed at his lands as though reassuring himself of all that he owned. He turned again and stared at her.

"Your duties aren't only in the bedchamber," he said.

He dominated everything in the house, and thought that because he dominated her physically, he controlled her. He confused lust with power.

She stood up too quickly and a wave of dizziness washed over her. Gripping the back of the chair, she stammered, "I – I don't want to get in Tess' way. She doesn't like me." Bannock moved closer to offer support, and she resisted the urge to pull away. "I've no experience managing a household," she continued.

"Tess and Simon will teach you."

"They don't trust me, and Bertrand follows me around like an old hound sniffing out a rabbit." She cast about for a way to defend herself. "I'm not at ease here. Chateau Brèche was different. It had...luxuries, and beautiful decorations. This house is newer, but it lacks the finer details."

He looked around in surprise. "What? This isn't comfortable?"

"Perhaps for a man used to living in an ancient keep." She pointed to the walls. "Stones are cold." Being careful not to offend, only to throw him off, she said, "This room should have wood paneling and a mantle over the fireplace."

His eyes narrowed suspiciously.

"It would make Bannock Manor more like the home of an established nobleman."

"You think my home is too rough for you?"

There was no point in trying to explain her feelings to a man as solid and cold as the walls. She missed Chateau Brèche, her father, Jacques, and everyone else she'd grown up with. Suddenly she was in tears, longing for her homeland. Sleepless nights and nauseous mornings, fear that he would notice her swelling belly were sapping her resolve to be strong.

"What is it you want?" he asked.

If she told him she was pregnant, perhaps he would leave her alone at night. Desperate for sleep, she spread the palm of her hand over her stomach and said, "It's too soon to be certain..."

She saw the flicker of hope in his eyes.

He held her at arms' length and looked her up and down. "I knew you would be fertile." His chest swelled like a rooster, and he smiled broadly. "I knew it!"

"It's too soon to get your hopes so high. Sometimes...." Lorraine swallowed. "I fear you may cause harm – during the night – when you need me." Her eyes filled with tears again. "Please don't let anything happen to this baby."

His touch turned gentle. "Of course, you need more rest. There's no need for you to take on any responsibilities. Tess and Simon can handle running this house."

Trying to hide her relief at his eager acceptance, she said, "If I could make this room more like what I had in France, then the other changes might be easier."

"I will talk to Tim Carpenter. He's a gifted artisan. I'll tell him to create whatever you want." His hand slid from her shoulder to her wrist. "But you will continue to spend your nights with me."

A few days later when Tim Carpenter came to Lorraine's room, she handed him a sketch she had drawn of acorns and oak leaves, copied from the original design in her father's room at Chateau Brèche.

He looked at her work thoughtfully. "I can tell you've studied art. This is good."

Flattered, she asked, "Can you do it?"

He told her about the furniture and paneling and elaborately designed doors he had crafted for his wealthy patrons. "If only Lord Bannock appreciated those things. Your husband is a fighting man and sees no difference between what I do and a common laborer." He shrugged. "Anyone can learn to make a plain door, but I make it look like folds of linen."

Lorraine sensed his frustration. "Then why aren't you doing that kind of work?"

"I have to take my jobs as I find them."

She gave him her friendliest smile. "Perhaps I can help you."

Tim Carpenter came every morning and worked steadily until dark.

Lorraine waited and watched, observing his diligent and quiet manner. After a few weeks, when the oak mantle surrounding the fireplace in her chamber was nearing completion, she took a chance and said, "There is another project I'd like you to consider." She led him into her dressing room. "It's hard for me to feel safe in this house." She studied his eyes, trying to discern his reaction, but they revealed nothing. "I'm not used to living outside of castle walls," she continued, taking a chance. "I want a hidden room built at the back of this space."

The carpenter's eyes lit with understanding. "I saw a secret room like that in a castle once." He inspected the walls, nodding to himself. After several minutes, he said, "It could be done if I first build a hollow wall to hold a sliding door. Beyond that will be another door, concealed in the paneling and strong enough to withstand a battering ram. If someone should discover the antechamber, they'll never find the next one."

"My husband...." She looked over her shoulder and made sure they were still alone. "Lord Bannock cannot know about this."

He backed away, tight lipped, shaking his head.

"In return," Lorraine promised, "I'll persuade him to give you plenty of work. He'll come to see that talent like yours is valuable."

For a few minutes he stared at the floor. Finally, he ran his hands over the walls, studying the space where he could build the room. It would make her dressing area half its previous size.

It was too much to ask, and now she was scared.

"It's just that Lord Bannock supports the Duke of York over King Henry, and if there is a war –" Lorraine knew she was risking both their lives. She placed a protective hand on her swollen mid-section and whispered, "I need a hiding place to protect Lord Bannock's heir if we are attacked."

The carpenter pulled a string from his leather apron and measured the length and height of the wall. He wrote the dimensions on a scrap of parchment. He wouldn't look at her.

"If anyone else knows, and there is an attack, well, people can be forced to talk." Stammering, she hurried on, "I'll be safer if only you and I know the room is here."

Tim Carpenter scraped at the mortar between two large blocks of stone. He was probably thinking about what might happen to him if Lord Bannock found out. Finally, he turned to face her. "Your husband ordered me to build whatever you want. I can make you a hiding place no one will ever find."

The carpenter was gone for a week, and when he returned he brought back seasoned wood from the nearby countryside. When the local supplies were gone, he went farther abroad. After six weeks he was ready to begin transforming her private chamber into a suite that would rival anything France had to offer. Bannock was told only that she had asked for a more gracious room, suitable for nobility.

When Bannock was home, Lorraine went willingly to his room so he would have no reason to enter hers and interfere with the construction. She brought her needlework or read while he reclined on the settle.

One evening as Bannock watched her, he said, "Give me a son."

"God willing, you'll have an heir before the harvest."

He studied her face, and she was glad she had learned to disguise her emotions. She was agreeable toward him while keeping most of her thoughts to herself. Often when they were in bed together, he reached for her, finished quickly, and lay back against his pillows, falling fast asleep. When that happened, she left his hand where it lay around her middle. He was gentle, but she couldn't help thinking about how different it would be if Jacques were beside her.

Lorraine pretended, for Bannock's sake as well as her own, that she was content.

She spent her days with Matilde, sharing meals, chatting in French, and reminiscing about life at Chateau Brèche. They sewed baby clothes, diapers, and even embroidered a gown for the baptism. The softest wool was made into blankets.

As the weeks progressed, Tim Carpenter built a thick wooden wall across the middle of Lorraine's dressing room. Half of it was hollow, and the other half slid in a groove, disappearing inside the hollow portion. When it was working perfectly, he installed high baseboards along the bottom of the bedroom walls, and ornate moldings against the ceiling to attract the eye.

Once the first room was done, he divided it again, building a second secret room. If someone got into the first room, they would still have to discover the innermost chamber. The surrounding walls were of the thickest, hardest oak, and the door that opened into the second part of the chamber was narrow and studded with iron. The inner door was so well disguised that a person standing in the antechamber could hardly detect it in the elaborate linenfold paneling.

When he was almost finished, the carpenter asked Lorraine to come into the innermost room.

"I've added a shelf so you can store supplies," he said.

Lorraine was grateful. She wouldn't have thought of that detail.

As she turned to leave, Bannock's voice boomed. "Where are you?"

Tim Carpenter jerked, eyes wide with fright.

"Wait here." Lorraine pushed him back, and slipped into the antechamber, closing the door between them.

"Lorraine!" Bannock's voice came from within her room.

She didn't have time to get out of the antechamber. If he knew she had a secret room, he'd have it removed. If he knew she'd been in it alone with the carpenter, he'd have the man killed.

"Lorraine!" He sounded angry.

The only thing separating her from his wrath was the heavy, sliding wall. Would he notice that her dressing room was half the size it used to be? All she could do was hide until he left.

He yelled for Matilde, his swearing sounding more distant as he moved into the corridor.

For a few minutes, Lorraine stood there shaking, not daring to move. When Bannock's bellowing sounded like he was traveling down the stairs, she opened the false wall and dashed across her room and into her husband's. From there she glanced into the corridor, saw it empty, and quickly made her way to the garderrobe.

It didn't matter that the stench was obscene. She was safe – for the moment. Pulling up her heavy skirts, she sat down, needing desperately to relieve herself. If only she could hide out until he left the house again, but it was afternoon, and there was no guarantee that he would.

Resolving herself to be calm, Lorraine ventured out.

A moment later, Bannock's heavy steps were on the stairs again. "Where were you?" he demanded. "Didn't you hear me calling?"

She cast a glance over her shoulder at the garderrobe door. "If I had answered you, would you have joined me inside?" She smiled to take the sting out her sarcastic words.

To her surprise, he laughed. "I'll teach you to overcome your shyness one day, you'll see." He reached for her and gave her a pinch.

She endured it, only wincing slightly. "I suppose you'd like me to be as rough as one of your men-at-arms."

His tone softened. "No, no. I only wanted to show you a colt that's been weaned. I couldn't find you, and I began to think you'd stolen away."

"I'll go out with you now," she said.

"Fetch your cloak."

She didn't dare hesitate. To her relief, he waited in the hall. She grabbed her cloak and cast a glance toward the alcove. Tim was still within the inner chamber. He'd have to wait there a while longer.

§§§

The incident so unnerved the carpenter that he didn't come back for three weeks, and Lorraine began to fear he'd leave the rooms undone. The two hiding places were almost complete, the doors were in place, but there were no locks.

Lorraine waited. Finally, Bannock left for an overnight visit at Berkeley Castle, and Matilde was sent to fetch Tim.

"Please finish," Lorraine begged. "I'll see that you're paid handsomely."

He looked sheepish. "I didn't mean to make you fret. I've been working on something else," he said. "I'll bring it tomorrow."

When he returned the following day, another man was with him, helping him carry a large cradle. "This is for your child," he said.

Lorraine caught her breath. "C'est magnifique." Tentatively, she gave it a small push and set it in motion.

The cradle had decorative spindles, and a finely carved canopy extended over the headboard.

"It will protect your baby if the cradle is overturned," Tim said.

She admired the footboard, embellished with the Bannock crest, two stags leaping over the letter B. Since she'd arrived in England, no one had been so generous. Tears sprang to her eyes as she watched the cradle rock smoothly on its runners.

"Truly, you've given me – us – a kindhearted and thoughtful gift."

Tim Carpenter stared at his feet. "Honored to do it, mi' Lady."

The silence deepened and stretched.

"I'll never forget what you've done."

"I'll get back to work on your chamber," he said.

As he left, she recognized his companion. The other man worked in the bake house and was deaf and dumb. Tim had been careful in selecting his helper, and for that she was doubly grateful.

A few days later, Lorraine stood on the hillside between the manor and the castle. The fields were being ploughed and the air hummed with the twitter of nesting birds. She was looking for a familiar rider, or any sign that Jacques might return to her. But as the months progressed, so did her doubts. Would it be safe to run away when she was more than halfway to term? Her eyes scanned the horizon, but there was nothing to see besides fields, grazing animals, and the thatched huts of the peasants. It was the same peaceful view she looked at every day.

She sat down on the hillside and opened her bag of art supplies. Before she realized what she was doing, she unrolled the parchment and began to sketch Jacques. In her mind's eye, he smiled back at her with his crooked smile and gleaming amber eyes. She filled in the curly, brown hair, the long neck and broad shoulders, his woolen tunic. Next, she drew his muscular legs, his boots, and then, at his waist, she added the Bonville dagger.

She looked up and saw Bannock coming toward her. Hurriedly, she stuffed the parchment under her legs and spread her gown to cover any telltale edges. Picking up a second piece of parchment, she quickly sketched a rabbit and then some hedgerows.

When he got close enough, he said, "Let's see what you have there." She handed him the picture and he smiled. "You're rather clever with a pen and ink, my dear. I thought you might like to walk along the battlements with me." He reached down to pull her to her feet.

It had been foolish to sit in the open and draw Jacques' image. There was no telling what Bannock would do if he saw it. Scared, she hesitated. "I'd like to finish the rabbit first, if you don't mind." She smiled coquettishly. "It's a gift, you see."

He nodded, pleased at the implication that she was making a gift for him. "As you wish." He left her then, climbing the hill to be with his soldiers.

She finished the painting with extra care, adding in an image of Bannock in the distance on horseback. Later, she would have Tim Carpenter build a frame for it. It seemed that when she wasn't thinking of Jacques, she was devising ways to keep Bannock happy.

§§§

By the time the work was finished, Lorraine was so heavy with child that she could barely squeeze through the innermost door.

The carpenter showed her the locking mechanism between the two chambers. "If you push right here, on this wedge of wood, it will slide up and reveal a compartment holding a key."

She followed his instructions and was delighted to find a large key. "But where is the lock?"

He pushed the adjacent segment of wood and an iron square with a keyhole in its center appeared. "When those pieces of wood are in place there's no evidence of the door, the key, or the lock." The carpenter proudly pushed the narrow door open and beckoned her inside, pointing toward the ceiling. "I made an air shaft. It's almost invisible from outside." Reaching onto the shelf, he grasped a second key and said, "Keep one in here so that you can lock the door from inside if you're in danger. The other key should remain in the compartment on the outside of the door."

"Another thing," he said, as he knelt down in a corner of the room. "I've made a place to keep jewels and money." He used one of his tools to pry up the edge of a floor board and revealed a hiding place.

"Your cleverness always amazes me."

He dropped the board back into place. "The walls are so thick that once you're inside, no one will know you're here. You will be safe, Lady Bannock." He replaced the key on the shelf, and they slipped back into the antechamber. He shut the door, locked it, placed the first key back into its hidden compartment and then slid the covering panels back in place. "When you are in that chamber, a battalion of knights cannot get to you unless they find this key – and they won't."

"I can't thank you enough, and I'll make sure you have work here for as long as you want it." She peeked through a narrow opening in the sliding door, made sure the dressing room was empty, and then pushed the door wide enough so that they could exit.

§§§

In August of 1453, Lorraine was sitting with Lord Bannock when a courier delivered a letter with news of King Henry's mental collapse. The king had been struck by a fit while at his hunting lodge. Queen Margaret tried to sequester him, but word had reached London that he was like an idiot, oblivious to those who addressed him.

Lorraine wondered how the king's health would affect their lives at Bannock Manor.

"The nobles around the king are disorganized, and the House of Lancaster may destroy itself from within." Bannock began to pace. "I'm not leaving until my son is born."

She focused on her needlework. "Men aren't needed to deliver babies." She felt his eyes on her, studying her shape, measuring the growth. "And I'm not due for many weeks."

"You're a small woman. Perhaps that's why you look ready to deliver soon. The next two months might be difficult, and I have business to keep me here."

§§§

The following week, on a hot afternoon, Lorraine went into labor. Her water broke, and the household went into a frenzy. It was hours before the contractions became regular, and then the pains grew excruciating. Her muscles tightened involuntarily, and she clenched her teeth against the screams.

Tess fretted about the risks of an early delivery.

"Her mother died in childbirth," Matilde whispered nervously. "It will be better for her if the baby comes early."

Lorraine groaned as the next contraction gripped her. When the ache in her back became unbearable, she clutched Matilde's arm and slowly walked around the room, doubling over for each contraction. She wore only her chemise, and rivulets of fluid ran down her legs. As the afternoon wore on she tired, clutching the back of a chair as sweat dripped down her face. "I need rest."

"Women survive childbirth every day," Tess said. "It's hard while it lasts, but then you have the baby and life goes on."

How would she know? Lorraine thought. She'd never had a baby!

"You're not going to have any rest until the baby is born." Matilde rubbed Lorraine's back. "Not much afterward, either."

Soon the pains were so intense that she couldn't think of anything else, and believed she was going to die.

At dusk, Bannock returned from his business at Berkeley Castle. He rushed into Lorraine's room as though his son would be born at any minute.

Tess hurried him out again, telling him to fetch Mary Nolan, the best midwife in the county.

Just before midnight, a woman Lorraine had never seen before came into the room. Heavy, dark circles rimmed the woman's eyes, and her once-white apron was spattered with blood. Lots of blood.

Lorraine curled on her side and wrapped her arms around herself. "Stay away from me," she screamed. Another contraction gripped her and squeezed the wind from her lungs. She reached for Matilde and pleaded, "Don't let her butcher me." The sight of the midwife's blood-soaked apron reminded her of every story she'd ever heard about women dying in childbirth.

Her screams brought Bannock through the door.

"Lord Bannock, you can't be in here." Matilde quickly stepped between him and the bed. "We'll call you when it's time." She guided him out and ordered, "Tess, give Mrs. Nolan a clean frock and have her wash up." She soothed Lorraine. "You'll be fine and your baby as well. Don't be afraid."

Matilde kept up a soft banter, but Lorraine stopped listening as the next contraction overtook her. She lost track of time.

At the sound of more voices she opened her eyes. Tess and the midwife had slipped back into the room. The rotund little woman was now presentable in clean clothes.

The midwife walked to the bedside and lifted the covers. "Let's have a look. The first baby is always the hardest." She examined Lorraine, and announced, "Not even a tuft of hair yet, darling. You have a ways to go."

Lorraine's throat was dry, and her lips cracked. "It's been too long already."

"Have a sip of ale, dear. It brings in the milk. Careful. Too much and it'll all come up." She held Lorraine's hand for the next contraction, all the while giving orders. "Just a few sips. It will go easier if you stay calm. Tess make sure we have hot water." Mary Nolan gulped down vast quantities of the ale herself, and then suddenly dropped into a chair. Within minutes, she was snoring.

By daybreak Lorraine was beyond exhaustion, and according to the midwife, the baby's head still had not crowned. She whimpered, tensed for the next pain, and then dozed for a few seconds before the rhythm began again.

During the second afternoon, a strong hand clasped hers, and she opened her eyes. Bannock was there.

"This is so hard for you," he said. "I pray it'll be over soon."

Her voice was barely a whisper. "What if I don't give you a son?"

"Lorraine, please...." He turned his face away, trying to hide his emotions. "Just deliver this child and be well."

But as the long summer day passed, her body grew weaker. Matilde followed Mary's instructions and fed her spoonfuls of broth, but she couldn't keep them down. Tess came and went on silent errands, and the contractions continued through a second night. Her hands cramped into permanent fists, and her legs ached. She wished Donna-Marie, her old herbalist, was there. Donna-Marie would have made a tonic or tea to soothe her.

Weakly, she raised her head. Matilde and Mary were dozing by the fire. She groaned, and then, suddenly, she was panting, and her body, of its own accord, pushed hard. A viselike grip of pain squeezed. Her hips felt as if they were being ripped apart.

Mary got up and lifted Lorraine's gown, and then ordered Matilde to climb into the bed and support her from behind. "It's time," Mary announced.

Matilde began to pray loudly. "Mon Dieu, aidez l'enfant." She asked God to assist the baby before it was too late.

Lorraine's head fell back against Matilde's chest.

"You're strong," Matilde coached. "Men fight their wars but the suffering of battle pales next to the pain of bringing a child into the world."

Lorraine would have fallen into a stupor, but the rapid contractions would not let her rest.

Tess' voice broke through the haze of pain. "Lord Bannock wants to know how she is doing."

"Tell Lord Bannock to offer his prayers," the midwife called. "We need God's hand in this."

Lorraine wanted to pray but couldn't – the ache in her womb consumed her. She shuddered again and again. Coldness stole through her, turning her limbs to ice. Matilde was at her head, and Mary was at her bottom, looking between her legs.

"What can I do?" Joan asked, as she rushed in the room and shut the door behind her.

The midwife pressed several lengths of clean linen into her hands. "She's bleeding, and we need to deliver the baby now. Hold her legs."

Mary Nolan's face was nearly as pale as the cloth. She bent to Lorraine. "My dear, is there anything you would like to say, anything at all that you would ask of me?"

Lorraine struggled up through the fog of agony. *They think I'm going to die.* She heard it in the tone of Mary's voice. She saw it in the way Tess bit her lip, and in Joan's wide eyes, and she felt it in the way Matilde held her and sobbed.

Mary Nolan was asking if she wanted to tell her anything. She was not a priest, it would not be a confession, but this woman was offering her the chance to ease her conscience.

Lorraine shook her head. No. There were a million things she wanted to say. She wanted to scream at them to find Jacques and bring him to her. She wanted to cry out that this baby was his and that he should be here to receive it as his own. No. She closed her eyes and felt Matilde's hands on her shoulders. She was aware that Tess and Joan were holding her legs. Mary's fingers probed deeper than before, entering, tearing her apart. Then it felt as if Mary pushed her whole hand inside, and Lorraine screamed long and hard.

§§§

Bannock knelt in the castle's chapel. Every time he closed his eyes, he saw Lorraine's face twisted in agony. Her screams tormented him. He was afraid she would die in childbirth, afraid the child would die with her. It was coming too soon, and it might be gone before he had a chance to look upon its face.

He prayed for a son.

Hours ago, the midwife had cautioned him, "She's a tiny woman, not good for breeding. Spare her too many births after this one."

Pain could be tolerated. He had survived more wounds than he could count, and sometimes when he was injured in battle, he didn't notice it until the fighting was over. But this was different. The midwife had already been with Lorraine for two nights and a day. He clasped his hands, bowed his head, and wondered what God would ask of him in return.

Finally he left the chapel and made his way up the stone steps to the castle's wall walk. It was early morning, and the summer sun was climbing above the horizon. From the battlements, Bannock saw the shepherd boys herding sheep across the pasture.

He stared down at his house and noticed smoke coming from the chimney above Lorraine's room. *A baby will keep her tied to me, and a safe home will keep her tied to the land.*

He watched his soldiers at practice. With war likely between the Duke of York and King Henry, it was a good time to improve his fortifications. He would extend the outer wall at the back of the castle and build another courtyard, a walled enclosure big enough to hold a new practice ground for his men-at-arms. He nodded to himself, satisfied with his plan.

War waited for no one. Why must he wait so long for this baby?

Bannock hurried down the hillside to the house, and was about to dash up the stairs, but Simon intercepted him.

"Don't go up just yet." Simon placed a restraining hand on Bannock's arm.

"What's wrong?"

From the floor above they heard the screams. Bannock looked at Simon's worried face and felt the blood drain from his own. He pushed past him and ran up the stairs. He had heard wounded men shriek, heard death moans and the pleas of the dying, but he had never before heard anyone scream like that.

§§§

The pressure on her pelvis was unbearable, and her breath came in panting gasps. She felt a tear, and then the pressure shifted. It was different now, sharper, more insistent.

"There," Mary breathed. "Here it comes."

Lorraine's womb continued cramping, but this time each spasm seemed to have an effect. She exhaled in a long, low moan.

"I can see the head," Mary cried. "Push down hard with each pain."

Lorraine felt an irresistible urge to push. She bore down, and as her body moved the baby, another pain tore at her, but she held her breath.

"Now I have one shoulder," Mary called. "Here it comes."

The pressure vanished, and Lorraine saw the midwife hold up a bloody, squirming mess of wrinkled flesh. After a moment's hesitation, the baby let out a protesting squall.

"It's a boy!" the midwife announced triumphantly.

Lorraine sobbed with relief, and as soon as she had the baby in her arms, she admired his tiny fingers and toes. He cried with his eyes tightly closed, and she wondered if he would have Jacques' amber eyes. She stroked his fine brown hair, grateful that he was alive.

"He's quite a large boy." Mary Nolan looked from Lorraine to Matilde with a knowing expression. "It's good that he came early."

The midwife tugged on something, and it hurt. Lorraine looked up in alarm.

"It's all right. The afterbirth is supposed to come out now." The midwife soothed, "Everything has come out the way it was supposed to."

Lorraine closed her eyes and visualized Jacques beside her, gazing at his son. She barely registered when Matilde took the baby from her arms. From a distance she heard the women scurrying about the room, but she paid them little attention until a voice broke into her dreams.

"Can you hear me?" Joan whispered urgently in her ear. "Mary can't stop the bleeding."

Lorraine looked up as Mary held a needle over a candle's flame to thread it in the light. "Hold her tight, Matilde." The fear in the midwife's voice was unmistakable.

"No," Lorraine screamed. "Leave me be."

A searing heat pierced Lorraine's flesh, and she grabbed at Mary Nolan's hands, trying to fight her off. Matilde's strong arms pinned Lorraine down as the midwife, intent on the task at hand, worked her needle in and out as though darning a stocking.

She must have fainted. When she was aware again, Mary was bending over her.

"His father's coming for him," Lorraine murmured.

"What did you say?"

"Hush," Matilde said. "Lorraine, wake up."

She blinked and sought Matilde's face for reassurance. Matilde had tears in her eyes as she brushed the damp hair from Lorraine's brow.

"Where's my baby?"

"Joan has him." Matilde shifted her weight on the bed. She'd been there for hours, bolstering Lorraine, and now she climbed down stiffly. "Thank God, the bleeding has stopped."

§§§

Bannock couldn't wait another moment for the news. Mercifully, the screaming had stopped, and now he heard the women talking. He opened the door and saw Matilde holding a tiny bundle wrapped in swaddling. At the foot of the bed, the midwife was setting aside her needle and thread. Next to her was a basin full of blood-soaked linens.

The midwife wiped her hands and gestured toward the little bundle. "Lord Bannock, your son."

The infant was mewling, the face pinkish and wrinkled. His son. That tiny creature was his son? He laid a hand on the baby's blanket and tried to pull it open, but the cloth was tightly wrapped.

"Let me do it," the midwife said. With expert hands, she unwound the blanket and exposed the baby. The end of the freshly cut birth cord was blue. The baby started crying.

Bannock looked down at the swollen red testicles. A boy.

He moved to Lorraine's side and went down on one knee. "God has heard my prayers." He kissed her cheek.

She smiled weakly and held out her arms for the baby. Mary wrapped him up and tucked him against her.

"I shall give you anything your heart desires," he said.

"Let me tell you his name."

He frowned. She had named him already? But she looked so intent, and the flush on her damp face was so beautiful, he relented. He heard the name, nodded, and carefully picked up the infant.

Bannock carried him out of the room. At the top of the stairs he looked down at Simon and the servants. Some of his knights had gathered, and Bannock held up the baby for them to see. "Julian Bannock," he announced. "My son and heir."

Chapter Twenty-Five

The baby was snuggled into the crook of her left arm, and with Lorraine's free hand, she fluffed the chair pillows and then unbuttoned the front of her gown. As soon as she sat down, she released her breast. A tiny hand waved in the air, and the baby's mouth began to pucker and suck in anticipation. Lorraine enjoyed everything about motherhood, and though she sometimes had the wet nurse feed the baby, she loved this intimacy.

"So hungry already?"

The dark brown eyes stared at her with such intensity and wonder. Lorraine was surprised at the depth of her love for her four-month-old daughter.

Julian tried to shove his sister off her lap and claim it as his own. "Mama, pick me up."

"When I'm done feeding Elizabeth, I'll hold you."

"No. No. Pick me up!"

At two and a half years, Julian was the image of Jacques, long and lean with silky brown curls and golden-brown eyes. Her feelings for him were so powerful she had worried she wouldn't have enough love for another baby, but she adored both her children.

Matilde stepped over the wooden blocks and carved animals strewn about the nursery floor, and pulled Julian away. "Let's go outside."

He stopped pushing his mother and began to tug at Matilde's skirt. "We go outside," he chirped. He ran full speed toward the nursery door, on the brink of losing his balance with each step.

The door flew open and slammed against the wall, narrowly missing the toddler.

Julian stopped in his tracks. "Papa?"

Bannock stood in the doorway, his face dark with rage, staring down at the boy. The happy atmosphere of the nursery was suddenly charged with fear, and Julian began to cry. Matilde scooped him into her arms and mumbled something about taking him to the garden. Bannock made no objection as they slipped past.

Lorraine tried to appear calm as she sat poised on the edge of her chair, waiting to hear the cause of his wrath.

His fists were clenched, and his eyes bored into her. "Joan says you've cuckolded me, and everyone knows it."

"Joan." Lorraine grimaced. "She brings us nothing but trouble. I've asked you to send her away." She used her finger to break the baby's suction and secured the front of her gown. She busied herself patting the infant's tiny back, helping her burp while avoiding Bannock's accusing eyes.

He slammed the door closed, stalked across the room, and lifted the baby from her arms. He laid their daughter in her cradle and then turned on Lorraine. "Julian is that bastard's son, isn't he?"

She did her best to keep her voice from trembling. "You bed Joan, and she's jealous. She's trying to get rid of me."

He yanked her to her feet, and his face was inches from hers. "Was Julian fathered by that wretched dog's meat?"

"He calls *you* 'Papa' and follows you everywhere." Her mouth was dry. "He even mimics your walk."

He gripped her shoulders and shook her. "Tell me the truth!"

"You're hurting me!"

He shoved her against the wall and she fell to the floor.

"Why do you believe her?" she cried.

"Just look at him." Bannock stood over her, flecks of spittle on his lips. "He's no child of mine." He drew his foot back and she braced herself, but he deliberately kicked the wall beside her.

To still her shuddering limbs, Lorraine wrapped her arms around herself. Ever since Julian's birth she'd tried to imagine what she'd say, what she'd do, if Bannock confronted her. She never had an answer. The child was, in every way, Julian's. Lying wouldn't work.

"He doesn't look anything like me." His shouting frightened Elizabeth, and the room filled with her piercing screams. He grabbed Lorraine's hair and yanked her head back so that she had to look at him. "I want him out of this house!"

She'd seen her husband angry before, but this time was different.

He switched his grip to her arm and pulled her to her feet. "I wish I could kill you." He was twice her size and could easily have delivered a fatal blow, but he settled for giving her one more violent shake and then shoving her away. He looked into the cradle at the squalling baby. "At least I know this one is mine." He turned to leave.

"Wait." She grabbed his arm. "What are you going to do?"

His look was full of hatred. "I haven't decided."

"Don't you dare touch Julian, or I'll..." *How would she punish him?* "I'll make sure you never have a moment's peace again."

He laughed. "I'll put you off my land, and the boy, too."

Bannock refused to speak to Lorraine for the next several weeks. She slept in the nursery and kept Julian out of his sight. She thought about hiding in her secret chamber, but when she came out again, Bannock would demand an explanation. She would use the chamber only if he threatened to harm Julian. She'd barely been able to eat or sleep, and it took all of her patience to care for the children.

Joan, a mere servant, had drawn the battle lines, and in a household full of servants, it was impossible to keep matters private. Simon was sullen and avoided her. Tess took a position of neutrality. She didn't want to take sides against Lorraine, but she had to guard against the possibility that Joan might be elevated above her. Poor Matilde was just plain terrified that she'd be thrown out of Bannock Manor, and there was no safe place for a French woman alone in England.

One afternoon Lorraine passed Bertrand in the corridor. He gave her a look of disdain and shook his head as though his suspicions had been confirmed. His haughty look seemed to say that he had been right all along.

Joan stayed out of her sight, but Lorraine knew her rival was spewing accusations and turning the servants against her, and there was little she could say to defend herself.

Bannock simply refused to be in the same room with her, and if their paths crossed, he looked at her with loathing. She felt as isolated as on the first day she had arrived, but at least then she had thought she could leave. Now she had children, and they had to be protected at all costs.

For three years she had waited for Jacques' return, had spent countless hours fantasizing that he would one day overpower Etienne and take her and Julian back to Chateau Brèche. But all of that had changed on the day Elizabeth was born.

Bannock Manor was her home now, and it was where she wanted to raise her family. She couldn't take her daughter away, and wouldn't voluntarily leave her behind.

She had nowhere else to go.

Bannock kept busy with his estate during the day, but every evening he had Tess bring Elizabeth to him. When the infant began to fuss, she was sent back to the nursery, where Lorraine waited anxiously.

One evening when Tess came for the baby, Lorraine stopped her. "I'm going to talk to Lord Bannock. Elizabeth is to stay here with the nurse."

"If I don't bring her," Tess stammered, "he'll knock me about the head."

"You wait here," Lorraine ordered. "I must talk to him. He's had enough time to brood."

Outside his door she hesitated, and her hand shook as she reached for the latch. Tonight she would do everything she could to negotiate for the survival of her family. She straightened her shoulders, drew a calming breath, and opened the door.

Bannock sat by the fire and didn't look up.

He looked like he'd aged ten years in the past few weeks. She saw no hint of the battle-hardened baron. The man before her had more gray than red in his beard and he looked tired.

When he finally turned toward her, she expected to see anger, but his eyes held only despair. "Don't talk, unless you're prepared to speak the truth." He returned to staring at the fire.

"I never meant to cause you pain," she said. "I was seventeen, my life in France had been destroyed, and I seized the chance for love." His hands balled into fists, but she pressed on. "I didn't know I was with child until after the wedding. If I'd known, I would have told you so that I could leave. If Jacques had known, he never would have brought me here." She knelt before him and grasped his fists. She tugged at them like a child might, trying to force him to listen. "I've been living with the hope that someday I could go back to France, but I was wrong."

She thought about all the times she had been unable to return his affections. "You are my husband, and I want to stay with you. I beg you – think of Julian as your son, and I will do whatever pleases you."

His expression remained impassive. Finally he shook free of her and rose to leave.

She threw herself in front of him. Her dignity vanished. She wrapped her arms around his waist and pleaded, "Please, tell me what I have to do."

"You've been a fool to wait for that French bastard." His voice was hoarse. "I bought him off with a handful of coin, and he's never coming back – not even for his son."

"Why didn't you tell me? Why did you let me wait?"

"And you made me believe the boy was my son." He stared at her coldly. "He is not my heir. His existence mocks me."

The child that had given her life meaning was the same child that had brought disgrace to Bannock. Nothing she could say would appease him. "What do you plan to do with us?"

"Elizabeth is mine and will stay with me, but I do not want to deprive her of a mother's care. When she's older, I'll send you and Julian to live somewhere else."

The thought of being sent away terrified her. She had not been off Bannock land since she'd first arrived. Desperately, she grabbed his arm. "Please don't send us away."

He studied her face, and then spoke deliberately, as though he had already decided on his terms. "I want my own sons. A son of my blood will be my heir, not Julian."

She had suspected he would never permit Julian to inherit once he knew the truth, but the agony she felt at his words overwhelmed her. She let go of him and slumped into the nearest chair. She remembered Jacques coming to Chateau Brèche, so young and alone, because he could not live at his father's home. People called him a bastard. Was that to be Julian's fate as well?

Bannock threw his cup into the fire and yelled, "I have no son."

Frightened, she backed away. "What if I don't have another son?"

"You've had two children in three years, and they're both healthy. I'm sure you can bear more boys."

"If you elevate another son above Julian...."

"A bastard will never inherit from me. My first legitimate son will take my title and my land." His expression softened a little. "When the matter of the next king of England is settled and I am no longer needed by York, then perhaps I will go to France and fight Etienne Dannes. Chateau Brèche was supposed to be mine, but I may let Julian live there."

She bit her knuckles and forced herself to meet his gaze. His eyes bore into hers, and with awful clarity, she finally understood that she was no match for him.

He poured himself another cup of wine. "That's more than he'd ever get from your beloved Jacques."

She flinched at the insult, but had to bargain for her son's future. "If I agree, what will be Julian's status? How will you treat him?"

"He'll not get my title."

"You expect me to bear more sons while you pass over my first born? It's my lineage that will give your sons nobility!" She stood abruptly, anger pulsing through her veins. "If you want more children from me, then banish that whore of yours!"

"A man needs the comfort of a woman. Joan takes pleasure in my body, and I in hers." He smirked. "That's something you haven't been willing to do."

"I want her gone." She had little to bargain with, and after a moment's indecision, Lorraine lowered her head and leaned against his chest. "Send her away and I will accept your terms."

§§§

The solar on the third floor of the manor was usually filled with chattering ladies and children, but on this summer's day, after weeks of rain, everyone was outdoors enjoying the sunshine. Bannock stepped into the oriel window at the end of the room and peered down at the garden where Lorraine walked with the children, their nurses and Matilde.

At Lorraine's insistence, the once barren hillside had become a terraced garden surrounded by a tall stone wall. The section closest to the house was planted with flowers, and a breeze carried their perfume through the open windows. The estate was more beautiful than ever, and with four children Lorraine was settled, tied to her family and to him, dependent upon his wealth and protection. The sight of his children in the garden warmed his heart, but after six years of marriage the dream of his own son still eluded him.

Elizabeth was three now, a quiet child with Lorraine's dark hair and wide, watchful eyes. Anne, thirteen months younger, was almost as tall as Elizabeth, but she had his red hair, his white, freckled skin, and a bold, sunny disposition. She had been conceived on the first night of his truce with Lorraine, and she was his favorite. As Bannock watched, her nurse caught her moments before she would have toppled into a flower bed. She was adventurous, with his temperament as well as his looks. Denied her objective, she pulled a bloom from its stem and shredded the petals.

Sophie, the baby, was as healthy as her sisters, but every time Bannock looked at her, he was filled with disappointment. After her birth he had locked himself into his room and wept. How could God grant him such power and wealth and then deny him a son?

Julian was six. Every day he grew taller and stronger, and every day he looked more like Lorraine's cursed Frenchman. Bannock had knifed and buried him, but he lived in his son. His eyes were neither dark like Lorraine's nor blue like his own, but a shade of brown so light that in the sunlight they appeared golden. The ladies exclaimed over him, but the boy's looks were visible proof that Lorraine had come to their marriage carrying another man's baby. Three daughters and a bastard son.

Julian worshipped him, but sometimes Bannock looked into those eyes, the eyes of another man, and wanted to strike him. When that feeling came over him, he ignored the child.

Simon appeared at his elbow, and Bannock asked irritably, "What is it?"

"A messenger from the Earl of Warwick to see you."

"Warwick's man is here?"

"He is in your justice room enjoying a cup of ale."

Bannock focused his wandering thoughts. He could not afford to be distracted. Warwick's holdings stretched from Cornwall to Yorkshire and all the way to Wales. Bannock ruled one manor and one castle, but Warwick had twenty castles or more and hundreds of manor homes. He was rumored to be as arrogant as he was wealthy, but riches were not enough for him. The Earl of Warwick wanted to choose the next king of England, and he had decided that Richard of York should have England's throne.

Bannock descended the stairs and slowed to a stately pace as he entered the justice room.

The messenger wore a scarlet surcoat with the Earl's white bear and ragged staff emblem. He bowed and got right to the point. "Our army is gathering at Warwick Castle. The Lords Salisbury and Norfolk are with us."

"What about the queen?" Bannock poured ale for himself.

"Her ally is the Duke of Somerset. She also has the loyalty of Buckingham and the Tudors of Wales. You must come at once."

So there was to be another battle. Once again he was to risk his life without the assurance of a legitimate heir. Bile filled his throat. The messenger departed in a flash of scarlet, and he slammed his cup on the table.

Simon cleared his throat. "Shall I make preparations for travel?"

"In three days' time." Bannock stormed out.

§§§

Lorraine was enjoying Matilde's conversation as they strolled in the garden with the children and their nurses. With servants and soldiers, peasants and land tenants, there were at least two hundred people living on the Bannock lands.

The first few years had been difficult, but Matilde was now accepted by the other servants, and she was Lorraine's primary source of gossip. When Sophie became too heavy, Lorraine handed her to the nurse, but the baby bawled and stretched her arms toward her mother. As usual, she gave in too easily and took her back.

"You have spoiled them all," Matilde scolded. "How can her nurse properly train her if you always give in?"

"Why make her sad? Life will be hard enough when she is older."

As they walked, she admired the garden. She had designed it herself in the fashion of the gardens at Chateau Brèche. The walls rose to six feet on all sides, and the beds were terraced down the hillside. Fruit and nut trees had been planted at the highest levels, where their roots held the soil stable and the steep drainage prevented root rot. She had bought new varieties of fruit trees that would begin producing in a few more years. The five middle terraces were planted with vegetables, and flowers grew on the lowest level, protected from the wind and scavenging deer by the tall walls.

"I should have paid more attention to Donna Marie's teachings about herbs and potions," Lorraine said. "I have seen so much need for her skills here." They seldom dared speak of their lives in France.

Matilde frowned. "Do you suppose she survived the attack? She was a good woman."

"I never imagined I would be so cut off and that we would never hear from anyone again." She shifted Sophie to her other hip as they continued their walk. "I don't think we will ever know what happened the night we left Chateau Brèche."

They were heading back down the hill when Bannock emerged from the house, and by his expression, she knew he wanted to talk to her. She handed Sophie to Matilde and turned to the other children and their nurses. "It's getting cold. All of you – it's time to go inside."

Bannock waited until they were alone and then escorted her to a nearby bench. He looked grave as he said, "There is going to be more fighting."

"When must you leave?"

"In three days." He squinted into the sunshine. "Before I leave, I hope you will be with child again."

"But Sophie is just a year."

"You promised me a son."

She had wanted to stay composed, but she whirled on him. "Do you forget your daughters? They are your children!"

"You have not given me an heir. I'm going to battle, to risk my life, and for what?" His sweeping gesture included the manor and the hillside, and then he jabbed a finger toward the castle. "I could die knowing that all of this might go to another man's son. There is nothing I can do to protect my name."

"Julian has your name," she whispered.

He looked so angry she was afraid he might strike her. "Do you want me going to my grave knowing that I am the last of my line?" He stood abruptly. "I'll see you in my bedchamber within an hour."

The children were inside with their nurses, and she wanted to go to them, but she slowly followed Bannock down the hill to the manor. She would order a bath and change into a clean gown. To please him, she would wear the pearl necklace he had given her. And when he took her to his bed, she would do her best to satisfy him.

§§§

In the darkened room Lorraine stood before the fire with her back to him. Beneath her chemise, Bannock could see the swell of her hips and rounded buttocks. She was fleshier now than she had been when younger, and the change pleased him. At twenty-four years she was half his age and looked as beautiful as ever. He only wished she would respond passionately to him. He longed to feel her reaching for him, longed to feel her nails biting into his flesh the way Joan's did.

He smiled at the thought of Joan. The wench had no shame. She liked it from behind as well as from the front, and if he slapped her a bit, well, it was just in the heat of passion. He had set her up in a small cottage west of Tetbury, and he saw her several times a month. He had meant to quit after his bargain with Lorraine, but Joan was with child by then. Her bastard son was two years old now, but he wasn't convinced the boy was his and refused to acknowledge him.

He moved closer to Lorraine and felt her tense when he placed his hands on her shoulders. He kissed her neck, her cheek, her ear, and whispered, "I am pleased to see you are wearing your pearls." She turned and reached under his tunic to loosen his clothing, but he stopped her. "Not so fast." He buried his face in her hair and inhaled. The scent of her made his knees go weak. Joan aroused his coarser instincts, but it was different with Lorraine. He wanted to savor her. He cupped her breasts and milk leaked out. The nipples stiffened, but so did she. He tasted the nectar that nourished her babies and then swept her into his arms.

Instead of taking her to the bed, he sat on the bench before the fire. The back of the settle was up, holding the heat in, and he placed her on his lap and cradled her. She put her arms around his neck.

He murmured, "When I am alone in my tent, I want warm memories of you. You have no idea how rough a battle camp can be." He moved his hand under her chemise and slowly caressed her, working toward her center. She closed her eyes and pressed her face against his shoulder. After all this time she was still shy. He stroked her flesh and teased her thighs apart. "You are different from any other woman." She shifted on his lap and he groaned as she pressed against his arousal. This was always the moment that required his discipline. He wanted to throw her on the bed, take her quickly, and then take her again as he would a common girl. But there was nothing common about Lorraine. She was still across his lap, still had her arms locked around his neck, but her legs parted slightly. Her breathing changed, and she was pliant now. He raised his head, and she met his lips. He wanted her to understand, and he whispered, "You mean more to me than anyone." He kissed her but still did not take her to bed. She freed him from his clothes, and he shut his eyes, willing himself to go slowly. He lifted her so she could straddle him, and her fingers bit into his shoulders as she resisted. He cupped her buttocks, supported her weight, but did not force her. "I'll always take care of you. I shall never abandon you or your children."

His words had the desired effect. She softened and finally lowered herself. It took her body a moment to adjust to his size, to accommodate him. When he was completely within her, he eased back against the settle, trying not to rush. Gradually, her body began to move. She rocked her hips a little, and he groaned. "More," he urged. She moved on him timidly and then with vigor as he swelled to fill her even more. And then it was as though the rhythm possessed her, too, and they were moving as one, moving with a common intent. His arms came around her, supporting her as she arched backward. He felt the delicate ripples in her body moments before his own release, and then he held her tightly as a long, pleasure-filled groan escaped him. Even before he caught his breath, he was already growing hard again. He refused to withdraw. He grabbed a blanket from the back of the settle, threw it on the floor before the fire and lowered her, bracing as he stayed within her, stayed over her.

Her arms clung to his neck. She was not fighting or resisting, and he did not stop to question whether it was spontaneous or calculated. She was willing, and he drove himself into her again. She looked into his eyes, drew his face to hers, and kissed his lips, kissed his forehead. Then her head dropped back even while her hips arched to meet his, and he strove to possess her completely.

§§§

On the eve of Easter in 1460, Lorraine skimmed Bannock's long letter. He was garrisoned in the south of England, awaiting Warwick's return. The Duke of York was still in Ireland, but Yorkist troops were gathering in both the north and south. Bannock asked her to send news of the manor and of her pregnancy, but she set his letter aside. She would write to him soon, but now she dispatched a messenger to fetch Mary Nolan. Her fifth child was ready to be delivered.

The spring weather was raw, and throughout the rainy evening, Lorraine paced in her sitting room. Soon the contractions would be too strong and she would have to lie down, but it helped to walk a little. Would this child be Bannock's long-desired son? She hoped not. In spite of Bannock's assurances, she feared for Julian's safety, and she had been secretly relieved with the birth of each daughter.

Matilde was making the usual preparations, setting the cauldron of water over the hearth, making sure clean linens were close at hand. She offered comforting words. "Your girls came easily, and it should be the same this time."

Lorraine crossed the room, taking slow, deliberate steps, her hands supporting her lower back. "If I have another girl, Brian will be furious." She lowered herself to a chair as the next contraction began its tight grip across her middle. "I have spent the last seven years carrying and nursing babies, and I can't keep doing this."

"You have a wet nurse." Matilde was matter-of-fact. "Why do you insist on nursing the babies yourself? Margaret sits and eats all day, and she has an ample supply of milk. Let her do the feeding." She stood behind Lorraine and began massaging her shoulders. "The nursing has not helped you avoid another pregnancy."

"If Bannock does not give me a rest, I shall be a toothless old woman by the time I am thirty."

"If only you could see the way he looks at you, the way his eyes follow you through a room," Matilde said wistfully. "I have never had a man look at me with such longing." She sighed. "It's the kind of thing minstrels sing of."

The night progressed, and so did Lorraine's labor. Matilde stayed at her side, sponging the sweat from her face as they waited for Mary Nolan. At midnight the church bells tolled the arrival of Easter, and the storm lashed the windows and forced smoke back down the chimney. Lorraine coughed, then groaned with the next contraction.

It was late when Mary finally showed up. "I almost turned back," she said, propping her hip on the bed. She casually lifted Lorraine's chemise. "This one is coming fine, and it will be here soon."

The baby boy, his head covered in bright orange fuzz, was delivered just after dawn. Lorraine held him as tears streamed down her face. She had given Bannock his son. And she had sealed Julian's fate. He would grow up as his father had, a boy without land or a title, with nothing to his name.

§§§

Bannock was sick of the garrison. The rain would not stop, and it was hard to tell where the muddy ground ended and the soggy shelter of the tents began. He wasn't the only one going crazy from boredom. His best knights were used to hardship, but the common soldiers were not as disciplined, and as the wait grew longer, their patience whittled away. Soon they were picking fights over little things or over nothing at all. Bannock was impatient for word from home. Cragmoor Castle was under the command of Sir Robert Armstrong, but Bannock wondered if the small troop he had left behind was enough to protect his family and estate.

He heard a commotion outside and emerged from his tent, surprised to find himself face to face with Robert. "What do you mean by coming here?" he demanded. "Have you left my family undefended?"

"You have another son!" Robert yelled, grinning broadly. "I traveled with only a few men, just enough to make a safe journey and bring you the news."

Rain pounded on their unsheltered heads and drenched their clothes. The news so stunned him that Bannock stood frozen while muddy rivulets ran around his boots. "A son? A son!" His voice caught. "I have a son!" He roared the joyful news above the downpour, grabbed Robert's arm and dragged him into the tent.

He wasted no time making arrangements to return home. He left his men-at-arms under the command of one of his knights and sent a messenger to inform Warwick that he would soon return.

They traveled by day through torrential rain, and set up camp each night on the driest ground they could find. The soil was still saturated, and all of their supplies were damp and moldy. Two of the men had fevers and could barely keep up.

Across the land, storms had beaten crops until they drowned in their furrows. Everywhere he went, the land was flooded, the grain smashed.

Bannock grew somber as he reached the edge of his own water-logged land.

On a familiar rise, he stared down at a tiny flock of sheep. Some of the animals were huddled in a stone shelter, but one of the walls had collapsed, leaving them exposed to the wind.

He reined in, and the others drew up beside him. "Why hasn't that wall been repaired?"

"Some of the households have fever," Robert said. "We dig trenches for the bodies, but the ground is so wet they don't always stay buried."

Grimly, Bannock asked, "How many households are afflicted?"

"Most of them. The crops are ruined, and the tenants complain that their stores are full of mold. Their gardens are drowned, and there is not enough grain left from the last harvest to feed the animals. Unless they can replant, you'll lose another year's grain rents."

They rode further into the valley, and Bannock stopped again. The smallest cottage belonged to Ross Jones, the man Bannock had once disciplined for beating his wife. Jones had never been as careful with his land and his flock as some of the other tenants.

"They butchered the last of their flock over the winter," Robert said. "Simon told him he owed you a harvest fee, but he said he had to feed his family. After they slaughtered and ate the last of their animals, they packed their belongings and moved on. I let them go, mi'lord. I figured we'd have fewer bodies to bury. A man cannot eat when he has no crops and no livestock."

"I didn't think I'd leave the garrison behind only to find things worse at home." He tugged on the reins. "I have to see my wife and newborn son."

At Bannock Manor he barely paused to draw off his cloak and sword belt. He pulled off his gauntlets as he ran up the stairs.

Lorraine was in her room, seated by a roaring fire. She looked thin, her face a little pale.

Overcome with relief, he pulled her into his arms and held her tightly. "I got here as soon as I could." He lowered his head and searched her face. "I saw the land, the fields ruined by the rain. I was worried for you and the children."

"I begged Simon to open up the castle stores and let the tenants have some of our food, but he refused."

"He was right. We have to safeguard our supplies."

Lorraine nodded sadly and led him toward the nursery. "Come and see your son."

Margaret, the wet nurse, hastily drew a shawl across her ample breast and handed him the swaddled bundle. He drew the blankets away so he could see the baby nude, and gave a shout of laughter. He cradled his son protectively.

Lorraine said, "He does not yet have a Christian name."

"My son is to be named Brian Blake Bannock, and we shall call him Blake."

The following morning, Bannock awakened Lorraine with kisses and pressed a carved wooden box into her hands. "Wake up." He stroked her hair. "I've kept this for you."

She rubbed the sleep from her eyes, sat up and lifted the box onto her lap, then opened the carved lid. Inside were her possessions he'd kept hidden since she had tried to run away.

"I thought I'd never see these things again." As though she couldn't believe it was real, she picked up a sapphire ring and held it against her heart. "This was my mother's." Her tears overflowed. "Now that I have daughters of my own, I feel her loss even more." Slipping the ring onto her finger, she stretched out her hand to admire it. "Someday, it will belong to one of our girls."

Brian watched as Lorraine picked up a small book of verses. She didn't open it, but set the book beyond his reach, as if afraid he would take it back. He didn't read French, and didn't care what books she had.

It was Lorraine's reaction to the cross that bothered him. Instead of being happy, she looked sadder than he'd ever seen her. She held the golden cross to her lips and cried as if she could never be consoled.

Chapter Twenty-Six

Three months later, in the summer of 1460, Lorraine received a hastily scribbled note from Bannock informing her that York's troops had crossed London Bridge and entered London.

"On the second of July, the commoners opened the gates," he wrote, "but before we got into the city, we had our soldiers take down the rotting heads that our enemies had left on spikes as a warning to us. We were greeted with welcoming cheers."

Within days of securing London, Bannock and his men were heading north again with Warwick's troops.

Lorraine had learned to work with Simon, and together they managed the estate and its farms. Their tenuous relationship had strengthened over the years, and she had gradually taken over more of his duties. At first they had worked on the accounts together, but now she handled the rents and other finances by herself, and when Bannock was home, the ledgers were always in order for his review.

Her alliance with Tess was stronger, too, and as the estate grew, so did the size of the household staff. Lorraine took in peasants willing to work for a few shillings per year just to keep food in their bellies and a roof over their heads. Some had no other home to return to, while other families were so overburdened they pressed their children, often as young as six years, into service.

There were many nights when she barely slept, worrying about hungry tenants, squabbling servants, or a feverish child. She was always exhausted, but at least she had a solid roof over her head. Most nights, that was more than Brian had.

As she did each morning, Lorraine accompanied Tess on her rounds. The first room they came to on the ground floor was full of young girls plucking chickens and geese. The birds, sheltered in coops and subsisting on table scraps, stayed hardy even in the poorest weather. The manor had poultry and eggs for the table, feathers for bedding and pillows, fletching for arrows, and rendered goose fat for cooking. Lorraine allowed nothing to be wasted, and even the egg shells were ground up and used as grit for the chickens.

Next they came to a small room where two women were pressing honeycomb.

Lorraine dipped a finger into the sticky, golden honey and licked her lips. "Mmm. I can taste clover and apple blossoms." She smiled. Just last evening Sophie had licked the golden goo off her bread. Honey was a favorite of the children. The wax, which had a sweet scent and burned cleanly, was made into candles for the family. The servants used candles made from rendered animal fat, which smoked as it burned and gave off a rancid smell that clung to the walls.

In the hot, steamy laundry room, eight of the older girls were hard at work. Their chattering stopped abruptly when Lorraine and Tess entered. It would be nice to have someone other than Tess and Matilde to talk to, someone more her age. The ladies at Chateau Brèche used to sit in the solar and embroider as they talked about travel, or fashion, or their children's antics. She missed the laughter and camaraderie.

She shook her head, knowing that she was lucky to be alive.

This home was safe, and the modern innovations made all of their lives easier. In front of her was a long stone trough, fed by a nearby stream. It saved the girls from hauling buckets of water from the well. Each of its three sinks were filled with varying degrees of clean water for washing clothes.

Lengths of rope were strung across the ceiling rafters and hung with drying bedding and clothes. One girl rotated small iron triangles on and off a hot platform positioned over the fire, and two other girls used the heated irons to press out the damp wrinkles. Lorraine watched their progress, and one of the girls, probably nervous from the attention, accidently burnt the side of her hand.

"Be careful!" Tess snapped.

Chastened, the girl bent her head over her work, cheeks as red as the burn.

"Hold it under the cool water," Lorraine said.

Tess hated it when she intervened, but it was no good letting the burn fester.

Obediently, the girl did as she was told.

In a corner of the room, an older woman mixed potash, leached from wood ash, into a bowl filled with lard. When the mixture cooled and hardened, it would be cut into bars of lye soap. She also kept her head down, appearing to concentrate on her concoction, obviously hoping to avoid Tess' notice.

Lorraine and Tess stepped outside, and in their wake, the prattle of the girls resumed. They strolled along the covered walkway that Lorraine had built the previous year. It linked the bake house to the main house so the food reached the table while it was still hot.

Tess said, "I don't know if that new girl will work out. She's clumsy, distracted. You barely looked at her and she burned her hand. And I suspect she's with child." Her voice was full of scorn.

A strict hierarchy was in place among the servants, and Tess ranked at the very top. The future of all the female servants was in her hands, and Lorraine shouldn't interfere with her decisions, but she pitied the new girl.

For the second time that day, she risked intervening. "Show her some charity."

Tess frowned. "We have enough to do without taking on immoral girls."

"Their lives are hard enough," Lorraine said. "Must we make them even more miserable?" It was as far as she could go without giving Tess a direct order.

They passed two barefoot boys carrying buckets of water. The boys nodded respectfully without slowing their pace.

The cows were being herded from the barn to the pasture; the milking was finished. Immediately, three boys disappeared into the barn to begin mucking it out. A pig had been culled from the sty and was on its way to the butcher.

Everywhere Lorraine looked, people were hard at work, but some of the peasants complained that summer had abandoned them. All year they had been beset by storms, and now several men were digging trenches in an attempt to drain the flooded vegetable garden. Some tenants had given up and abandoned their plots, hoping for a better living farther south.

Without peasants to replant the fields, this year's harvest would be even worse than the last, but Simon had refused to grant charity to the tenant farmers. The castle had stores put by, and the manor cellars were stocked, but they had to conserve food for their large household and for Bannock's troops.

The cycle of famine and disease would prevail another year, and there was little Lorraine could do to alleviate the suffering, except to offer work and shelter, warmth and food to those who lived on their estate.

§§§

By fall, word reached the manor of more fighting between Warwick's army and the royal forces. At Northampton, Warwick won decisively, but although the Duke of York proclaimed himself the rightful heir and ruler of England, King Henry still held the throne.

Bannock returned home at Christmas, boasting of victory, and he was in such high spirits that for a short time no one mentioned the bad weather or the stores that were in short supply.

Instead of new clothes for the servants and knights, Lord Bannock gave them sacks of dried fruit and nuts. A few of the highest ranking among them also received cones of sugar. It was their poorest Christmas feast in years.

As the holidays passed and the men stayed home, Lorraine once again adjusted to Bannock's presence in the manor. He inspected everyone's work, from the baker to the blacksmith, and bellowed whether he was pleased or angry. He was proud of his children and happy to see them unless he was busy, distracted, or tired. Lorraine did her best to read his moods.

One afternoon in January, Lorraine sat with Bannock in the withdrawing room. Even with the roaring fire and thick tapestries on the walls, the room was cold. She wore layers of woolen clothes, and Bannock kept his cloak on.

A messenger entered and bowed hastily. "My Lord Bannock, I bring grave news. On the thirtieth day of December, Richard of York and his eldest son were lured from their castle and slain on Wakefield Green. Their heads are on spikes at Micklegate Bar in York City, and there is an empty spike intended for the head of the Earl of Warwick."

The color drained from Bannock's face. "My good friend is dead?"

"York's second son, the Earl of March, will take up his father's standard," the messenger continued.

"I know Edward. He's too young!"

"He is eighteen, and has the right to succeed to the throne. He's already raising an army to avenge the deaths of his father and brother."

Would the killing never end? Lorraine didn't want to betray her emotions in front of the messenger, but Bannock would no doubt leave again. She didn't realize how badly she was shaking until Bannock's warm hand covered hers.

"Tell Edward he can count on my support," Bannock said.

The messenger bowed and left.

"If you hadn't come home for Christmas, it might have been your head on a spike," she said bitterly.

"England must be unified under a strong king, and I will continue to back York, or risk losing his patronage. If the Lancastrians win the throne, our holdings may be confiscated, and I can't let that happen."

"You've barely spent any time with the son you wanted so badly." She moved to stand by the fire, keeping her back to him so he wouldn't see her tears. She knew he didn't like to be confronted by her fear and frustration, but she couldn't keep silent. "What if you're killed? We'd be left helpless."

"I've survived more battles than I can count."

Perhaps he cared more for his precious land than he did his family. She turned around. "Will you abandon your estate just before the planting?"

"The troops are heading toward York, and I must be with them."

She could tell that his mind was made up, and she had nothing left to lose except her dignity. "I'm begging you not to go."

"I will support Edward." He pounded the table. "His father and I were friends, and I cannot leave this business unfinished.

This home is your world; you don't understand the importance of king and country."

Furious, she folded her arms and glared at him. "When are you leaving?"

"As soon as we gather supplies – day after tomorrow."

"It does not matter that I need you?"

"Fighting is how I earned my title." He sighed impatiently. "Long ago I made my will and left it with Lord Berkeley. If something happens to me, he will become the legal guardian for you and the children. I trust him." As he strode to the door, he added, "I'm going to write an amendment so that when Blake reaches his majority, he will assume control of my estate. I'll teach him to care for his mother and sisters, and he will be generous with Julian."

Tears and pleading were wasted on Bannock; she fixed a smile on her face. "Make sure you come back to us."

§§§

Bannock awoke, dressed quickly, and climbed the path to the castle. A light dusting of snow covered the ground. The forge was crowded with men mending their swords or repairing their saddles and harnesses. The chimneys of the bake house billowed with the yeasty aroma of extra bread that they would eat on their journey. Inside the bailey, the white snow was trampled into mud as wagons were loaded with tents, barrels of ale, rounds of cheese and dried meat. He was responsible for feeding his own men, and food was always scarce in the villages surrounding an encampment.

In the castle great hall, he found Robert, his second in command, shouting orders at a group of the older boys. "In a week's time you will be facing your first battle. Do not stare into the face of your foe. Never hesitate with your sword. Strike fast or die!"

Bannock drew him aside. "Robert, we leave at dawn. We'll take every boy over twelve, and every man under fifty. See that they're outfitted and ready. Leave a small contingent here to guard my home."

"There are men still nursing wounds from the last battle. It's best to leave them behind. They'd only slow us down anyway."

"Take care of it," Bannock said.

"Yes, my lord." Robert cast a knowing look at a group of soldiers. "All will be ready."

After several hours of preparations, Bannock returned to his justice room. He and Simon drew up plans to have walls built between the vaulted areas in the cellar. Once the area was divided into separate rooms, doors would be locked to protect the food supplies. The time had come to begin rationing.

As Simon was leaving, Bannock said, "I have letters to write. Have a trusted messenger here in the morning. Their safe delivery is vital."

"I will make sure of it, my lord."

The first two letters were easy. Lord Bannock wrote to Lords Mowbray and Norfolk, informing them that he and his troops had departed for York. He wanted them to be assured that young Edward had his support. His third letter was to Lord Berkeley and took more thought. He explained to his old friend that Julian was not his son and would not be his heir. If Bannock did not survive, then his title would pass to his infant son, Brian Blake. He cautioned Lord Berkeley not to think poorly of Lorraine. She was a good wife, and he was pleased with her. She was now five and twenty, had delivered five children, and had earned the respect of Tess and Simon. He signed the letter, held the sealing wax over a flame, and let it drip onto the folded parchment. He carefully pressed his seal into the soft wax. He left the three letters in the center of his desk.

That evening, the children gathered around him in the withdrawing room. The girls all talked at once, and he listened to the stories that made up their day. Sophie climbed onto his lap, her tiny hands clasping his large fingers. He turned to listen to Elizabeth, but Sophie was competing for his attention. She stood on his lap, grabbed his beard with both hands, and pushed her face against his. She reminded him of a miniature Lorraine, petite, with dark eyes and hair. Now that he had Blake, he no longer resented his youngest daughter. Her determination to have her father all to herself charmed him.

Bannock looked at his family, safe and comfortable in the house he had built to shelter them. Blake and Anne had his fair skin and red hair, while Elizabeth and Sophie resembled Lorraine. He suddenly longed to stay home. Then his gaze fell on Julian.

Julian smiled hesitantly. He didn't crowd forward like the others but waited for Bannock to speak to him.

Instead, Bannock turned to Lorraine. "I have written to Lord Berkeley. The matter is settled."

She had dark circles under her eyes. Too much work and worry had taken a toll on her. Instead of responding, she stalked from the room, but not before he caught the look she cast at him, a glance full of bitter resentment. He continued to hold Sophie, continued to watch his children, but their chatter grew tiresome, and he felt weary.

When he joined Lorraine in bed later that night, he held her but didn't make love to her. He listened to the gentle sound of her breathing and resisted the urge to tell her how much he loved her. It would sound weak and embarrass them both.

Just before dawn, he kissed her, but she didn't awaken. In the darkness, he stood over the bed and watched her. He wanted to touch her but just looked at her for a long time, trying to memorize her exactly as she was at this moment – her eyes closed, hair tangled on the pillow. His heart constricted; he knew her intimately, the feel of her breasts, the shape of her hands, her legs.

He dressed, pulled on his boots, and threw a cloak around his shoulders.

In the corridor, he lit a candle and moved silently toward the nursery. The door was ajar, and he saw the outline of Margaret, the wet nurse. She sat by the banked fire holding the baby.

She started awake when he touched her shoulder. "My lord, is something wrong?"

"Give me my son."

He cradled little Blake and gazed in wonder at the very likeness of himself. The baby stretched, and the little mouth opened in a yawn. Bannock looked into the blue eyes then pressed his cheek to the soft, soft skin. He kissed the baby's brow, and chuckled when the infant found his thumb and began to suck. He handed him back to the wet nurse and left, too overcome to speak.

His soft boots made no sound as he moved to the next room. A young nursemaid lay on a pallet in the corner with little Sophie sleeping peacefully beside her. Elizabeth and Anne shared a bed, their heads inclined together, one dark and one red, both of them fast asleep. He studied them the way he had studied Lorraine, looked at their small forms until he knew each of them by heart. Then he silently retreated. Julian's room was at the end of the corridor, and Bannock looked in that direction, but did not go inside.

He walked silently through the house, out into the courtyard, and then climbed to the top of the hill overlooking the manor. The castle with its battlements and turrets rose strong and solid, gray stone against gray sky. The manor, outbuildings, fields and farmland stretched before him. Everything he owned, everything he had built, everything he valued extended in all directions into the misty dawn. He knelt and prayed to God to protect his holdings and his family, and he prayed that God would see him safely through another battle.

In the courtyard, his men were already saddling their horses for the trek northward. When all was in readiness, Bannock donned his armor, mounted his horse, and gave the signal to depart.

§§§

Lorraine awakened and peered out the window. It was still early, but she saw smoke rising from the chimneys, and knew most of the servants were up. Two young girls carried pails of milk from the barn, but the courtyard was empty of soldiers. She didn't have to search the house to know that Bannock and his troops were gone.

He hadn't said goodbye.

She hurried to the justice room and saw Bannock's letters on his desk. She picked up the one addressed to Lord Berkeley, broke the seal and read the letter disinheriting Julian. She carried it to her room. Messengers were sometimes robbed, and letters were not always delivered. So many things could happen.

Bannock didn't understand the impact of his decision. There would be scandal, feuding, brother against brother. What if Blake didn't survive? He was not yet a year old, and so many infants never lived to see their sixth birthday. She made the sign of the cross.

If Julian was disinherited, some distant Bannock relation could claim the estate, and they all might end up destitute.

She closed her bedroom door and locked it, and then went into her dressing room. Quickly, she lifted a corner of the beautiful tapestry she'd brought from Chateau Brèche.

She remembered Bannock's confusion when she'd hung it in the closet.

"To protect it from fading in the sunlight," she'd lied.

"I'll give it a place of honor in the great hall," he offered.

"No. It's too sentimental." For just a second, she'd felt guilty, but then added for good measure, "I want it close to me in memory of my father."

She slid the oak paneled wall in its groove until it almost disappeared inside the hollowed wall. Once inside, she felt around in the dusky light for the opposite wall and the wedge of wood that hid the key. She knew just where it was and her fingers found it easily. She unlocked the narrow door, but before going inside her secret room, she smoothed the tapestry and then moved the sliding wall back into place. The first chamber was instantly dark; it felt good and safe. She breathed a sigh of relief.

The inner chamber was lit only by a shaft of light coming in through the air hole. Going straight to the corner where Tim Carpenter had so cleverly made a hiding spot, she lifted the floor boards and stuck Bannock's letter deep inside the hollow space.

Julian would not be humiliated as Jacques had been, at least not as long as she could prevent it. It could be months, or even years, before Bannock again talked to Lord Berkeley. They would never know what had happened to the letter.

She left the chamber, carefully locking it up again. When she was outside the antechamber and everything was back in place, she stood and stared at the tapestry.

It was done, and she would take that secret to her grave.

§§§

The days and weeks that followed were so demanding that the rest of the winter passed quickly. But by March of 1461, the fickle breezes brought more than spring buds. A fever raged in many households. Last year's sickness had felled the poorest and weakest tenants, but now even the strong succumbed. Simon and Tess placed extra pallets at the far end of the castle and did their best to sequester the sick, but every day, more servants died.

The elderly Sir Bertrand, who had never come to like or trust Lorraine, was among those who passed away. She was surprised to realize that she missed his cantankerous ways.

Lorraine kept the children inside on all but the warmest days, and then she let them run off their energy in the walled garden. Most days they stayed in the nursery with their governess and tutor, and when they grew restless, she cleared the great hall so they could run and play.

Julian, almost eight, led the others into pretend battles as they galloped across the room on stick horses. Five-year-old Elizabeth and four-year-old Anne shrieked and screamed as their big brother defended them with his small wooden sword. At two and a half, Sophie ran circles around them, dragging her favorite cloth doll and ignoring their protests when she crossed invisible enemy lines. Baby Blake held Lorraine's fingers and attempted to walk. It was almost Easter again, almost time for his first birthday.

§§§

Lord Bannock and his men traveled a mile north of York city before they found an empty field to make their camp. From this distance, he could still see the tall, elaborately carved spires of York Minster reaching into the clouds.

On Sunday, the twenty-ninth day of March in 1461, he awoke shivering in his tent. It was Palm Sunday, and a snowstorm was raging. Word had come to prepare to march, and so he dressed in layers of wool and leather, and his squire helped him with his armor. All around him, men were braced for battle, and tensions were high.

Edward had been newly proclaimed King Edward IV, but Henry VI, his queen and their son had taken refuge inside the city walls. The opposing armies of Lancaster and York filled every field with archers, knights and foot soldiers. He had never seen so many men gathered for one battle. Edward had at least twenty-five thousand soldiers, and the Lancastrian scoundrels numbered as many or more even before their reinforcements arrived.

Henry sent word asking for a truce but he was refused. Edward had the popular support. People already called him king, and he would not rest until he had secured his throne.

Bannock's men gathered around him. "Your service shall be remembered," he shouted. "Fight for God and for King Edward!"

The men cried in unison, "God and King Edward!"

The march began and by late morning they reached a ridge near the village of Towton. The massive Lancastrian army spread across a high meadow. Bannock's breath steamed from his mouth and nose. His muscles vibrated with energy. He felt as he always did before a fight, alert to every sound, every smell. He heard the creak of leather saddles, the rattle of armor and swords. Many of the men looked scared, but he was excited. He sat his horse lightly, holding the reins easily. It began to snow harder, and the wind-driven flurries made it difficult to see. From the ravine below, he heard the roar of a flooded river. Then the order came for the archers, and with the snap and twang of bowstrings, they began their deadly work. Snow found its way under his armor and stung his skin.

The enemy fell back under the onslaught of arrows, regrouped and made their charge.

From the ranks around him, a cry went up. "For God and King Edward!"

Now they were rushing to meet the oncoming Lancastrian army, plunging down the hill and into the meadow, but the press of men was so fierce he could hardly maneuver his horse. He cut with his sword first to one side and then the other, clearing a jagged path through the mayhem. Under the hooves of his horse, the snow turned red.

Bannock sensed his knights flagging, pointed his sword toward Edward's standard, and urged them onward. He spurred his mount toward the rise behind the main line, dismounted and dropped his reins. His men followed suit, and they rushed back into the fray on foot. In the thick of the battle, young Edward had also dismounted, crying out for his men to stand with him.

Robert and a squire were at Bannock's back, and the snow cleared just enough for him to see that his men had gained a little ground. They fought back and forth across the bloody meadow, but neither side held the upper hand. Beneath their boots, the ground was slick with gore. His squire screamed and went down, his helmet caved in by an axe. Bannock stabbed his sword at the foe, and the point found its way through the padded jerkin. He felt the flesh give way and rammed his sword in toward the heart. The man gave a guttural cry and fell. Bannock jerked his weapon free, dropped his shield, drew his dagger and fought relentlessly with a blade in each hand. He was spattered in blood, and under his armor, his woolen tunic was soaked with sweat, but he refused to yield to exhaustion. He continued fighting as the din of warfare rang through the valley.

It was dusk when the cry came from a distant rise. "Norfolk is here!"

Fresh troops bore down on the enemy, and the tide of battle turned. Bannock did not pause to rest. He raced for his horse and spurred it after the retreating Lancastrian army, and his flush of victory turned to rage.

"Spare the commons!" Someone yelled for mercy, but the victorious army ignored the order and continued to slay the retreating men.

On horseback, Bannock cut down those running before him and pursued others into the ravine. They ran for the plank bridge across the icy Cock Beck river. Some of the fleeing army tried to cross the surging stream on foot, but the heavy current swept them away. The Lancastrians were in full retreat, but the fighting was as heavy at the bridge as it had been in the meadow above.

Once more Bannock dismounted and surged into the mass of struggling bodies. He wanted the fighting to be finished. Let war be over and a new king declared by all. The planks of the wooden bridge groaned and swayed. He made another sword thrust and pulled his blade free from the gut of a surprised looking youth.

The bridge shuddered and the wood began to splinter.

He fought to the middle, and the soldiers of Lancaster and York pressed in on him from both sides. He struck again with his sword, and then the crack of timber drowned the cries of dying men. The bridge collapsed beneath him, and he was plunged into the water. The air was ice, the water was ice, and his bones were turning to ice. The river churned with bodies. He pulled off his helmet, gasping for air. Wet flakes of snow touched his face. Still the thunderous tide of men came pouring into the river.

The oncoming horsemen, seeing that the bridge was gone, plunged their mounts into the stream and galloped across the bridge of bodies. Bannock's armor weighed him down, and he scrambled on dead men below him. The hooves of a horse smashed into his chest and forced him down again. He sank, grabbing at the legs of men still thrashing on the surface, their armor gleaming against the dull, dark water. Far above, men still fought. Bubbles escaped his mouth and nose as the river dragged at him. He clamped his lips and flailed, his movements growing weaker as he touched the silt at the bottom of the riverbed. He could no longer recall what had been won, or what had been lost, only that he would never see his infant son again.

Chapter Twenty-Seven

Simon entered the justice room, cleared his throat and announced, "Sir Robert Armstrong."

Robert staggered in, his eyes rimmed with red, his clothes spattered with mud. "Excuse my appearance, mi'lady. I've been riding day and night."

Simon hurried to push a chair toward him, but he ignored it. The knight wouldn't meet Lorraine's eyes.

The quill pen dropped from her fingers as she stood, terrified to hear what he had to say.

"King Edward is victorious." Robert delivered the message without joy, and then faltered. "We won at Towton…"

Her voice caught. "Lord Bannock?"

The knight's eyes flashed from Simon to Lorraine, and then he studied a spot on the stone floor. Finally, he looked up, but whatever he was seeing, it wasn't her. "It grieves me to tell you that Lord Bannock is dead. He drowned."

Lorraine's trembling legs wouldn't hold her, and she sank back into her chair. "Drowned?" He couldn't be dead. In her mind, she saw him confident, seated gallantly on his horse, indomitable in his armor.

Simon glanced at Lorraine.

He was deferring to her and she had to stay in control. "I want to know everything."

"The Lancastrians were routed, and Lord Bannock pursued them as they fled across a bridge." Robert raised his hand as though reaching for something, then let it fall to his side. "The wood couldn't bear the weight of so many men and horses."

Bannock couldn't be dead. It wasn't possible.

"Most of our army was lost," Robert said.

Simon looked ashen. "Did you bring his lordship's body home?"

"There must have been twenty thousand slain. All in mass graves." His finger tapped rapidly against his leg, as though counting the dead. "After the bridge collapsed, I never saw Lord Bannock again."

Simon grasped his shoulder, and Lorraine saw Robert's eyes slowly regain their focus. He looked around as though surprised to be standing in a room and not on a battlefield.

Lorraine could scarcely comprehend the tragedy. She cleared her throat. "You saw him?" She waited for Robert to meet her eyes. "Before he drowned, you saw him on the bridge?"

"He fought bravely," Robert said.

Bannock would have been at the heart of the battle. It wasn't in his nature to hold back.

"He wouldn't let them retreat," Robert said quietly.

Brian, you stubborn fool. Why risk your life for a battle that was already won? To Robert, she said, "Thank you. The cook will give you something to eat, and then you can rest."

He bowed deeply and stumbled out.

Simon helped himself to the empty chair. She read the devastation in the deep lines on his face and in the pallor of his skin. He seemed to have aged years in a matter of minutes.

"What should we do?" she asked.

For once, Simon seemed incapable of answering.

All her worries about Julian and the letter were suddenly replaced by the realization that all of her children were now vulnerable to the whims of a man she'd never met. How could she, a foreign born woman, hang on to this estate long enough for one of her sons to reach majority?

Simon looked up, almost as if he'd read her thoughts. "Everyone must be assured that the house of Bannock is strong."

"Yes." She nodded slowly, staring him in the eye, trying to read his thoughts. How much did he know? She needed a plan. Now that Robert had returned, word would spread fast. "Send for Lord Berkeley at once, to solidify the family's position."

They'd been left weakened and in danger, and she had to prove that she could manage the estate. She was reminded of when she first came to Bannock Manor. Everyone had been watching her, trying to measure her, judging what kind of mistress she might be. They would watch her again now, perhaps judge her even more harshly.

Would the tenants respect her authority? Did she have enough men-at-arms to protect their land? If what Robert said was true, then most of their army was lost. She remembered her last year at Chateau Brèche, the hunger, the fear, and the feeling of being powerless.

Her gaze fell on the basket weave pattern of tiles on the floor. The intricate and clever pattern was no accident. Brian had been so proud of the way it hid his strongbox, and she wondered how much money was concealed there.

Simon was still struggling to hold back his tears. "He was always so sure of himself. Invincible."

Brian Bannock was part of everything; his presence filled the house. Somehow, in spite of the stubborn, willful girl she had been when she left Chateau Brèche, in spite of her determination to remain loyal to Jacques, she had grown to care for him. "I relied on him to come home," she said.

"We all did." Simon's lips trembled. "We lived for him."

Lorraine said, "He was devoted to you, too."

Confusion filled Simon's eyes as though he couldn't understand how death had gotten the better of Bannock.

Lorraine looked at the desk – Brian Bannock's desk. She ran her fingers along the leather spines of the ledgers. They contained an accounting of the wealth of the estate, and it was her duty to protect it. She wanted to put her head on her arms and weep, but another thought consumed her.

Which one of her sons would inherit?

§§§

Four days later, Lord James Berkeley and his wife, Lady Isabel, arrived. The Bannock household was deep in mourning as Simon ushered their guests into the withdrawing room and offered refreshments. Lorraine curtsied, smoothed her gown, and tried to conceal her nervousness. Lord Berkeley was in his sixties, and it was unlikely that he would live long enough to see either Julian or young Blake grow to manhood. Why had Bannock appointed such an elderly gentleman to be their children's guardian?

Bannock had been home so little during the past year, and the children didn't really understand what had happened. Their voices carried from the gardens through the open windows. They had no idea that their way of life rested in the hands of the man now standing in her drawing room.

"Your husband was my dear friend, and I admired him greatly." Lord Berkeley nodded respectfully and took her hand. "Without Bannock and his men, we are both in a weakened position."

She was surprised by the strength of his grasp. He might be old, but she could see the intelligence in his face. He murmured something about being honored to be entrusted as the guardian of Lord Bannock's heir.

Lorraine's heart fluttered. "When was the last time you and Lord Bannock discussed the guardianship?"

"Oh, it must have been over a year ago." He looked out the window where the children were visible. "The last time I saw him, he was very proud of his growing family and wanted to be sure you would be protected if anything happened to him."

"You saw him a year ago? Before the birth of his second son?"

Berkeley turned from the window and smiled. "As I recall, he was worried that he might have another daughter. He did not want to arrange four marriages and four dowries, but fortunately, you gave him another son."

"But you never discussed our welfare after our second son was born?" Lorraine pressed.

"I assure you, I know Lord Bannock's wishes." He took a seat stiffly. "And I am prepared to honor them."

Lady Isabel sat in an armchair beside her husband. "You needn't worry that my husband will interfere unnecessarily."

"My duty is to keep the title and property intact for the heir," Berkeley said. "He will have control of the estate when he is twenty."

Lorraine tried to appear impassive while hanging on Lord Berkeley's every word.

When she remained silent, her guests shifted in their chairs. "I can help with the boy's education, of course," Berkeley offered.

Lorraine watched Simon. He moved about the room offering refreshments to the guests, but he avoided looking at her.

"Lady Bannock, this estate will be handled according to your late husband's wishes," Lord Berkeley said. "I intend to make sure that it passes to Julian without complications."

She exhaled deeply, not realizing she'd been holding her breath. "That means everything to me." Slumping into the nearest chair, she resisted asking him to repeat himself. "Thank you."

Simon silently poured wine.

"It may seem like an indelicate subject." Lord Berkeley glanced at his wife. "But your property will be better protected if you remarry quite soon. A woman without a husband is always in danger."

Lorraine had been about to suggest that the Berkeleys might enjoy a tour of the grounds, but she didn't dare rise, didn't want her guests to see how horrified she was. It had taken her years to feel affection for Bannock, and she had managed it because she loved her children.

Lady Isabel was already making plans for Lorraine to visit their castle. "Our sons are grown, and William, the eldest, is thirty and still unmarried." She smiled. "Of course, it will have to wait until your mourning is over."

"You're very kind," Lorraine said. She would fight to the death to protect the estate for her children, but Jacques was the only man who could tempt her to get married again. Perhaps, in time, news would reach him of Bannock's death, and he would come back to her.

Simon returned from escorting the Berkeleys to their room, and Lorraine waited for what he had to say. She recalled her first days at Bannock Manor when every word between them had been a battle, every act of disobedience part of a larger war. She didn't try to keep the challenge out of her eyes this time either.

"Lord Berkeley would like to meet with Julian later," Simon said. Whatever his thoughts about her deception, he kept them hidden behind an inscrutable expression. "Also, he will need to go over the household accounts with you."

"Yes, of course."

He cleared his throat. "Perhaps you should…"

She leaned forward, waiting to hear his threats.

"Consider the Berkeley's request and meet their son," he said. "Your estate and family will be better protected if you find another husband."

His agreement that she should marry again caught her off guard. Simon had been more devoted to Bannock than anyone. She could hardly imagine how hard it would be for him to serve another master. What would the cost be to him if another man became lord of the Bannock household?

"Simon." She braced for an argument. "I have no desire to get married again."

"We need an alliance with the Berkeleys." As usual, Simon was putting the practical needs of the estate before his own feelings. "We've lost most of our army, and they have only a small defensive force. Together we can fortify both families."

"Another husband will want his own heir."

Impatience flashed in Simon's eyes. "Let's be sure that you have an estate to pass to your… heir. Your first duty is to protect us, Lady Bannock. Other nobles may try to take advantage of your weakness."

He might be right, but it galled her. Julian was just a boy, and Lord Berkeley was an old man, and between the two households they couldn't even raise an army.

At least for now, Simon seemed prepared to keep her secret.

§§§

For the next five days, Lorraine entertained Lord and Lady Berkeley. She showed them around the property and spent hours with Lord Berkeley in the justice room, where together they worked on the required inventory of the estate. He seemed surprised and then relieved at her grasp of business.

Each evening, instead of eating in the nursery with the younger children, Julian was allowed to join them for supper in the dining room.

Lord Berkeley took a keen interest in his young charge. "Julian, tell me about your studies."

Julian sat up straighter and answered seriously. "My tutor is teaching me Latin, reading, and numbers. I can speak French to Mama and Matilde."

"I often speak French to the children," Lorraine said. "It's part of their heritage, and I don't want them to forget the Bonville lineage.

Lord Berkeley leaned closer to Julian and asked, "What do you enjoy most?"

"Arithmetic."

"Besides your studies." Berkeley placed a gentle hand on Julian's shoulder.

Lorraine saw the tension ease from her son's face. He relaxed a little and grinned up at his guardian. "I like to play outside," he said. "I want a horse."

The older man continued to smile warmly. The more he listened, the chattier Julian became.

He looked over at his mother. "I'm going to grow up and protect Mama."

"I plan to help you do just that," Lord Berkeley assured him.

Lady Isabel renewed her invitation for Lorraine to visit Berkeley Castle. "It's less than a day's ride," she said, as she nibbled on a squab leg. "I can't understand why Lord Bannock never brought you."

Lorraine thought of dozens of reasons. Because Bannock hadn't trusted her enough, because he was afraid she might try to run away, because the babies had come in rapid succession, because there had been battle after battle to support one king or another. The years had passed, and she had never left her husband's property.

After dinner, the three little girls and the baby joined them in the withdrawing room. As her children charmed her guests, Lorraine studied the Berkeleys. They seemed warm and generous, but they also had their own interests at heart.

§§§

Lorraine closed her eyes and leaned back against the bench, relishing the warmth of the July sunshine on her shoulders. She heard Anne's young voice laughing and reluctantly opened her eyes. The little girl hopped in and out of a puddle, splashing muddy water. "Anne, stop," Lorraine called. "Your gown is getting dirty."

Anne's dimpled cheeks made her look like an imp. The four-year-old ran over and snuggled into her mother's lap. Lorraine kissed the top of her daughter's red hair and wiped the sweat from her brow. "Would you like to watch Julian at sword practice?" She grasped the small hand, and together they walked up the hill. It was slow going as Anne stopped and looked at every bug.

As they passed the dovecote, she pulled Lorraine's arm and begged "I want to see the baby birds. I want to watch their mamas feed them."

"It's dirty in there," Lorraine said. "Let's find Julian." But the child continued tugging her toward the dovecote door. "Oh, all right, but take care not to touch anything."

She unlatched the door, and they entered. The octagonal building was forty feet tall and about twenty feet around. Once inside, they looked up to see dozens of wooden nesting boxes attached to the inside walls. Small openings allowed the doves to come and go freely, and the sounds of wings flapping and birds cooing seemed amplified within the confined space. The lowest nests were five feet from the ground to prevent foxes and rodents from feeding on the young. She picked Anne up so that she could look into the lowest nests. The air was stifling, bird feathers softly fluttered to the floor, and the stench of bird droppings made Lorraine's eyes water. She tried to hold her breath. When the hatchlings were large enough, most of them were collected and cooked for dinner. Squab was one of her favorite dishes; watching them grow was not one of the things she enjoyed. After just a few minutes, she hurried Anne outside to the fresh air.

"They stink!" Anne rubbed her nose.

Lorraine brushed the feathers and dust from their gowns. "So, why do you always want to go in there?"

Instead of answering, Anne ran ahead.

Julian was at the top of the hill, brandishing his wooden sword, probably organizing another charge of his imaginary army. She watched her son's deft, confident movements. He only ever fought one battle now, always pretending to save the man he thought of as his father.

Lorraine looked down at the manor house. The chimney pots were arranged along the roofline in clusters of four, reminding her of rows of marching men. She prayed that neither of her sons would ever go to battle, and yet they would both be trained to defend their family, their land, and their king.

Squeals of laughter sounded as Elizabeth ran from the house. Matilde chased after her, scolding in French. Although she was only five, Elizabeth took advantage of most situations and didn't stop running until she was at Anne's side. She grabbed onto her sister and they both tumbled to the ground.

Matilde caught up with her. "Sophie and Blake are sleeping," she said, struggling for breath, "but Elizabeth wouldn't leave them alone." She grabbed the child's shoulder and shook her. "Why must you be naughty?" Matilde settled herself on the grass beside the girls.

"Can we visit Papa," Anne asked. "I want to see him again."

It had been two months since their father's death, but Lorraine wasn't sure the girls understood. They entered the cool interior of the chapel, and her daughters admired the colored light filtering in from the round, stained glass window above the altar.

"I want to see Papa," Anne demanded, stomping her foot.

Lorraine led them to the stairs that descended beneath the chapel. Elizabeth hesitated, and Matilde took her hand.

The crypt contained an empty tomb topped with a marble effigy of their father. The figure of Bannock was a testament to the strength he had displayed in the flesh. He wore his sword at his side, his head rested on a sleeping lion, and a dog lay in repose at his feet. He lay as though in slumber, but it was easy to picture him alive, red-haired and passionate in word and deed. The marble was cool as she ran her fingers over the shoulder-length locks of hair, the full lips and rounded cheeks.

Lorraine knelt down and pulled Anne and Elizabeth to her side. She pointed to the words that were freshly engraved and read out loud, "Lord Brian Bannock, Baron, Husband and Father. Died 29 March, 1461 at Towton Battle." Below that was the verse she had written shortly after Sir Robert had delivered the news.

> A blush is on the meadow
> A calm is on the field
> No glimmer of the battle
> No ring of sword on shield
>
> The blood that stained the soil
> Runs in the sap of trees
> That line the bending river
> That drowned the dying pleas
>
> My soul released from armour
> No more the weight of war
> Some men have other seasons
> I'll pass this way no more.

Brian Bannock had wanted to insure a final resting place befitting a baron, and he had lived just long enough to see the chapel and his tomb completed. But his body hadn't been recovered, and the tomb was empty. How would his soul ever find peace in a mass grave?

Elizabeth's high voice cut into her reverie. "Mama, can we paint the statue colors so it will look more like him?"

"Let's do, Mama. Please." Anne pointed to her own hair. "His hair should be painted red like mine."

A horn on the wall walk blasted three long notes, and Lorraine looked at Matilde. "The alarm!"

Lorraine grabbed the girls' hands and bolted toward the stairs. "Quickly! Let's get back to the house!" She rushed them up the crypt stairs and out of the chapel.

The warning sounded again, and she saw men running toward the castle. She looked down at a dark stain spreading across the valley. Horses and riders, fifty or more, were coming fast. She saw the billowing cloaks of the mounted men and for a fleeting moment thought it might be the king's army, but she searched for a banner and saw none. Frantically, she looked around. Where was Julian? She spied him running down the other side of the slope, toy sword raised as he headed straight toward the oncoming horsemen.

A chill rose on her skin, and she screamed. "Julian!"

He was too far away to hear her.

From the direction of the stables, Tim Carpenter came running. He reached them and snatched up Anne and Elizabeth, one under each arm, and began racing down the hill. "Lady Bannock," he yelled. "I'll put them in the chamber!"

"Get Sophie and Blake," Lorraine called to Matilde. "I'll meet you there."

The horn blasted another note, and she saw Sir Robert taking charge of what was left of the Bannock army.

She set off at a dead run, calling out to her son, but people were screaming as they ran for safety, and Julian continued his charge toward the invading soldiers. She caught up with him and pulled him into her arms, struggling to carry him.

Julian kicked and tried to wiggle free. "Put me down!"

He was too heavy. "Run." She yanked on his arm. "Faster!"

They raced toward the manor house, and as they came around the side of the chapel, she saw the horsemen crossing the bottom of the valley. Tim, still clutching the girls, had reached the manor, and Matilde was right behind them.

The attackers urged their mounts forward, fanning out as they galloped closer. Lorraine screamed, and urged Julian to run faster. He heard the panic in her voice and started to cry. She clutched his wrist and half-dragged, half-carried him so that his churning legs lifted off the ground.

Julian fought her grip and choked on his tears. "Let me fight!"

They weren't going to make it.

Hanging onto her son, she changed direction and headed back inside the chapel. They ran down into the crypt and crouched behind Bannock's tomb. She could hardly catch her breath as she whispered, "Hold still. Don't make a sound!"

Within minutes, she heard boots stomping down the stairs. She was trembling and Julian's eyes were wide with terror, but he stayed quiet. Footsteps crossed the dark room, and suddenly Julian was snatched up by his tunic. He squirmed and twisted, squealed and kicked. The soldier shook him like a rag doll and then tossed him into a corner.

He pulled Lorraine to her feet, and pushed her so that she was pinned between his body and the wall. Fighting for her life, and her son's, she wrenched an arm free and dug her elbow into his gut. He gave way just enough that she almost broke free, but he grabbed her and flung her across the room. Her head struck Bannock's effigy.

"Don't give me trouble," he warned. "Or I'll take it out on your bastard."

Cowering, eyes bulging, Julian made a strangled sound.

"Please," she begged. "Don't hurt him."

She lunged to get to Julian, but the back of the soldier's fist caught her across the face and she went sprawling.

"Don't worry so much about that one." The soldier moved over her, his boot clamping down on her wrist. "It's the other boy we're after." He looked over his shoulder and spat at the tomb. "The mighty Lord Bannock," he said. "Fitting that he should be here too."

"Who are you? What do you want?"

He bent down and grabbed her hair, twisting her head close to his face. "I've got a message to deliver, and your bastard son is going to see why he's unfit to ever claim this estate."

Julian dashed toward the stairs, and the invader cursed and ran after him. Lorraine was on her feet and grabbed a trowel.

He caught Julian and his arm tightened around the boy's neck. "Put it down." Julian's face turned purplish red, and his eyes watered.

She threw it on the far side of the tomb so that if he went for it, she could rescue Julian, and maybe reach the stairs.

Shoving the boy away, he ordered, "Lie down woman, so that I can use you like the whore you are."

Julian landed on his hands and knees, gasping and choking.

She forced calm into her voice. "Crawl behind Papa's tomb. Close your eyes and block your ears. Don't come out until I tell you."

He started to cry.

"Please, Julian." He seemed too frightened to move. Ignoring the lewd glare of her aggressor, she pulled her sobbing son out of view.

The stranger laughed again. "I'll make sure he never forgets this day." He stepped toward her, his finger curling, beckoning her closer.

She backed away from him, deeper into the crypt, further from the door. When she felt the wall behind her, she held up her hands. There was no way to escape. "Please. Leave us alone."

Moving faster than she could react, he grabbed her shoulders and threw her to the floor. He yanked up her skirt and she fought back. Then he was on her, his knees pinning her down, his weight making it hard for her to breathe. In one vicious jerk, he ripped off her undergarments.

Her fists pummeled his arms, his chest, his stomach. She heard Julian whimpering, and twisted to see him.

A blow landed on the side of her head, and she was stunned. Her ears rang and the metallic taste of blood filled her mouth. Her head, and neck, and jaw vibrated with pain.

Above her, the soldier opened his pants and began massaging his cock. "I'm going to take my time with you. Keep you out of the way until we've got what we came for."

"Why are you doing this?"

He continued to stroke himself. "Remember a wench named Joan? Her bastard has a striking resemblance to your Lord Bannock. Some might say he's next in line to inherit this estate."

"Joan has no claim here!" Lorraine was sickened by the sight of the soldier's dirty foreskin. She remembered the plump housemaid. She'd been gone for years, and she'd never heard of her having a baby. "Joan's a liar," she said.

"That's not what Squire Winthrop thinks. He's agreed to be guardian of her son. You could say he was offered the opportunity to look out for the boy's interests." He positioned himself between her legs and began to thrust awkwardly.

Lorraine tried to roll away, but his thumbs dug into her shoulders, pinioning her.

"As long as you kept having girls there was no problem, but you can't keep your legs closed, can you?" He wedged her legs apart with his knees and ground against her. "And now, your youngest stands in the way."

He was forcing himself inside. More pain. Everything hurt.

"She wants me to give you a message." Brutally, he grunted a word with every thrust. "You – are – a – French – whore – who – deserves – to – be – punished."

His breath smelled of decay. His stench was sweat, and dirt, and fouled clothing. She tried to push him off, but could hardly move through the agony.

They were here to get Blake. To kill him.

The realization got her moving again, and she tried to buck him off, got her hands free and dug her nails into his face. She tried to gouge his eyes, but only scored his cheeks.

He lifted her by the shoulders and slammed her back down, knocking the breath out of her. Bile rose in her throat.

He stiffened, thrust again and finished inside of her. A moment later he was on his knees and lacing his pants. "Want more? My friends are waiting outside." He got to his feet and nudged her bare hip with the toe of his boot and laughed again. "They may want to pass. You don't look good."

She opened her eyes and saw the top of Julian's head as he crept forward. She lifted a hand and tried to wave him back, but he kept crawling closer. "No." It came out as a groan.

Julian rushed the brute, swinging his arms.

"I can just as easily kill you too." The soldier laughed and shoved him, sending him sprawling backward. Julian landed hard against the wall.

"Don't!" Lorraine sat up, pain in her abdomen and where he'd stretched her arms, pain where he'd knelt with his knees digging into her thighs. She wanted to rip his head from his neck and smash it against the wall, but she had to think; her children's lives depended on it.

"Maybe your next bastard will be mine." The soldier slowly finished fastening the front of his pants.

She heard Julian throwing up in a corner. Pulling her skirt around her legs, she said, "Get out of here and leave us alone."

Outside, men were shouting, but the terrified screams of women had lessened.

He watched her, his expression unreadable. "Joan's son has a rightful claim on this estate, and he will be the next baron." He glanced at Julian, and shook his head in disgust. "At least her boy looks like Lord Bannock." He spat as he delivered his last warning. "Joan will get Bannock Manor for her own."

Grinning lewdly, he said, "I'll come back too." He kicked her again and stalked out of the chapel.

She crawled over to Julian but he wouldn't look at her and cringed away when she tried to touch him. Finally, she coaxed him into her arms and held him, stroked his head, and rocked him. Tears streamed down his face. She wanted to cry but couldn't, not yet. Not until she was certain the attackers were gone.

They hid behind Bannock's effigy until the screaming died down to absolute stillness. Not even birds twittered or chirped. There was nothing she could do right now but hold her son and pray for everyone else. She had to survive for the sake of her children, and they had to survive to make her life worth living.

When the silence was as deep as a grave, they ventured out. Sir Robert's body was draped over the battlements, his blood staining the gray stone. More broken bodies lay at the base of the stairs, her guards all slaughtered.

Julian shuddered, and clung tightly to her hand as they slowly walked down the hill.

The front door, made from stout oak, had been shattered by axes. Blood was splattered across the floor. She hesitated at the threshold, afraid more men were waiting inside. Perhaps Joan wanted her to see this carnage, make her want to leave Bannock Manor with her children and never come back.

Lorraine gripped Julian's arm. "Stay by my side."

She moved past the splintered wood and broken crockery in the front hall, and then she covered her nose and mouth. Someone had defecated in the middle of the corridor.

The ground floor rooms were full of blood and sprawled bodies. Cupboards had been toppled, dishes broken, and trunks hacked apart, the contents torn and trampled. Anything of value had been stolen, the rest left in ruins.

Had anyone else survived? She wouldn't go straight to the secret chamber until she was sure it was safe. She was shivering, walking stiffly, aching everywhere.

She looked into the justice room.

"It's Simon," Julian said, his hand tightening on hers. "They killed him."

Blood was everywhere. Simon's skull had been bashed in, and clumps of his hair and brains lay in a dark pool. He'd been loyal to the end, first to Bannock, then to her. She made the sign of the cross and whispered a quick prayer as guilt and grief flooded her. He'd tried to warn her this could happen.

Julian was staring at the corpse and tugging on her arm. She hardened herself for what was to come, turned his head away and led him out of the room.

The body of a girl, one of the young servants who worked in the laundry, lay sprawled on the landing of the stairs. A baby was wailing and she found it in a basket buried under a pile of linens.

A fresh shudder passed through her. The girl who had been pregnant, the one she'd let stay had had this tiny boy just a few months back. She gathered him up, trying to soothe him. If Tess had dismissed her, the mother might still be alive.

Upstairs, bedding had been torn open and tossed aside, the hems of her gowns ripped, the bottom of each trunk broken.

Where were her own children? Her lips quivered and her stomach cramped as she got closer to the secret chamber. The infant squalled piteously against her shoulder.

Please dear God, let my babies be alive.

She turned the corner into the dressing alcove and her knees almost buckled.

Julian began to scream.

Tim Carpenter's body lay crumpled at their feet. He was face down, a stream of blood trailing across the floor. A tiny hand stuck out beneath his chest. It was motionless, and she knew it would never move again.

She tried to pass the crying infant to Julian, but he was hysterical, shaking, and he started backing out of the room.

"Take this baby." She shook his shoulder, demanding that he obey.

His mouth hung open and he began to gasp. Never taking his eyes off the body on the floor, Julian raised his arms and she placed the wiggling infant into them.

"Hold him tight," she ordered. "Wait in the corridor." She turned him around and gave him a little push.

When she was certain Julian had gone, she braced herself and tried to roll Tim's body over without crushing the child beneath him. He barely budged. The hem of her skirt dragged through his blood, soaking it up.

Sobbing, her heart breaking, she heaved two more times. The weight of him was too much for her; she needed help but there was no one, no one at all. She had to move him, to free her baby.

She bent her knees, shoved her hands beneath his torso, and, ignoring the slack wetness of his body, lifted him with all her strength. Finally, he flopped over.

A long, shrill wail ripped from her soul and curled up through the rafters, up through the clouds, heavenward. Everything in her begged that her child was alive.

Sinking to her knees, she pulled little Sophie into her arms and rocked back and forth. The beautiful little eyes were closed like she was sleeping, but instead of pink cheeks and lips, they were white.

Lorraine kissed her over and over, caressing the black curls, brushing tendrils away from the baby's forehead. There was a stillness, a slackness to the little body.

The other infant cried, but she didn't care. She wanted her own baby to cry, to be alive.

Her agonized shrieks drowned out all sound. Her fury and anguish obliterated all thought.

"Damn you for leaving us defenseless, Brian Bannock! Damn you and your whore to hell!"

"Mama?" Julian stood in the doorway, tears running down his cheeks. "This baby won't stop crying." He moved beside her and touched the top of her head. "Maybe you should feed him."

"I don't think I can," she said, but her breasts were engorged and tender, and leaking milk left wet circles on her blouse.

"You have to," Julian answered. "Or he might die too." His eyes were the mirror image of Jacques', wise beyond his years and full of pain. "Where are Elizabeth and Anne? Where are Blake and Matilde?" He tried to hand her the squalling baby, but she shook her head.

Lifting Sophie's hand to her lips, she kissed the palm and touched it to her cheek, felt the tiny fingers as they brushed against her tears. Two years of life wasn't enough. She couldn't let her go.

Had Matilde saved the others?

Her children were the fabric of her existence. She stared at the back of the alcove. The tapestry hung as it always did, covering the entrance to the secret chambers.

Chapter Twenty-Eight

Todd Woodbridge stood in Bannock Manor's drawing room as family and friends listened to another update from Officer Stiles. The goal of the search had switched from finding Laura Bram alive to recovering evidence – finding the body. The bloodstains on the stairs and the scattered knives pointed to murder.

The image of her smile came into his mind and then was crowded out by fear. It was incomprehensible. She couldn't be dead.

He glanced at Laura's father and saw a change come over him, so visual and readable, like watching a silent movie. First disbelief and astonishment, followed by anger that hardened briefly into rage, and then the face of the tall, handsome, middle-aged man went from red to gray and crumpled into despair. He broke down and sobbed openly.

Choking back his own emotions, Todd briefly placed his hand on the older man's shoulder. He wanted to offer words of comfort but there was nothing he could say.

"We're looking at all possibilities," Officer Stiles said. "Not just with Laura, but with Eleanor Colfax Bram and Winifred Wilcox."

"Why didn't you consider all possibilities earlier?" Laura's older brother, Edward, stood beside his father, his teeth clenched. "My sister made numerous calls, even brought evidence to you. How is it that now, now that she's missing, your department gets serious?"

Todd had searched side-by-side with the family for the past six days. They had possessed a deeply ingrained belief that they could control the outcome of most situations. Until now, this kind of violence, this vulnerability was simply not part of their experience.

Officer Stiles' response was drowned out as the others present, a dozen friends and neighbors, voiced their concerns just as loudly.

Outside the window were fifty to sixty volunteers who'd been helping with the search, and camera crews from at least four television stations, all waiting to hear the formal announcement.

He'd heard enough and slipped out the back door. There were still places he hadn't looked. He walked along the lane, and then up the hill, hoping to notice something that the previous searches had missed. When he reached the crest he turned around; this was the best view of the house.

Shoving his hands deep into his pockets, he stared back at the house, wracking his brain to think of where she might be. Perhaps she'd fallen into an old well, or maybe she was being held hostage in some remote building. But the truth was that the police had already dug up every mound of loose dirt or sunken bog searching for her body.

Every time he thought of Laura, every time he breathed, pain stabbed his chest. Her smile, her easy laugh, the way her eyes sparkled with that mischievous look that was so uniquely hers. So – Laura. Pictures of her filled his mind and sliced into his heart. As each hour passed the odds of finding her alive grew slimmer. He had to keep moving, keep looking, or he'd fall apart too.

He followed a path that ran along the hillside, his feet sinking into the loamy soil as he stepped over fallen branches and bracken. The afternoon sun glared into his eyes. He tripped over a large root, lost his balance, landed on his butt and slid two feet in the mud.

Shit!

But he didn't get up right away. Resting his elbows on his knees, he sat and pondered the house. Where was she? He was letting her down, failing, and it was killing them both. She was meant to be with him, and he couldn't lose her now.

In the past week he'd searched everywhere from the roof trusses to the cellar cupboards, but there'd been no sign of her anywhere. For the first time in his life, Todd understood the desire for vengeance. He wasn't a violent man, but whoever had hurt Laura was going to pay. He'd make sure of it.

Rising to his feet and wiping his muddy hands on his jeans, he decided to examine the western wall first. For over an hour he painstakingly studied the Georgian side before shifting his attention to the medieval section.

The old part of the manor, dating to the 1400's, was four stories high with thick granite walls partially covered in ivy. There weren't as many windows and doors, making it less vulnerable to attack. He walked slowly, examining every angle. The windows had most of the original glass, dozens of tiny, diamond-shaped panes rippling and buckling with age. They caught and scattered the light.

At the third floor level something sparkled against the wall, but it was too far away for him to see it clearly. Probably just something a bird had stuck in the ivy. He pulled his binoculars out of his backpack, focused them and scanned the foliage, methodically searching one section at a time, shifting his gaze in tiny increments until he spotted it again.

Tightening the focus, he zoomed in for a closer look but still couldn't make out exactly what it was. A popped metallic balloon? A wad of aluminum? Upon closer inspection it appeared to be shaped like a cross. He studied the wall behind the object, and saw what looked like a drain hole or vent, but there were no windows nearby. Whatever was reflecting the sun so brilliantly reminded him of the isolated beam from a lighthouse, a warning to pay attention.

Staring through the binoculars, he analyzed the placement of the windows on that floor, calculating where in the medieval section of the house he could get closest to that spot from the inside. When it came to medieval homes, he had more expertise than anyone, and if Laura was still in the house, it was up to him to find her.

He made his way downhill.

The press conference was over and there was no one in the kitchen or the foyer, but Bernard and Edward were probably around somewhere. He'd been given permission to search anywhere on the property, and he silently made his way to the arched door that led into the oldest part of the house.

The medieval great hall looked the same as the last time he'd been there with Laura. The police search hadn't disturbed much, and this part of the house still had the musty, unused smell of a place that had been shut up for too long.

He climbed the stairs until he reached the third floor and then moved carefully, taking his time, studying the walls in each room and counting the windows. The two chambers farthest back were larger than the others and connected by an interior door, obviously designed for the highest ranking family members. He went inside the first one and examined the inside surface of the exterior wall. Most of it was covered with ancient oak paneling. Was the hole he'd seen behind the wood? He scanned the entire room until he reached the corner where the exterior wall continued into an alcove.

Laura had briefly shown him this room, and the torn tapestry hanging on the back wall, but she'd been uneasy, and when he'd started to ask, she'd changed the topic and guided him away.

Leaving the tapestry undisturbed, he returned to the larger room, examining the exterior wall and its windows, but nothing seemed unusual. Once again he analyzed the window placement. The glittering object had to be on this level, on the outside wall of one of these two rooms. He paced the distance from the doorway to the wall in the first room, and then measured the distance again for the second room. There definitely was a space that was unaccounted for between them, and it had to be behind the alcove. He looked at all the nearby walls, even lifted a corner of the tapestry, but couldn't discern anyway to access the area.

Laura had to be somewhere, and he had to find her. His neck and shoulders were tight. Today, it had to happen today.

His mind kept circling to the shining object in the ivy near the mouth of a vent hole, and the unaccounted for space between rooms. He measured the walls again, looking for a hidden entrance. Priest's holes were always carefully disguised.

The most likely spot was behind the tapestry hanging against the ornately carved wood paneling. Todd lifted a corner of the fragile cloth and studied the wall. There was a tiny gap along one corner. He pushed it and was amazed when it slid sideways in a groove hidden behind the baseboard.

Shoving it as far as it would go, he exposed a closet about four by six feet.

It was empty. Another dead end.

He closed his eyes, trying to stem the rush of disappointment. It was a priest's hole all right, a fancy one at that, with oak paneling carved to look like linen, but Laura wasn't in there.

If she didn't care so much about this damn house he'd tear it apart room by room until he found her. Why had she insisted on staying after what had happened to her mother and Winnie? And why had he encouraged her? Her life was worth more than this place.

Struggling to stay calm, he took several deep breaths and then walked into the corridor. He looked in both directions. Where in the hell was she? His fist slammed the wall. He circled through every room on that floor, and then the one above. Nothing but empty rooms. He even shone his flashlight down the garderrobe, relieved when there was no sign of her there.

If there was nothing else to go on, then he might as well try to track down that hole in the wall again. He made his way back to the bedchamber with the alcove and slipped into the small room behind the tapestry. He knew enough about medieval architecture to know that there had to be a logical, practical reason for that small hole in the wall, and it was most likely for ventilation.

It was highly unusual for the inside of a closet to have such finely detailed paneling. Examining it closely, he started at the top and worked his way to the bottom. Along the sides of the room, the accumulated grime looked like it hadn't been disturbed in years, but in the center, there were shoe prints, modern shoes with a patterned sole, and very different from his own. Someone had been in here recently.

He peered more closely at the dust, and his pulse began hammering. There was another set of footprints, too small for a man. They were fresh, too new for any more dust to have settled in them, and they were the prints of someone with bare feet.

Hope surged. Finally, he was seeing something new, a sign of life that couldn't have been made by the cops.

He examined the wall, feeling along the baseboards, and discovered a small gap where the wall wasn't flush with the floor. The bottom edge was rough as if it had been gouged, and a piece of paper poked out. He pressed his forefinger onto it and pulled. It was bigger than he thought, and he worked at it gingerly until a whole page of parchment, about ten inches by twelve, gradually eased out from under the wall. The brittle page was covered in flowery script. It was old, ancient even, and he was astounded at the find. How had it gotten in the wall, and how long had it been there? He began to read.

It was almost dark on the December afternoon in the year of our Lord, 1452, when I first set eyes upon Bannock Manor. I had never seen a nobleman's home without protective castle walls. It was newly built, and I wrongly assumed the walls would come later.

Our journey had taken weeks and had been fraught with danger. So many had died, and most of what I held dear had been left behind in France. We were three weary fugitives who stood in the freezing rain and looked across the valley at the house. I was terrified to enter those doors.

Looking across the valley at the house.

Whoever had written this must have been standing near the top of the lane. He had the strange sensation that he'd been there with them, looking at the house, afraid of what was going to happen. An enormous sense of loss enveloped him, like something closing in that he couldn't stop.

He looked from the page to the wall panels, and then back at the delicate old parchment. It was valuable and historic, but right now, finding Laura was the only thing that mattered.

There had to be another small room behind this one. Probably the real Priest's Hole.

Lying on his belly in the dust, he maneuvered as close to the wall as he could get, focusing on the tiny gap at the bottom of the paneling. When he got his face down next to it, he smelled decay, and his stomach lurched. Cold sweat flooded his armpits. He drew back, choking, praying it was just a dead rat, but the smell...it was too foul.

He needed to call the police. He'd promised them that if he found anything he wouldn't touch it. Pulling his cell phone out of his pocket, he started to dial 999, but there was no reception. He threw the phone down, not caring about anything except finding Laura.

Even though he couldn't see a door or latches, he knew there had to be access to the space, but when he pushed against the panels, he felt no give. He tried smaller areas, pressing along the carved design, pushing in every direction, searching for a piece of scroll work that moved. Finally, about halfway up one wall, an inch wide piece of the carved oak slid down and revealed a keyhole. He grabbed his flashlight and tried to look inside, but it was blocked.

Using the keyhole as an anchor point, he found the outline of a door cleverly disguised in the wood decoration. Destroying such a masterfully carved piece of history went against everything he believed in, but there was no time to waste getting planning approval on this one. He was going to deface an ancient door on a Grade II listed building.

If Laura was in there, he had to get to her.

He knew where Paul stored his work tools in the basement, and he ran for them. No one seemed to be around as he dashed through the house, and down the basement stairs. He threw screw drivers, pliers, and a drill into his backpack, tucked a crowbar under his arm, and carried a sledgehammer in his other hand.

He was sweating and out of breath by the time he got back upstairs, but didn't even pause. Grabbing the drill, he jammed it into the keyhole. A deafening squeal erupted when he turned it on, metal grinding on metal.

His arms burned with the force, but the door still seemed impenetrable. He kept the pressure on until the drill bit snapped. He inserted another and went at it again. The drill was smoking now, the handle getting hotter, but he ignored it. His back ached and his shoulders were on fire, but he didn't let up until the drill's battery ran out of juice. Throwing it aside, he grabbed the crowbar and wedged it into the gash he'd whittled in the iron lock. Slowly, using all of his strength, he twisted the metal. Bits of iron broke out and fell to the floor and the keyhole got bigger. He could see how large and elaborate the locking mechanism was, and it was still holding tight.

Impatient, he picked up the sledgehammer and with trembling arms swung it against the door. With a snap like a rifle shot, a ragged, uneven crack split the grain of the beautiful old wood. Todd felt a moment of regret, but he had no choice.

He swung the sledgehammer again, and the wood split even more. His hands shook as the outline of the door became more obvious.

He shoved the long crowbar into the widening gap. With a metallic shriek that set his teeth on edge, the latch began to pull away from the wood. The wood groaned, and then the latch tumbled out, landing at his feet. He kicked it aside, shoved his hand into the hole and pulled.

The door swung open to reveal a hidden chamber. Todd stood frozen by the horror of what lay before him.

She was dead.

Laura was sprawled on the floor, dressed only in a blood-smeared nightie. Her hair was matted with dark, dried blood, and she had blackish circles under her hollowed eyes.

He raised a shaky hand to his mouth, bit down on a knuckle, and blinked back stinging tears.

She couldn't be dead.

There was another body too, a heavy man, his skin gray and mottled, bloated with decay.

For a moment, he could only stare at Laura, so helpless, so violated, and that thing, that almost inhuman lump beside her on the stone floor.

Who was it?

Around their prone bodies, blood and other fluids made sticky puddles. He fought down the urge to vomit.

She could have lain there for decades, undiscovered, and like the skeleton in the courtyard, no one would have ever known what had happened.

Was that guy to blame for Laura's death?

Moving slowly, deliberately, he stepped past the man's body and moved to her side. He did his best to ignore the smells, the other body, all the signs that her death hadn't been easy. His heart seemed to press against his chest until he didn't think he could keep all of his grief inside. He needed to scream, break something, hurt someone, but he just knelt over her. It chilled him to think that she'd held out until recently. If only he'd tried harder, or figured this out sooner – a few hours might have made a difference.

He swiped at some tears and blew his nose on the tail end of his shirt. He touched her cold hand. Her nails were broken off at the quick, and her fingertips were raw, as if she'd been trying to claw her way out. She was dressed for bed, and her bare arms and legs made her look even more vulnerable. Covering his nose with one of his sleeves, he quickly glanced around. On the floor was an ancient-looking manuscript. The large, leather-bound book lay open beside her, and he touched the vellum, comparing it to the page he'd found under the door. It matched. She'd been trying to signal someone for help, had probably scratched at the wood until she could slip the page beneath it.

She'd tried as hard she could, and he'd let her down.

He needed to tell someone that he'd found her, but he also wanted to spare her father and brother the pain of seeing her like this. She was awkwardly sprawled, and so he straightened her legs. They were cold, but her skin wasn't as stiff as he would have expected. He had nothing to cover her face, and just kept staring at her.

It seemed as if there was a brief flicker of movement beneath her eyelids, and he bent closer. It must have been his imagination because she remained perfectly still. Then he saw a tiny flutter of eyelashes.

His hopes soared, but he steadied himself, whispering warily, "Can you hear me?"

She didn't react.

Placing his ear against her chest, he heard a faint heartbeat. His own heart was pounding as he bent closer to hear if she was breathing.

"Jacques?" Her lips had barely moved, but her eyelids flickered again.

He'd made it in time. She was still alive. He touched her cheek. "I'm here."

"I waited... so long ..." Her voice was raw, and when she spoke bright red droplets of fresh blood welled on her cracked lips.

"Six days," he said. "You've been lost six days." He looked around frantically, wanted to scream for help, but was afraid to startle her. A puddle of blood had coagulated beneath her head. He touched her arm, trying to comfort her.

"Are they all right?" Her eyes got the frightened, dazed look of someone who'd been through a disaster. She shifted, tried to rise, groaned and fell back.

"Lie still," he said. Gently, handling her like he would a baby, he carefully lifted her onto his lap and wrapped his arms around hers, trying to give her warmth.

She must be dehydrated, near starvation. The jagged edges of the gash on the back of her head looked red and infected. She probably had other traumas he couldn't see. She'd gone limp again, and he prayed for her to hang on, prayed she wouldn't lose her will to survive now that she'd been found. He stroked her cheek, and her eyes opened again.

She studied his face, and he thought she might speak, but she lay quietly, watching him. Finally she said, "So many years, but you came back."

She was delirious and confused. "You're going to be all right," he said, hoping it was true.

She mumbled so softly that he had to lower his ear to her lips. "Have you seen Julian? He looks like you." Suddenly she panicked and tried to sit up. "What happened to them?"

He had no idea what was she talking about, so he gently held her hand. "Your family is fine," he murmured.

She closed her eyes, and he felt her relax. It must have been the right answer. He shifted uncomfortably, easing her weight, wondering how fast he could get help. Her breathing was shallow and irregular.

A shaft of sunlight lit the chamber, and he looked up. There it was, high in the wall, the hole he'd been looking for. On the floor he saw broken tendrils of ivy, and he could guess what had happened. She'd tried to climb up and had fallen.

"I'll be right back," he whispered.

Her eyes popped open. "No! Don't leave me again."

He couldn't leave her, not with that terrified look in her eyes. "All right. I'm just setting you down for a second." He'd have to get her out of there by himself.

Getting them both through the narrow door was going to be tough. He brushed away the wood and metal debris, then placed his hands beneath her shoulders. Her head was badly cut, and he tried not to touch the wound, or move her neck. He dragged her carefully, slowly backing though the door. When they were in the antechamber, he lifted her, trying not to jostle her, letting her head rest in the crook of his arm.

He thanked God for keeping her alive until he found her.

Through the large room and along the corridor, he carried her cautiously, going sideways down the wide stone steps, bracing his weight against the railing. He didn't want to put her down, not even for a moment.

As they crossed the great hall, her eyes fluttered open and she looked around. She stared at the ceiling with a bewildered expression. He didn't pause. She needed medical attention as soon as possible. They reached the passage that led into the main part of the house and just as they entered it, she tensed. He shifted her weight.

She squirmed as if trying to break loose. "Take me back."

"It's okay. I just need to open the door."

"No." She tried to wriggle free. "Not through there."

Struggling to hang onto her and get the heavy arched door open, he leaned forward to grab the knob.

She became frantic, almost sliding out of his arms. "I have to go back!"

Afraid she was going to get hurt, he dropped to his knees and held her tightly. "We're going for help."

She was sobbing now, still scrabbling in the opposite direction. "You're going the wrong way."

She was delusional, not making sense. "Listen to me. Please." He pulled the door open. "Help us," he hollered. He rose and staggered a few more steps, carrying her through the passage and into the newer side of the house. "Help," he yelled. "I found Laura."

Chapter Twenty-Nine

Laura awakened and tried to clear her mind. She didn't know where she was. Something was covering her mouth, trying to suffocate her, and she gasped for air.

Her father's face swam into view, his hands clasping hers, his voice soothing and kind. "It's all right, princess. I'm going to make sure you're okay."

Where were her children?

Frantically looking around, her gaze settled on her father's worried face.

She was his daughter.

But she was a mother too.

Lying back against the pillow, she readjusted the plastic oxygen mask that she'd been trying to tear off. A high-pitched tone behind her head started beeping, and she tensed.

"It's only the machine that monitors your vital signs and the I.V. drip," he said. "One of those bags needs to be replaced. That's all. Nothing to worry about."

She twisted around to look, and the I.V. needle taped to the back of her right arm tugged painfully.

"It's normal to have panic attacks after what you've been through," her father said, stroking the side of her head. "Your system released a lot of adrenaline and all those fight-or-flight chemicals."

In the dim light of the hospital room, the lines in his face seemed deeper, his eyes looked bloodshot, and his hair, which had been salt-and-pepper, seemed to have a lot more gray.

"Thank you for being here, Dad."

She had vague impressions of people coming to visit. Gertie and Amy had been there, and then she awoke another time and Todd was beside her bed. And always, when she opened her eyes, either her father or Edward was there, standing guard, ready to reassure her.

Once, she woke up and found a police detective staring down at her. "Had you ever met Oliver Colfax prior to the night he accosted you?" he asked.

"No," she mumbled.

"What did he tell you?"

She squeezed her eyes shut, fighting back tears. "That he'd killed Mum, and he was going to kill me too. Somehow..." The image of him lying on the floor, dying, bragging about what he'd done was crystal clear. "Somehow, he thought he would inherit the house." She bit her lip, struggling to remain composed for her father's sake. Guilt was eating her up, and there was nothing she could do to make amends. "I should have gotten the Wilcoxes out of there sooner. It was me who was supposed to get electrocuted that day, not Winnie."

"That's enough," her father's voice cut in. "Let her rest."

The next time she opened her eyes, her father was dozing in a chair beside her hospital bed. His chin was on his chest, shoulders slumped, his soft snoring punctuated by the beeping of her I.V. monitor.

A nurse came in to change her I.V. bag. She took Laura's blood pressure and made a note in the chart. "Pretty soon you'll be able to go home."

"How long have I been here?" Laura asked.

"Two days now." The nurse held a cup with a straw to her lips. "Have a sip of this."

Laura sat up and tried swallowing. She coughed, and then sipped a little more. The cool water soothed her raw throat. "Thanks." Carefully she lay back down, trying not to rub the sutures on the back of her head.

The nurse left and Laura waited until her father stirred. He shifted and wiped a hand over his face.

"Dad," she said, "Something happened when I was trapped in the chamber."

"What?" He came more fully awake.

"It's as if I could see the past, vividly. Like I really experienced things."

"It was just a dream, honey. You were starving and dehydrated, and you have a serious infection on your scalp. Any of those things can cause hallucinations. But it's over now, and you're going to be fine."

"No. It wasn't like that. Everything was so clear."

"A head injury will do that to you. It took fifteen sutures to close it."

"I saw Bannock Manor the way it used to be when it was brand new."

He cleared his throat. "After the antibiotics have had more time to kick in –"

She looked at her father's face, saw that she was scaring him, and decided to drop the subject.

Closing her eyes, the pictures immediately began to replay. She saw each of the little girls, and knew their individual personalities. There was Julian running through the walled garden, and then maneuvering gracefully at fencing practice. She was nursing Blake in her bedchamber. Like short home movies, she saw snippets of their lives.

"Hey, Sis." Edward walked into the room. "What's the matter? You look so sad."

"Just thinking about stuff."

Edward glanced at their father, then back at her. "You feeling okay?"

"A lot better, but please tell Dad to stop worrying."

"That's like telling a banker to stop counting money."

"I heard you two plotting to take me back to Boston, but I'm not going."

"Laura –" Her dad and brother protested in unison.

Weak as she was, she needed to take a firm stand. "I'm not going to walk away from Bannock Manor."

Edward opened his mouth to say something but closed it without making a sound.

"I have to figure things out," she continued. More of the images – or were they memories – came back to her. Making candles, baking bread, mending clothes and keeping the children warm. She missed them. But was it her life?

She refocused on Edward and her Dad. "I need to do this."

Edward's face mirrored his emotions, his old desire to protect her battling with his habit of taking her side.

Her father, looking tired and beat up, said, "The house isn't safe."

She turned onto her side, facing him, needing him to understand something she couldn't even explain. "I can't leave it. Not now."

Her father started talking about money and security and taxes.

She wanted to look like she was listening, but her eyes drooped and her thoughts drifted to Bannock Manor. Not recently, but when she'd first seen it. She was young and in love, and willing to sacrifice everything for Jacques. He was all that mattered to her then.

The next time she woke up, Todd was sitting in the chair beside her bed. "Your color's coming back," he said, as soon as he noticed she was awake. "You're looking stronger."

"Thanks to you."

"I always wanted to be somebody's hero."

"You are now. You knocked Edward right out of the slot forever." She smiled at him, half teasing. "I don't know how he's going to take it though."

He slipped onto the edge of the bed, leaned over and placed a kiss on her forehead. "I'm so glad I found you in time."

"Where are my sentinels?"

"I convinced them that between me and the hospital staff, you'd be all right if they went back to the house for a shower." He smiled, raising one eyebrow. "It wasn't easy getting you alone."

She'd been waiting for a chance to talk with him privately, and she stroked his cheek, freshly shaved and smooth beneath her fingers. His brown eyes had flecks of gold that she'd never noticed before. There were so many things she wanted to ask him. "When you found me, did I say anything – odd?"

"You wanted to know why it took me so long." He said gently, "I would have asked the same thing, if I'd been the one trapped in a closet for a week."

"The chamber," she said firmly. "You must have seen or felt something." She watched his face, trying to read the slightest clue. "Tell me exactly what you saw."

"That...body was in there." His eyes begged her to let it drop.

"Besides him." She was making Todd uncomfortable, but she had to know. "Did you feel any kind of presence?"

"You mean like a ghost?" He looked surprised. "No. I don't really believe in that kind of stuff. Why?"

"What did I look like?"

"You were in there a week. Do you really want the physical details?"

"I know I sound crazy, but this is important."

"I thought you were dead." He swallowed hard. "My heart felt like it was breaking, and then you opened your eyes." He frowned, seemed to be searching his memory. "You called me… Jacques?"

She shifted, tried to look out the window, but it was already dark, and she couldn't see outside. The window reflected the hospital room back at her. "I don't know who to talk to," she said.

"You can talk to me." He edged a little closer.

"I have to understand," she said. "I want to know what happened – to some people – a long time ago."

"Is this about Oliver Colfax? Do you want me to help find someone?"

"In the chamber, I saw things, felt them, lived them…" She twisted the thin blanket between her hands. "I tried to talk to my dad, but he thinks I'm hallucinating."

"What do you think it is?"

"Never mind."

"I'm not doubting you," he said. "I'm just wondering how to classify your experience."

"I can't classify it."

"There has to be a logical explanation."

"You've been in old houses. Have you ever seen things you can't explain?"

"I've been spooked a few times, but nothing like what you're describing."

She'd been leaning toward him, eager to hear whatever he could tell her, and now her shoulders and the back of her neck ached.

"You were in pretty bad shape," he said. "It's normal to have some confusion for a while."

She knew that wasn't the answer. "Maybe that's what happened." Sighing, she settled back against the pillows. "When

Dad and Edward come back, don't mention this conversation. They can't handle it."

She'd been hoping that he'd also felt that sense of déjà vu. But it was more than that, it was like traveling to a medieval time zone where she'd reset the clock. She knew Lorraine's life as if she'd lived it. Fight-or-flight chemicals in her brain didn't explain how she could see faces and remember details of their lives. Dehydration wasn't the explanation for the deep-seated love and loyalty she felt for a family that had lived at Bannock Manor five centuries earlier. She couldn't wait to do some research, to compare the details she remembered with facts she could substantiate.

Todd was studying her, and all of his compassion, his love and concern were easy to see in his wide brown eyes. He was on her side, even if he couldn't understand.

"How did you know where to look for the chamber?" she asked.

"I spotted the cross you pushed through the vent hole."

"I was trying to signal my location, but it didn't work. Jacques' cross got tangled in the ivy and never reached the outside wall."

He stared at her. "Why do you think it's his cross?"

"I just know it."

He looked uneasy. "That was the first clue I followed. It led me to the room behind the tapestry – and to you."

"I was trying to fling it through the air vent, but it got stuck. It never made it outside."

"I looked at the house from the hill using my binoculars, and I saw it glinting in the sun."

"I believe you," she said. The ghost had been in the chamber with her, and it wouldn't be the first time he'd intervened in her life. "I knew about the room behind the tapestry and sliding panel, but I didn't know there was another room behind that." She paused as images of Tim Carpenter and Lorraine planning the construction bubbled to the surface of her memories. She recalled the feeling of control Lorraine got from her secret chamber. "How did you know there was a second room?"

"I found a page out of an old book," he said. "If you hadn't pushed it under the door..." Todd picked up her hand, brought it to his lips and kissed it tenderly. "That was the second clue that led me to you."

She closed her eyes, savoring the sensation, remembering the way Jacques used to kiss her – first the back of her hand, then the palm, and then each finger.

Todd turned her hand over and placed another kiss on the center of her palm.

Her eyes blinked open. For a moment she'd been convinced it really was Jacques' lips on her upturned palm. Todd's eyes met hers as his lips moved to her thumb, her index and middle fingers, and then he kissed her ring finger and even the pinkie. She held her breath, never breaking eye contact, looking at Todd and feeling Jacques, feeling him as though he were right there on the edge of her bed.

Jacques had promised to come back for her. Could a soul keep that kind of promise after all this time?

Todd lowered her hand. As if he'd been reading her mind, he asked, "Are you going to tell me who that guy is? Any competition I need to know about?"

"It's always been you." She couldn't explain the depth of her feelings for him without going into the very distant past.

He pressed his lips softly to hers, and then their kiss deepened. When he pulled away his fingers stroked her hair. "I had to find you."

"We're getting a second chance." She kissed him again and something settled in her heart, like a missing piece finding its place. "We have time now."

His eyes had a faraway look. "God, Laura, I really thought you were gone." He shook his head as if to cast away the bad memory. "Then you woke up, and it was like – you came back from the brink of death."

"That's what it felt like." Maybe he understood a little after all. "It was like I'd been away for a long time."

Beneath the worry and concern, she saw his curiosity. He was puzzling it through, trying to figure out what it meant, and she wanted to explain it, wanted for both of them to understand.

It would be easy to lie, to say she knew about those lives because of what she'd read, but she knew details that couldn't be in the memoirs. "I read a little," she said. "I couldn't escape, and I was trying to distract myself. I didn't want to think about what might happen."

He gave her hand a reassuring squeeze. "You must have been terrified."

If she didn't tell him now, then the lie would always be between them, and she hadn't been through the ordeal just to come back and pretend. "I think," she began, "there's something in us that's bigger than any one lifetime."

He leaned back a little.

She wanted to plead with him to keep an open mind, but whether or not he believed her was up to him.

"Something extraordinary really did happen while I was in the chamber, and it helped me survive."

A nurse came in and waved her hand, signally for Todd to move out of her way while she went through the routine of checking vitals and changing bandages.

Laura wanted to tell him about everything she'd experienced, but now she was having second thoughts.

Todd seemed to sense the change in her mood, and when the nurse left, he switched to a new topic. "Are you really going to keep the house?"

"Yes."

A look of disappointment flashed in his eyes. "I was hoping I could talk you into moving closer to me."

"Did my dad put you up to that?"

"I don't think your dad is ready for you to settle on the west coast any more than he wants you in England." He grinned, still playing with her fingers. "I'm being selfish because I don't want to risk losing you again."

"I don't want to lose you either." She felt like she was walking on a tight rope, and falling to either side was going to hurt. "But, I need to stay here and fight for the survival of Bannock Manor."

"I can't afford to quit my teaching job, but I want to be with you. For now, I can come back every break. Thanksgiving and Christmas, between semesters, and a long time in the summer." He sounded disappointed, and doubtful. "I know it's not much."

"There has to be a way to figure this out. I want us to have a chance. We just need time."

§§§

The next morning Laura was eating breakfast when Edward showed up.

"Hey, sis. How ya doing?"

"Day three?" she asked.

"Yep."

She was getting better at tracking time.

"Do you need anything?" He raised a paper coffee cup. "Want some?"

"How much of that stuff have you been guzzling?"

"You could fill a moat with all the coffee I've been drinking." He tried to make it sound lighthearted, but she sensed his weariness. "You're not making this any easier on us," he said.

"Day three, round six of the family saga." She put her spoon down. The mushy porridge wasn't very good anyway.

"You'll have to give in, because Dad's not giving up."

"It's my house," she said simply. "I can't give up."

"But why –"

"That guy is dead," she said, cutting to the heart of his objections. "He tried to kill me, and I killed him instead." She'd awakened today feeling stronger and even more determined. She didn't want to waste her energy fighting with her father and brother. "I'm not leaving Bannock Manor."

"Okay." Edward sounded resigned.

"You're agreeing?" If he was giving in, then there had to be some kind of trick.

"Negotiating, more like."

"Uh-oh." Her father and Edward were savvy businessmen. They wouldn't cave without something in return.

"Since you're so stubborn, Dad and I are moving to plan B."

"And that is?"

Edward held up a finger. "Part one. Dad's going to hire some people – housekeeper, handyman, security. You can't live alone in the house."

She bolted upright. "No way!"

"Part two." Edward continued in his want-to-be-a-lawyer tone, holding up a second finger. "Since Dad's paying the wages, they'll work for him."

"Then they can live with him – in Boston."

"He's at Bannock Manor now. I believe he's down to the final choice between a husband and wife with great credentials and a sweet elderly couple with a St. Bernard. Dad kind of likes the dog. You know, same name and all that."

"Are you kidding?" She could tell by the serious look in his eyes that he meant every word. Now she was really irritated. "He can't replace Winnie and Nigel."

"He's not trying to replace anyone. He wants to be able to sleep at night knowing you're not alone. It's called help, Laura. Can you accept a little of it?"

She bit her tongue to stop herself from snapping in return. Her father meant well and he wanted her to be safe. If it didn't work out, well then, she'd let them go. Besides, he couldn't pay their salaries indefinitely, and she certainly didn't have the budget for any staff.

Edward was watching her, and when she gave a small nod, he continued. "Part three. Paul's moving in today. He's already picked out his room."

"That's. Just. Great." She infused the last word with all the sarcasm she could stuff into one syllable. "Anything else?"

"Dad's having the alarm system fixed. That's also as much for him as for you."

She flopped back on her pillow. "Ouch!" She'd forgotten about the stitches. "Dad is being his bossy self, but if this will ease his mind, then I guess I'll cooperate."

"And if you change your mind and want to sell–"

"I won't." She had a sense that she'd fought this battle before, struggled with every ounce of courage to keep the house. Before she could try to put her feelings into words, there was a brief rap on the door.

"Mind if I interrupt?"

The sound of Todd's voice made her pulse speed up. "I'm glad you're here." She couldn't hide the excitement in her voice and didn't bother to try.

With a groan, Edward got to his feet. "Take my seat. You two can talk about sugar and spice and everything nice, while I go deal with the snakes and snails and St. Bernard tails."

§§§

Edward stepped out of the bright sunlight into the dark interior of the White Hart pub. Laura was due to be released from the hospital at the end of the week, and he hoped Megan's networking would come through. They needed to organize a support team. As his eyes adjusted, he spotted several of her friends, and a few people he didn't know gathered at a table. Their animated conversation quieted when he approached.

His chair scraped as he took a seat. "Thank you all for coming on such short notice."

Kit, the bartender, waved a hand, cutting him off. "Excuse me, Mr. Executive. This isn't a board meeting."

"Yeah, I guess my first clue is that everyone has their hand wrapped around a pint." He smiled and started again. "Laura's determined to stay in Tenney Village, but she's going to need help." He glanced from face to face, attempting to read their reactions, trying to discern how much he could count on them once he left. "Dad's hired a live-in couple, but I'd like her to have friends around as much as possible."

"We wish we could have done more to protect Eleanor and Winnie." Megan cast a look around the table, her lower lip quivering. "Thankfully, we get a second chance with Laura."

"I'll be around day and night," Paul said, pulling a folded sheet of paper out of his pocket. "I had a long talk with your father, and he gave me a list of everything he wants me to do."

"Ah, that's probably just for the first week. You might as well know, his lists never stop growing and can never be completed." Edward hid his smirk by taking a sip of ale. If Paul had to answer to Dad, he was going to be working harder than he ever had before.

"Oh. All right. I'll keep plugging away then."

"Did he mention finishing the repairs on the water line?"

Paul looked a little embarrassed. "I'm calling my friend Barry this afternoon. He's a real plumber."

"Good." Edward would rather have called a plumber himself, but he didn't want to make Paul look incompetent in front of the others. "I'll cover that expense," he added.

"Laura can stay with me until she's fully recovered," Megan offered.

"She's determined to be home," Edward said. "But she's still weak, and that house is a lot to handle, even with extra help."

Kit wiped the table with a grungy rag. "I'll send up care packages."

"I'll help with the shopping," Gertie said. "And Ben and I can pitch in with the odd jobs."

The vicar was seated beside Megan, and he spoke for the first time. "With your permission, I'd like to bring a group from the church over to do some cleaning."

Currently, the manor was a disaster. The police had finished gathering evidence, but dirt was tracked everywhere. Some of the walls still had signs of the attack, and whenever Edward looked at them, he felt shaken, thinking how it must have been for Laura. He had a catch in his throat and couldn't respond right away.

"The new couple will be busy getting settled," the vicar continued, "and we'll want everything looking spiffy when Laura walks in the door."

The last bit of Edward's business façade drained away. This simple act of kindness from a church that Laura didn't even belong to got him choked up. For the first time, he saw the village from her point of view, like an extended family.

Maybe she'd be okay here, after all.

Chapter Thirty

Her father opened the car door, and Laura stepped out and stared up at the manor. The Georgian façade along the front looked foreign, as if it didn't belong. The porch steps and front door were not the same ones Lorraine had used so long ago. That passage had been swallowed up by successive renovations.

Turning slowly, her gaze traveled across the grounds. Generations ago, long after Bannock's time, shade trees had been strategically planted about the expansive lawn for a tidy, yet random effect. The garden walls had changed little, and she knew that inside the roses would be in full bloom, hanging their heavy heads in the afternoon heat. Up the hillside, the chapel and the graves that surrounded it held more memories than she could process. More than her own memories; she had Lorraine's now too. It wasn't logical, but to her those thoughts were real.

She clutched tightly to her father's arm, and then her eyes alighted on the tall, carved cross that had been Lorraine's memorial to Jacques. Lorraine had never known what had happened to him, but Laura did, and now she knew where she was going to re-bury his skeleton.

The breeze picked up, and she shivered.

"Are you cold?"

She rubbed her arms, wondering if anyone had ever been able to change the past. "Just a bit nervous. That's all."

"Kate and Miles are waiting to meet you." He collected her overnight bag from the trunk and slammed it shut. "Let's go inside."

Closing her eyes, she tried to settle her mind in the present. "I wish they hadn't started so soon."

Strangers moving into the house seemed wrong, like you could hire new people to replace the ones you'd lost. Tears welled up, and she took a deep breath, forcing herself to calm down.

Her father walked slowly, matching his pace to hers. "They come well-recommended and have experience in a National Trust house. Kate loves to cook. I think it's going to be a good fit, honestly."

Her mind slipped back again and she saw Simon haughtily staring down at Lorraine that first day she'd arrived here. His expression had been scornful, taking in the details of her soiled clothes and shabby carriage. And then he glared at Jacques and said something dismissive, his tone, rather than his words conveying that they were not welcome.

"I'm sure they're very nice people." Laura wished she could sound more upbeat for her father's sake. He was being generous, and she really did appreciate it.

"You're a little pale," he said, looking worried. "Let's get you inside."

"The fresh air feels good."

She scrutinized the ornately carved front door. She couldn't control when the visions came, but she was learning to regulate how long they lasted by focusing on something in the present, like the rail on the hospital bed or the dashboard in the car. She needed to keep her edge, to prove to herself and everyone else that she was capable of handling things.

She paused just inside the entry hall. The furniture looked freshly polished and an enormous flower arrangement stood on the hall table. She smelled the roses and read the card.

Welcome back to your castle, Princess. Love, Todd.

He and Edward had left yesterday, and she already missed them both. Brushing away a tear, she mumbled, "I swear he did this just to make me cry."

"Todd's a great guy." Her father cleared his throat, his emotions as close to the surface as hers. "Thank God he didn't give up."

"I think he's... the one."

"No need to rush a relationship just because –"

"We won't be rushing anything, Dad." She stood up straighter, hoping to look healthier than she felt. "I'm ready to meet Kate and Miles now."

Together they walked down the corridor and into the kitchen. A breeze wafted through the open windows and the yellow curtains fluttered. She'd always loved this room, and today the sun was pouring in, giving everything a buttery glow.

The man seated at the table stood up and made a formal bow. "Miles Simmons," he said. "At your service." He was the tallest person she'd ever met, had to be close to six feet, six inches, and very thin.

She shook his hand. "Pleased to meet you."

His wife, Kate, also introduced herself. She too was tall, but more muscular, with very short, sandy blond hair. "Mr. Bram thought it best we start in here since you prefer a more casual arrangement," she said, as if offering an apology for the circumstances.

"It's a lovely idea," Laura said. The whole meeting seemed a little too orchestrated. Just the type of thing her father would do.

"I'm sure we'll all get on just fine." Kate sliced into a large sponge cake smothered in double cream and strawberries, and then lifted generous pieces onto plates. "This job is just the challenge we've been looking for."

Laura sat down at the table and looked around. Kate had already turned the kitchen into her own space. The battered old breadbox, the half dozen canisters, and Winnie's pile of writing tablets were all gone. The counter tops were cleared, the Aga polished to a shine, and the collection of silly little magnets had been taken off the refrigerator. The kitchen seemed emptier, more like she'd expect to see in a restaurant, or a magazine ad. It didn't feel like Winnie's kitchen at all.

Kate set a teapot on the table and began arranging cups and saucers.

"Where did you find this teapot?" Laura asked.

"At the back of a cupboard." Kate sounded uncertain. "Is it sentimental?"

"I haven't seen it in years. When I was a little girl, Winnie used to serve tea in this pot. It was just for the two of us – here in the kitchen." Even Nigel wasn't allowed to partake in their little parties.

"I'll put it away if you'd prefer not to use it."

Wrapping her hands around the warm pot, Laura held it tightly. It was as if Winnie were welcoming her home. "I'm glad you used it today."

She glanced toward the staff apartment, knowing that during her absence, Kate and Miles had rearranged the rooms. The Wilcoxes' old clothes and furniture had been hauled down to the cellar, and Nigel's bedroom was now their private sitting room. According to her father, they had painted walls, bought new draperies, and installed wall-to-wall carpeting, scrambling to get it all done within a few days. They were industrious people, the kind he liked to have working for him.

Turning her attention to something less emotionally charged, she took a bite of the sponge cake. "Did you bake this yourself?"

"Just this morning." Kate smiled. "I wanted something special for your homecoming."

"How does it feel to be back?" Miles asked.

She didn't know how to answer. The last time she'd been in the kitchen, Oliver Colfax had been chasing her, trying to kill her. "Lots of emotions," she said honestly. It was far more complex than she had anticipated or could explain.

Her stamina was fading and she half-listened as Kate chattered on, telling her father all the plans she had for the house. Not just cleaning and cooking, but painting and repairs. Laura expected her father to remind Kate of the budget, but instead, he was nodding his head in approval.

Why was he agreeing with Kate when he'd always been adamant that he wanted Laura to sell the house and move back to Boston? She didn't have the money for interior decorating. Trying to get his attention, she gave him her look that said, *What the heck?*

Finally, he turned to her. "What's the matter, sweetheart?"

Everyone stopped and stared at her.

"I thought you said cosmetic renovations were a bad idea." She could hear how petulant she sounded. But why was it suddenly a good idea because Kate wanted it? She put her fork down, feeling guilty. Her father was being kind, but as far as she was concerned, Kate and Miles were only here temporarily.

"We should save all this for another time," her father said. "You look a bit wilted, Laura."

"I'm fine."

"I think a nap is just the ticket," Kate chimed in as she refilled Bernard's teacup. "Why don't you have a lie down while we get some work done?"

She didn't like being told to nap as if she were a toddler, but she did want to be alone. She stood up. "It was nice meeting both of you."

"Dinner will be served in the dining room at six," Kate said. Her whole demeanor seemed to be directed toward impressing Bernard.

So much for the agreement to keep things casual, Laura thought as she went up to her bedroom. After she closed the door, she announced out loud, "This is my home."

Her head was pounding and she pulled three vials out of her overnight bag: antibiotics, anti-anxiety medication, and something for pain. Swallowing one of each, she lay down on the bed and closed her eyes. The uncertainties of the future scared her, and the past, oh the past, it beckoned, as if she couldn't move forward in this life until she was finished with Lorraine's.

The next time she opened her eyes, the bedside clock read 2:14 am. Someone had left a tray on her dresser with a sandwich and a carafe of lukewarm tea.

Ignoring the food, she went to the window and pushed it open. Outside, a full moon cast an ethereal glow on the castle walls and the last round tower. The chapel and surrounding headstones stood out in silhouette. Once, a long time ago, Lorraine had gazed down at this very courtyard and plotted her escape.

Escape. Escape. The word repeated like a mantra.

Her thoughts wandered to the chamber and how time had seemed to shift in there. She couldn't explain how tangible, how real the experience had been. But something had happened to her, and now her very essence was changed.

Her beautiful old home had given up one of its secrets, and now she knew what the ghost had always been trying to show her. A mysterious power had been lying dormant in the very heart of her home.

§§§

Laura endured the next week as her father took charge. She was used to it, had grown up watching him give commands, and now that she was safe, he was going to employ every tool at his disposal to keep her that way. He tried not to come across in his typical, overbearing manner, but she knew him too well, knew his gentle suggestions could quickly turn into dictates if he thought it important enough. He was on a mission, setting up security, making To-Do lists with Kate and Miles, inspecting and re-inspecting the progress of the plumbing repairs. She waited for Paul to quit under the pressure, but he didn't.

Laura had neither the strength, nor desire, to challenge him. She could afford to be patient; his time was limited. He was heading back to Boston this afternoon. She was grateful for his help and would miss him, but it was time for her to get on with her own plans.

Last night they had eaten in the dining room again, six sharp. It was ridiculous and pompous. Bernard, a single father and a busy man, had always made meals with her and Edward an intimate time. Dinner especially was for having Dad's uninterrupted attention. That's what she wanted last night, but instead, it was another formal dinner where Kate showcased her culinary skills and Miles stood around analyzing their use of forks. Laura deliberately used her utensils the American way, switching the fork between hands when she needed the knife. It was more awkward, and she'd been trained to eat in the British tradition, but something rebelliously juvenile welled up in her when the Simmons were around. She was actually getting tired of her own bad attitude.

Bernard's suitcase and coat were waiting in the foyer, ready to go, but he still hesitated. "Laura, don't neglect to set the security system when you go out. Or when you're in for the night."

"Don't worry. I'll be fine." She opened the door and a persistent beeping started up. "How could anyone forget with that noisy reminder?"

"Keep your cell phone in your pocket – at all times."

"If you don't get going, you'll get stuck in the afternoon traffic."

"Laura –"

"I'll be okay. I promise."

He made it to the car, but wavered before opening the door. "I –" He stared into her eyes, searching for a sign of weakness, some hesitation, and then he looked up at the house. "You don't have to prove anything. If you want to come home – just come."

"And you have nothing to worry about except missing your flight." She gave him an especially tight hug meant to reassure him. "Thank you for being here when I needed you."

"I love you, princess." He stood there uneasily, so unlike his usual self.

"I love you too, Dad." She opened the car door for him. "Have a safe flight." It took a lot of will power to turn and walk into the house without looking back, but she didn't want to see the tears in his eyes. She felt guilty enough for what she'd put him through.

§§§

Laura waited until Kate drove into Dursley for groceries, and Miles scooted down to the cellar to resume organizing the chaos.

She unlocked the arched door, then slipped quietly into the passage leading to the medieval wing. As soon as she was in the great hall, she could visualize it filled with people, fifty or a hundred and fifty, eating and working, chasing after children, celebrating life, mourning death.

Her footsteps made a hollow sound, and she was saddened that the beautiful room had been mostly empty and unused for the past century.

The marble stairs were broad and shallow, and she went slowly, taking in every cornice and balustrade. She wanted to touch everything. On the landing she paused, catching her breath and listening for any reverberations from the past. After a moment, she felt the familiar soft brush of fingers on her skin, giving her goose bumps. Just as she'd done when she was a girl, she followed the pocket of cold air down the corridor to the master bedchamber, and then into Lorraine's room, and the alcove.

She paused again, excited, yet nervous. Between her shoulder blades the soft pressure intensified, but she resisted. "No," she whispered. "I'm not ready. I just want to know if the power is still there."

She wanted to experience more of Lorraine's life, but at the same time was afraid the details of the massacre would be too horrible. If she could just have a tiny glimpse…

Instead, unwanted memories of Oliver filled her mind. It all came back – the terror of being chased, the fight, and the aftermath, being trapped with death and decay. Her skin crawled as she remembered his touch, and the sticky warmth as his blood sprayed over her. She had been forced to sit and listen to his labored breathing in the cold and dark.

Bits of police tape still clung to the door and sagged onto the floor. While she'd been in the hospital, the chamber had been the focus of an investigation, and then everyone except Laura seemed to have forgotten about it. They'd taken Oliver's body away, but no one had cleaned the room. The stench of decay hung heavy in the airless space and a dried puddle of blood still lay in the middle of the floor.

At her feet, some of the wall panels lay in pieces, smashed beyond repair, and the ancient tapestry that had always hung over the alcove wall was now only hanging by one corner.

She gripped the upper edge and held it up. An image wove itself through her mind – Michel hurrying to take it down before the attack, and packing it with his own hands into one of Lorraine's trunks.

"So that you will always remember Chateau Brèche," he'd said.

Laura smiled, grateful for the memory, and said a brief prayer for Michel: *may he rest in peace.* For some that was a cliché, but for her it carried a profound plea.

Following that memory was another. She remembered how ardently Lorraine had waited for Jacques to come back for her, but then little by little, as the years went by and her family grew, Lorraine had become tied to England and this house.

Laura understood what it felt like to be pulled between two places and two lives. She'd always been torn between

Boston and Bannock Manor, and now, standing on the threshold of the chamber, she teetered between Lorraine's world and her own. She wanted the consciousness of both. To prove that she knew more than what was written in Lorraine's memoirs, she had to finish reading it. And perhaps someday she could also prove to Todd and others that what she'd experienced was more than imagination.

Ignoring the foul air, she stepped inside and a wave of dizziness swept over her. As her knees began to buckle, she groped for the wall and caught her balance, but a headache struck, blinding her.

Her skin turned hot, so hot she was burning. Flames licked her body, her hair was on fire, and when she inhaled, searing heat scorched her lungs.

I beg you father, show us mercy.

Save me.

Please, don't burn us alive.

Rough, scratchy voices vibrated in her mind, and she bent nearly double, trying to catch her breath as sweat broke out on her skin. Horrible screams echoed in her ears, going on and on, until they were swallowed up by the roar of flames.

Gasping, Laura stumbled out of the chamber and fell to her knees. The acrid scent of smoke filled her nostrils and tight spasms gripped her lungs. Coughing so hard she was choking, she crawled to get enough distance between herself and the room. Gradually, her head began to clear and the tightness in her chest eased. When she could breathe again, she sucked in cool air, her mind reeling from what she'd seen and felt.

She leaned against the wall on the far side of the alcove, still feeling faint. Her temples throbbed as she searched her memory. Nothing about what she'd just experienced resonated with Lorraine's life. Slowly the scent of burning hair and flesh was fading. She tipped her head back and closed her eyes.

Before she could fight them off, more images formed in her mind.

The gates of Cragmore Castle opened and a horse drawn cart appeared. Bound in the back were six women, and snatches of their pleas could be heard above the wailing. "God have mercy on us." At the level spot, halfway down the hill, they came to a stop, and one by one, the women were tied to thick stakes set in the ground.

"We're innocent," they screamed, spitting and kicking at their captors.

The gathering crowd jeered, "Burn the witches. Burn the witches."

Piled nearby were stacks of firewood and bundles of thatch for kindling. Men layered it around the women's legs as they continued to beg for mercy.

When all was ready their lord arrived, sitting haughtily upon his stallion. Ignoring the screams, he announced, "Wife, I saw you with my own eyes doing magic, and teaching your daughters the spells your mother taught you."

"You're lying. You want to marry someone younger and beget sons." His wife turned on the crowd, straining against the ropes that bound her. "You stand by and let him burn his own daughters?"

The youngest daughter, barely more than a girl, cried for her father's compassion, but he shook his head, then turned to the man holding a lit torch and motioned to him. The kindling was lit and the first small flames appeared.

The daughters screamed in terror, but the wife shouted angrily, "Our ashes will taint your soil. This spot is forever cursed." Flames raced up her skirt and the heat turned her face bright red. "I curse you all to Hell."

The crowd backed away, frightened, making the sign of the cross.

The fire spread quickly and gathered momentum until the screams and the flames roared together.

They had been burned on the very spot where the manor now stood.

Laura swallowed hard, her throat parched, and she wiped perspiration from her brow. Those women were as real as Lorraine. She'd felt their anguish, but they weren't a part of her in the same way.

Had her own trauma given her access to their memories?

She didn't want to know the suffering that others had endured. It was too much.

When she stopped shaking, she got up and backed carefully away from the chamber. She'd get the cross and the memoirs another time.

§§§

Laura couldn't stop thinking about the chamber. Just as she was coming to terms with Lorraine's memories, she'd been bombarded with memories from another era. The chamber was the common denominator. She scoured the Internet, looking for anything she could find about hauntings and curses. Some of the reports talked about energy, stuck energy that clung to a place and changed it. There were similar stories all over the globe. There were also scientists refuting them and calling the believers quacks. If they had experienced what she'd seen, they wouldn't be so certain.

Women had been burned at this site. She felt it. She knew it. There was no doubt in her mind.

Maybe someone else could go into the chamber and experience the past the way she did.

She wished she could share these experiences with Todd, but he might think she was crazy. Perhaps after they'd spent more time together, she could start with little bits and see how he took it. But he wouldn't be back for another two months, and she had to find out now.

Paul was the only other person she could trust to go with her into the chamber and not sell her out.

It took five days before she got up her nerve to go back, and then she had to wait until both Kate and Miles were gone. As far as Paul knew, they were going to clean the chamber and retrieve some valuable artifacts.

Back and forth through the medieval hall, up and down the stairs, they lugged buckets of water, a ladder, a shovel, soap, sponges, rubber gloves and a bottle of bleach. When all the supplies were assembled in the bedchamber, Laura tied a bandana around her mouth and nose. She dabbed it with peppermint oil, and then passed the vial to Paul. "Here. Use a lot."

His bandana was already in place, making him look like a bandit, but over the cloth that hid his nose and mouth, his innocent, puzzled eyes stared at her. He'd wanted to hire a professional company, and didn't understand why she insisted on doing this herself.

Partly it was because she wanted to know if he'd have any paranormal reactions, but also, she felt embarrassed – it was her house, her mess. And most importantly, she wanted to make sure every trace of her ordeal with Oliver was erased. If there was some kind of power, she didn't want it tainted by him. On a more practical level, she couldn't take chances that some idiot would take photos and sell them to the Daily Mail.

Paul's presence was an insurance policy if things went badly after she was inside.

"All right," Paul said. "Let's do it."

She appreciated his loyalty, the way he offered his help unconditionally, even when he clearly didn't want to do the job. He began shoveling the worst of the debris into large trash bags, clearing a path to the small door of the inner chamber.

The drilled out lock lay on the floor, and she bent down to examine it. The shaft and teeth of the broken key were jammed in the lock. Turning it over, she looked at the sheared, sharp edges. The very thing that had trapped her had provided her with a weapon.

"I'll go in first," she said.

The peppermint oil did nothing to mask the fetid air. Holding her breath, Laura peered at what had been the site of her torture for so many days. She gagged, backed up and bumped into Paul who was close behind her.

He caught her arm. "Do you really want to do this?" His voice was muffled by the bandana.

"Yes, I do." She clamped her lips against the stinking air. There was no point trying to explain, talking used too much air, and it was hard enough to breathe.

With another step, she was standing beside the spot where Oliver had died. The outline of his body had been drawn twice, first by bloodstains, and then by police chalk. She intended to erase every sign of him.

Setting to work, she doused the room with soapy water, swishing the mop and then wringing it out every few minutes. It didn't take long for the water in the buckets to turn pink and frothy.

"I'll empty the buckets and bring up more clean water," Paul said. He didn't show any signs that the chamber was affecting him.

They repeated the process over and over, until the thickest stains were washed away. Laura was now ready to concentrate on the remaining residue, and pulled on a second pair of rubber gloves. She got down on her hands and knees and attacked the floor with a scrub brush and bleach.

Her anger resurfaced in successive waves as each memory struck – Mum, Winnie, herself – all of them victims of that sadistic bastard. She pushed the brush harder, scrubbing until her shoulders ached and her nose burned, and even then she kept the brush whisking back and forth, slashing at the stains the way she'd slashed at him, fighting for her life.

"Take it easy," Paul said, tapping her on the shoulder. "Why don't you take a break, okay?"

Using her sleeve, she wiped away the tears she hadn't realized were there. "I'm all right."

He looked like he didn't believe her. "How about we finish this another day?"

"You go on. I can't leave it unfinished." Her tone was clipped and edgy. "Sorry, but I haven't been sleeping well. I need this to be done." She stood up and nudged his shoulder. "Go on. Go. You've been a great help and I'm almost done. Just don't tell the troops where I am, all right? I don't want them snooping around over here."

"I could use some fresh air," he admitted, but he looked worried.

As soon as Paul left, she pushed the ladder into place under the airshaft. The last time she'd been up here, she'd been balancing on the ledge and she'd fallen. That wasn't going to happen now, but her legs were shaky.

A few days ago, early enough to catch the rising sun, she'd taken the binoculars and hiked up the hill, standing in roughly the same place that Todd had described. Focusing on this wall, she saw the glint of gold, but it could have been anything. She had to see for herself if the cross was the way she remembered it – stuck in the air vent, tangled in the tendrils that blocked the opening.

When she was level with the vent, she squinted through. Near the outer edge, much farther back than she could have pushed it, she saw the belt. She needed a tool of some kind to reach it.

Climbing down, she hammered a nail into the end of the broom handle and bent it into a hook. Back on the ladder, she shoved it through and pulled the ivy out of the way, hurrying to retrieve the cross before Paul came back. She didn't want him to insist on doing it for her.

Finally, she hooked the belt and dragged it toward her a little at a time, stopping every few inches to peer though the shaft until the cross finally came into view. She tugged a few more inches, and the pendant appeared from where it had been dangling.

The cross had made it through to the outside, just as Todd claimed.

But that was impossible.

Dragging it carefully, she eased the belt the rest of the way out until the cross and chain slipped into her hand. As soon as she touched it she thought of Jacques. She could see it hanging around his neck, and remembered the day he'd placed it around hers.

The passion they had shared was like a shooting star, superheated and then gone. By comparison, her relationship with Carl was like the moon, cool and distant. Lorraine had felt the same about Brian Bannock. Upon reflection, she could see how Brian and Carl were alike.

Todd Woodbridge was the sun, full of promise for a new life. He was warm and caring, conscientious, steady. He was worth the wait. She would be patient, no matter how long the time between his visits. Having the right man part of the time was better than living with the wrong man.

While she was on the ladder, she looked over at the shelf and saw the rolled parchment with Jacques' picture on it. Lorraine's memoirs were there too.

Laura climbed down and placed them safely in the outer room, then loosened her bandana to take a good look. Immediately she felt the temperature drop, and she stared intently for any sign of a presence, but there wasn't one.

She found a wobbly old chair, sat down and lifted Lorraine's heavy book into her lap. Turning the pages, she ran her fingers over the yellowed parchment and faded ink. It was easy to find the place where she'd left off, and she flipped back through all that she'd read about Lorraine's life, searching for details, and noting what wasn't there, like the siege of Chateau Brèche.

During the siege, Lorraine's thoughts had been with her father, and with Jacques. When the fighting began, she was caught up in the panic of avoiding Etienne's soldiers. In Lorraine's journal, she barely mentioned Michel, except to say that he bid them farewell.

Laura remembered things differently. She knew Michel's story, understood him as if she'd read his memoirs too, as if she'd been right beside him when the walls of the chateau were overrun with the king's soldiers. The faithful steward had faced death as his duty, and he'd fallen not far from the body of his beloved Marquis, slain by a mercifully brief slash from a broadsword.

Putting a hand to her stinging throat, she could feel the residue of pain, the sensation of metal biting into her skin.

She felt like she was sinking, falling, and a rush of vertigo made her head spin, and then the pictures began, her mind filling with glimpses of people she recognized, and others she didn't, faces and clothing from different eras. An onslaught of smells filled the air: roasting meat, rotting carrion, roses, baking bread, and waste. They were distinct: sweet, pungent, or spicy. She heard horses screaming, someone calling her name, but which name she wasn't sure. One after another, emotions broke over her until she was drenched with the sensations of those other lives.

She slipped off the chair and onto the floor, clutching at the smooth floorboards for stability. Her stomach churned and she tried to lift her head, and then, without warning, she threw up. She lay still, breathing shallowly, waiting for the spinning sensation to ease. Closing her eyes again, she rode wave after wave of images – too many, too much all at once. The chamber held more than one life, more than one era. Life and death whirled around her. The chamber was like the eye of a storm that swept across time, and she was caught up in those lives, open to the tempest spinning through that secret room.

"My God, Laura, what happened?" Paul knelt beside her, then scooted back when he realized she'd been sick. "Did you get hurt?"

She had no idea how long she'd been lying there. "Too soon for me to be doing heavy labor, I guess." There was no point trying to explain. He wouldn't believe her anyway.

"I'm going for Kate." Fear plastered his face.

"No. Don't!" She sat up, trying to control her trembling limbs. "I'll be okay. Will you help me to my room?"

"Yeah. Sure." He stood up, rolled his shoulders. "You gave me a scare."

She was pretty rattled herself and could barely hide it as he pulled her to her feet. "I think I'd better rest now."

Chapter Thirty-One

It was mid-afternoon, London time, when Todd made his way through the long queue snaking through British customs. He cleared the passport checkpoint and then picked up his luggage. Once he got beyond the security barriers, he started looking for Laura.

She was smiling and waving, and as cliché as it was, he couldn't help thinking she was the woman he'd been waiting his whole life to meet. Her blond hair was tied back in a girl-next-door ponytail, and it bounced around as she jostled to get his attention. She looked so much better than when he'd seen her two months ago lying in a hospital bed, peering at him with anxious, sunken eyes. He brushed away the unhappy images. She was better now; he could see it in the way her eyes sparkled.

"Thanks for coming to pick me up." He wrapped her in a hug. "I could've rented a car."

"I couldn't wait, and anyway, I haven't been out of Tenney Village for months." She grinned up at him. "Had to dig my lipstick and blush from the bottom of a drawer."

The thought of her putting on make-up just to meet him at the airport made him smile. She was all he thought about. "You look great," he said, forcing himself to loosen his hold so they could move on.

In the car park, she slipped in behind the wheel. "Are you tired?"

"Hungry. They barely feed you on planes these days." He touched her shoulder. "Finally, we get to talk in person."

She started the engine. "I always like talking to you, by phone, computer – it doesn't matter."

"It matters to me," he said. "Skyping doesn't do justice to your smile."

"You're making me blush." She drove confidently through the London traffic, one hand on the wheel, the other resting on her thigh as she negotiated a complicated intersection. "This week's going to go by fast. There's so much I want to show you."

Lightly, he traced the back of her hand. "I'm all yours – nothing on the agenda but you and me."

She merged onto the motorway. "Except, Kit's having a party at the White Hart tonight."

Inwardly, he groaned. He'd been looking forward to spending a quiet evening alone with her. "It'll be nice to see everyone again," he said, trying to sound enthusiastic.

Her sideways glance said it all; she understood his reluctance. "If I didn't agree to tonight, we'd have to wade through a steady stream of visitors all week long."

"It'll be fun – really." Maybe it was a good idea. A party would force him to slow down. But before they got back to the manor, where her attention would be claimed by other people and bigger problems, he at least wanted an hour or two alone. "Instead of going straight back to the house, why don't we do something first, maybe see some sights?"

"Sure. What do you have in mind?"

He had two things on his mind, and food was one. Lunch would be good, but he was tired of sitting, didn't want anything formal. "Maybe a picnic?"

She frowned thoughtfully. "We could have lunch in the gardens."

"Have you ever been to the long barrow outside of Uley?"

"Hetty Peggler's Tump." Her face lit up. "That's a great idea. I haven't been there in years. We'll stop in Dursley to get snacks."

That's what he loved about her, her spontaneous enthusiasm. She was one hundred percent authentic.

At the grocery store he pushed a cart while she selected cheese, crackers, and apples. He picked out a six pack of ale. She went for pastries. He liked walking around the market with her. It felt domestic, like they were a real couple.

As they headed back to the car, she asked, "Have you seen the town square? There's a building here you might appreciate from the medieval woolen market days."

"Can I at least have an apple?"

She pulled one out of the bag and wiped it on her shirt. Smiling, her eyes teasing, she took a bite, holding it against her lips longer than necessary.

He dove for her, grabbed her wrist and tried to bite the apple in her hand. She squealed and tried to wiggle away as he wrapped her in his arms. She turned, her back pressed against his chest, holding the apple at arm's length, out of his reach. He nibbled on her neck instead.

"That tickles!" She squirmed, and the apple fell to the sidewalk and rolled away.

They were laughing and acting like fools in front of the other pedestrians. She bent to retrieve the apple, but he held her more tightly. Breathless, she turned and faced him.

Holding her in his arms, he knew he would do just about anything to be with her, even give up his job, his career plans, his country. The realization was startling. He brushed his hand along her cheek and leaned in to kiss her.

An elderly lady pushed by with a walker, her little dog barking incessantly, straining against its leash. "There are better places for that kind of behavior," she huffed.

"Sorry," Laura said, straightening up and pulling her shirt back into place. She smoothed her hair, not looking at him. "You'll give me a bad reputation."

"And I'll enjoy every minute of it." Staring at the old woman's back, he crossed his eyes and stuck out his tongue.

Laura doubled over, snickering. "Stop it!"

He wanted to make her laugh, wanted to see that look, that softness come into her eyes that he remembered so well from their first date.

Laura tugged on his arm and they began walking toward the center of town. "We have to see the old woolen mill. Wool was big business in medieval times, and wool from the Cotswolds brought a good price. A lot of local landowners got rich."

He gazed up at the old buildings that lined the streets. "Do you miss teaching history?"

"I feel like I've been living it."

That smile was back, the one that made her look like she was keeping a secret, waiting for him to guess the answer to a riddle.

"What did all those landowners do with their money?" he asked.

"They bought more land, raised more sheep, and paid to have churches built."

"So, are there a lot of sheep farmers in heaven?" he asked, gently poking her in the ribs.

"That's what they were hoping for." She pointed out a stone building elevated a good twenty feet above street level, supported by four great pillars. "They stored the wool up there."

Todd studied it appreciatively. "I never get tired of looking at these villages. Imagine building this without heavy equipment."

They strolled through the undercroft holding hands; the touch of her palm against his made his heart expand. In a shadowed corner, he turned and pulled her closer, finally giving her the kiss he'd been yearning for since their first hug at the airport.

"I couldn't wait another minute," he said.

"I'm glad you didn't." She clung to him, returning his kiss.

"I've waited so long to see you again."

She swayed against him. "I'm glad you came back. I was afraid you might not." Her lashes came down, shuttering her eyes, and when she opened them again, they seemed slightly unfocused. She blinked a few times, looking confused. "For a moment – I thought –"

"What?"

"Nothing." She shook her head as if trying to clear it. "We might just have enough time to catch the sunset if we leave right now."

Laura was silent as she drove them up the winding roads. He looked at the scenery and then back at her, but he couldn't tell what she was thinking. Sometimes she was a mystery. They reached the top of a hill and she pulled into a car park and turned off the engine.

"When's the last time you took a day off?" he asked.

She thought for a moment. "The day we went to Castle Combe."

"But that was months ago. We need to build more fun into your life."

The setting sun bathed her face in a golden glow. "Okay, I'll practice all week with you."

"I'm going to hold you to that."

"You're pretty good at keeping promises." Her voice was so low he almost didn't hear her say, "Even if it takes a while."

They got out of the car but didn't unpack the picnic. Instead, they walked across the grass covered ridge, and he put his arm loosely around her waist. They stood side by side, staring out across the Severn Vale. Picturesque farms dotted the rolling land, and sheep grazed in fields bordered by low stone walls and ancient oaks. Villages were clustered here and there, and on the horizon the sun glinted off the River Severn and its estuary.

"This view is better than I remembered," he said, shielding his eyes from the glare.

"When were you here?"

"On one of my research trips." He turned and gazed at her. The longing he felt was probably as easy to read as a first-grade primer.

He kept his arm around her as they wandered over to the ancient burial tomb. They read the small brown sign that described Hetty Peglar's Tump as a prehistoric barrow. It was mostly subterranean, its walls made of carefully placed stone slabs.

The breeze picked up, and he slipped out of his jacket and wrapped it around her shoulders. She snuggled into it, her cheek grazing his collar like a caress.

"Do we really have to spend the evening at the White Hart?" he asked.

"Long enough to be polite. You're the guest of honor."

He groaned, then dropped a kiss onto the back of her neck. "How late do we have to stay?"

"You're making it very hard for me to think." She edged away from him, and cast a teasing glance over her shoulder. "You said you were hungry."

They unloaded the car, and she began pulling the food and napkins from the grocery bags. They sat on the grass, and he noticed the way her hands moved, the way her shoulders bunched and relaxed as she set out the bread, cheese, and apples. Every little gesture seemed to mesmerize him, and he couldn't stop watching her.

"No blanket, and we forgot forks and knives." She sighed.

"I'll be right back." He went to the car and dug his pocket knife out of his luggage. "Ale first." He opened two bottles, then switched to one of the small cutting blades. Using the bread wrapper as an impromptu plate, he sliced the wedge of cheddar and passed her a piece. As their fingers met, that feeling sparked again. Slowly, he withdrew his hand, and just as slowly, she raised hers to her mouth and nibbled the cheese. He passed her some bread, and then a crisp wedge of apple, feeding her a morsel at a time.

Her smile was back, enticing and mysterious.

Gently, she eased the knife out of his hand and just as he had done, she sliced a hunk of cheese, a wedge of apple, and broke off a piece of bread. He also ate slowly, his eyes never leaving hers.

They took turns feeding each other, moving a little closer every time the knife changed hands. By the time they were full, the sun had dropped low and it was growing cold. Todd drew her into his arms and kissed her.

Her hands wound around his shoulders. "I like the way you do that."

Once again he claimed her lips, lowering her gently onto her back. He was aware of the grass beneath them, the breeze blowing, and then his focus narrowed just to her: the feel of her skin, her face under his fingertips, the way her hair sifted through his hands. He felt the wide, jagged scar on the back of her head. "Is it still tender?"

"A little."

He turned her head and kissed the nape of her neck. "Everything about you is special, even your scars." He was ready for more, but wanted to keep the tenderness they were sharing. He lay back and closed his eyes. The wind cooled him just a little; he needed that, to cool off.

She sat up and bent over him, traced his lips with a blade of grass. Everything slowed down. She grew still and when he opened his eyes and looked at her, he saw the same look of love on her face as when he'd found her in the chamber. She'd opened her eyes and called him Jacques.

"Do I still remind you of Jacques?" he asked softly.

"In some ways. You both have dark hair and light brown eyes. You're both tall." She drew her fingertip from his hairline, down his nose, across his lips, and stopped at the tip of his chin. "You have similar profiles too." She lay down beside him and nestled close. "I think I'd like to see you in a tunic."

"You'll have to wait for Halloween."

§§§

At the pub that evening, he'd never seen an atmosphere so changed. People pressed toward him from every side, looking nothing like the frightened villagers who had glumly waited through Laura's disappearance. Folks he didn't even know pumped his hand and clapped his shoulder.

Kit waved them to the bar and offered the first round on the house. After a rousing chorus of cheers, Kit leaned closer so he could be heard over the din. "I've never bought the house a round before." For a moment, Todd was afraid the slender barkeep was going to get sentimental and mushy, but Kit managed to pull himself together. He raised his glass. "Welcome back. Take care of our girl."

"Thanks." Todd was feeling a little emotional himself, and quickly swallowed a long draught.

Gertie appeared at his elbow. "How long are you going to stay?"

"Only a week this time, but I'll be back."

"Nonsense!" With a wave of her hand, she dismissed the rest of his life. "You should move here."

Mr. Pickney bustled forward. "I've advised Laura not to take on too ambitious of a project, at least to start. A house like that is a lifelong commitment." The pale solicitor raised his whisky glass. "Good luck to you both."

Todd's head was spinning.

Laura rescued him and led him to a table. "I should have warned you. The whole village has plans for the manor. They think there's no time to waste."

"What plans exactly?" He pulled out a chair for her, letting his hands linger on her shoulders as she sat down.

"Oh, everyone has their own ideas." She picked up her glass. "Like the ale, advice is bottomless around here."

"Apparently, they think you're an integral part of their economy." He admired her rosy cheeks. The fresh air had improved her color, or maybe it was the alcohol.

Paul elbowed in. "I've drawn up a list for the cottage. Electrical, then plaster and painting. We'll get started tomorrow morning. See you around nine." He bounded away, heading back to the bar.

Todd glanced down at the scrawled list that Paul had tucked under his glass, then looked at Laura. "Was he talking to me?"

"Hmmm...yeah. You're the structural engineering type, right?"

"I can handle a hammer, but what's the plan?"

"Once I get the gardener's cottage fixed up and rented, it'll bring in a small income, hopefully enough to pay the utilities. My utility bills are huge."

Todd liked the idea of more people living on the property, people she could trust and who paid rent. He took another sip of ale. Just as he thought they were going to have a moment of peace, Kit approached with another tankard. "If that's for me," Todd said, "you'd better give it to someone else."

"Not very sporting of you to refuse the gesture." Kit ignored Todd's protest and set down the drink.

"And if I keel over, how would that look?"

"Meeting a real life hero makes people feel good." Kit patted his shoulder. "Having a pint with a friend makes people feel good. We're both fixing the world in our own way."

An hour later, Todd was hoarse from shouting and his head was fuzzy from alcohol and twenty-plus hours without sleep. He leaned toward Laura. "I need to get a little air."

"Time to go," she said, standing up.

He tried to pay the tab, but Kit waved him away and raised his eyes in the direction of a table crowded with Laura's friends. "It's all taken care of."

Todd recognized Gertie and Ben, Megan, Mr. Pickney, and a few others. "That's really generous of them, of all of you." Todd was glad he'd let Laura talk him into this. "Thanks for the party. I'm honored."

It took a while to work their way to the door because he and Laura had to pause by each table, but eventually they made it outside. He drew a deep breath. "Is everything a collective effort?"

"Sometimes it seems that way." She laughed.

He took her hand, gave it a squeeze. "Everyone was so nice."

"I need to walk a little."

"Good idea." They were probably both too unsteady to drive right away.

They walked along High Street until they reached the village church. The Norman tower rose tall against a backdrop of dark clouds.

"This is where Lorraine married Brian Bannock," Laura said. She tried the doors, found them unlocked, and they slipped inside. In front of the baptismal font, she paused. "Their children were christened here too. She had five in all, but only four of them were Bannock's. Her first son was fathered by Jacques."

"Why didn't she marry him?"

"He was illegitimate, without title or land. He didn't have anything, and his brother killed Lorraine's father. If Etienne got ahold of her, he'd either kill her too, or marry her. Jacques had to get her out of France. Tragically, he kept the promise he made to her father and brought her to England, and straight to Lord Bannock."

He was treading in sensitive territory but he had to know. "Did you read about this in the manuscript?"

They took seats in the first pew, close enough to see the gilt-trimmed altar.

"Some of it." She stared up at the stained glass window, and he could tell her mind was focused on the past. "As the years went on Lorraine adjusted. She had to."

He waited for her to tell more of the story, but she fell silent. Laura was doing the same thing as that other woman she talked about. She was adjusting to her circumstances, not because she wanted to, but because she had to.

They sat quietly for a long time, and when she looked at him again, she had tears in her eyes. "I keep thinking about little Sophie. The last time I saw her, she'd been brutally slaughtered. Her small body was just outside the chamber." She shook her head. "I can't get the pictures out of my mind."

She was visibly struggling, and even stranger, she'd started talking in first person, as though she were really there all those hundreds of years ago. He didn't know what to say, so he sat quietly, holding her hand.

"I don't know if the other children were safe inside or not." A tear dropped off the end of her nose. "There was a massacre."

"What about Lorraine's memoirs? Have you read all of them?"

"Someone must have had something to hide because pages have been hacked away at the end of the book. They're just gone."

"Can you tell how much is missing?"

"Probably the last third – shortly after the massacre. Whatever happened next was removed."

As gently as he could, he said, "It must be terrible to think about, to know that those people suffered, but why does it matter now, after so long?"

"It matters because when I'm alone at night, half asleep, I... I get stuck between... sometimes..." She looked into his eyes, searching for understanding. "I can't sleep." She sighed, as though there were so much more to convey, but she didn't have the words. "The tension builds until I have to get up and walk around. Have you ever been an insomniac?"

"Not really. I guess I'm lucky." The truth was he could hit the hay and fall into a coma-like sleep, and stay asleep. No dreams, no nightmares, no problem. Clearly that wasn't the case for Laura.

Something flashed in her eyes and was gone almost before he'd registered it. Underneath the fatigue and turmoil, she was terrified. Her fear, the rawness and depth of it, worried him. For the first time he began to consider that maybe what Laura was going through was more than post-traumatic stress. He had to be careful. Her happiness seemed fleeting. One moment she was radiant, excited, and in the next she got quiet and pensive. She was healing, he reminded himself, and she would be doing that for a while.

"I hate to see you suffering," he said. It sounded lame but he meant it. He would do anything to make her feel safe again.

"I don't expect you to understand." Her words cut him, but she gave his hand a reassuring squeeze. "I'm still trying to figure things out, waiting for life to feel normal again. Please don't think I'm crazy."

Even though they'd been together so briefly, he knew her better than he'd ever known anyone. "You're not crazy." He didn't believe everything she was saying, but he hoped it would become clear in time. He put his arm around her, wishing he had something more profound to say, some theory that could ease her mind, and his. "We can work through this."

Laura folded her hands in her lap and closed her eyes. He thought she was praying, and so he remained quiet. The church was like a private world. It could have been modern day or five hundred years ago, and he was beginning to understand what it had been like for her in the chamber. Not the part about being trapped or starving, but the sense of timelessness. No wonder she'd been so caught up in the lives she'd been reading about. They had lived in the same house, had wandered the same village lanes. It was uncanny.

It was close to midnight by the time they got back to Bannock Manor. Todd could barely keep his eyes open.

Laura parked the car, and as they walked into the house, she said, "Being with you makes me feel grounded, in the present."

"That's the first time I've had that effect on a girl. Usually they think I'm way too intellectual." He followed her upstairs and they stopped in front of an open bedroom door. He hoped she would invite him to sleep with her.

"Kate made up this room for you. You'll share the bath across the corridor with Paul. Fresh towels are in the cupboard."

"Is it because I'm wrinkled and whiskered?"

"I didn't want to make assumptions." She indicated the doors on either side of his. "Paul's room is down that way, and mine is over there."

"Couples on Match.com would've been married by now."

"Really?" She gave him a quick peck on the cheek and went down the hall to her own room.

He unpacked and then went into the bathroom. Paul's stuff was all over the counter and damp towels were on the floor. Todd kicked the towels into a corner and turned on the shower. Standing under the tepid spray, he stretched as he washed, trying to work out some of the fatigue, and then dragged a razor across his cheeks and around his jaws. Raising his head, he carefully shaved his neck. After he dried off, he splashed on a tiny bit of aftershave – just in case.

With a towel wrapped around his waist, he stepped into the corridor and glanced towards her room. What would she do if he knocked? She must have heard the shower shut off, because as he stood there, the knob turned and the door creaked open.

The hall light illuminated a portion of her face, and she mouthed 'oh' like she'd been caught. Then she smiled and stepped back into the shadows, disappearing.

That was all the invitation he needed. Cautioning himself to go slowly, he moved just outside her door, pushed it open a little wider, waited, and then stepped inside.

"Laura?"

Her silence offered no clues.

Softly, he shut the door, blocking out the light from the hall. He could barely see her, outlined against the partly opened window. She stood looking out, and a gentle breeze riffled her hair. Her nightgown was short and shimmery, with the tiniest little straps at the shoulders, not the type girls wear when they want to be left alone.

"Is this all right?" He wouldn't push her if she wasn't ready, even though he ached for her.

She turned toward him. "Yes."

It took him only seconds to close the space between them. Her bare skin felt cool as he caressed her.

She shivered, then leaned into his arms and snuggled against his chest. "You smell good."

He kissed the top of her head, glad he'd taken the time to freshen up instead of collapsing into bed. Gently, he lifted her chin and kissed her mouth, his tongue barely touching her lips, teasing, offering himself, but not pushing.

She kissed him eagerly as her hands roamed up and then down his back. The towel fell away and he was naked. As smoothly as he could, he guided her toward her bed. "Let's do this right."

Through the dim light he caught a glimpse of her smile, but she said nothing, just crawled inside the covers.

Climbing in beside her, he traced his fingers along her cheek and under her jaw. He was exhilarated by the feel of her bare legs next to his. He began stroking her, long caresses starting at her shoulder and lingering on her breast, her waist, all the way down to her thighs. He moved his hand up to her shoulder and began again, slow sensual petting that made her murmur with pleasure and press more tightly against him.

Her lips moved like a whisper of silk against his neck. "Sure you're not too tired?"

In answer, he slid his hands around her hips, under her gown, and then pulled the satiny little number over her head. She was naked, and his fingers played lightly on her skin. He dropped the lightest of kisses into the hollow between her breasts before moving on to her nipples. They were puckered and erect, and he suckled them gently.

"This feels so right." The smell of her hair, the touch of her face intoxicated him. He moved on top of her, melted into her, and the world stopped in that moment. His soul linked with hers. "We were always meant to be together," he said, wondering where the thought had come from, knowing it was true.

Her eyes were shut, her hips moved slowly, sensually, then her legs wrapped around his thighs, pulling him closer. She began moving more urgently and he fought to hold back, but his pace increased until they were both panting.

Her moan began, rolling like low thunder. He felt the shudders deep within her, and he strained to enter her more. She was pulsing beneath him, the tension ebbing but not fading completely.

Finally, he could let go, and his passion and longing erupted as their bodies fused. She was his world, his life.

Chapter Thirty-Two

Laura felt self-conscious the following morning as she walked into the kitchen with Todd. She had stalled, taking a shower and blow drying her hair as poor Todd waited for her with his stomach growling.

Paul leaned against the counter gripping a mug of tea. "Sleep good?"

Laura blushed, then turned to Kate. "I'd like you to meet Todd Woodbridge."

"I've cooked up a full English for you, so I hope you've got an appetite." Kate nodded toward Paul. "And it's been tough going keeping his hands off it."

"Wonderful." Todd pulled out chairs for Laura and himself.

"It's set up in the breakfast room, love." Kate bustled out the door carrying a platter laden with food.

Todd tracked her like a bloodhound, and Laura had no choice but to follow. The table was set formally for two. There was even a vase of roses.

The sideboard held an array of steaming dishes and Kate began lifting off the lids. "What would you like? Sausage and bacon? Mushrooms? Grilled tomatoes?"

"Breakfast is my favorite meal and no one does it better than the British." Todd had a grin on his face as wide as a melon slice. "I'll eat everything you put on my plate."

"How many eggs would you like, Mr. Woodbridge? Two, three?"

"Oh, please, call me Todd." He looked almost giddy with anticipation. "Three will be great."

Laura was reminded of the old adage: the way to a man's heart is through his stomach. It certainly seemed appropriate here.

Paul had followed them in. "Mind if I join you?"

"Of course not." Laura collected another place setting out of the cabinet.

Kate, her back to them, visibly stiffened. In her rule book, Paul was staff, he had crossed a line and Laura had encouraged him. It was a game they played; the daily battle against pretentiousness.

"I'll serve myself, Kate. Thank you." When they were alone, Laura said, "I liked it better when I cooked for myself."

"But, Kate did all this work." Todd slathered jam on a piece of toast. "Why don't they use these little toast racks in the U.S.?"

Paul filled his plate and sat down. "Around here, there's dishes for fishes, and dishes for their bones. Kate scolded me one day because I used a soup bowl for cereal. My sister-in-law, Gertie, loves all the china in this house."

"I don't feel welcome in my own kitchen anymore" Laura said. "Now it's her territory."

"Our Kate likes to follow protocol," Paul concurred. "Miles is just as bad. Doesn't say much but his expressions read like a novel."

Laura heard movement on the other side of the door and put a warning finger to her lips. "So what's on our agenda for today?" she said, speaking loudly. "Would you like to go to Stratford?"

"I thought I was helping Paul on the cottage."

"This is your vacation."

"I love renovation projects."

She wasn't ready to share him. "Let's play today and tomorrow we'll both help Paul."

Since Mum and Winnie had passed, she'd almost forgotten what it was like to enjoy the local sights, but now that Todd was here the urge to go exploring was coming back. He probably knew the country as well as she did, but she wanted to show him her England, the one she'd grown up with.

In Stratford-Upon-Avon they rented a boat. After an awkward start, Todd got the hang of it and rowed them slowly along the River Avon. The branches of ancient willow trees dripped into the water and swans glided smoothly past, barely causing a stir. The dip of oars and the occasional fish breaking the surface were the only disturbances on the glassy surface.

Laura lay in the boat watching clouds float by and listening to the birds. It was like a day in paradise, no destination, no time constraints.

"You look delicious," Todd said lazily. "I'm tempted to tie up to a tree and ravish you."

Just then another boat passed them, the four passengers inside drinking wine and laughing.

"Tempting," she agreed. "But probably a little too public. We were scolded for that yesterday."

"People love to see romance. We'd be doing a public service – sharing bliss."

"It is idyllic, isn't it? I feel like I'm in a Jane Austin novel."

"Give me swashbuckling over high society."

"Sir Walter Scott?"

"If you must know, my favorite character was Robin Hood, and I read about him in every version I could get my hands on – old English and modern remakes."

"It makes so much sense," she mused. "Unfairly cast out of society, forced to steal." She closed her eyes for a moment and felt the sun, warm against her face. Were people's tastes in the present always shaped by the past?

"Don't fall asleep," he said. "Not when I'm working so hard to impress you."

She raised her head. "You don't have to work at it," she said. "I'm already impressed, and I've always had a soft spot in my heart for the underdog." She loved the sound of his laughter. "My students were always lured by that part of medieval history, as though warfare were nothing more than gallantry and good deeds, but they forget to consider the long term consequences." She hadn't meant to sound so intense, but the past did that to her, stung her when she wasn't expecting it.

"I wish I'd had a history teacher like you," he said.

She gazed at up him gratefully. He always seemed to know when she was a little too sensitive, and he found a way to make it easier for her.

"It's so much work, but I do miss my students." She fell silent as a surge of homesickness coursed through her, sharp and sweet.

"What's your favorite age to teach?" he asked.

"I started off with middle-graders." She laughed. "I was convinced they were the most fascinating kids, always on the verge of exploding into something. We just never know what." She dragged her fingers through the water. "The last two years I've been at the high school. They're so optimistic and adventurous, convinced they can conquer the world. And you know what, I believe they will."

"That's because they had you for a teacher."

"It's because for the most part, they believe they can control their destinies." She turned her head away, pretending to watch a swan. Had she ever been in control of her destiny? It seemed a life time ago that she'd believed her decisions were her own, but that had been naïve. Lorraine had also learned about sacrifice and compromise.

Todd asked quietly, "Do you think you'll go back?"

"My year's leave of absence will run out before I get things settled here. Then I'll have to let the job go." The prospect of losing it – all those eager kids with their energy and optimism – filled her with sadness. It would be another complete break with her old life, her previous self.

Above her, afternoon clouds gathered in clusters. She sat up, pulled on her jacket and stuck her hands in the pockets. The day's idyllic haze had vanished, leaving her thoughts in turmoil. She'd made up her mind to stay, but then Todd had waltzed in looking perfect, feeling perfect, and she started thinking crazy thoughts like leaving England to be with him.

Casting about for a safer, saner subject, she asked, "Do you like Shakespeare?"

"Since we're in Stratford-Upon-Avon, we have to see one of his plays." He rolled his shoulders. "And, my arms are getting tired. I'm probably not as macho as I led you to believe."

At the next wide bend in the river, he turned the boat around and rowed them back to the village pier. It was easy to find the Royal Shakespeare Company, and they were able to get tickets for that evening's performance of *A Midsummer Night's Dream*.

"Thank goodness we have time for dinner," Todd said, rubbing his stomach. "With all that exercise I worked up an appetite."

They chose a restaurant with a terrace overlooking the river and settled in with a bottle of Chardonnay. Fairy lights wrapped around the nearby trees and candles twinkled on the tables. They dined on filet of sole and wild rice.

"It's so serene here," she said. When she was with Todd, the tightness coiled in the pit of her stomach began to unwind, and she could relax. She sat back, fingers on the stem of her wineglass while she contemplated the soft lights reflecting on the water.

Magic.

The word floated into her consciousness. That's what today had felt like.

"It was all a dream," she murmured, thinking of the play they were about to see, a story of fairies and magic.

"Hmm?" Todd looked as relaxed as she was. "What are you dreaming about?"

"I was thinking about Shakespeare, how people fall asleep under a fairy spell and wake up believing it was only a dream."

"I know how it ends," Todd said. "Each lover finally wakes up in love with the right person." He paid the tab, and as they walked hand-in-hand to the theatre, he said, "You were right. It was a good idea to spend the day here."

In the theater, Laura was lulled into the story of mixed-up lovers and fairies, romance and charm, and in the end, after much confusion, a triple wedding. She had seen it before, and yet tonight it seemed different.

"Shakespeare was a genius," she said.

"Lord, what fools these mortals be!" Todd quoted, taking her hand as they walked out of the theatre. "Sometimes it's difficult to follow those old speech patterns."

Part of the magic for her had been the familiarity of the old English. It felt comfortable. Maybe that was it; she wasn't just seeing it but hearing it in a different way. So many things in her life felt that way now. "Let's try to see one of his plays every time you visit."

"I'd like that," he said. "I'll finally learn where all the clichés came from."

It was late as he drove them home, but it seemed the magic came along for the ride. Romantic oldies played on the radio, and under clear skies and a full moon, the road, like the River Avon, seemed to go on and on.

There was no pretense of separate bedrooms when they got back to Bannock Manor. She helped Todd gather his clothes and move into her room. She didn't want to spend a single minute apart from him. After she washed up, he was already waiting for her, and she slipped into bed naked, the sheets cold and soft, his body muscular and firm.

He took his time, first kissing across her shoulders, then caressing her back. Slowly, his tongue traced each one of her vertebrae, sending shivers of pleasure across her skin, filling her with delicious anticipation. The entire day had been foreplay, and by the time his lips reached her lower back, she was eager for him.

She explored his skin with her fingers, her lips, her tongue, inhaling his scent, savoring everything about him. Gently, he moved above her, and her eyes locked with his as their bodies connected. It felt perfect, like coming home from a long trip and seeing all the comforting things again, knowing that everything she loved was right there waiting for her.

His hands roved over her breasts, her waist, her thighs, caressing and stroking, moving slowly as if he intended to make love all night long.

She got on top and stared down at him. Her senses were heightened; both the old visions and her present sight became superimposed, like seeing two photographs at once. She was Lorraine bending over Jacques; she was Laura kissing Todd. She knew everything about Jacques, but she was still learning the feel of Todd's body. And then the memories winked out, and all she saw was Todd.

When she couldn't wait another minute, she pulled him over her, and they began moving as one. His heart beat against hers; his body covered hers. She felt herself falling deeper in love, except she had always been in love with him, and now they had found each other again. She held him close and didn't let go until she was shuddering against him.

His body arched as he followed her to climax. After a moment he whispered, "You are amazing, and mysterious, and so beautiful."

The weight of him felt right. "I've dreamed about you my whole life."

He kissed her forehead, her eyebrows, her cheeks, her chin. "I love you." He sounded surprised at his own admission.

"I love you too." She wanted to say it over and over again. I love you, Todd Woodbridge.

He curled around her, spooning her, holding in the warmth. She hadn't felt this safe in a long time.

During the night, she awoke with a nightmare. Todd's arm was around her. "It's okay. You're safe now," he whispered in her ear.

But she knew he'd be gone in five days. His job was waiting. "What if something happens to keep us apart?"

"Nothing can keep us apart. I'll come back in November for the memorial. I promise." He rubbed her back until she drifted off to sleep again.

§§§

Something about the filthy old gardener's cottage intrigued both Todd and Paul. They acted as if they were having the time of their lives as they spent the next three days working in the old building. Laura hoped it would be ready to rent before winter set in, otherwise it might sit empty until spring.

The afternoon was warm, and she thought about how nice it would be to finish early and hike up to a secluded glen with a picnic supper and a bottle of wine.

"What's that sneaky smile about?" Todd asked. A smudge of grime extended from his brow to his jaw.

She wiped his face with a paper towel and kissed him. "Things we could be doing instead of this." Her hand waved like a wand as she pointed at water stains and flaking paint, cracked window glass and the sagging doors. "If I had a fairy godmother, she'd make the rodents do the work, and I'd run away with you, my prince."

He nodded toward the other room where Paul was pulling up old carpet. "You don't want to stop the momentum now, do you, Cinderella?"

"I guess I'm not Sleeping Beauty anymore." She pretended to pout. "Since I haven't gotten any sleep all week."

Todd seemed to have endless energy, grubbing around the outbuildings by day and making love all night long.

"Mushy talk," Paul complained as he backed out of the bedroom, dragging a roll of moldy carpet. "Pick up the other end, will you?"

Todd hurried to help, but not before he gave her a lustful look. "Later," he mouthed before Paul turned around.

She grinned back at him, then scooped a small batch of wet plaster onto her putty knife, pressed it into a crack in the wall, then feathered the edges smooth. For the first time in months she was starting to feel like her problems were manageable. Little by little, things were getting fixed. With new carpet and fresh paint, the cottage would be adorable, and she might even find a renter who would also become a friend.

Paul returned and inspected the walls. "Almost ready to paint."

"I think we have enough for this room, but we'll need more paint for the kitchen and bedroom," she said. "I haven't had a chance to go into Dursley."

"Hmmm. I wonder what's taking all your time?"

Todd interrupted, sparing her having to answer. "You want to finish up what you're doing while Paul and I go for supplies?"

They left in Paul's truck, and she continued working alone, rolling crisp white paint across the walls of the living room. The fresh, clean expanse promised a new beginning for someone, and steady income for her.

Her shoulder burned from the continual motions of daubing up paint and spreading it on the walls, but she didn't quit until the room was finished. She looked around, sore but satisfied. She had put in a good day's work.

The guys had been gone for a couple of hours, and Laura started getting worried. She kept watching through the door and listening for Paul's old truck. Later, she climbed the hill to the chapel to watch for them coming over the rise. After another half hour, there was still no sign of them.

As the afternoon began to fade, she went inside the chapel, blinking as her eyes adjusted to the dim interior. It was quiet and calming, and she focused on the soft twilight coming through the stained glass windows. On a whim, she knelt in front of the five-tiered candle holder.

A few days before her mother's funeral, Winnie had purchased a large box of votive candles and then spent hours cleaning the fifty red glass holders in the black iron rack. Winnie had always shown love through her handiwork.

Neither of her parents had been regular churchgoers, and Laura had never been very religious, but she was tempted to make the sign of the cross. She wasn't even sure she knew how. It was so Catholic, and she was not.

But Lorraine had been.

Laura wanted to pray, wanted the solace that people of faith talked about, and she shook one of the long matches out of a box, struck it, and began lighting the first row of candles. The wooden match blackened and curled, the flame crept closer to her fingertips, but she didn't blow it out until she felt its heat. She got another match and lit the second row: ten for Mum and ten for Winnie. She missed them both. Nigel too.

The odor of sulfur swirled around her head.

Slowly, she lit the remaining thirty candles, watching as the tiny flames flickered inside the red glass cups. Closing her eyes, she tried to empty her mind but memories whirled like smoke: Mum's funeral, Winnie's body lying in the cellar, Oliver's greasy hair and clammy, pudgy hands, the chamber, the cold, the blood...

Rage erupted from somewhere deep inside and she wanted to scream, to throw the red jars one by one and watch them shatter, watch the melted wax slide down the wall, turning from warm to cold, and then congealing.

Trying to calm down, she began taking deep, rhythmic breaths. She stared at the fifty tiny fires until her vision blurred.

It hadn't always been like this.

Once there was a door.

And stairs to the crypt.

Laura tried to summon her earliest childhood memories. She was sure the candle rack had always been there. Narrowing her eyes, she squinted at the glowing lights, trying to remember.

There had been a door there. She was sure of it. Moving closer to the niche, she examined the walls. Wrought iron panels covered all three sides, ostensibly to prevent the candles from starting a fire. The upper half of each panel depicted a biblical scene in relief: Jesus on the cross, Jesus emerging from his tomb, and Jesus rising into the clouds.

Laura started blowing out the candles, coughing from the smoke and wishing she hadn't lit all fifty of them. Her eyes burned and watered until all the votives were finally extinguished, and then she grabbed the front of the rack and yanked it hard. It moved half an inch. She jerked it from side to side, and a shrill scraping noise assaulted her ears as she slowly pulled it forward. Her back and shoulders ached, but she couldn't stop.

Somehow, she was certain that when the chapel was built, this niche had been the landing that led down into the crypt.

Once the rack was out of the way, she studied the door-sized, iron panels. In the half-light it was hard to see, but she knew exactly which wall the opening would be on, and she traced her fingers down the corner seam until she felt a series of hinges. Pulling the outside edge, she felt a little give, and she tugged until she heard the low grinding of rough metal hinges. She yanked and pulled until she could peek behind it. The iron panels hadn't been intended to hide access to the crypt, but the space had been filled with the candle rack, and the crypt had been forgotten.

She heard Paul's truck in the drive and was relieved. Smoothing her shirt, she ran outside and down the hill, calling, "Hey, can you give me a hand?"

"Hope you haven't been waitin' long." Todd was smiling, looking relaxed. "We thopped ...stopped by Kit's."

"Wanted to make sure he enjoys his –" Paul grinned stupidly. "Vacation. What you digging around in this time?"

She looked down at her shirt, covered in swathes of white paint and black smudges of soot. "The chapel."

"I'm done for the day," Paul said, staggering toward the kitchen door. "One project at a time, I always say."

"I want to show you something," she said to Todd.

He looked at her blackened hands. "What have you been doing, Cinderella? Cleaning chimneys?"

"I found the door that leads into the crypt."

He gripped her shoulder to steady himself, and lowered his head so he could peer intently into her eyes. "Did you know there was a crypt?"

"Not really."

"Another one of your cryptic answers." Once he started laughing at his own joke, he couldn't stop.

"How much did you guys drink?"

"A pint or three. Or more. Kit's my best friend, after Paul."

Anxious, she pulled him up the path and into the chapel. The hinges squealed eerily as she wedged open the iron door that led into the crypt.

"Sure you want to go down here?" Todd asked.

"I do." She turned to look at him. "Scared?"

"Nope. I'll even go first."

She hesitated; he wasn't in the best condition to go exploring.

Todd took the stairs cautiously, and Laura followed. As they descended more deeply into the crypt, the last of the light from the doorway faded and they moved slowly, feeling the way with their feet. The floor leveled out and they shuffled forward, Laura clutching the back of Todd's shirt.

When she figured they were beneath the altar of the chapel, she put out a hand and touched a marble effigy. She moved around it, letting her fingers trace the figure, remembering what she'd seen in another lifetime. Slowly, her eyes adjusted until she could see what her hands had discovered.

The man carved in marble wore chainmail and had a great broadsword by his side. He was lying on his back, a sleeping dog at his booted feet, his head resting on a lion. His hands were clasped in prayer above his heart.

She touched her finger to his lips, lips that had once curved in a smile and said her name. *Lorraine.*

Todd unclipped a penlight from his keychain and directed the beam across the figure. He gave a low whistle. "Who is that?"

"Brian Bannock, but the tomb is empty. His body was never recovered from the Battle of Towton."

Laura circled the monument again, and in the dim light she made out another tomb a few feet away. It was topped with the carving of a woman wearing clothes that had been fashionable centuries ago. A faithful dog also rested at her feet, and her head reposed on a sleeping lamb. Her hands were also folded in prayer, and her expression, like Bannock's, was peaceful.

Through the shadowy light she could barely read the nameplate. *Lady Lorraine Bannock. Born February 6, 1438, Normandy. Died February 11, 1493, Bannock Manor.*

"She lived to be fifty-five years old." Todd's voice was full of amazement. "How much of her life do you know about?"

She wanted to be honest, to share everything she saw and felt, especially now that he was showing a glimmer of belief. It was hard trying to hide the pieces of Lorraine's life that slipped into her mind, and sometimes she wasn't exactly sure where Lorraine's thoughts ended and hers began. "My memories stop a year or two after Bannock died," she said. "Lorraine had this memorial made in his honor."

"And her tomb? Who made that?"

"I don't know." There was so much she still didn't know, so much that could have happened during the remaining years of Lorraine's life.

Close to Lorraine's tomb was a smaller one, topped with the effigy of a sleeping child, and the name Sophia Catherine was carved into the base. Under her name were the words of her favorite prayer. *By day I'm in the shepherd's sight. At night the angel's hold me tight.*

Night after night, they'd whispered the words together, and then Sophie would cling to her for one more hug.

Sleep tight, little Sophie.

Laura's heart ached, but she blinked away her tears, not wanting Todd to see them. She moved deeper into the crypt. There were other tombs, some raised and topped with effigies. If Lorraine's other children were buried down here, then she would finally know how long they had lived, and whether they had survived the attack on the manor.

Moving from tomb to tomb, brushing off centuries of dust and dirt, her fingers traced the engraved letters as she searched for the familiar names. Her throat was tight as she circled the crypt twice. "I can't find their names. The other children aren't here."

"Tell me what to look for."

"Julian, Elizabeth, Anne, and Brian Blake Bannock." Their little faces and silky hair, their smiles and whims came back to her in vivid detail.

Marble slabs marking other tombs were embedded in the floor, and Todd wiped away the dust. "Maybe they're buried outside, in the cemetery."

"They're not. I've already looked a thousand times." Thunder rumbled through the room, and she stiffened. "Did you hear that?"

"What?"

The rumbling continued, making the ceiling shake, and her heart hammered just as hard. "Hurry. We have to hide."

She clutched at his hand but he didn't seem to understand. He just stood and stared at her as the ground shuddered and the thundering came closer.

Why was he just standing there?

Trembling, she dove behind Bannock's tomb.

The ground vibrated beneath them and plaster fell from the ceiling. The sound grew louder and everything began to shake. Dozens of horses were bearing down on them, and outside she heard the terrified cries as people tried to scramble to safety. Julian crouched beside her, and she whispered, "Hold still. Don't make a sound."

She heard the shouts of men, the hammering of weapons upon the gate, footsteps on the stairs, and then suddenly Julian was snatched up. He cried out to her, and then the man was on her, holding her down, grappling with her skirts, ripping off her undergarments. She kicked and scratched harder, thrashing her head as the man between her legs clawed his way in.

"Laura." Todd's voice called her back. "Laura, it's all right." They were sitting on the floor and she was battering his shoulders, furiously trying to break free. He held her tightly, his legs locked around hers. "Stop fighting me."

Gradually, her terror faded and she came back to the present, shivering uncontrollably. "You pr...probably think I'm crazy," she said through her chattering teeth.

He gathered her against his chest and wiped her tears with the hem of his shirt. "I love you," he whispered. "I hate to see you in pain."

Taking another shaky breath, she said, "Lorraine was raped down here." She swallowed, trying to talk past the tightness in her throat. Her body ached as though the beating had been real. "Julian saw the whole thing."

"It's over now," he soothed.

She pushed away from him, the memories of the violence too fresh, too real. "That attack on the manor – that's the last day I remember."

Gently, Todd said, "Whatever you're tapping into, you have to shut that door." He tried to pull her back into his arms, but she resisted. "What happened in the past is over," he said. "Let it go."

She couldn't let it go. It was a part of who she was now. Sooner or later, he was going to have to understand that.

§§§

Later that night, Laura lay awake with Todd's arm around her. He held her gently, but the weight of his hand seemed too heavy, and she had to resist the urge to shrug it off. It might wake him, and it would only hurt him more. For the first time since he'd arrived, they hadn't made love. She couldn't relax.

She slipped out of bed and took another shower. She'd taken one earlier, trying to wash away the memory of that soldier's touch, but it hadn't helped. Neither did talking with Todd. He was trying to be logical and practical, but his rational thinking only irritated her. There was so much about her that he didn't get.

She pulled on her heavy terry robe and left the room, and before she realized it, she was at the door between the modern house and the medieval section. Angrily, she pushed through. The great hall was cold and dark, and she hesitated. It was the last place she should be in the middle of the night. She paced back and forth, barely registering when her bare toes stubbed against a raised tile edge. Fury drove her, and she muttered curses at Brian Bannock for caring more about the next king of England than protecting his home and family.

Why was she still so affected by Lorraine's life?

Could she stop it?

Did she want to?

After a while, the tempo of her pacing changed. No longer furious, she slowed her steps, and instead of walking up and down the hall, she began moving in a large circle. With each turn, she contemplated another memory of that day in 1461.

It was July, a sunny and warm day. She held Anne's hand as they looked inside the dovecote. Julian was at sword practice. She'd spent the morning reading to the children in French. Three little girls ran through the house, laughing, Matilde chasing after them. These were the memories she had to cling to.

It was Sophie's last day alive.

Grief slammed into her, and she took a step back, and another, physically pushed by the agony of losing her child.

Reach for something else, a happier recollection, another day. Sophie playing with a doll, smiling and robust.

Laura stopped walking. Not even the man wielding the sword had set those events in motion. She stared at the floor, trying to understand. The fabric of life was made up of thousands of destinies woven together, and hers was one small thread. Bannock's life was one piece of the pattern, and Lorraine's was another, all caught up and tied together.

Through the window, she watched the sky lighten to orange and blue streaks, the dawn giving way to pale daybreak. She'd been up all night. A band of clouds lay on the horizon, but rays of sun streamed through. A new day – a fresh start.

Deep down, she was grateful for the richness of Lorraine's experiences. Perhaps it really was a gift to have her modern education and understanding, and Lorraine's firsthand knowledge of the medieval world.

But to have a healthy life now, she had to let go of the trauma. She had to do what Todd was coaxing her to do, and somehow put the painful experiences into context, detach from the memories, and disempower them.

Shivering, she clutched her robe tightly around herself and went into the kitchen to make coffee.

Todd had two more days, and she didn't want to spoil them. She had to make it right for him and breakfast in bed would be a good start.

She found the eggs, heated the skillet, set the toast in the rack while the eggs were cooking. Not as fancy as Kate's full breakfast, but it would do. When the eggs were done she arranged everything on a tray and carried it upstairs.

"What's all this?" He sat up, rubbing his whiskers. "You didn't have to."

"I wanted to. I'm sorry I was so... distant."

"Hey, it's okay. This looks great." He kissed her, and then, true to form, gave his full attention to his food.

She smiled and did the same. Suddenly, she was starving.

When they were done eating, she took the tray and set it aside, then crawled back into bed.

He looked surprised. "I thought you'd want to get back to the cottage, make sure we get it finished."

"The cottage can wait. You've done all the repair work you're going to do on this vacation. The next couple of days are about us."

"Anything special you want to do?"

"I thought maybe we could go hiking and explore some of the footpaths."

"That sounds like fun." He untied her robe. His hands touched her and she started to tense. He stopped. "It's okay. We can wait."

"I want to. Right now." She kept her eyes open, riveted to his. He was Todd, and she was Laura.

He made love to her slowly, pausing every few minutes to make sure she was okay. When she began to get nervous, he stopped and held her.

She listened to his breathing, listened to his heart, anchoring herself in the present.

Chapter Thirty-Three

Autumn always brought transitions, Laura thought as she hurried toward the gardener's cottage. The oaks and sycamores had turned orange and brown, the larches golden, and the alders yellow. It got dark earlier and once the sun set, pockets of cold air hovered among the trees.

Fumbling with the key, Laura unlocked the door. With only twenty minutes to spare, she turned on lights, lit a fire in the hearth, and popped some pre-made yeast rolls into the new oven. Everything had to be perfect before the couple arrived.

Furniture had been brought over from the manor, smaller items, a sofa, table and chairs, lamps, a bed. The cottage looked cozy now. Lace curtains hung over the new windows and a bunch of mums were in a vase on the table.

At 6:15 Laura pulled the rolls out of the oven, nibbling one as she waited.

When the potential tenants were forty-five minutes late, Laura went outside for more firewood. A hearty wind had kicked up and crisp, dry leaves blew like snow flurries. The temperature was dropping, and there were no headlights in sight. She gathered another armload of wood just as it started to drizzle. If they stood her up, she wasn't going to take anymore night appointments. It was too much work.

She swept up the debris she'd tracked in, straightened a hanging picture, and then checked her cell phone again. No new messages. She ate another roll. They were as cold as rocks and the fresh baked smell was gone.

Finally, she heard a car's engine. She waited behind the closed door until they reached the porch, not wanting to seem anxious. After a quick knock, the couple stepped inside, cold air swirling around them and mud clinging to their boots.

"We had a hell of a time finding this place," the man said, stomping his feet on the new doormat. "Passed the turn off twice, had to turn around and start out of the village again."

"It's not hard once you've been here," Laura said.

The woman glanced around the sitting room, and then went into the kitchen. "It's a bit small."

Laura followed, ready to point out the new appliances. "I could lower the rent if –"

"Our life style wouldn't fit here." The woman shook her head dismissively, her decision clearly made. They left without bothering to look in the bedroom. They were the third prospects this week to reject the cottage.

Laura dropped onto the faded sofa. Now she'd have to wait for the fire to burn down. Her asking price seemed fair. She'd spent more money than she'd planned to, and it'd take a year's worth of rent just to break even. It shouldn't feel like a personal slight, but it did.

Maybe she should move into the cottage and turn the manor over to a historical trust, let the experts worry about the upkeep. She looked around, seriously considering the idea. The small pile of glowing embers made the room feel snug and homey. It wouldn't be so bad living here. In a way, it was more pleasant than the manor; the space felt intimate and safe.

As the fire cooled to a soft gray afterglow, her thoughts turned to Todd. The incident in the crypt had alarmed him, and ever since things had been different. She couldn't put her finger on it, but the tone of his calls conveyed less romantic yearnings and more business advice. She appreciated his expertise, and she was working hard to follow his practical suggestions, but more importantly, she needed to prove that she wasn't irrational.

More than anything else, she didn't want to lose him, and when he returned next month, she was going to make certain that their relationship got back on track.

Finally, juggling her flashlight, umbrella and the bag of rolls, Laura stepped outside into the icy wind. Walking quickly, sluicing through puddles, she turned the bend and the manor came into view. A few lights shone in the windows, barely masking the emptiness. Miles and Kate were in there, but after six on most nights they disappeared into their apartment off the kitchen. As usual, Paul was at the pub.

The house looked massive and strong, but she knew from personal experience, hers and Lorraine's, that safety was an illusion. No matter the place or time, if you had something of value, there were those willing to steal it.

As she neared the back side of the medieval wing, beside what had once been a kitchen exit, she spotted the ghost shimmering in the lamplight. Lately, he'd been around more. He wanted something, but it was one more thing she hadn't figured out.

She got ready for bed and then skimmed the pages of a home improvement magazine as she sipped a cup of tea. Just as she did every night, she thought about Todd. Would he want her to move to California so that he could pursue his career at Berkeley? Would he find someone else, someone more predictable? Her stomach was in knots, and so were the blankets twisted around her legs. She kicked her feet free. There was no way she was going to fall sleep anytime soon so she climbed out of bed and got Lorraine's memoirs.

Plumping the pillows, she got back into bed and placed the heavy book across her knees. She turned the pages, reading the familiar script, occasionally pausing to touch the vellum and ink as though she could feel her own hand forming the words. At the beginning, Lorraine had written more about her devotion for Jacques. In later years, she wrote about her family and their lives, about running the estate, making purchases for the household, about the crops and the livestock.

Laura loved reading the book, feeling a connection with that former life. Lorraine's words brought back vivid images and memories. Everything had value and even the struggles seemed meaningful. It wasn't just about money and paying bills. Lorraine's life was colorful and rich, so full of people. Lorraine had never been lonely.

Laura's head dropped onto her chest and she dozed, but she was awakened later by the sound of creaking. It wasn't the typical sound of the house settling down for the night; it wasn't footsteps or tree branches but something rhythmic and steady.

She got up and eased open her bedroom door. The sound increased slightly. Tiptoeing down the corridor, she leaned her ear against the closed door of the next bedroom. She waited a minute before turning the knob and peering inside, but nothing was out of place and there were no unusual sounds.

At Paul's bedroom, she heard him snoring. She hesitated, wanting to wake him, but knowing he'd over react. She only half believed she was in danger; the calmer part of her mind told her to knock it off and investigate for herself.

It was probably nothing, just a rat, or a leaking pipe, or the breeze rattling a loose shutter. Old houses were full of eerie sounds. She'd check the rooms on this floor herself and then go back to bed. Creeping along the hallway, she opened each door, peering into darkened rooms, flicking on lights. Nothing.

Near the stair landing it sounded louder, like a squeaky gate, or an old hinge. The noise drifted from the floor above.

The hair along her arms began to prickle, and then she felt it – the softest touch of a cold breeze. She whirled around, but there was nothing to see.

Did the ghost want to help her, or warn her?

Listening intently, she climbed the stairs to the third floor. The tempo of the creaking quickened, but the timbre remained the same. Whatever was making the noise was staying in one place. It was higher still, in the attic, wafting like music from a scratchy record.

Clutching the handrail, she started up the plainer, narrower stairs, ready to turn and run at the first hint of danger. She hadn't been up there since her experience in the chamber; she didn't like small spaces anymore. The wood floors were gritty beneath her bare feet.

She approached the room where the old toys were stored, certain the strangely familiar sound came from inside. Her fingers trembled as she forced herself to turn the knob. The hinges whined as she pushed the door all the way back against the wall. Scanning the room, she saw shelves full of toys, baskets of playthings.

In a far corner, the empty cradle rocked back and forth, back and forth.

"Damn it! Leave me alone," she shouted.

The speed of the rocking increased.

This was how the ghost did things, and it made her look more closely. For the first time, it dawned on her that this was the same cradle Lorraine had used. There was no mistaking the ornate wooden canopy or the Bannock crest on the footboard that Tim Carpenter had so carefully constructed.

The memory made her hunger to hold a baby again, to smell the sweet scent of a newborn, and feel the comforting weight of an infant in her arms. She wanted to keep the cradle close to her in the hope that more memories would come.

She began tugging, but it was heavier than it looked, and awkward to grasp. She managed to drag it to the stairs, but had to pause every few minutes on her way down to catch her breath, bracing the end against her thigh. It hurt, and she'd have bruises in the morning, but once she started she was determined to get it back to her room.

"Are you trying to wake the dead?"

Laura jumped, her foot slipped on the stairs, and she let out a high-pitched scream, barely catching her balance.

Miles stood on the landing below her, tying the sash of his robe. "Or, are you organizing a jumble sale in the middle of the night?"

"You scared the crap out of me." She'd been waiting for something creepy to jump out and startle her, and it pissed her off that it was Miles who did it, while managing to make her look like an idiot at the same time. "I wanted to bring this to my bedroom," she said, hoping it sounded somewhat rational.

He raised his brows. "Are you expecting a baby?"

"No. I just like it." Her back felt like someone had shoved an iron bar between her shoulder blades, and the heavy cradle was ramming into her thigh.

He blocked the way, scowling in irritation. "And you had to get it right this minute? You couldn't wait until tomorrow to move furniture?"

They remained in an awkward stand-off until Miles, shaking his head, walked away without offering to help.

This is my house.

She stomped down the rest of the stairs, the cradle clunking loudly behind her. Miles and Kate were exasperating, and if her father wasn't paying their salaries, she'd have let them go already. They had a way of making her feel inadequate, and she was tired of living with them skulking about.

She dragged the cradle into her room and placed it next to her bed. Dozens, maybe hundreds of babies had been rocked in this cradle, but Lorraine's babies had used it first. The intense love she'd felt for them was powerful and sustaining. It fortified her. Unconsciously, she gave the cradle a gentle push and set it in motion again.

They were my babies and I miss them.

As she watched, the pace of the rocking increased.

The ghost wanted her to make the connection between the cradle and Lorraine.

"I've got it now," she said out loud.

The rocking stopped for a moment and then resumed. She grasped the side railings and brought it to a standstill. "I said, I've got it now. I understand the connection. Will you please go away and let me get some sleep?" She rolled up a blanket and tucked it around the curved wooden base so that it couldn't move.

Finally there was silence.

Lorraine's life continued to seep into her own. Like the ghost, it couldn't be rationalized away. She peered down into the dark courtyard, and pressed her hand against the window pane as though she could break through from this world into the medieval one.

§§§

Laura tried to be patient as she listened to her father's advice over the phone. He always assumed she wanted, and needed, his opinion.

"It's better to liquidate the art now," Bernard said. "Homes in the states aren't designed to accommodate large collections. People don't want to live in mausoleums over here. Get rid of as much as you can."

"The man from Christie's is not going to give me free appraisals on everything in the house." She looked out the sitting room window. It had begun to rain again. "The most they'll consider is eight items per visit."

"He's a salesman. He can spend more time if it benefits him."

There was no point explaining that she'd done more research than her father had. Or that for weeks she'd been following the antique auction sales. She and Megan had even spent two days in London scouring art galleries and asking questions about the resale market for old paintings. She'd tolerated haughtiness and suspicion, and had quickly learned to convey that she was an heiress with something of value to sell.

It was sadly comforting to realize she wasn't the only heir forced to sell old masters and ancestral portraits to pay the tax man.

"This appointment wasn't easy to get, Dad." She flipped through one of the Christie's Auction House catalogues. "They book seven weeks out, and before I could even get on their calendar I had to provide them with photos and measurements. They wanted documentation of each painting too. I found some old record books in the library, but there wasn't much. For proof of ownership, I had to get a letter from Mr. Pickney."

"Remember Laura, they'll want to buy low and sell high. Be careful."

"Their company works on commission. It's in their best interest to get a higher price."

They'd been talking for forty-five minutes and she wanted this conversation over with. "I've got to go, Dad."

"Speaking of the library, show him some of those old books."

"I'll call you in a couple of days and let you know how the meeting went." She had to change before the man from Christie's showed up.

"I'm going to buy your plane ticket today," he said, before she could hang up. "How long do you want to stay when you come home for Thanksgiving?"

"I told you I can't come to Boston this time – maybe next year." A lump formed in her throat. It was the same conversation she used to have with her mother. *When are you coming home?* "Dad, please... I'm sorry, but there are too many things going on. I just can't make it."

"But you and Edward always spend Thanksgiving with me." He paused, his disappointment hanging between them. "It's our family tradition."

"The art dealer just pulled up. Think about coming here instead."

She hung up the phone and looked down at her scruffy jeans. Dressing like a gardener wasn't the best way to do business with someone who'd come all the way from London. She waited a minute, hoping Kate would get the front door so she could slip upstairs and change. When the chime sounded a second time, she swore under her breath. It seemed whenever she wanted help from Kate, the woman pulled a disappearing act.

With no other choice, she opened the door herself. "Hello," she said in her most gracious, lady-of-the-manor voice. "Please come in."

Mr. Cromley, the appraiser from Christie's Auction House, London branch, maintained a blank expression. He stepped into the foyer and swiftly scanned the furniture, the photos, the paintings, even the rug on the floor. She imagined his instantaneous assessments: yes, no, yes, maybe, junk, replica...

"The works you've come to see are in the drawing room," she said, picking up her clip board and leading the way. Perhaps he would think her faded jeans and plain white tee-shirt were intentionally casual. Shabby chic?

"The nouveau riche adore these massive paintings of aristocracy on horseback," he said, pointing to the painting over the fireplace. "Old money looks for The Masters." He moved around the room slowly, stopping at each painting, his magnifying glass never far from his face. He took photos and made lots of notes. "Where is the Griffier?"

"It's upstairs, in the library." The Jan Griffier was probably the most valuable painting in the house, but he seemed to be on the lookout for other possibilities. "Do you want to see it now?"

"In time." He lingered for another twenty minutes before wandering into the dining room. "Gainsborough, Fleming, Poussin... Do you have any of that caliber?"

"I've got a Chesterfield."

He looked confused. "Van Dyck did paint the Countess of Chesterfield."

"I'm referring to a painting by George Chesterfield. He was a personal friend of the family. Albeit, only a generation ago."

"I've never heard of him." His attention landed on a pair of marble busts.

"They're Roman Senators," Laura said. "One of my great-uncles brought them back from his Grand Tour. He was killed in the war and so my grandfather inherited."

"And now you," he said, with a practiced, sympathetic smile. "Are you interested in parting with them?"

Unlike the paintings, which would leave patches of vibrant wall paper surrounded by faded walls when they were gone, she wouldn't even miss these empty-eyed, cold faces. "What do you think I could get for them?"

"What else can you tell me about them?"

"They're from Italy."

He raised an eyebrow but didn't answer. It was obvious he wanted them.

Not wanting to appear eager, she pursed her lips and frowned. "Let me show you the Griffier," she said, heading toward the stairs.

He paused at the landing and admired the life sized portrait of Lorraine Bannock. "That's magnificent." He got so close his nose almost touched the gold frame. "I can definitely find buyers for that."

"It's not for sale – and never will be."

He stared back at her, clearly surprised. "Are you certain?"

Tugging at the hem of her white cotton shirt, she remembered how beautiful she'd felt in the green, satin gown. It had been a hot summer and the dress was heavy and ornate, but she didn't mind posing long hours for the artist. "I'll never part with that one. It's very special to me."

They continued into the library, and he couldn't contain his excitement when she showed him the Griffier landscape. And he didn't bother hiding his disinterest in the Chesterfield that had been painted by her mother's admirer.

By the time he left five hours later, Laura had signed a contract hiring his firm to represent her in selling eight paintings, the two busts, and a Chinese urn.

§§§

"So they came, did they?" Megan said, getting right to the point as she came through the door.

"Just as promised." Laura took Megan's coat and hung it in the foyer closet. Mr. Cromely's crew had come to collect the selected art work exactly two weeks after their initial meeting. "I've never seen so much bubble wrap, and they built a custom packing crate for each item."

Megan bee-lined straight into the drawing room and then stopped abruptly, her mouth hanging open. "Your mother was always so careful when she sold something. She never wanted it to be so…obvious." Her shoulders slumped, and then her whole body seemed to sag. "It's rather sad to see the estate being dispersed like this."

"I had no choice but to go for the more expensive things." Laura thought of all the missing furniture upstairs. "Selling bedroom suites wouldn't bring in enough to pay the inheritance tax."

"I understand," Megan said, lowering herself into a chair. "Honestly, I do." But she was clearly shaken. "Have you talked to Nigel?"

"Yes. He's very excited to be coming home."

"I mean about the paintings."

"Oh, that. No, I didn't mention the art work. What's the point of upsetting him now? He'll see it for himself when he gets here."

Kate came in, carrying a tray. "Tea and biscuits for you ladies." She set it on the table and filled two cups.

Megan took one and added three spoonfuls of sugar. "How is it going to be with Nigel back in the house?"

The question hadn't been directed to either Laura or Kate, but Kate was quick to answer. "Hopefully, he can take care of himself because I didn't sign on for nursing."

Irritated, Laura sprang to Nigel's defense. "He's always been very self-reliant." But she thought about the accidents he'd had, the bad fall and all of the doctor's appointments.

Kate left the room, and Laura set down her cup with a bang. "As if I'd ask her to do anything for him."

Megan glanced around, making sure Kate was really gone. "What about Nigel's old room?"

"I can't ask Kate and Miles to leave the apartment. Besides, I think it would make Nigel depressed to be in there without Winnie."

"Well you don't want him going up and down the stairs."

"I painted the ground floor office and put his favorite chair in there. It has a nice big window that overlooks the garden."

Megan leaned forward and helped herself to another cookie. "He'll need a bed."

"Paul and I have been working our butts off. We moved a giant, old-fashioned wardrobe into the room and his same old bed is waiting for him. I was tempted to get him a new mattress, but there are just too many other expenses right now."

She'd also scrounged around the cellar until she'd found the boxes of his personal items. He'd been carted off so suddenly after Winnie's funeral that most of what he owned had been left behind. His clothes were now freshly laundered and waiting for him in the wardrobe.

"I found some old photos of him and Winnie and put them in frames," Laura said. "It was fun to see snippets of their lives. They're on his dresser now."

"You're doing right by him," Megan said. "Your mum and Winnie would be proud."

"I love him like a grandfather. I need him as much as he needs me. That's what families are for, right?"

Megan looked away, her face suddenly stark and unreadable. "I've always made my own way," she said quietly. "We do what we have to."

Chapter Thirty-Four

Todd drove up to Bannock Manor and parked behind a delivery van. Two men in tight pants, their short, spiky hair standing straight up despite the persistent drizzle, were unloading large flower arrangements under Kit's animated directions.

As he shrugged into his jacket, Todd wondered how much product it took to keep your hair poking up in the rain. More than he wanted to use.

Another truck was backing up beside the first, and he spotted Paul guiding it with two hands, like he was directing a plane on a runway.

Cranky from the long flight, the long drive, the bad weather, Todd looked around, anxious to see Laura. He'd tried to talk her out of staging a funeral for someone who'd already been dead half a millennium. It wasn't like there were any friends or family left to mourn a box of bones. Mostly he worried about the impact of another funeral on Laura and her unpredictable hold on reality.

Satisfied with the truck's position, Paul lowered his arms.

Another pair of guys jumped down and raised the rear door. Chairs, about a hundred of them, were stacked together.

"Can you help set up?" Paul called to him.

Todd was wearing dress shoes and his feet sank into the lawn as he walked over to help. "Where's Laura?"

Paul pushed a hand truck into place. "She's talking to Reverend Graham."

"I thought this was supposed to be an intimate memorial."

"Kit called a few of his contacts from the press and kicked off a coverage competition." Paul wrestled with tangled chairs. "Laura threatened that it would be his funeral if he didn't rein it in, but it was already too late."

"Kit did this to get PR for the pub?" A damp chill crept up through Todd's socks and he started to shiver. "Who's paying for all this stuff?"

Paul started pushing a hand-truck full of chairs up the hill. "Kit. He's even holding the Celebration of Life reception at the pub straight afterwards."

Pushing a second load, Todd followed Paul, and as they neared the chapel, he spotted Laura. She was talking to Megan, her blue eyes bright over her rosy cheeks. Her collar was zipped up to her chin, and strands of her hair escaped from under the hood of her rain slicker. The sun broke through the clouds and the droplets of mist that covered her sparkled. She looked vibrant, and just watching her took his breath away.

She spotted him walking toward her and a smile lit her face. She brushed away wisps of her damp hair. "I'm glad you're here. I've been watching for you."

He stepped closer and took her hands. Her eyes pierced him, sending a heated barb into his heart and setting off a chain reaction that made his whole body tingle. The noise, the cold, the commotion faded. He loved her. With everything he had to give, he loved her. The other distractions, the tension, all the things he didn't understand, none of that made the slightest difference. "Laura –"

She walked into his embrace, her arms wrapping around him, her cheek nuzzling his neck. "I don't dare admit how much I've missed you."

"Laura, I'll need to get going." Reverend Graham stood in the chapel doorway. "If I could have just a few more minutes..."

"Oh, yes. Sorry." She held onto Todd a moment longer, and he felt her reluctance to leave him. "Can you take care of yourself for a bit? We're finishing up the details for tomorrow's service."

A short distance away, near the tallest stone cross, a couple of men finished digging a small grave. They began laying strips of artificial sod around the perimeter to prevent the guests from sinking into the mud.

"What do you need me to do?" he asked.

"Rest. You've just had a long trip. I'll wrap it up here."

When Laura couldn't think of another detail that had to be done, they walked together toward the house.

"Hungry?" she asked.

"Starving." He took her hand and pulled her in for a kiss. "For you."

She smiled but her expression was worried. "Some people think this memorial is a silly idea, but I need to see it through." She looked into his eyes, as if searching for his opinion. "I would have done it quietly, and privately. Kit's going to pay for his interference this time."

"It'll be fine," he said, but he wasn't sure either.

Inside the foyer, Nigel hovered, leaning heavily on his cane. "You'll get sick tromping about in the rain all day."

"Don't worry so much." Laura patted his shoulder.

"It's good to see you again, Nigel." The relationship between Laura and the elderly butler was so caring and gentle that Todd was glad to see them back together. "Are you feeling well?

"Quite well. Quite well indeed," Nigel said. "Thank you for asking."

Laura led Todd directly to her room, and when the door was closed, she leaned her head onto his shoulder, suddenly still. "I've missed you so much."

She raised her head, and her desperate kisses dispelled any doubts that her world was full enough without him.

He caressed her back and marveled at her soft skin. She'd put on a little more weight and her ribs no longer poked through. Everything about her seemed healthier. She had the curves of a woman and the strength of a survivor.

"We should get ready for dinner," she mumbled, even as she snuggled more tightly against him.

"How about if Kate serves us supper in bed?"

"She planned something special and I don't want to cause a scandal."

It took a lot of will power and another ten minutes before he could let her go. They walked into the dining room late for dinner.

"It smells wonderful," Todd said, as Kate began to serve them. "I fantasize about your cooking as I eat my fast food meals. Would you consider moving to the States?"

"I've cooked a nice roast and potatoes," Kate said. "They might be a bit overdone now." She turned to set a platter on the sideboard.

In a way, he and Kate were allies, and her formal dinners gave him time to relax with Laura over a nice meal. He appreciated the home cooking, and it was fun watching Kate bask in his praise.

When they were alone in the dining room, Laura said, "I shouldn't blame you for flirting with her. At least she feeds you. All I do is make you work."

He'd barely tasted his first bite of roast when Miles appeared in the doorway.

"Dr. Jocelyn North has arrived," he announced, in a voice that always reminded Todd of Alfred Hitchcock.

Laura glanced at Todd. "She's bringing *him* back."

He was curious to meet Jocelyn, but it was strange to think of her transporting human remains.

She strode in and shook Todd's hand. "It's nice to finally meet you."

Kate reappeared, added a place setting and topped off their wine glasses.

Todd concentrated on his food as Laura and Jocelyn caught up on the details of their lives and work.

"I made a documentary about our research," Jocelyn said. "I think you'll find it interesting."

Todd started to squirm. It didn't take much to stir up Laura's PTSD. Too much talk about the skeleton might give her nightmares. He tried to shake off his trepidation. Laura was sensitive about the past, and she got pulled back into it so easily.

When dinner was over, he followed the two women, still chatting like best girlfriends, into the drawing room, and they all settled on the couch.

Jocelyn pulled an iPad from her purse. "It's all on here." She opened a file, and a video began to play.

Laura's lips compressed, like she was trying to keep her thoughts to herself.

The video opened with a long shot of the manor, and then the camera panned the grounds and zeroed in on the well. Todd studied the pictures of the open trench and the partially exposed skeleton. At first it was like looking at an exhibit in a museum, but as more of the skeleton came into view, and the camera moved in for a close-up, his gut clenched. It didn't feel like looking at inanimate bones, it was more like evidence of human suffering. Seeing the skeleton, knowing it was here at Bannock Manor, made it personal.

Laura shifted, and he took her hand.

The scene changed to a view of Jocelyn's lab, and a program slowly developed a graphic reconstruction. Detail by detail, a picture emerged of the medieval man as he might have looked when he was alive.

Laura was leaning forward, and when the last piece of the reconstruction fell into place, she whispered, "Pause it."

Jocelyn stopped the video, and Laura continued to stare at the reconstructed face. "I knew it was him. His hair was a little curlier, especially on the ends." She looked at Todd. "And the shade of his eyes was a little lighter. He was handsome, and this doesn't do him justice."

Todd didn't say anything. She was speaking as she did sometimes, like she had some special knowledge about the people in the past. But then she often crossed a line and started talking like she knew them personally. It was the coping mechanism that had helped her stay alive in the chamber.

Jocelyn leaned back, her eyes narrowed slightly, watching Laura. Her gaze flicked to him, but she gave nothing away. He recognized the look; she was observing, like a good scientist, staying neutral.

"You don't believe me," Laura said softly, a hint of sadness in her voice.

"I just don't see how you can know what happened five hundred years ago," Todd said. "Except for what you read in the manuscript."

"I don't understand how, exactly, but at least now I have proof that what I know is real."

"I never said –"

"It's all right." She shook her head. "I know how it sounds to you, to Dad, and anyone else I've tried to explain it to."

"Try me," Jocelyn said. "I've been studying those bones for months. Is there something more I should know?"

"He was a young Frenchman, Jacques Dannes, who brought Lorraine Bonville to live here. He loved her, but the man she was betrothed to murdered him."

"Do you have records?"

"I've got something even better. I'll be right back."

As soon as she was out of the room, Todd turned to Jocelyn. "She's convinced she knew him in a past life."

"Let's try to keep an open mind," Jocelyn said. "It's important to her."

Laura returned holding a rolled parchment. "I found this when I was in the chamber. I – Lorraine drew it."

Todd wanted to believe her, if only because she was so certain.

Carefully, Laura unrolled the scroll. The drawing was pen and ink, so old the ink had colored to a rusty brown, but the picture was clear. The young man in medieval garb looked amused, like he was humoring the artist, holding still for the portrait even though he didn't want to.

"Do you see?" Laura held up the scroll. "Look how alike they are."

Todd leaned forward, and Jocelyn did the same. There was an uncanny similarity between the drawing on the parchment and the image on the tablet.

Jocelyn got up and took the parchment, handling it carefully. She turned it over. "It says Jacques Dannes in the orchard at Chateau Brèche."

"Chateau Brèche is in Normandy. It was owned by the Bonville family until the middle of the fifteenth century, and then it became the property of Etienne Dannes, Jacques' brother. Some of that is probably in historical records."

Todd's skin prickled. Could it really be possible that the man in the picture, the one she called Jacques, was the same man whose body had been buried beside the well?

"Let's look at some other evidence." Jocelyn took a padded envelope from her satchel, opened it and drew out the contents, revealing a metal blade and a carved scrimshaw handle. "This is the blade that was found with the bones. We know from the score marks on the ribs that it was most likely the murder weapon. And this," she said, holding up the handle, "was the hilt. The metal fragments in the handle are a match to the blade. They were absolutely once joined together." She glanced between Laura and Todd. "Most likely the blade snapped with the force of the blow that was dealt to your fellow."

"May I?" Todd picked up the old hilt and studied the intricate carving. "A griffin," he said. "It's a beautiful piece of craftsmanship."

Softly, in a whisper barely above a breath, Laura said, "It was yours."

The words settled like ice in his stomach, cold and jagged. Todd glanced up to see if Jocelyn had overheard, but her expression revealed nothing. Laura wanted him to agree, but he wasn't willing to go that far. She still seemed to be struggling with what was real and what was trauma.

"Do you see the dagger in his belt?" Laura pointed to the drawing. "Look at the design. Also a griffin."

"Do you really think it's the exact same knife?" Todd asked, hoping to rein in her certainty.

"It belonged to him," Laura said. "One of Bannock's servants stole it, and they used it against him."

"Sounds like he was murdered with his own knife," Jocelyn mused.

"But it doesn't add any proof that the skeleton and this man," Todd pointed to the parchment, "are the same."

Jocelyn placed the parchment and the two halves of the dagger on the coffee table. "A picture drawn centuries ago is a very close match with the reconstructed image of the skeleton. The parchment is very likely authentic. I can have it and the ink analyzed. I've already had the dagger tested, so I can verify its age. It is contemporary to the time period of the bones. The carving on the hilt looks identical to the dagger in the picture. A finely carved dagger of this quality would have been valuable. Made by hand, of course. The odds of having two daggers that looked alike with this amount of detail are infinitesimal. And then of course, they were all found on the same property."

Todd needed time to think, time to absorb all of the pieces that Jocelyn had so logically laid out. The bones, the picture, the dagger. If it was true then perhaps some of the other things Laura was saying could be verified. But was he being sucked in because he wanted to please Laura? Or because the evidence was compelling?

He didn't believe in past lives. Laura wanted him to be Jacques, and he wasn't. He needed a life with her now, in the present.

Laura looked like she was waiting patiently for him to figure it out. She said softly, "We get another chance."

He looked into her bright blue eyes, full of hope and promise, and the cold knot in his stomach melted. Whatever else was going on, the trauma she was healing from, that would get better. She was strong and intelligent, not the type of person to latch onto flighty ideas.

"We can figure this out together," he said.

"Yes," she said. "We have time now."

Jocelyn stood up, breaking into their private moment. "The remains are in my van."

"Let's take them to the chapel," Laura said. "I have a casket ready."

She got a couple of flashlights, and they put on their coats and gloves and stepped into the cold night. The rain had stopped, the clouds had cleared, and the sky was spread with stars. Jocelyn started to pull a box labeled Human Remains out of her van.

"I've got it," Todd said. The box was lighter than he'd expected.

Laura and Jocelyn went ahead holding the lights, and Todd followed the yellow splashes of their beams, stepping carefully to avoid stones and tree roots. In the chapel, Laura lit two candles and placed them on either end of the altar.

Todd set the box on the floor in front of the altar and stepped back. Laura and Jocelyn shut off their flashlights, and the small chapel was illuminated only by candlelight.

"We should say something," Todd said. "A prayer for him."

"I've never been very good with that sort of thing," Laura whispered in the dark.

Todd inhaled the cold, still air. "The Lord is my shepherd, I shall not want." He hesitated, looked at Laura to see if she was okay with it. She nodded, and he continued. "Even though I walk through the valley of the shadow of death –"

Jocelyn moved into a circle with them, and they all clasped hands.

"I will fear no evil, for you are with me." He squeezed Laura's hand. He wasn't sure he knew all of it by heart, but praying for this man seemed important. Whoever he was, the guy had died young. Part of his life had been stolen. "My cup overflows. Surely goodness and love will follow me all the days of my life, and I will dwell in the house of the Lord forever."

"Amen," Laura whispered.

Jocelyn echoed, "Amen."

They held hands for a moment longer, and then let go. Laura stepped to the altar, bowed her head, and then a shudder seemed to shake her. She took a deep breath and blew out the candles, first one, then the other.

They stood quietly, enrobed in the darkness.

A gust of wind blew the door open. Todd's jacket was open and the icy blast stabbed him in the chest, seemed to blow right through him. He caught his breath as the cold air froze his lungs. His chest ached, his heart skipped a beat. For a second he wondered if he was having a heart attack, and then the wind died and the pain eased.

"Let's go," Laura said, turning on her flashlight and leading the way.

§§§

The next morning, Jocelyn peered out the front windows. "The press is here. It's time for the news conference."

"Laura went up to the chapel," Todd said. Fortunately yesterday's storm had ended, and the day was clear and cold.

Laura had gone to oversee the transfer of the remains from the box to the casket, and Todd hadn't asked to join her. He was still unsettled by everything that had happened last night. She seemed to have some kind of inside knowledge about another lifetime, and pieces of evidence were surfacing to support her claims. And he couldn't explain that odd feeling in the chapel, that sense of being stabbed. He rubbed his chest and found it was still tender. He suppressed a shiver. What better place than a medieval chapel to get spooked?

"Shall we join Laura?" Jocelyn asked.

"Guess so," he said, grabbing his suit jacket and heading outside.

Several camera crews were unloading equipment, snaking cords and swinging boom microphones into place. Paul was right in the thick of it, although it looked as though the crews were doing their best to work around him.

"Give a hand, will you?" Paul was taking large protective sheets of plastic off the chairs, and his impatient shout pulled Todd out of his reverie. "We need to help the press set up their sound system," Paul added.

"Who's going to be here?"

"Papers, TV, bloggers and every Tom, Dick and Harry with nothing better to do."

In spite of Paul's complaints, he seemed to thrive on the excitement. A canopy had been set up and a cordoned area had a sign that read "Press."

A guy in coveralls was busy at the podium, probably rigging a microphone.

"Laura, come and tell me where you want this." Paul held a picture and stand.

"By the podium," she called back.

'Here?" He tried it on one side. "Or here?" He moved it a few feet.

It was the parchment drawing from last night. Somehow, Laura had managed to get it into a frame with glass. Now people could view it, but it would be protected from the weather and sticky fingers.

"It's better on the right," she said.

"They might want to interview you," Jocelyn called to Paul. "You're the one who found the bones."

"I don't know how to act in front of a camera. Todd can talk to them."

"My specialty is old wood." Todd said. "I don't know nothin' bout bones."

"I don't think it matters," Jocelyn said. "Looks like all eyes are on Laura."

Laura was wearing a black dress that clung to the curve of her waist and hips, and accentuated her long legs. He'd seen her shimmy into it an hour ago, and he'd helped her fasten the clasp on the pearl necklace. Three different microphones were pointed at her.

What if she said that she believed she was the reincarnation of Lorraine Bannock? Would people laugh out loud, think she was crazy? Todd moved closer. He wasn't sure he could help, but he wanted to be there if she needed him.

"I'll be all right," she said, patting his arm. "You don't need to worry."

Little by little, he recognized the local people arriving: the Barnes family, Megan, Pickney and Kit. Well before noon, hordes of other people showed up, and the seats began filling.

"We'd better take our seats," Jocelyn said, coming up beside him.

Laura   stood before the tall stone cross, the perfect backdrop for the cameras. She looked poised and elegant as the interviews continued.

At noon, Reverend Graham stepped to the podium, ready to begin.

Laura closed down the interviews and took her seat beside Todd. Briefly, she leaned against him, but her focus was on the vicar.

"Good morning, friends." Reverend Graham's voice boomed over the crowd.

Todd turned and looked over the rows of chairs. Every seat was filled, and those who had arrived later stood in the back and along the side.

"A funeral is always a somber time," the vicar began. "But we are gathered for a different kind of service today. This is not so much a time of grief, as it is a ceremony of giving grace."

People settled and gave him their attention.

The vicar read a prayer and then nodded to Laura.

She took her place at the podium, at ease as she began to speak. "This year we've buried too many loved ones at Bannock Manor." The sound system carried her voice over the crowd. "I'm sure many of you are wondering why we have to do this again." She fingered the double strand of pearls at her neck. "This person deserved to have his life acknowledged, and his death mourned, just as we all do. But no one grieved when he was murdered, and he was never given a proper burial."

She looked out over the cemetery, and continued, "We discovered the remains of Jacques Dannes last spring because he was interfering with my plumbing."

Laughter rippled through the crowd, and Todd began to relax.

"That tall stone cross, which will mark his final resting place, was always intended as a monument to his memory." She held up the gold pendant, and like everyone else, he strained for a better look. She'd shown it to him up close, how the design matched the standing stone cross in the cemetery.

"I discovered this when I was trapped in the manor, and I'm sure it belonged to this man." At the mention of her entrapment, the crowd stilled.

Laura's voice caught and she paused, visibly struggling to contain a wave of emotion, and then her words rang out again. "This small cross signifies eternal life, and it was passed down through many generations."

Beside him, Jocelyn dabbed at her eyes.

Everything seemed to be connected in a way Todd didn't understand. Centuries ago the stone cross had been erected in honor of the man in that picture. The dagger and the cross had been his. Whoever had placed the cross in the cemetery had been waiting for the murdered body to be discovered – and Laura had found it.

And he'd found her with the help of the cross.

Laura continued, "All of life follows a cycle of birth and death. Crops are planted, and we gain nourishment from them after the harvest. Branches that bud in the spring give us brilliant beauty in the fall, and then go dormant in winter. Winter's ice gives way to the summer streams. We are all caught up in the stream of life, and we may take comfort in the ebb and flow, the beginning and the end. Today I would like to acknowledge the journey, and give thanks for second chances."

Todd was transfixed by the words that Laura was saying so beautifully. Could a soul return – could two souls return – to complete what hadn't been finished?

Laura paused, looking over the crowd and then her gaze settled on him. She smiled, and he smiled back. He knew what she was trying to tell him.

She took a deep breath, and opened a small, leather bound book. "This book of poetry also belonged to our medieval man, and it's also been handed down from generation to generation. I'd like to read you one of his poems."

The crowd stilled and even the reporters stopped jostling as Laura began to read:

> At evening time we rest as one
> A moment's grace when work is done
> All quiet under lustrous night
> When souls are healed and set to right
> The angels share their peace and then…

Todd kept his eyes closed, concentrating on the words, on the sound of Laura's voice. In his mind's eye he saw a quill dipped into ink, and the words took shape on the page. He whispered, "The angels share their peace and then we gently walk as two again."

Todd opened his eyes and watched Laura's lips as she said the final line. "The angels share their peace and then we gently walk as two again."

Jocelyn was staring at him. "You've heard it before," she said.

"Yes." He didn't try to explain how he knew the words, just as Laura couldn't really explain how she knew the man whose bones were in the casket. Laura hadn't read the poem to him, and yet he knew the lines before she spoke them.

Then the image of an old inn came into his mind. He saw a crackling fire, and a dark haired woman stretched out before it. There was bread and wine, and desire. Only he was the one reading the poems.

With a final prayer, the casket containing the remains was lowered into the ground. Laura took a rose from one of the bouquets, held it to her lips for a moment, and then tossed it into the grave.

When the ceremony was over, Todd walked up to the grave. A carved headstone read, *Jacques Julian Dannes, Normandy, France, 1431 – Tenney Village, England, 1453.* He knelt and took a clump of earth from the mound beside the grave. "Rest in peace," he whispered, tossing it into the hole.

A breeze stirred the trees, the bare branches thin and skeletal. But in the spring they would bud again and another season would take bloom. Todd looked across the hillside and a feeling of contentment settled in his chest. Sunlight warmed the brisk air, and he opened his jacket, took a breath, smelled the earth.

The reporters and the guests all trudged off to the White Hart, just as Kit had planned, and Jocelyn gave Laura a tight hug.

"There's something I've been wondering about," Laura said. "You once mentioned that you worked on the excavation of the mass graves from the battle at Towton."

"That's right."

Todd edged a little closer, curious.

"Brian Bannock was killed at Towton." Laura looked into Jocelyn's eyes. "I was thinking what a crazy coincidence it would be if you had handled his remains too."

"No one knows the names of most of the men who died there," Jocelyn said. "You did a good turn by learning about your fellow."

"I'm glad you're the one who helped us."

"Me too. I'll come for another visit, if that's all right."

"Absolutely." Laura waved goodbye to Jocelyn, and then turned to Todd. "Ready to go inside?"

"You go on. I'll finish with the cleanup."

He watched Laura walk down the hill to the house, hugging the picture of Jacques to her chest. There was a crack in his belief about having only one life to live, but that was it, just a tiny crack. He didn't understand the concept of multiple lives; that idea belonged in foreign countries and eastern religions. It didn't resonate with his sense of self. Laura had such certainty, but he didn't share her conviction, and he didn't want to fake it. They both had to be honest.

When he got back to the manor, Laura was in the kitchen fixing dinner for Nigel.

The old guy sat at the table, sipping a cup of tea. "Glad I didn't have to deal with that mess up there," he said by way of greeting Todd.

"Is Laura a good cook?" Todd asked.

"She's wonderful." Nigel's gaze fell on Laura. "If I'd only found someone like her sixty years ago I would've gotten married."

"It's never too late." Todd pulled out a chair and sat down beside him, enviously looking at his tea.

"What about you?" Nigel's boney, crooked fingers pointed at Todd's chest. "If you're waiting for the perfect Miss, she's standing at the stove."

Laura and Nigel were both staring at him, and he wanted to slip unnoticed out of the room. "Wow. The pressure's on," he mumbled.

"He's just teasing you," Laura said. "Pay no attention."

"I'm being perfectly honest," Nigel burst out.

Paul barged into the kitchen. "Is there anything to eat?"

"Tea and cheese sandwiches," Laura said. "If you want more, you'll have to go to the White Hart."

"So much ruckus over there now. A bloke couldn't have a decent game of darts. Even Kate and Miles are down there for the party."

"I know." Laura set a plate of grilled sandwiches on the table. Paul served Nigel and then himself, and Todd grabbed the last one. "I'll make another batch," Laura said, chuckling. "Since I have no intention of going to the pub and validating Kit's behavior."

After they were all fed, Todd helped Laura putter around the kitchen. Nigel went off to bed, and Paul decided the pub might be all right after all, and left for the village.

"That's the last of the dishes," Todd said, hanging up the tea towel. The spacious, old kitchen was dated, but comfortable. No fancy stainless steel appliances or granite countertops here, and he liked it that way.

They wandered into the drawing room and he knelt in front of the fireplace. "Your eulogy was so heartfelt and meaningful." He stacked kindling and logs, then lit a fire.

She curled up on a sofa. Her skin glowed in the firelight. "Thank you."

"It was beautifully written." He settled in beside her and picked up her hand.

She leaned her head on his shoulder, and sighed.

"There were layers of meaning," he continued. "I can't quite explain it."

She laughed softly, relaxed. "I've almost given up trying to explain it."

"Don't give up," he said, placing a kiss on the back of her hand. "Don't give up on anything yet – especially me."

Chapter Thirty-Five

After the warmth of the fire in the drawing room, Laura's bedroom was cold, and Todd felt her shiver as she moved into his arms. She wasn't wearing much, just a silky robe over her negligee, and it fell away as he untied it. Slowly, he eased the straps of the gown from her shoulders, and then slid his hand lower, cupping her breast, and then fingering the lace on her thin panties. Her hips were already angling toward his, her arms curling around his neck, her movements languid as their bodies aligned. Massaging lightly, he moved his hands across her back, and she nuzzled closer. His lips whispered across her shoulders, her graceful collarbone, up to the hollow of her slender neck.

Notions of loyalty, and vows, and always, sprang into his mind. He was surprised at how comfortable these new sentiments felt, and he wanted them.

He inhaled the scent of her hair as his tongue circled the rim of her ear. "You are impossible to resist," he murmured.

"Mmm." Her lips were against his neck. "Take me to bed."

"In a moment." He wanted to savor her like this, sexy and relaxed, and hungry for him.

He clasped her hips as she pressed against him, trying to keep just a fraction of space between them. He was hard and swelling more, but he wouldn't be rushed, not even when she tugged off his tee shirt and smoothed her hands over his chest, her fingers outlining his muscles, her palms moving lower, dipping into the waistband of his jeans. She unfastened his button and lowered his zipper an inch at a time, each little tug increasing the exquisite pressure.

"You're torturing me," he groaned.

"Take me to bed."

Each time they were together, he discovered a new side of her. She was like the manor, full of intricate secrets and unexplored regions. He swept her into his arms, placing her in the middle of the still-made bed. There was no time to get under the covers before she had his jeans open and was stroking him.

His need to love her completely helped rein in his passion, holding him back just enough.

Her lips parted, her tongue flicking lightly, inviting him in. His tongue met hers and moved gently inside, claiming her that way first, until he was lost in her kisses. When he could think again, he kicked off his jeans and yanked the covers down, but he paused before drawing the warmed blankets around them.

"I want to look at you," he breathed.

"And I want to touch you," she whispered. Her hands roamed over his back, around his hips.

He was poised above her, ready to enter, but fought the surging heat. His fingers grazed along the flesh of her opened legs until she squirmed with desire.

"I need you," she pleaded.

He dropped kisses down her chest, pausing at one gorgeous breast, and then the other, taking each one lightly into his hand, and suckling the nipple, teasing and rolling it with his tongue until she moaned.

Love pulsed through him at a depth he hadn't known existed. His mouth moved down her stomach as it rose and fell with each sharp intake of her breath. His lips nuzzled along the crest of her pelvic bone, and his hands slipped beneath her hips, raising them so that he could kiss the delicate triangle that hid her center.

She tugged his hair and tried to pull him up. "Come to me, hold me." Her body writhed against his.

He lingered at her center a moment longer, whispering his love as he breathed the very essence of her, tasting her fragrant beauty before he allowed her to draw him up.

Moving alongside of her, he reached between her legs, feeling her soft parting, the luxurious, spreading dampness. He rolled over her until his tip was at her opening. Slowly, he slipped into her a little at a time, filling her and pulling back, and then sinking in again.

She surrounded him and it was more than he could bear.

§§§

Laura pressed her palms to the muscled planes of Todd's back, rising to meet his thrusts, closing her eyes and waiting for the double vision, the moment when she felt Todd and saw Jacques. She longed for it; she was afraid of it.

Her whole body responded to his exquisite rhythm. Todd kissed her shoulders, her breasts, his fingers playing over her heated skin. Every nerve ending was sensitive to his touch as he moved slowly, provocatively.

He gazed down at her, and she took his face in her hands, and hungrily drew his lips to hers. His tongue teased while he nibbled her lips, and then he kissed her passionately, claiming her with his mouth and his body. She rose to meet him, and they joined, each stroke filling her and opening her more.

She was on the brink, and he seemed to know it. He held back, prolonging the moment when they were most fully coupled.

A vision formed, but this time it was of her and Todd walking hand in hand across the hillside. They turned to gaze at the castle, its walls aglow in the setting sun, and then he kissed her. Laughing, sunlight glinting on his face, he began tugging her down the hill, toward the manor.

In her dreams, in her mind, and here, in her bed, it was Todd.

Grasping his shoulders, she moved with him, each thrust staying inside of her longer, pushing deeper. She felt his heart beating over hers. She reached for him with her mind and her body, stretched to bring him closer until her whole being sizzled.

He took her past the brink, filling her deliciously, claiming her again and again until her toes flexed and her back arched. Mindlessly, all thought swept clean, her body melted and gave way as his low moan filled her ears.

§§§

Todd stirred and opened his eyes. He'd fallen asleep with his arms curled around Laura. During the night they'd shifted; now her head lay on his shoulder, and his arm was trapped beneath her, tingling with pins and needles. Gently, he eased it from under her, rolled onto his side and watched her sleeping.

Through a gap in the curtains, a silvery band of moonlight washed over her face, illuminating her porcelain skin and dark eyelashes. The furrowed brows were gone and she looked peaceful.

He wanted to protect her. He wanted her to be happy, truly happy. The past few days he'd watched and listened as she shared her hopes and dreams. He thought about everything she said, her ideas, her concerns, her fears. Her mind shot from project to project. Sometimes, he could barely keep up.

One thing was certain, she wanted to own her problems, and handle them herself.

He forced himself to hold back, to not jump in too soon with suggestions. He gave her the space she needed and waited for her to ask his opinion. It hadn't taken him long to gather that between her father, her brother, and her previous boyfriend, Carl, she'd had enough of people telling her what to do.

He admired her strength and independence, and could adapt to whatever she wanted.

A breeze kicked up and the curtains stirred; they must have left the window open. The room was cold, and he tugged the duvet up over their shoulders, scooching closer to Laura. She was toasty warm and smelled of shampoo, and soap, and sex. He nuzzled her neck and inhaled deeply.

The temperature seemed to be dropping; even the top of his head was cold. Slipping out of bed and pulling on his shorts, his bare feet touched the icy wooden floor. He went to the window and felt for the sash. It was already down. He looked around, wondering where the draft was getting in. The bedroom door was closed. The windows were closed. And yet it felt like a breeze was blowing.

Shivering, he slipped on his tee-shirt. It had to be the small window in the adjoining bathroom.

Laura murmured in her sleep, turned and settled again.

On his way to the bathroom he bumped into something in the center of the room. A sharp pain shot through his thigh. "Damn it!" He'd almost fallen over a piece of furniture, and his toe was throbbing. He felt the wooden spindles of the antique baby cradle. When they'd gone to bed a few hours ago, it was against the wall.

Why had Laura moved this darn thing into the middle of the room?

Irritated, but unwilling to interrupt her sleep, he grabbed the cradle, and as quietly as possible, dragged it back against the wall. Limping slightly, he went into the bathroom and flipped on the light. Yep, there was going to be a nasty bruise on his thigh.

He almost forgot to look at the bathroom window, but when he did, it too was closed. Rubbing his arms to warm them, he crept back into bed and scooted close to Laura.

Just as he started to doze, something began creaking. He swung his legs over the side of the bed and jumped up, his fists balled and ready to punch. He stared into the dark room, waiting for the sound to come closer. The persistent, thawap, thawap, thawap on the floorboards reverberated through the bottom of his feet. Through the shadowy light he saw the cradle rocking. Nothing was near it, nothing that could keep that insistent pace going.

The hair on the back of his neck prickled. He stepped forward, jerking the cradle to a halt.

The curtains fluttered again, but he knew the windows were closed; he'd already made sure of it.

Letting go of the cradle, he pulled open a curtain, and looked down into the courtyard. Everything was still; no wind, not even a breeze. From this vantage point, he could see the difference in the surface where the trench had been filled in after the water pipe was replaced. The new area was wider where the old well had been capped off – and where the skeleton had been so carefully excavated.

The cradle started to rock again, just barely, but still noticeable.

His stomach quivered with a ragged, greasy feeling. And although he was cold, his back broke out in a sweat.

The cradle picked up momentum.

Maybe there was a vibration coming from pipes below. He concentrated, determined to find a reasonable explanation. He stilled the cradle a second time, then waited. After several minutes of quiet, he slowly backed into the bed and climbed under the covers. For over an hour, he alternated between watching the clock and watching the cradle, waiting for something to happen.

Laura liked the cradle because it reminded her of people in the past, but he was tired of bumping into her medieval world every time he turned around. It was 3:15 a.m., he was exhausted, and his neck and upper back were knotted tight.

The second it started to wobble, he jumped up. He wasn't wasting any more of the night messing around. Grasping the cradle on either side, he pulled it across the floor, propped the bedroom door open, and pushed the darned thing into the hall.

"Todd?" Laura's voice was sleepy. "What are you doing?"

"Getting this damn baby bed out of your room."

"Why?" She sounded hurt. "What's the matter?"

"It... was...rocking."

"Yeah, it does that sometimes." She didn't seem surprised. "It belonged to Lorraine," she added, as though no other explanation were necessary.

"It's keeping me awake." He wasn't about to admit that he was really rattled.

She started to get up. "I suppose we can put it somewhere else."

"I'll take care of it." Quickly, he pushed the cradle into the empty room across the corridor. Before shutting the door, he dared it to move, but it remained still.

He crawled back into bed. "I need to get some sleep."

"He's trying to tell me something," Laura said.

"Who?"

"The ghost."

He didn't want to talk about the ghost like it was real, but gave in because he had no better explanation. "What's he trying to tell you?"

She didn't answer right away, but finally whispered, "You won't believe me."

"Try me. I saw it rocking."

"It has something to do with my – with Lorraine's children. It was their cradle."

He needed her to be Laura, just Laura, and he wanted her to concentrate on their future and stop dwelling on the past.

Between this Jacques fellow and the ghost it was no wonder she had nightmares and they both lost sleep.

"Tell him to go away," he said. "Permanently."

§§§

Todd walked into the enclosed courtyard of the Victorian era stable block. The four two-story buildings were about a quarter of a mile from the main house. Just far enough away to prevent the stench of manure from disturbing the gentle senses of the aristocracy, but close enough that they wouldn't have to wait too long for their carriages to be brought around.

Phase One of Laura's business plan was to establish Bannock Manor as a destination for weddings. The medieval great hall would be the venue for receptions, but constraints by the Planning Authority made it almost impossible to install modern conveniences in the old part of the house. Those would have to be located here, in the stable block.

He pulled out his tape measure and walked the length of a dozen horse stalls. The partial walls were sturdy and ornate, and would work perfectly to divide into separate bathrooms. Adding plumbing and electrical would be a headache though.

As soon as he started visualizing trenches and pipes, he couldn't help but think of the skeleton again. He'd been uneasy since the memorial. That line of poetry had popped into his mind moments before Laura read it aloud. He wasn't the type to have premonitions, had no idea how he'd come to know those words, but he did and it bothered him. A lot.

He jotted down measurements and then moved into the next building. In this one, the main floor was open, ideal for the commercial kitchen. Food was more critical to weddings than the grooms.

He chuckled to himself. Grooms for brides and grooms for horses; they could all stay here together.

On the third side of the courtyard the building housed five two-story apartments. They were all the same, two rooms up, two down, gloomy, with small windows facing front and back. He ducked out quickly. The families who had lived here a century ago probably had eight or nine kids each.

No fancy cradle for those babies.

Todd hated to acknowledge that he now believed in ghosts. And he'd never admit it to anyone except Laura. Since the cradle incident a couple of nights ago, he'd been harassed constantly. Something would tug his hair, or a draft would kick up and blow dust in his eyes. Last night his glass of water fell off the nightstand all by itself. The day before, a painting dropped off the wall just as he walked by. That had really made him jump.

He didn't even want to be in the house anymore.

It was better out here. The ghost didn't seem to care about the stable block. Todd was tempted to ask Laura if they could camp here for the rest of his stay, but then he'd have to admit that he was nervous.

The upper level on the fourth side had been used for storage, with remnants of burlap and straw still on the floor. Todd bent down to inspect a piece of an old bridle. It had been gnawed through by a rodent. He sighed.

A scrap of paper caught his eye and he picked it up.

Old Mrs. Bram sat on a wall. Old Mrs. Bram had a great fall. One funeral today, one more ahead. Soon all the poor Colfaxes and Brams will be dead!

Todd stood rooted to the floor, and a shudder rippled through him.

That bastard!

He had no doubt who'd written this sick poem; the guy who'd tried to kill Laura. Carefully, he folded the note and put it in his pocket. It was evidence, and he should probably take it to the police, but it was going to stir up all Laura's fears again. She knew that creep had been lurking about, spying, and plotting to kill her family, and finding more evidence was going to upset her.

Todd rubbed the back of his neck. Since Oliver was already dead, maybe there was no good reason to dredge it all up again. Laura was excited about the future and he didn't want to spoil that for her. He wanted them to concentrate on building her dreams.

He glanced down at the tape measure in his hand. It would be helpful to have a blueprint of these buildings so that he'd know where to knock out walls and open windows.

§§§

Laura repeated into her phone, "You're sure? They aren't going to change their minds?"

The art dealer chuckled. "He's wiring the money tomorrow."

After thanking him and hanging up, she sat stunned, her phone pressed between her palms like a religious medallion. If this deal really went through, there would be enough money to pay the first installment of the inheritance tax and catch up on the mortgage payments.

Rolling her shoulders, she stretched and popped her back. She was finally getting a break.

Todd walked into the library, but halfway across the large room, he stopped. "You have the strangest look on your face. Everything all right?"

"Good news, actually. Two of the paintings sold."

"Already? Can I ask how much?"

"Six hundred and sixty-thousand pounds." It was hard to wrap her mind around so much money. It wouldn't make her solvent, but it bought precious time. "I don't want to get too excited until I see it in my bank account."

"Wow." He sat beside her on the sofa, and picked up her hand. "That's awesome."

"I'm still shaky about it." Leaning back, she stared at the empty spot above the fireplace. "It was the Griffier landscape that brought the big bucks."

"Any regrets?"

"Oh, not at all." She smiled. "I'd sell all the art if that's what it took to keep the house."

"Then let's celebrate your windfall." He walked over to the liquor cabinet and poured them each a small glass of Port. "And they have how many more pieces to sell?"

"Right now, six. Plus two Roman busts and a Chinese urn, but I don't expect that kind of money from the other pieces." There was so much to consider, she couldn't sit still. Pacing the room, she asked, "Do you think we could get the commercial kitchen and restrooms built in the stables for two hundred thousand?"

"If you're not extravagant. There's plenty of space, but start small and add gradually."

"I want to get on it right away."

"Funny thing." He grinned. "I came in here to look for old blueprints. I'm ready to start playing around with designs." He pointed to the wall that was mostly covered in book shelves, with long drawers along the bottom. "Let's search in there."

"I don't think anyone's looked in those in years. I'm not even sure what's in them." She counted twenty drawers. Kneeling, she pulled out one in the center and began leafing through it, didn't see anything useful, shut it, and opened the next one. Inside were stacks of maps, the large, old-world prints that people in the U.S. framed and hung in their offices. She held one up.

"That's a good one," Todd said. He moved a few drawers to the left and began sifting through the contents.

Laura's third drawer offered up original water colors of birds and flowers. It wasn't until she was searching her seventh drawer that she found some drawings of Bannock Manor. "Jackpot!" Carefully, she extracted a large, rectangular diagram of the estate buildings and handed it to Todd. "There's more." She removed another one, the layout from a different angle. "Let's spread them on the table."

They lined up the illustrations end to end until they ran out of room.

"Look how the buildings have changed over the years," Todd said. "You can see how the additions were added. It's fascinating."

Laura continued to dig carefully through the drawer. Near the bottom she found a folded parchment sealed with a blot of red wax, the impression of the sender's mark still clearly visible. With a shaking hand, she lifted it out and stared at it, turning it over.

"What have you got there?" Todd was behind her.

Her vision blurred, wavered, and then it became clearer. She saw a parchment letter in her hands, the lines of writing, the way the ink had smeared, and the signature at the bottom.

"I have to go back," she said, her voice sounding strange to her own ears.

"What?" Todd crouched beside her, began to take her arm.

She pulled away. "I have to go into the chamber."

"Laura, I'm not sure that's a good idea. You're pale."

She stood up. "I hope it's still there."

He was going to get sick of this happening, but she couldn't stop it, didn't want to push it away.

"I'm coming with you. You're not going in there alone."

Todd stayed with her as she ran through the great hall, took the stairs two at a time, and then hurried along the corridor to what had been Lorraine's room. When she was in the alcove, she stopped in front of the tapestry that still covered the sliding wall of the antechamber. It was closed. She hesitated, debating whether she was willing to go inside again.

She remembered the stench of decay, and Oliver's bloated body. Shuddering, she bit back a groan.

Todd tugged gently on her arm. "There's nothing good in there," he insisted.

A long time ago, she'd hidden something away for safekeeping and now she wanted to get it. It was all the proof she'd ever need. Shaking off his hand, and her fear, she straightened her shoulders. "You can wait here if you want to."

"If you have to do this, I'm going with you," Todd said. "No matter what you decide, I'm here."

She pushed against the moveable wall.

Todd put his weight into it, and they shoved until the wall slid open.

In front of her, the narrow door that separated the two parts of the chamber still hung crookedly from the hinges. The inner room smelled faintly of disinfectant.

She ducked inside and dropped to her knees, knocking against the floor boards in rapid succession, trying to remember which ones lay over the hiding spot.

Todd knelt down beside her. "What are you looking for?"

"Lorraine hid a letter under the floor. It's around here somewhere." She brushed her hands back and forth, and then used her knuckles, methodically rapping each plank.

They both heard the hollow ring.

She pressed down hard on one end of a board, and the opposite end lifted a fraction. "I need something to pry it up."

Todd opened his pocket knife and pressed the blade under the edge, and several boards lifted together. A hatch door. Lying flat on his stomach, he peered beneath it. "All I can see are cobwebs."

"It's there." The memory was clear in her mind.

He reached in gingerly. "Hang on. Let me get some of this gunk out of the way." He pulled out a handful of sticky, silken threads and wiped them away on the leg of his jeans. Using the light on his cell phone, he peered inside. "I think I can see it now. It's really far back." He reached under the floor and plucked out a piece of folded parchment.

He handed it to her. "Is this what you wanted?"

She nodded, her throat so dry she couldn't speak. Gently, she brushed off the coating of brown dust. The paper had yellowed, the edges were stained with watermarks, but the red wax seal of the Bannock crest was still attached.

Swallowing, she gave it back to Todd. "Bannock wrote this letter."

Her stomach churned the way it had all those years ago when she'd put the well-being of one son ahead of the other. The despair, the grief and helplessness, the agony of Lorraine's decision threatened to tear her apart all over again. "I couldn't bear the thought that Julian would be disinherited the same way his father had been. I read the letter and then I hid it where Bannock would never find it."

His jaw dropped. "You're speaking like you're her."

She felt like Lorraine. "I know what she went through."

"You read her journal..."

He held the past in his hands, and if that wasn't enough to make him believe her, then there was nothing else she could do. But she needed the man she loved to understand that they'd been together before, and that the bond they shared was all the more precious because it had survived for so long.

"You saw the cobwebs, the dust." She met his questioning gaze. "Do you think that letter was handled recently?"

Todd held the parchment carefully by the edges, inspecting it. "If anyone had touched it, there would have been fingerprints."

"If you want to read the journal, you'll see that this letter isn't mentioned." She watched his face as he scanned the chamber. She knew him, knew he was picking through the evidence, analyzing the details, needing something tangible.

"I'm going to tell you what the letter says. The first line is, Be it known that these are my wishes…"

Gently, he turned the letter over.

"I read it – back then – in 1461. Open it and you'll see it was written from Bannock to Lord Berkeley."

Slowly, he unfolded the brittle pages, scanned the writing, and then read aloud, "Be it known that these are my wishes. My estate shall pass to Brian Blake Bannock, my son and heir."

"I did what I thought was best." The headache was starting, the blurry vision, the wavy lines that made it hard to tell whether she was seeing the past or the present. "I don't know if it turned out right, or wrong."

The room began to spin. She had just enough time to put her hands on the floor on either side of her and brace for support. The sensation of falling came next, like a giant roller coaster making the big dip, and her stomach roiled up and down, around and over. Taking measured breaths, she fought the nausea and willed herself not to faint. Memories poured over and through her, filling her mind, ravaging her body: the attack, the slaughter, the gutted, broken lives.

The rape.

She moaned and bit back a scream.

Julian was by her side. "I need to get you out of here." He sounded different, older, worried.

More images battered her mind.

Sophie's lifeless body.

An orphaned infant in a basket.

Tim Carpenter's severed neck.

A low, keening wail filled the room. "Please, please, help me." This was her pain, her grief. The howling came from her.

The sense of spiraling out of control settled and she found herself sprawled on the floor. The chamber was dark. She could just make out shadows huddled in the corner. Matilde sat, wide-eyed, clasping a sleeping infant. Wedged behind her, barely visible, Anne and Elizabeth rubbed their eyes as if just waking from a nap.

Julian shook her shoulders.

"They need me," Lorraine told him, pressing her cheek to the back of his hand.

Her daughters rushed her, wrapped their arms about her, touched her face, attached themselves to her as they wailed their fear and relief.

"You're safe now," she whispered, trying to hush them. "It's over."

Matilde was crying, her tears falling on Blake, who slept in her arms. "Sophie panicked as we were closing the door." She made the sign of the cross, blessing herself and the infant in her arms. "Tim Carpenter went after her, but there was no time. They were coming for us. He slammed the door and locked us inside."

This was Bannock's fault. He'd left them defenseless, and his whore had wasted no time trying to destroy them and claim the estate. Agony fueled her hatred. *Damn you, Brian Bannock!* Silently, she uttered the savage curse again. *Damn you and may you never have a moment's peace.*

From a distance, someone called her name, but she was too consumed with pain and grief to listen.

"You did your best," Lorraine said, extending her arms, motioning for Blake to be handed over. She needed to hold her son. The girls had quieted and she didn't want to upset them all over again.

"Mama," Elizabeth asked. "Where is Sophie?"

Julian's wide gaze was on her.

"Hush," she said, bidding him keep silent. She answered Matilde's questioning look with a slight shake of her head. Later, she would explain it to the children. "She's sleeping now," she murmured.

Matilde lowered her head and her shoulders shook as she muffled her sobs in her apron.

A strange voice whispered urgently, "I'm getting you out of here."

A man grabbed her from behind and dragged her out of the chamber. She kicked and clawed to break free. In desperation, she sank her teeth into the back of his hand.

"Damn!" He didn't loosen his grip. "Stop biting me!" He hauled her across her bedroom and into the corridor.

She kicked hard, aiming strategically, and twisted, prepared to gouge his eyes. A hand caught her arm. The face looking down on her seemed...

She stopped fighting. She took in his clothes, and her mind made the adjustment.

"I'll let go of you if you promise not to hurt me."

"All right." Shaken, she crawled a few feet away and sat down with her back to the wall.

Todd released a long breath and sat beside her. "It's as if you were possessed."

"My soul, my mind." She paused as the full realization of what she'd done sank in. "My very essence went back to the exact day and time where I'd last been Lorraine."

He touched her hand. "Your body was here, but the girl I love was gone. You became someone else." Gently, he brushed strands of hair away from her face. "You were wild with emotions."

"I didn't know I could do that. Go back." She closed her eyes, trying to hold on to the images and feelings. Now she knew who had survived the attack. If she went back again, she could learn more, perhaps watch her children grow up.

Todd lifted her chin, turned her face toward his. "It's not good for you to go in there. I think it's dangerous." His expression was serious, his voice firm. "I think we should close the chamber. Permanently."

She already wanted to go back. "No, I can't lose my connection to those people."

"You have to let that other life go. It's not healthy."

"I can't."

"Laura, please listen to me."

Looking into his eyes, she knew he was reading her mind, feeling her temptation.

"I've only got a few days left here, and I can't leave knowing you might climb back into that other life."

"All right." she said. "For now." Later, she'd find a way to go back inside.

"Forever."

Down the hall, something crashed, and they both jumped to their feet.

Laura felt the chill and her skin prickled. *He's here.*

Cautiously, they moved toward the end of the corridor. The crash had come from the stairs. Near the landing, a medieval sconce had broken away from the wall and lay on the floor. Large iron nails rolled in different directions.

They edged closer and the cold became more intense.

The ghost had often revealed itself as a pressure on her skin, a drop in temperature, an unseen presence. Until now, she'd never known his identity. This time as she watched, mist gathered and solidified.

Brian Bannock towered over her.

She smelled wood smoke and horses and leather, the familiar, musky smell that was uniquely his. His long tunic was slit at the sides, richly embroidered at the collar and cuffs. His red hair flowed around his grim face, his cheeks ruddy as though he'd just come in from the wind.

You robbed my son.

His words materialized in her head. Understanding hammered in her consciousness, but she was Laura, not Lorraine.

I know who you are.

The ghost moved closer, his gloved hand reaching toward her. The side of her face went cold, and she stepped back. "I did what I had to," she said, "to protect our family." Lorraine's rage stormed inside of her. "You left us, and my baby died!"

The air around Bannock seemed to quiver. *That bastard wasn't mine.*

"Didn't you care about your other children?"

"Laura!" Todd was beside her, gripping her shoulders. "You have to get out of here."

Ignoring him, she kept her focus on Bannock.

Bannock pointed at Todd, his wrath palpable. *Get him out of my house!*

"He doesn't want you here," she said to Todd. Facing Bannock again, she seethed, "It's my house now."

"Tell him to go to hell," Todd said.

"He's never fought me like this," Laura said. "He's always protected me."

"No," Todd said. "He's used you. He can't keep you safe. He didn't protect you from Oliver Colfax, and he didn't save your mother or Winnie either, did he?" Todd's face was red with fury, and his words came through clenched jaws. "Why are you listening to him? He wants you to be as trapped in this house as he is."

"It's you he's angry with, not me. To him, you're Jacques."

They were at the top of the landing, and the cold pressed around them. Bannock moved closer and Todd retreated.

"Look out!" Laura yelled.

Todd's foot came down on one of the large, iron nails from the broken wall sconce, and he reared back, off balance.

Laura shoved herself between Todd and Bannock. The cold pulled at her, slowed her movements as she stretched a hand toward Todd.

Scrambling to catch the banister, Todd twisted, and his hip hit the railing hard. He began to pitch head first over the side.

Laura grabbed the back of his shirt and yanked so hard that her fingernails punctured the fabric, tearing it all the way to the hem. She wouldn't let go. Bannock had killed Jacques, but he wasn't going to get Todd.

Todd was half over the banister, the stone floor of the great hall forty feet below. With strength she didn't even know she had, she held on, struggling against his weight, hauling on his shirt until both of his hands were on the banister, both of his feet solidly on the stairs.

Terror flashed through Todd's eyes, and he was shaking. "That fucker just tried to kill me."

Bannock would stop at nothing to get rid of Todd. She realized that now. She had to make him understand that she was in charge. Todd's safety depended on it.

Slowly, she climbed the stairs, waiting for the temperature to drop, but she was so hot with anger that the cold melted away from her skin. She couldn't see Bannock now, but sensed him hovering.

"Get out of here," she spat. "You have no power over the lives in this house."

This is my home!

His image solidified once more, moving away from her. He was in the corridor, halfway between the top of the stairs, where she stood, and the entrance to the master suite.

"It's mine." She walked toward him, stretching to her full height, knowing she was at least eight inches taller than

Lorraine had been. She wanted him to see the difference. "You belong to a different time."

I belong here.

"Brian Bannock is dead. He died at Towton battle defending his king and country."

Behind her, she heard Todd moving toward her, but she motioned for him to stay still. This was between her and Bannock.

"Lorraine cursed you," Laura said. "And she regretted it. Your soul never found peace." She took several more steps toward his shimmering form. "I'm Laura, not Lorraine. Her life ended too."

His wavering image grew stronger. *I loved you.*

She knew what she had to do. The only thing he would understand. "If you don't leave, I'll sell this estate and never come back." She meant it. Too many people had sacrificed their lives to preserve the house.

She'd almost been one of them.

He swirled closer. *You can't leave.*

"Oh, but I can. I'm free to live my life as I choose."

He was directly in front of her, and he raised his gloved hand.

She stood her ground. "You did what you had to," she said. "You made your choices, and Lorraine made hers. Now I'll make mine. I will not allow you to hurt or interfere in my relationship with Todd."

Slowly, he lowered his hand and his form grew fainter.

"Go in peace," she whispered, hoping with all of her heart that he would find it at last.

He drifted down the corridor until he reached the master suite, and then his essence vanished.

"He's gone, isn't he?" Todd asked.

"Yes, but I don't know for how long."

Chapter Thirty-Six

Taillights of a car disappeared around the bend as Laura walked from the cottage back to the main house. The trees were mostly bare, their branches rattling in the brisk November evening. A carpet of brown, brittle leaves scrunched under her feet.

Despite having just signed a lease on the cottage, she felt apprehensive, like every time something good happened, something bad, really bad, followed. Selling the paintings and signing the lease should have eased her tension, eased it a lot, but none of that mattered if she lost Todd.

Finding Bannock's letter under the chamber floor had finally given Todd the physical proof he needed that she knew private details about Lorraine's life. He didn't try to deny or explain away the ghost's impact on the rocking cradle or the freezing pockets of air. Todd was a believer, all right. He could probably have lived with those things.

Even though there had been no sign of Bannock since the confrontation two days ago, both Todd and Laura were miserable. Todd didn't like being in the same house with the ghost. He wanted to annihilate both Bannock and the chamber. He'd spent all his time sealing up the chamber, his hammer colliding with such violence that the impact reverberated through the hall. In the past, he would have cared about permits and planning approval, about preserving the historic integrity, but now thick sheets of plywood, braced by excessive amounts of two-by-fours, were good enough. Somehow he thought that pounding on the house was hurting Bannock.

At night, in the darkness of her room, their love-making had become awkward and tense, as if someone were watching, or they were about to be threatened. Their laughter and spontaneity had dissipated just as silently as the ghost.

Laura knew that Todd probably wanted to leave early, but he'd stuck it out, edgy and angry, a trooper without a target.

His flight was booked for tomorrow morning and he couldn't wait to go. All morning he'd been preoccupied. After lunch, he said he had things to take care of and left without her. He'd been gone ever since.

Blinking back tears, she looked up at the clear sky. A full moon, giant and orange, was just cresting over the hill. Behind her, on the ground, her shadow followed.

What if Todd never came back? Or didn't ask her to join him in California? What if it was over and she didn't get a chance to make it work?

She'd kept her phone in her pocket the whole time, fighting the urge to call him, afraid she'd sound whiney and smothering.

Todd had never called her once.

She stopped walking. She wanted to delay the moment she saw him, afraid of what she'd see in his soft brown eyes. He'd probably be too nice to tell her to her face; he'd wait until he was back in the States, so that when she fell apart, he wouldn't have to deal with her pleading and tears.

For him, it would be a clean, complete separation.

She sat down on a low stone wall. Cold from the rocks infiltrated her jeans and crawled into her bones.

What if, before he left in the morning, Todd gave her an ultimatum to choose between the house or him? In her heart, they were linked. Without him, she knew, she would never be happy.

On the other hand, the estate harbored the remains of so many people she loved. The manor's building blocks were part of her DNA. Why should she have to choose if she was willing to give one-hundred percent of herself to both?

She picked up a dead branch and snapped it in half. It was impossible to give one-hundred percent of herself to opposing interests. She would always be pulled in two directions – just as she always had been.

Her mother had faced the same dilemma. And if the outcome wasn't so painfully crucial, Laura might have been able to appreciate her mother's choices, but the correlation only emphasized the importance of getting it right.

The chamber was another unsettling dilemma. She couldn't be the only one who'd gone in there and encountered such experiences. What if she sold the house and something terrible happened? Who knew if, over the centuries, other people had gone in and relived the past?

What had her mother known? Was the chamber's power the reason she'd given custody of her only child to an ex-husband who lived so far away?

Her cell phone rang and startled her. It was Todd.

"Hello." *Please, please, please don't let him be angry or distant.*

"Where are you?"

"Just coming back from the cottage. A young couple signed a rental agreement. They're moving in on the first."

"That's great!" He sounded genuinely enthusiastic.

She stood, her backside cold and stiff. "Are you all right?"

"I am," he said. "Can you see the top of the tower from where you are?"

"No. Why?"

"Because I'm waiting for you in the turret. There's a full moon and it looks magnificent from here." His tone was warm and inviting, and she couldn't wait to see him.

"I'll be right there." She started walking as fast as she could up the hill and then broke into a run as she neared the castle ruins. It was full dark now, and when the ruins came into view, she spotted a light coming from the narrow turret windows.

She made her way onto the wall walk, past the spot where Megan had found her mother's body. She didn't want to look down there. She kept the light in her field of vision as she carefully picked her way. When she reached the tower door, she pulled it opened and was astounded at the sight.

Lit candles glimmered on the outside edge of every step, winding up and around. They were in the red votive cups from the chapel. Rose petals had been sprinkled in the center of each step. She followed the flames up the stairs, higher and higher, her hopes soaring. It was the most romantic sight she'd ever seen, and knowing that Todd had done this, meant he truly loved her.

At the top, the turret opened into a small room. She found him inside, an impish grin on his face.

A Persian carpet of reds and blues covered the floor, along with several large cushions she'd never seen before. More candles had been set in each window seat, casting the room in a blushing glow.

"Your expression is priceless," he said.

"You've worked magic in here." She was so in love with him it hurt.

He pulled her into his arms. He was warm and strong, and she melted into his embrace. "I want to treat you like royalty, like a princess."

She laughed and her worries drained away.

Todd filled two champagne flutes, handed her one, and raised his to make a toast. "To our ever-lasting love."

She touched her glass to his. "To you," she said. "To us." Their eyes met as she took a sip. "Very nice."

"It's French," he said. "The real stuff."

She loved it that he'd thought of those details. "When you said ever-lasting, did you really mean forever?" She needed to know what he believed, exactly what he meant when he said those words.

"I may not understand everything the way you do," he said. "For me, it's like we're connected on a cellular level. Deep in our bones."

She was relieved that he understood. "Our bodies, our minds, our spirits share something." She took his hand. It felt so good to touch him. "When you went off by yourself and I didn't hear from you, I was afraid you were upset."

"As you can see, I've been busy. And I didn't want you asking a lot of questions about what I was up to."

She admired all his effort. "This is magnificent." He'd turned the turret into a beautiful room. She pointed to a tapestry hanging on the wall, one she'd never seen before. "Where did you get that?"

"I went to the gift shop at Warwick Castle." He made a bow and kissed her hand. "I bet you've never seen chivalry like this!"

"Honestly, I never have."

He guided her onto a floor pillow. "I never expected to find a woman like you, someone who means more to me than anything, or anyone."

"I feel the same." Her throat tightened when she thought of how she'd almost lost him. Again.

He seemed to read the emotions on her face. "Don't be frightened," he whispered. "I'll always come back to you. I promise."

"I'm counting on it." Her heart swelled with love as she settled back onto her cushion.

Todd began unloading a bag, pulling out a long baguette, wedges of cheddar and brie, olive tapenade, and grapes. "It's not roast venison, but I didn't have time to go hunting."

She accepted a plate of food, suddenly ravenous. "Thank you for saving us from another formal dinner with Kate in attendance."

He chuckled. "She's not so bad, but for tonight, I wanted intimacy."

As they ate, her denim-covered legs intertwined with his.

"When can you come back?" She was already thinking about his next visit, and she couldn't keep the eagerness out of her voice.

"December, after the semester ends." He met her eyes. "You know I'm going to come back every break until I can find a job over here."

She was afraid to hope for too much, but his intention gave her something to hang on to.

When they were done eating, she leaned back against his chest, reveling in his presence. She'd missed that the past few days, the comfortable, enjoyable, worth-more-than-anything-else-in-the-world companionship.

He kissed the back of her neck, ran his fingertips through her hair. He picked up her hand and laced his fingers through hers. Trying to sound casual, he asked, "How long would you have to know a guy before you'd accept a marriage proposal?"

She tried to match his carefully neutral tone. "I'd give it serious consideration after, say... five hundred years."

He kissed each one of her fingers in turn, and his voice was low, and warm. "According to a trusted source, I meet the criteria."

"You do." Holding her breath, she wanted to put her heart on the line and be honest, say what she had to say while she had a chance. She didn't want him going back to the States until he knew exactly how she felt. "I love you, you know that, right?"

"And I love you too," he said.

He pulled her to her feet and stared into her eyes. "I want to share my life with you." He dropped to one knee, extracted a small box from behind a pillow, and snapped it open. "Will you do me the honor of becoming my wife?" He looked up at her intently, his face full of hope. "I want to marry you."

Her heart was thudding loudly. The man she loved – the man she'd always loved – was there on one knee staring up at her with those eyes that she adored – a shade lighter then, a shade darker now – soft and brown, kind and understanding.

"Yes, Todd Woodbridge. I will marry you." All of her dreams seemed within reach. What she'd always wanted, what her soul had longed for, was going to come true.

He stood, took the ring from its case and slipped it onto her finger.

She looked at the glittering diamond, a large stone set into a white gold band, inlaid with a thinner ring of yellow gold.

"The two colors reminded me of your cross," he said. "And the blending of two lifetimes."

Spreading her fingers, she admired the ring a moment longer, and then she laid her cheek against his chest and listened to his heart. Finally she could merge all the facets of her life – English and American, past and present, Laura and Lorraine. "I'm happier right now than I ever thought possible."

Chapter Thirty-Seven

On Christmas Eve, a light snow sifted down, turning Bannock Manor into a scene from Currier and Ives. Laura stood near the Christmas tree, the branches heavy with ornaments and hundreds of tiny, twinkling lights. A fire blazed in the hearth, and the room held the kind of magic that usually only children can sense. She admired the silent scene a moment longer, and then began lighting dozens of candles.

Her father wandered in and placed a few more presents under the tree. His hair had turned completely gray, and the creases around his eyes were a little deeper. He wore a gray suit with a bright red tie, and his broad smile reflected his contentment. "Are you almost ready?"

"I wish." She blew out a match.

Edward, Paul and Todd barreled in, snowflakes sprinkled in their hair.

"You've got to come outside," Edward said. "You're not going to believe the fantastic job we've done."

The three men lined up like a row of students waiting for her to grade their Christmas project.

"All right," she said, laughing as she put on her coat. "But I've only got a minute to spare."

Todd grabbed her hand and pulled her outside and into the winter twilight. "Don't look back yet."

Together, the four of them trotted partway down the drive, and when they were far enough back, Todd turned her around to gaze at the house.

The roofline and windows were swathed in strings of lights, twinkling white against the deepening night sky. A large wreath hung on the manor's front door. Inside the house, the rooms were lit, and she could see through the window to the drawing room fire.

"It's gorgeous." Her breath came out in a frosty cloud. "You guys did an amazing job." She wrapped her arm around

Todd's waist. Three years ago she couldn't have imagined things turning out so wonderfully.

Todd kissed her, their cold noses touching. "The kids are going to be so excited," he said.

Edward punched Todd on the shoulder. "We've got to get cleaned up before everyone arrives."

"You mean Jocelyn, right?" Todd shoved back.

An hour later, Todd and Laura had the two year old twins dressed and ready to go downstairs, Julia in a red velvet dress with a white lace collar, and Jordan in a matching vest and gray shorts.

The doorbell rang just as they reached the first floor landing. "Hold Mummy's hand," she cautioned.

Todd hurried ahead to get the door.

Megan, wearing her best wool dress, came in juggling an armful of wrapped presents. "I've never seen the house look so alive," she said to Todd, before glancing up and spotting Laura coming down the stairs, steering a toddler with each hand. "There are my babies!" She snatched up Julia and smothered her with kisses, before turning her attention to Jordan. "Yumm, yumm, yumm. I could eat you up."

"No Auntie Megan, eat cookies." Jordan wriggled out of her grasp. "I show you."

Laura and Kate had been baking all week, and the sideboard in the dining room was spread with plates of decorated cookies, bowls of trifle, and dozens of little tarts. Platters of hors d'oeuvres covered the dining room table.

Edward and Paul were already there, stuffing their mouths with turkey sandwiches.

"Hey, little man, what do you want to eat?" Edward picked up Jordan and flew him around the room like Superman. "Liver pate?"

"Yuk. I want cookies."

"Salmon and capers?" Edward tipped the child's head close to the fish.

"Cookies."

"How about Brussels sprouts?" Edward continued to tease his nephew.

They heard voices in the foyer, and Laura said to Edward, "Keep an eye on these rascals so I can greet the guests. No

Figgy Pudding either – it has alcohol." She handed each of the children a sausage roll.

Julia was hanging on Paul's leg.

Suddenly the foyer was full of people. Miles was busy hanging up coats, and Kate collected purses and scarves.

Gertie and Ben came in, along with Amy.

"Merry Christmas," Gertie chimed. "What do you need me to do?"

"Just have a good time," Laura said, knowing Gertie preferred to keep busy. She'd lost count of the times the Barnes family had come to her rescue. "I want you to know how grateful I am for everything you've done," she said, touching the older woman's shoulder. "Not just for me, but for my mother, and the Wilcoxes."

Gertie waved away her thanks and wandered into the drawing room, but Ben lingered for a moment. "Some people are saying the ghost has gone."

She glanced over at Julia, remembering the last time she'd seen her daughter looking up at thin air, smiling and chattering.

"Who are you talking to?" Laura asked.

Julia didn't answer. She didn't have the vocabulary to describe a medieval knight, but her hand touched her cheek.

Laura shivered at the memory. Bannock wasn't gone, but she'd keep that to herself. "I haven't seen any signs of him for a while."

"I never doubted that he was the one who saved you as a tot," Ben said. "And he was there to signal again when you were trapped in the chamber."

"He can be protective," Laura said.

"Where are the kids?" Amy cut in. At fifteen, she was their part-time nanny.

"In the dining room, filling up on cookies. You'll have a hard time settling them down tonight."

Mr. Pickney walked up the front steps, brushing snowflakes from his coat. Behind him, Kit chatted amiably with Reverend Graham and his wife. And beyond them, Laura saw a half dozen other folks from the village. Everyone was ushered in, and the house filled with their conversations and laughter.

Bernard stood beside the Christmas tree, talking with Megan. Now that he was a grandfather, he spent a lot more time in England, helping Laura and Todd establish their business, and doting on the twins.

Laura overheard Megan say, "It doesn't look so bad without those paintings since they've re-plastered and put up new wallpaper."

"And the tax man's been paid in full," Bernard replied.

Julia and Jordan darted between guests, stopping here and there to administer hugs or receive a pat on the head. Nothing slowed them down for more than a few seconds until they saw Laura coming after them. Squealing in delight, they threw themselves against their grandfather's legs and hung on.

"Oh, they can stay up a little longer," he said, taking their side as usual.

Laura was about to argue when Jocelyn arrived.

"Thank you for inviting me." Jocelyn ruffled Julia's sparse blond hair. "The dynamic duo has doubled in size since I last saw them. And Uncle Edward can't stop bragging about how smart they are."

"Right here," Laura said, holding up her little finger. "They've got him wrapped tight around their pinkies, and he'll do anything they say."

"Where is Edward?"

"We show you. Come on." And they were off, dragging a smiling Jocelyn with them.

Nigel was looking dapper as he delivered a plate of canapés to one of the widows from the church. That old bachelor might surprise them all and get married one of these days. Even walking with a cane, he had a spring in his step now. Probably because he had to look lively when the twins were scampering underfoot.

Todd was circulating through the room, a bottle of red wine in one hand, and a bottle of white in the other. He smiled back at her, and her heart swelled. He'd joined her world and made it his own, and not a day went by when she didn't give thanks that they were together.

He was writing his third book, his first work of fiction, about a man who lived in medieval France.

Reverend Graham approached her. "How many weddings do you have booked for the coming year?"

"Fifteen in the next nine months."

"We'll have to start coordinating our calendars," he said.

"You're right. In addition to word-of-mouth referrals, we've amped up the website, and we've had some nice write-ups in the London papers. At this rate, I expect double that number by the end of next year."

A wedding reception in a medieval great hall was the ultimate venue. The bridal suite and apartments at the stables meant that their guests could celebrate and then stagger off to bed.

"I've got two family reunions booked for next summer," Laura told him. "I'm not sure how we're going to handle it all."

"It's good business for everyone," Mr. Pickney said, joining them. He took a bite out of his cheese and onion tart. "There's even talk in town of reopening the market."

Laura respected the tiny attorney. She hadn't always listened to his advice, but his skill in settling the probate, and helping her get a business license had been invaluable.

Kit sidled up to her, deftly uncorked a champagne bottle and poured two fizzing glasses. "To the most enchanting woman in England." He was more bubbly than champagne.

Laura returned his toast, but after a few moments she set her glass aside and went in search of the twins. She found Julia curled in Bernard's lap. He smiled as he watched his granddaughter sleep. What a good father he'd always been. She was glad he had another little girl to pamper and spoil.

Jordan was in the kitchen with Edward and Jocelyn, eating a banana.

"Doesn't this kid ever quit eating?" Edward asked when she came in.

"Only when he's sleeping." She wiped off Jordan's hands. "It's bedtime, buddy."

"No."

"Yes," she replied firmly. "Amy's going to read you a story."

Under Amy's attentive care, the twins were tucked in bed and fell asleep almost immediately.

Laura was finally able to sit down and relax with her guests. She loved seeing the house full of people. Everyone was having a good time, and their annual party was the high point of the holidays.

It was long after midnight when she and Todd said their last good-byes and shut the front door.

Todd grabbed two glasses and another bottle of champagne. "I've got one more toast to make before we turn in."

They climbed the hill to the castle ruins under a clear, starry night, the moon bathing the landscape in silvery shadows. When they reached the wall walk, Laura turned slowly, taking in the view of dark fields and stone walls in silhouette. She gazed down at the manor, outlined in sparkling lights.

Todd handed her a glass. "Merry Christmas, my darling, my love."

She raised her glass. "To the man of my dreams. Merry Christmas." She leaned into his kiss, her heart full of love.

When he released her, she turned again to gaze at the grounds of the estate. Lower on the hill she saw the tall stone cross where Jacques' remains rested, not far from her mother's grave. They were only a few yards apart, and yet so many centuries lay between them.

She studied the manor ablaze with lights, the old medieval section joined at right angles to the modern house, and thought of the untold lives of those who had come and gone, lived and died there. She was grateful to be one of them. Saving the manor was her way of preserving some of what they had accomplished. What she did now mattered to the past, and it would make a difference in the future.

Dear Reader,

This book is about love, and second chances. We began writing it together after each of us lost our mother. Losing our mothers rocked our world. Grief shook the ground beneath us, and set us on a journey as co-writers. Writing a book together helped us heal, and along the way we forged a fine friendship. We worked side-by-side and separately for years, bringing this project from dream to draft to published work. We hope you love it, and we hope you share it with your mom, daughter, granddaughter, friends and loved ones. We hope you believe in second chances, as we do.

Please let us know your thoughts. We're easy to find at our website:

www.TheChamberAndTheCross.com

Come and see the photos we used to create our settings, explore more of our writing, and get to know us, as we would love to get to know you.

Deborah & Lisa

Deborah Reed has always been fascinated by historical homes. During the past twenty years she has visited Europe over a dozen times, where she soaks up history, architecture and art. Many of those trips were to do research for **THE CHAMBER AND THE CROSS**. She can drive in England as easily as in the States. From the northern tip of Scotland to the coast of Cornwall, from the Welsh border to scenic Cotswold villages, there is no corner of this historic land she hasn't explored – and she always returns for more.

Her passion for travel has taken her to China, Italy, Germany, Austria, Spain, Belgium, Luxembourg, France and many other locations, and on her many adventures she has taken award-winning travel photography.

She and her husband Gene have three grown children and a granddaughter. They all live in San Diego. She honed her architectural expertise during her successful 27-plus years as a real estate Broker.

While writing **THE CHAMBER AND THE CROSS**, Deborah talked with British solicitors, stayed in medieval manors, and interviewed the owners of these historically designated homes.

Lisa Shapiro is an Assistant Professor of Business at San Diego Mesa College. She holds degrees in Management and Literature, and has also taught composition and creative writing in San Diego. Her published work includes three novels with Naiad Press. When it comes to writing, Lisa is still a student, and she has learned more from the co-writing process than from any class.

Deborah and Lisa traveled throughout Great Britain, dedicating more years than they'd like to admit to reading, writing, and researching **THE CHAMBER AND THE CROSS**. They walked historic battlegrounds, combed through castle ruins, and studied the procedures for exhuming human remains.